Vintage Movie Classics spotlights classic films that have stood the test of time, now rediscovered through the publication of the novels on which they were based.

Movie Adaptations of Fannie Hurst's

BACK STREET

1932: Produced by Universal Pictures. Directed by John M. Stahl. Starring Irene Dunne and John Boles. Screenplay by Gladys Lehman.

1941: Produced by Universal Pictures. Directed by Robert Stevenson. Starring Margaret Sullavan and Charles Boyer. Screenplay by Bruce Manning and Felix Jackson.

1961: Co-produced by Ross Hunter Productions and Carrollton Inc. Directed by David Miller. Starring Susan Hayward, John Gavin, and Vera Miles. Screenplay by Eleanore Griffin and William Ludwig. Academy Award nominee for Best Costume Design, Color.

Fannie Hurst

BACK STREET

Fannie Hurst (1889–1968) was an American novelist. Born in Hamilton, Ohio, and raised in St. Louis, Missouri, she graduated from Washington University in St. Louis in 1909. Hurst was a member of the Lucy Stone League, the Urban League, and was appointed to the National Advisory Committee to the Works Progress Administration in 1940. She was also a delegate to the World Health Organization in 1952. She published more than twenty novels and story collections in her lifetime.

BOOKS BY FANNIE HURST

BACK STREET

BACK STREET

Fannie Hurst
Foreword by Cari Beauchamp

Vintage Books
A Division of Random House LLC
New York

FOREWORD

By Cari Beauchamp

The name Fannie Hurst might ring a distant bell today, but in her time she was as famous for being herself as she was for the popular fiction she turned out with inspiring regularity. More than two hundred stories about her appeared in *The New York Times*, and her 1962 obituary made the front page.

Hurst lived a life that rivaled those she created on the page, and as she was inventing some of her most famous characters, she was reinventing herself. A Jewish fish out of water in her native St. Louis, she wrote her way to fame as a sophisticated New Yorker. She laughingly maintained she began collecting rejection slips at the age of fourteen and had amassed quite a pile before publishing her first national story in 1912, when she was twenty-one. By the time she was thirty-five, she was making more money than Somerset Maugham or Edna Ferber. Fannie's work was often serialized in the leading national magazines of the day, such as *Cosmopolitan*, *The Saturday Evening Post*, and *Collier's*, before they were published as novels or in a collection of short stories.

She created female protagonists who faced dilemmas rarely spoken of in polite conversation: sexual harassment, spousal abuse, and the plight of mistresses. She wrote of overtly sexual women who thought about the pros and cons of associating with married men, and the double standard that existed between men and women laced almost all her work. She was never a great literary figure, but rather a great storyteller, and for decades she was dubbed the reign-ing "sob sister" of American fiction.

Hurst was an active supporter of women's suffrage, civil rights, and the Lucy Stone League, which promoted women keeping their own name after marriage. Fannie not only did that, but she kept her marriage to the pianist Jacques Danielson a secret. They lived in separate apartments, breakfasted together twice a week, and bal-anced a schedule that included occasional weekends away together and many nights out with friends on their own. When, after five years, the marriage became front-page news, Fannie and Jacques found themselves advocating their arrangement, saying that since both of them needed hours alone for their work, they found it both productive and satisfying.

What stayed secret from her public, according to Hurst's biog-rapher Brooke Kroeger, was that during her marriage Fannie con-ducted a longtime affair with the anthropologist and Arctic explorer Vilhjalmur Stefansson. In her fiction, Fannie's female characters often found themselves waiting for their phones to ring, but in her own life, it was usually the men who did the waiting.

Fannie's widely read stories were obvious fodder for the bur-geoning film industry. Financial independence was important to her, and nothing was better than getting paid for work she had already done. She befriended the screenwriter Frances Marion when Marion adapted and directed a film based on Hurst's "Just Around the Corner" in 1919, and Fannie was pleased when Fran-ces was assigned to adapt her Jewish ghetto story of heart-tugging mother love, "Humoresque". Frances agreed with Fannie's sugges-tion of casting the Russian-born Vera Gordon as the mother in the film, and together the women laughed off the studio head Adolph Zukor when he chastised Frances: "If you and Fannie Hurst are so determined to make the Jews appear sympathetic, why don't you choose a story about the Rothschilds or men as distinguished as they?" Yet Fannie was "indignant" when she saw the first rough cut of *Humoresque* with a happy ending added, and demanded her name be taken off the credits. Frances talked Fannie down, explaining that while readers could handle a tragic ending, movie audiences needed "optimism and hope." To her credit, Hurst took to studying motion pictures, seeing as many as she could, and came to not only agree with Frances but to encourage her to adapt others of her works into films, using, according to Marion, "the skeleton of those stories in new garb especially designed for the screen." It didn't hurt that *Humoresque*, often billed as "Fannie Hurst's *Humoresque*," went on to win *Photoplay*'s first Medal of Honor, a precursor of the Academy Awards, as the best film of 1920.

Hurst's stories of women grappling with their lives, their desires, and their place in society continued to sell magazines, books, and movie tickets. *Back Street* would be made into a film three times (in 1932, 1941, and 1961). "Humoresque" was adapted twice, as was her most famous novel, *Imitation of Life*. By the time *Back Street* was going before the cameras the first time in 1932, more than ten years had passed since the first *Humoresque*, and a dozen more of Fannie's works had been made into films. Her short story "Back Pay" featured a classic Hurst heroine whose devoted small-town suitor loves her in her "little gingham dress," but she knows she has to leave for the big city because she has "a crepe de chine soul." Think of the young, dissatisfied woman in the hinterlands watching *Back Pay* in her local theater connecting, perhaps for the first time in her life, to a kindred spirit. She had been wondering what was wrong with her and she suddenly finds she isn't alone after all. This was the power of Fannie's stories.

In the book *Back Street*, Walter explains to Ray his ability to bifurcate his life: "My feeling for you and my feeling for my wife and children are things separate and apart." A simple declarative sentence explains it all, allowing Hurst and the film to focus on the agony and ecstasy of the mistress, a three-dimensional charac-ter. Fannie threads the needle carefully to make a role condemned by society into a complex and sympathetic woman, almost monastic in her dedication to her man.

In addition to selling her previously published work to Holly-wood, Hurst began writing scenarios directly for the screen when RKO offered her $30,000 for what she knew was only a few weeks' work. While Fannie was not directly involved with the filming of

Back Street at Universal, she was pleased that the director, John Stahl, and the writer, Gladys Lehman, stayed true to her story, including the dramatic ending. Fannie "adored" Irene Dunne as Ray, and the critics agreed.

If Fannie had made her peace, and her ever-increasing income, with the movies, a force much larger than the audience's need for "hope and optimism" was about to impact filmmaking. The Hays Office, created by the studios in 1922, had imposed a set of standards, but in 1934 the Production Code made censorship official. After the Legion of Decency, along with other Catholic and women's groups, loudly condemned "vile and unwholesome moving pictures" such as *Public Enemy* and "fallen woman" films such as *Red Headed Woman* and *Blonde Venus*, Will Hays's list of "dos and don'ts" gave way to what he called "a police department," and its new chief was the very Catholic Joseph Breen, a former public relations man who had transformed his push for the code's enforcement into a well-paying job.

Before the Production Code, films about adultery often centered on the "other woman" and told the story from her perspective. After 1934, films were limited in a myriad of ways. The focus was now on the cheating husband and the moral dilemma he faced. Sin had to be punished.

In the 1941 version of *Back Street*, Ray Schmidt becomes Ray Smith, and in the process sheds her Jewish background. However, Universal actively resisted some of Breen's suggestions, including the idea that Walter's death should be caused by his "disgrace" and then Ray should become a "cheap hag of a gambler." Directed by Robert Stevenson, who would go on to direct *Mary Poppins* and half a dozen other Disney classics, 1941's *Back Street* stars a strong but vulnerable Margaret Sullavan with a none too Midwestern Charles Boyer as her lover.

The cultural changes over the next twenty years are reflected in the 1961 *Back Street*, the film version that goes farthest afield from the novel. Ray (still Smith) has become the sophisticated Rae, an internationally successful clothes designer, and Walter owns a string of exclusive department stores. Together they are no longer in the "back streets," but in a comfortable country home and the best hotels in Rome and Paris. John Gavin and Susan Hayward make the most physically beautiful pairing yet, and their relationship is explained in part by the newly fleshed-out role of Walter's drunken shrew of a wife, played by Vera Miles.

Each film stands on its own, mirroring the time it was made. Now we can go back to the original novel, to pure Fannie Hurst, and discover anew that so much has changed and so little has changed since its original publication in 1932.

Cari Beauchamp is the award-winning author of *Without Lying Down: Frances Marion and the Powerful Women of Early Hollywood, Joseph P. Kennedy Presents: His Hollywood Years,* and four other books of film history. She writes for *Vanity Fair* and other magazines, is a two-time Academy of Motion Picture Arts and Sciences Film Scholar, and serves as the Resident Scholar of the Mary Pickford Foundation.

BACK STREET

BOOK ONE

BOOK ONE

1

One evening in one of those Over-the-Rhine cafés which were plentiful along Vine Street of the Cincinnati of the nineties, a traveling salesman leaned across his stein of Moerlein's Extra Light and openly accused Ray Schmidt of being innocent.

"I know! You're one of those cheating girls who act fly but aren't. You'll lead a man on, but you won't go all the way."

At the implication and all that went with it, Ray's hand flew to her tippet, color ran beneath her tan pallor, and as usual when under stress, she rolled her eyes and became flippant.

"Try me," was what she said, with little sense of the outrageousness of such a remark.

"That's exactly what I have been trying to do all evening," said the traveling salesman who, having exhibited what was for him an unprecedented astuteness in his summary of Ray Schmidt, now leaned to pinch her knee softly underneath the table.

Ray was forever being pinched underneath tables. As far back as she could remember, as a child and then as a girl growing up on Baymiller Street, boys had been fond of pinching and pulling her toward them for kisses.

"Spooning" was not unpleasant, particularly in the evening, when somehow the boys' faces receded out of a pimply reality into the velvet tunnels of Cincinnati's low kind of darkness. With the boys whose faces persisted in jutting lumpily, even out of cover of

nighttime, Ray simply had not the heart to follow the slightly disgusted impulse to push them away.

One "spooned" to be kind. It gave you the reputation of being
"fly," no doubt of that, particularly if, like Ray, you were endowed
with that subtle womanish dimension known as "style." Ray had
that. When she even so much as walked past the Stag Hotel, skirts
held up off the sidewalk with that ineffable turn of wrist which
again denoted "style," there was that in her demeanor which caused
each male head and eye to turn.

Sometimes they made kissing sounds with their lips, past which
she sailed with her head high.

But the fact was that more usually than not Ray had attired
herself, at length and with great detail, for this rapid sail past the
Stag Hotel. The turning of the heads set agog within her a sense
of excitement. It made life seem to quicken, as she felt the eyes
burn along her well-corseted back. It was as if she could feel, with
the very taper of her torso into a waistline that two ordinary hands
could come within an inch of spanning, the rhythm of being well-
proportioned. Nor was she above straining her ears from beneath
their pompadour for the bits of applause that were sometimes carried along to her.

"Hot baby!"

"You'd look sweet upon the seat of a bicycle built for two!"

"Sweet Marie, come to me!"

"She's a daisy!"

Ray's longish eyelids would properly drop like two slow fans,
and she would remark, if her stepsister Freda happened to be along,
"See anything green?" But deep within her would begin to run the
stirring saps of her body. The contour of her breasts, flung high by
corsets, felt beautiful, and so did the movement of her flaring hips
and the strength in the calves of her legs as, beneath two petticoats
and a Spanish-flounced skirt, they hurried her along in their strong
black cotton stockings.

Privately her own as were these sensations that lay warmly in
her body, the bold fact was that the eyes of the men seemed to bring
them pleasantly awake. It was a greater treat to the senses, even

more thoroughly delighting, than to indulge in her favorite habit of lying back in a warm bath with a copy of *The Wages of Sin*, by Lucas Malet, held open to its place and tied with twine to the faucet to facilitate page turnings.

These Narcissus-like delights of hers branded the daughter of old Adolph Schmidt, during the various stages of her girlhood, as boy-crazy, fly, swift, fresh, shady, gay, and even fast.

Men laid hands too readily on Ray Schmidt. She was not past slapping them off her thighs or the slim ledge of her hip, but the smile belied the fake anger in her gray eyes.

"Ray lets the boys get fresh with her," was the *sotto voce* indictment of Baymiller Street, even back in the days before she had lengthened her skirts, put up her hair, and developed to its fullest sense that promise of "style" which had already characterized her as a child.

It was well-known along Baymiller that Schmidt did not even try to keep (much less succeed in keeping) his daughter off the streets—that he let her run wild, as the saying went—that it was not unusual, indeed habitual, for her, at fifteen, to remain out on the stoop with two, three, and sometimes one of the boys; and more than one head in curlpapers, popping out of a window after ten, had beheld her kissing good nights, "spooning."

Boys carried home Ray's schoolbooks for her, just the ordinary boys who ran shouting about the streets after school, and stood for as long as an hour at the iron front gate, jiggling about in the spotty conversation of adolescence and ending with last-tag bouts and much body-mauling of Ray.

A fresh child.

When she was only thirteen, Bertha Auth, a neighboring child of a prosperous local builder, had already been forbidden to play with her because Ray kissed boys.

That hurt her, terribly. Bertha, forbidden, made Ray feel dirty and contaminating. You kissed boys, well, chiefly because you happened to be the sort of girl the boys wanted to kiss. True, the way it made you feel reminded you of the ice in the gutters when it began to thaw in spring and started to flow with that beautiful spiral glassy sound. The best part of it all though was the fact that the boys wanted to kiss you and got pleasure. They didn't clamor for the osculatory favors of Bertha or, for that matter, Freda Tagenhorst, who was prettier than Ray, and who at fourteen was to become Freda Schmidt by virtue of her mother's marriage to Ray's father.

This impulse to please was part of the very texture of Ray. It pleased the boys to kiss and fondle her. They breathed hard and were eager. Even when they had pimply faces, which offended her, and crusty hands from after-school chores and skating bare-handed on the canal, she bore with their embraces for the apparent ecstasy it was hers to bestow upon just an ordinary schoolboy of shuffling feet, unkempt hair, and ill-hung clothes.

It was not nice, and she knew it; and she suffered when the sweet and acquiescing friendship of Bertha was withdrawn, or when her stepmother bawled reprimands. But just the same, at nineteen, it was as characteristic of her as it had been at fourteen, that a traveling salesman, in the very act of making so acute an observation as, "You're one of those girls who act fly but aren't," should, unreprimanded, pinch her knee under the table.

How dared he? Why was she so acquiescent? Why, in the language of her stepmother, did she not "haul off" and slap the face of any man who dared get fresh with her? A man expected it. A man respected you if you did. Went on getting fresher if you didn't.

Ray knew that. She knew it as well as she knew she was sitting in a hall, Over-the-Rhine, being pinched on the knee by a traveling salesman who was no more to her than the ten or twenty others who streamed through her father's store each year.

This one's name was Michel Prothero, and he lived on Staten Island, New York, and was a married man, quite pretentiously so, and carried a photograph of his wife, with her two children's arms about her neck, in the lid of his watch. He represented a dress-lining concern with which Adolph Schmidt had carried modest account for over twenty years. The skirt in which Ray sat being pinched was lined in that firm's excellent grade of Frostilla sateen.

"If I was a married man, Prothero," she rebuked him softly, "it seems to me I would have something better to do than to try to get fresh with a respectable girl in her hometown."

He was not an unintelligent fellow. He was in love, after a fashion, with his wife, pompous and vainglorious about his children, and yet every time he came to Cincinnati he found himself admitting that here was the one girl who could bring him to the point of infidelity. Not that he ever thought much about her in the six-month intervals between his semiannual trips to the Middle West: it was her nearness that seemed to scoop him into a sense of security such as he had never known.

Great girl to bother about a fellow. She cared. It was pleasant to have a stunning, up-to-the-minute-looking girl like Ray Schmidt walk into a Vine Street restaurant with you and see her order, with one eye to a fellow's digestion and the other to keeping the check down. Sort of like having your cake and eating it too. Where could you find a girl of Ray's general layout who wasn't either a chippie or, as the saying went, all bound round with a woolen string? Ray was neither. She was one of the girls who would run around town all hours not bothering about the looks of the thing (Prothero would "break her neck" if he ever caught one of his own girls at the like of it); but, on the other hand, she wasn't out-and-out fast. Father one of the old-fashioned and respected merchants of the town. Small fry, but Schmidt's "Trimmings, Veilings, Dress Linings, and Buckram" was second only to Caldwell's, and, in lesser fashion, as much a part of staple Cincinnati as Rookwood Pottery, or Alms and Doepke, or the old canal itself.

Married man might do worse than be seen spending an evening with Ray Schmidt. Wife of a married man could thank her stars it was Ray Schmidt instead of a chippie. The difference between a fly girl and a fast woman was all the difference in the world.

"Yes, siree—you're just one of those girls who act fly and aren't."

She did quizzical things with her eyes and lips after the manner of one trying to appear enigmatic. It must be conceded that she succeeded. In her large pompadour hat, trimmed in two great panne-velvet splotches, one fuchsia, one purple, her gray eyes shadowed by black lashes, and a face veil with chenille dots, Ray Schmidt was sufficiently provocative of Vine Street's surmisings about her.

"A man like you, Prothero," said Ray, resting her chin in the palm of her hand and gazing at him across her glass of Moerlein's and one of Wielert's excellent tongue sandwiches embellished with cottage cheese, "divides his world into two parts—the half where he would take his wife and the half where he wouldn't."

"Nonsense. I'd bring my wife here to Wielert's any night in the week before eleven."

She consulted the silver watch held in place on her fine bosom by a garnet crescent.

"It's just eleven-forty-five. That's me."

"You're the darnedest!" he said, admiring her with his eyes where the watch rose and fell to her breathing.

"Darnedest what, Prothero?"

"Darned if I know. Man like me comes to your town once or twice a year, year after year, sees you sprouting up from just a youngster around your father's place after school hours, into about the toniest girl in town, but darned if I know any more about you now than I did when I used to pull your braids. A man, if he's any kind of a man a-tall, likes to know where he gets off with a fine girl like you. Not human if he doesn't. Hm?"

"I'm just about as you see me, Prothero. The kind of a girl you fellows get as fresh with as you dare," she said, without withdrawing her knee from the pressing palm of his hand.

"Well, that's just what I am trying to get at, Ray. How fresh dast he? How far dast he go?"

Strangely, this narrow, not unintelligent little traveling salesman, guilty, for the first time in an orderly married life of sixteen years, of the impulse to commit adultery, caught his breath from an inability to quite finish this sentence, because of an excitement almost more than he could bear.

How desirable she was, with all the stylish attributes of the toniest girl in town, and yet right down at rock bottom one of those girls you could talk to, straight from the heart! Not above a game of hazard in the back room of Chick and George's, long after the

chairs were piled on the table in the outer room and the family element had retired to respectability and discretion, and yet, withal,
a girl with whom you could discuss the homely eventualities. Life
insurance. The wife's erysipelas. Business ambitions. Baseball. The
youngest child's shoulder-braces. A girl who would take your mea-
surements and have you a chamois waistcoat made by a wholesale
firm that favored her, and think nothing of coming to your hotel
to administer a hot mustard foot bath for a cold contracted in an
overheated Pullman car. A girl who would jump on a train as quick
as you could say cock robin, and take a twenty-five-mile ride up to
Hamilton, and sit in Stengel's, nibbling pretzels and drinking beer,
while you called on the trade, and yet—why, a man would turn to
Ray Schmidt if he were in trouble.

As a matter of fact, two years previous something horrible had
threatened the equanimity of this narrow little salesman for ladies'
findings and dress linings. He had tinkered with his firm's funds. So
close to the bitter edge of tragedy had he faltered that he was on the
verge of being apprehended on a matter pertaining to five hundred
dollars, which if discovered would have meant ruin and disgrace to
the brood in the small house in the small street on Staten Island.

There had been one night, as he lay beside his plump little
snoring wife in the neat bedroom of their neat home, when the
idea of suicide had resolutely turned itself over in Prothero's mind.
Nowhere to turn—and suddenly out of his chaos had shot the idea
of this *gemütlich* girl in Cincinnati. The one who had once given
him a hot mustard foot bath the time he came down in the middle
of his trip with the grippe. The one who straightened his muffler
when he came into her father's ladies'-dress-findings emporium.
The one who let him kiss her and pinch her on her pretty, slender
thighs, and was willing, even at seventeen, to go over to Wielert's
with him, where Helene Mora, the girl with the baritone voice,
sang "Comrades," there to drink beer with him until mid-Victorian
dudes climbed upon the tables and with glasses held aloft sang "Little Annie Rooney" and "Down Went McGinty to the Bottom of
the Sea."

How she had happened to pop into his mind in the midst of a

duress that was threatening to submerge him in the lethal waters of suicide, was forever to remain a mystery to the small salesman who paid pew dues and recorded the births of his children in a Testament which his wife kept wrapped in a bureau drawer in a silk handkerchief. But pop she did into the whirligig of what threatened to be disintegration of his little life.

Ray Schmidt, that half-fast little near-chippie out in Cincinnati, would care enough to bother to find him a lifeline! She was like that. Cared like the dickens about folks. Not about him in particular. Didn't flatter himself. That was precisely the point. She just naturally bothered about a man's muffler, if he was subject to sore throat. Nothing extraordinary about that in a wife. But somehow—didn't expect it from a girl that fly. Cared about keeping a dinner check down just as if a fellow were her husband. Talked to a man about the value of endowment policy and nest egg as if she were the one to profit by it.

And so into the hour of his shameful crisis had walked the figure of this Ray whom he had not seen a dozen times in his life, and then for only a sporadic evening in a Vine Street café, concert hall or Heuck's Theatre for a melodrama.

She had actually responded with a money order for half the amount he had so frenziedly requested and a promise of the additional within sixty days. That had been two years ago, and Prothero had all but paid her back in small monthly instalments.

Fine gal. No questions. No pressing. Fly? Yes. Had to admit it. Did the things he would break his own daughter's neck for. But levelheaded as a wife, and a darned sight better looking than the run-of-the-mill of wives. (Not that he had any kick coming.) A girl with a nest egg in her sock. Never mind where she got it.

Saved it, no doubt. Leave it to those Cincinnati sauerkraut eaters. Girl like that working in her father's little concern—solid as Gibraltar—small credit, but never tell a thing about those thrifty Germans—salted away—well, never mind all that. Where the dickens though, did a man get off with her? Say, she was swell. If a girl like Ray would go the limit—say, would she? Had she? Say, had she?

Of course she had, and would. But had she? Darned if a fellow could tell. Darned if I know. Darned if anybody seems to know. Every once in a while some fellow at the Stag or Gibson House seemed on to a lot about the real truth concerning this girl and what she was—but usually you had the feeling that the fellow was spinning a yarn out of a half truth. Didn't know any more than you knew before. Just how far . . .

Just how far?

She darted her eyes, she nodded her head, she tilted her neck, and took a sip of beer through her veil, with her eyes continuing to roll above the rim of her glass.

The wife regarded drinking through the mesh of a veil as vile. What a girl. What a seductive feeling it gave you to see the veiling suck in against her lips that way. What a darned good-looker. Gray eyes. What made them so nice were the lashes. Black! Rather big, strong-boned face, as a matter of fact, but just downright the kind that brought you to your toes. The way those eyes were cut in. Couldn't exactly describe it, but it was a tasty face. The way olives and caviar and sardelles were supposed to be tasty.

Yessir, a darned good-looker. Style. Why, the girls in the East were just beginning to wear those light-tan box coats with the mandolin sleeves. And leave it to Ray to be among the first to venture one of those short-back sailor effects that were worn tilted to the angle of a toboggan-slide. Darn it all, when a girl answered a man's question, as to just how far he dared go with her, with all that rolling motion of her face and body, a fellow would be plumb crazy not to take his cue.

"Tell you how I feel about this thing called life, Ray."

They all began more or less that way.

"It's short."

"Sure is, Prothero."

"The Lord gives us all sorts of ways to enjoy happiness. I mean to do the right thing by the wife. That's me. And then in a class all by itself love another gal in those ways where the wife don't quite fill the bill. Sabe?"

"Yes, I sabe, Prothero. It's n. g. If you don't believe me, go over to any of the tables you see round here and put it up to the uphol-stered mamas you see there."

In the warm beer-scented security of Wielert's first-class fam-ily resort, the heavy harmonies of a full reed band, playing Wagner, Beethoven, "Ach, du lieber Augustin," "The Boat Is Com-ing Around the Bend, Good-By, My Lover, Good-By," flowed over table after table of Cincinnati's High-German, solid-as-Gibraltar citizenry, dipping mustachios into foam-crested mugs.

Into this old-world atmosphere of cream-colored walls, inscribed with German mottoes of epicurean source, there gathered, evening after evening, around the solid-mahogany tables, the firmly hewn bourgeoisie of this Munich-on-the-Ohio. Wielert's—"the true fam-ily resort in every respect."

Surrounding the table where Prothero and Ray were letting the foam on their glasses blink out sud by sud, were gathered the spine of the community. Sons and daughters of the Rhine, who could date their invasion back to that historic day when citizen Nicholas Longworth had first conceived the idea of transplanting his country-men from the sunkissed vineyards of the Rhineland to these similar bland hills of Cincinnati, whither he had migrated and prospered.

The vineyards did not quite come off; the transplantation did. Evidences of it and its progeny were everywhere in Wielert's. Fami-lies that dined out once a week. Sturdy, unstylish women with enor-mous busts, who ate and drank with relish but knew, to the penny, for how much less they could spread their groaning home tables with these luxuries of *Schmierkäse* and *Schnittlauch, Bratwurst* that had been fried without a prong of the exploring fork puncturing the sausage casing for loss of juice. Solid, thrifty men, in gates-ajar collars and congress shoes, to whom the *Turnverein* and *Sangverein,* the right lager, the virtuous wife, the virgin daughter, the respecting son, the well-tended business, were universe.

Yes, siree, it was possible, all right, sitting there in the preten-tious early-evening respectability of Wielert's pavilion, while a man in short pants, with braid running down the side seams, knee-shy stockings, and a small green hat with a brush in it, yodeled, to feel a little mad over the desirability of Ray. One tony girl.

And where there was smoke there must be fire. Ray Schmidt was to be had for the asking all right, if you knew how to ask. Girls simply did not run around that way, dressed to knock out a fellow's eye, unless—unless—

"How long is it, Ray, since I've known you?"

"More years than I'm going to admit, Prothero, that I've been gadding about with you boys as you come to town."

"I remember taking you to a baseball game in a feather boa that was one of the first I ever clapped eyes on. Remember, you helped me shop for one for the wife?"

"Yes, it was purple. Got it at Pogue's."

"All those years ago, and darned if I know one bit more about you now than I ever did, Ray. Good company. Girl, if ever there was one, that a fellow can turn to in a pinch; and yet—darned if I know. . . ."

"If I didn't know you for what I know you to be, I'd think you were trying to propose to me, or something."

"I am, Ray, trying to propose something."

"What's on your mind, Prothero?"

"Ray—would you sleep with a fellow—with me—"

For answer, she drew back her hand slowly, without surprise, and swung it with a hollow-sounding bang against the narrow cheek of the narrow Mr. Prothero.

2

Not but what every other man, sooner or later, by innuendo, had asked it. But never had anyone summed it up in the nasty little compact phrase that had issued from Prothero.

The shocking, stark-naked phrase, coming, it is true, off lips that she had more than once allowed to kiss her, had robbed her of her usual power of evasion. The hand that had struck out had been the hand of some violated inner being. Something private and away from the self that was being lived here in the unsacred everydayness of existence, in this town on the bank of a river, had leaped up hurt and banged in the crude form of fingertips against a human cheek, leaving imprints. One felt sick, with living.

A man named Henry Rathman, who at the time was already general shipping agent of the steamboat company that was ultimately to bear his name, had once walked her down Race Street as far as the corner of Longworth and tried to urge her into this narrow notorious lane, nodding significantly in the direction of the unlighted, heavily curtained second-story window of a narrow-shouldered house, one removed from the corner, Madame Yesska's.

That had seemed so horrible to her at the time (she was sixteen) that she always thereafter said of Rathman, without enlarging further, that he gave her "the shivers," although it is again here true that she had subsequently allowed him to kiss and press her and, on one occasion of a steam-launch outing of a Turnverein Society up the canal as far as Lockland, had permitted him to keep her head pressed against his shoulder for the homeward trip of the moonlit excursion.

He had wanted it. To withdraw was to bring conspicuous remonstrance. He had so palpably enjoyed that pressure of her cheek against his coat, where she could feel his heart make little swelling movements of increasing celerity. How easy it was to give pleasure. Your own pleasure was the result of giving that pleasure. To say "No" hurt more than the dilemma of granting a reluctant "Yes." That had always been Ray's particular predicament, although almost invariably there came the time when the "No" amounted to almost the explosion of disgust that had motivated her action in striking Prothero across the cheek.

And yet, the affair at Wielert's had been without precedent. No one had ever before summed up for her in words of one syllable, as Prothero had, the unspoken which lay in the eyes and along the moist lips of most of the men who regarded her. Letting rest these sleeping dogs that crouched in the eyes of men, you could relax, for instance, with your head against the coat of a man like Henry Rathman, all the way from Lockland down to Plum Street, filled with the none too restful consciousness that beyond the moment probably lay a situation that would have to be handled. Subsequently, Rathman would be almost sure to press her into a position where the ultimatum would either terminate their relationship, or merely postpone an inevitable crisis.

Apparently the fact that men were like that was part of the scheme of a universe into which she had been born, a girl.

At least men were like this where she—Ray—was concerned.

For the first time in her life, that night after leaving Prothero, seated, before going indoors, on the front veranda of the house on Baymiller Street, a doubt of her father crossed her mind.

Was her stepmother right, after all? Had Adolph, during those years following her mother's death, the formative years between seven and fifteen, let her run wild as a weed? Was she, in result, in the eyes of the miscellaneous men with whom she ran, just the potential chippie? What other so-called respectable girl in town could conceivably have been presented with the viscid question that had come to her off of Prothero's wetted lips? Ugh!

It was cold sitting there in the late evening on the front porch of the house on Baymiller Street. Damp November chill whitened the breath, sank through the roomy box coat, and ran up beneath petticoats and chilled her cotton-clad legs.

Papa, Papa! said Ray to herself, sitting down on the porch-railing and dangling one high-buttoned shoe. Oh, Papa, Papa! Her throat was hurting. She wanted to cry, but with a wilful sort of self-flagellation would not let herself, but sat there in the late chill of the silence of Baymiller Street, swinging her high-buttoned shoe, with its dangling tassel.

The Colerain Avenue car, dragging heavily along, threw a momentary light against the veranda; and the motorman, a new one named Fred Harley, leaned over and waved his cap. She threw him back a stiff-handed salute off her left eyebrow. Nice fellow. Didn't realize he was fresh. Held the car for her if she was late, mornings.

"Don't know he's fresh!" had been her stepmother's snorting retort to Harley's habit of waving as his car passed. "Don't know he's fresh! Huh! I'd like to see him so much as wave a finger, much less blow kisses, at Freda or any other girl on the block. A man knows quicker than a barometer knows, which way the wind blows in the matter of girls."

That was doubtless true. It was also true that in all probability there was not a girl on Baymiller Street who would have waved back to Fred Harley, or to whom Prothero would have dared utter that sickening question. For that matter, not a girl on Baymiller Street would have been found seated in Wielert's after eleven, unchaperoned, with a traveling salesman generally known to be a man of family.

No one would have been quicker than Ray, had such occasion arisen, to join in family prohibition against her stepsister Freda's appearing in a rôle which Ray permitted herself. Prothero would not dream of asking a girl like Freda to take a ride up to Hamilton with him and sit sipping beer and crumbling pretzels at Stengel's, while he visited the linings-and-dress-findings department of Howell's.

Freda had a demanding little way with her. She believed that the more you demand of a man, the more he thinks of you. It would no more have occurred to her, for instance, to admonish a suitor to put the seventy-five cents it had cost him to come bearing a box of bonbons, toward a savings account, than it would have to sit around Wielert's with a married traveling salesman.

Men respected Freda. True, they respected her chiefly because her mother did not trust one of them out alone with her. There lay the secret! Ray had been mother to herself during those years when men first began to lay hands upon her. Schmidt had trusted her, going his guileless, unobserving way and leaving it to his girl to somehow go hers.

Sitting there swinging her scalloped shoe, the thought smote Ray that, since her father's marriage to the widow Tagenhorst had been destined to happen anyway, it might better have happened sooner. True, when Adolph, newly widowed, had rented the house on Baymiller Street to the wife of the late Otto Tagenhorst, and he and his daughter had continued to live in the old home as boarders, Ray had come under the influence of the woman who was later to become the second wife of her father. Still, it had been too late. The interval of years when the widower had been courting the widow, and Tagenhorst had conscientiously and subtly "kept out of it" by not seeing fit to express her opinions of the lax social methods of Ray, except by the contrast of her own daughter's immaculately tidy behavior, had been the formative ones that had somehow clinched the point of view concerning the daughter of Adolph Schmidt. Ray was fly.

Now, although three months Ray's senior, there was something unspecked and protected about Freda's youth—something right and normal. The boys who courted Freda were the boys who, if not in a position, were at least in the mood, for marriage. It was not inconceivable that a certain Hugo Hanck, temporarily nothing more than a gas-meter reader, but the only nephew and heir apparent of one of the town's outstanding brewers, would finish off his courtship of Freda with marriage.

The fact was that, at eighteen, with the exception of Kurt Shendler, who owned a small bicycle-repair shop, and who had been at Ray to elope with him to Middletown ever since the days when she was fourteen and had ridden her bicycle into his shop for "pumping up" after school, Ray had never had an out-and-out offer of marriage.

No. The thought kept smiting her, as the cold poured in faster and faster beneath the mandolin-sleeves and against the cotton stockings, that if Papa had been less lax with her, or his marriage with Tagenhorst, since it had to come, had happened in the days when she was still young enough to be taken in hand by a step-mother, she would not be sitting out here sick with the nausea of disgust because a married traveling salesman had put into words the unspoken expectation which, encouraged by her general behavior, lurked in the eyes and manner of every man who enjoyed easy liber-ties with her and hoped for greater.

It was not that you could blame Papa. God love him, no! You could not expect caution of a man in whom mistrust had never been born. But if only—if only, somehow, some way, and still remaining Papa, just as he was, he had trusted her a little less. . . .

It was not wise to enter the house with her throat hurting so from pressing down tears, because Papa was still up. She could see him through the parlor window seated beside the dining-room table reading the *Volksblatt* through two pairs of spectacles. Seen through the lace curtain, the vista of dark parlor intervening, he looked as placid as the friar on his beer mug, his large shining hairless head falling forward now and then in intermittent fits of dozing. God love him. No amount of well-being could seem to spare her from the hurt of his seeming pathetic to her.

On one occasion she had wanted to appear to shed tears because she had succeeded in arousing a man, whose jealousy she momen-tarily coveted, into saying harsh things to her.

It was difficult for her to cry, because she was not feeling; and so she sat and thought of her father, and his inability even to think of her in terms of fallibility, and the way his face fell into benign sort of fat and adoring creases when he looked at her, and that lonely little fashion he had of sometimes rubbing his hand across the furrows of his brow, and immediately it was all she could do to keep the tears from turning into sobs.

Even back in those dim childhood days during the life of her mother, her father had set up a sort of perpetual hurt in his daughter. In the untranslatable coinage of a phrase that was frequently used in a local way to sum him up, Adolph was *eine gute Schnucke*.

It was the one linguistic atavism Ray permitted herself. She liked to call him *Schnucke*. It expressed some of her indescribable hurt over his darlingness.

A young reporter on the *Enquirer*, who had boarded at the house during the days when Tagenhorst had taken it over, had summed up the figure of her father, as they had once sat of a summer evening on this very same porch rail, regarding him through the parlor lace curtain. "Your old man sure is a character. Somebody ought to put him in a book." He was that. People often said to her, "Your father certainly is a character." Was it because he was as placid, by nature, as the friar he resembled? Well, if never to learn from all the bad things that happened to you made you into "a character," Papa certainly was that. Pa just wouldn't distrust. Let a bookkeeper cheat out his very eyeballs, as two of them already had, and Papa would go right on without precaution, trusting the next one and the next, just as if nothing had ever happened. Let Papa catch bronchial pneumonia two winters in succession from going out onto the sidewalk from the heated store without hat or coat, and Papa would keep right on stepping from one extreme temperature into another, just as if he had not almost lost his life from two serious illnesses thus induced.

Adolph was never tired of celebrating to his first wife the narrowness of his escape from the ensnarements of Cora Goebel. But did that prevent him from ultimately marrying this same Cora Goebel? It did not. An experience that had really seemed to cut deeply into Adolph, apparently had not cut at all. Seven decent years after the death of Lena, each bringing to the union a half-grown daughter, Cora Goebel Tagenhorst and Adolph Schmidt were married.

Papa lived life like that. Apparently nothing could really get at him. It was the same where Ray was concerned. His girl was a good girl, and go away with all your hocus-pocus talk from people who didn't have anything better to do. What had happened to girls before, did not make any difference. Ray was able to take care of herself. If Tagenhorst felt differently about Freda, and shushed over her like a mother hen, that was all right too. Everything was all right.

Well, Papa, this is how all right your all-right world is. A man has just asked me—a man has just asked me in dirty little words, the question every man I have ever known, except Kurt, has asked me with his manner.

The tears popped and hung in small diamond-shaped panes in the mesh of her veil. What's to be done about it, Papa? How can I start over being a different kind of me with men? . . .

A car lumbered by again, carrying one lone passenger huddled in a rear seat. This time the driver of the night's first "owl" leaned out, as the flash of its dirty yellow light fell against the Schmidt house, and, inserting two fingers between his teeth, let out a short, shrill whistle.

It was Harry Knorr, one of the older boys on the line. Poor fellow, that was a cold and lonesome job for you, running a Colerain owl-car. Fresh of him, though, to slow down and keep whistling. For goodness' sake, he'd wake up the neighborhood! Oh, poor fellow—lonesome . . .

What she did in the act of entering the house was to pause for a moment, place a kiss on the palm of her gloved hand, and blow it off in the direction of the Colerain owl-car, as it slowed down to what amounted to a standstill.

3

Gracious! Tagenhorst was forever leaving doors and windows open, so that when Ray entered at night, the draft of the hall door opening sent more of them slamming throughout the house.

The thought trailed through Ray's tired mind that she did it on purpose. As if to say: "Bang, bang, bang, here she comes! Well, it's not my say, I'm only her stepmother, and I'm not the kind that intends to get a reputation for being a nagging one! After all, she was dry behind her ears before I married her father. If it suits him it has to suit me. But if it were my Freda, God forbid, I'd rather see her dead. . . ."

Freda, with a stick of yellow braid over each shoulder, and ointment glistening on two chin pimples, was most probably up there in that room at the head of the stairs now, lying in bed beside her mother. Presently, half asleep, she would be gently shoved out, to patter barefoot across the hall into her own room. That would be when Adolph finally grew tired of his intermittent nocturnal habits of dozing, reading his German paper, and pouring himself another coffee or beer, and began hoisting himself upstairs.

My little bed warmer, he used to call his stepdaughter, and pinch her cheek as it blushed.

"Papa, such talk before Freda!"

It occurred to Ray, with something of a shock, during occasional of these ejaculations of hers, that actually she was three months younger than this stepsister whose innocence Tagenhorst was for-ever championing.

Three doors slammed throughout the drafty house, as Ray, with the two tears hanging against the diamond-shaped panes of her veil, entered.

It was difficult to remember to guard against those little on-purpose things. Oh, well, what did it matter? It made a lot of dif-ference, nit! Whoever wanted to know what time she came in, was welcome to the privilege.

Why on earth did Tagenhorst insist upon turning out the hall gas when she went upstairs? Papa never failed to stumble over the hatrack. The floor of Tagenhorst's heaven would be paved with small gas-bills. Last month, in an eight-room house occupied by four persons, the gas consumed had amounted to forty cents. Skinned shins and stubbed toes testified to that. It was right to be thrifty, of course, particularly now that Adolph's twenty-year lease on the store had expired and he had been obliged to undertake renewal at heavy rental increase. It twisted the heart out of one to see him sitting rubbing the wrinkles of his forehead, as if they hurt him. Tagenhorst's economies should be meticulously observed, but there was a difference between economies and smallness. Tagenhorst was the difference. It was small of her to go off to bed, leaving Adolph to stub his gouty old toes going upstairs. Small, small, small. In the few years since her father had remarried, it was a household of new smallnesses. Small of Tagenhorst to go off to bed, leaving Adolph the old end of headcheese, when she knew how he would have enjoyed slivering down into the yielding richness of the new one in the icebox. She stinted Adolph that way. Little things. If only he were not so good-natured it wouldn't hurt so to have him stinted out of his rights. Sometimes one found oneself wishing there was something downright mean about Papa. It would keep you hurting less for him. . . .

"My *Schnucke* is sitting in a draft," she said, upon entering, her precaution against his dangerous tendency for bronchitis, automatic.

He was already in the midst of an act that was his second nature.

Adolph loved to set a lavish table. He delighted in preparing and administering refreshment.

He was already cutting down through the hard heel of the cheese for a sliver which he would presently convey to her on a slab of the richly dark loaf of pumpernickel that stood end-up on the table. *"Naschen ein Bischen!"* She pretended to ignore him when he addressed her in German; and, strangely, the sole use he made of his native tongue, at least in the last brace of years, was the sentence or two he occasionally addressed to his daughter.

"Run and tell it to the Oberdorfers," was the retort with which she had weaned him to a more general use of English. The Oberdorfers were a family on Baymiller Street, five adult daughters and one son, all American-born, who spoke the pure Low-German of their parents and little if any of a highly impure English.

He poured the final contents of his granite coffeepot, which it was his habit to whiten and sweeten while it boiled, into his used cup, and handed it to his daughter, who took a sip and gave it back to him. She would do the same with the cheese on the slice of pumpernickel too, bite into it and return it to Schmidt, who would consume it with the coffee. Poor old Pa. The gas made his pallor glisten like paraffin.

"Who banked the stove, Pa? You shouldn't be sitting in this chill."

Tagenhorst had, of course. Well, what Father did not notice, did not hurt him, but how dared she, knowing his susceptibility to cold?

"Sit a little, Ray. It's not so late."

Not, Where had she been? Why had she been? It's past one. Shame! Everything she did was to him right and normal and as it should be.

If only it had not seemed so right and normal. If only it had struck him, back in the days when she had been the high-spirited, high-busted Ray Schmidt of fifteen and sixteen years of age, who was striking her gait as a lulu with the boys, because she found it so difficult to say no to them.

If only he had suspected her and corrected her and doubted her just a little, she would not be sitting there now, like one of the hordes of soiled pigeons that came home every night to huddle and bleat under the eaves of the post office in Government Square.

"There's a whole *Leberwurst* in the icebox, Daughter, that will melt in your mouth. I stopped by for it at Hamberger and Newburgh's. I'll fix you a sandwich with some beer."

Almost frugal at table himself, Adolph's eyes watered more readily than his mouth. Ever since she could remember, Ray had seen him come home laden with provender that had tempted his glance along the way. Cheeses, potted and pickled delicacies, smoked meats, tinned fish lurked in his icebox and even in his desk drawers at the store.

"I've just had tongue at Wielert's—with Prothero. How's that?" She knew it would be all right. All right in a way that was suddenly hateful and hurtful to her.

"MacQuirk was in, after you had left the store, asking for you."

MacQuirk was another salesman out of New York. Jets and passementeries. Sixty, if a day, sporty after the easy-spending, lavish-tipping fashion that had come to mean the New York manner. Married, of course. Grown daughters, in fact, and grandchildren. He was regarded as a crack amateur bowler, and liked to have Ray accompany him, on the one or two of his semiannual evenings in town, to the local alleys, where he attracted quite a gallery of spectators. Then, Over-the-Rhine for boiled beef and horseradish sauce, beer and pretzels, with Ray, whom he called the town's toniest.

It was galling to be tony to MacQuirk, who would not have tolerated her doings in daughters of his own. But then, it gave MacQuirk pleasure to walk along Vine Street with Ray. Tony girl with hips and a bust to her. Style. He was the kind of spender who made her feel special and excited and remote from the machinery of living. Waiters scurried before MacQuirk. Without consulting her, he started every meal with giant olives, celery stuffed with Roquefort cheese, and a short, new, provocative drink called "Manhattan cocktail."

Once, on a three-day, five-dollar-a-round-trip excursion to Chicago, which Ray had made with her father, they had encountered MacQuirk on Michigan Boulevard with his wife, a woman of at least sixty, with a cold, embittered face and none of the sporty bearing of her husband. It had been a quick, constrained little meeting, and MacQuirk had actually blushed over the introductions. Adolph, of course, had noticed nothing; but the immediate consciousness had stung Ray to the quick, that MacQuirk had hesitated over introducing his wife.

Was there ever a man of Schmidt's grotesque innocence? Sex was something that caused two people to marry, in order to enjoy desires that were thus legitimized.

Some day Ray would marry. Until then, complications, if they happened at all, were something that occurred to other people's children, and in the headlines of newspapers, from which Ray was somehow immune.

The way in which he sat there, informing her that an old roué, sixty if a day, married, a grandfather, had been sniffing around for the purpose of taking her to the baseball, the races, the bowling-alley, or Over-the-Rhine! Was there ever such insulation from certain realizations of life? It made you wonder that he had ever reached the point of marriage himself. His mind must have worked so simply. If at all.

A man had natural desires. He married a woman, usually with fewer of those desires, but acquiescence. Then home, reproduction, and family. Irregularities in this scheme were something that occurred, the town was filled with them, of course, but outside the wide arc of general conformity. Ray would marry the regular way. He hoped not soon. At least, he would have hoped, if underneath the thick cuticle of complacency anything about these taken-for-granted aspects of life had been called to his attention.

"Papa," she said suddenly, placing her hand over his, "Papa, do you ever think of me and the MacQuirks of this world?"

His lack of understanding was so complete that he reconstructed what he had heard into what he thought she meant.

"He hung around the store, waiting, went over to the Stag, and then dropped in again to see if you had come back. He was looking

for good company," said Adolph Schmidt, and regarded his daughter with the crinkles in his forehead moving up and down. His way
of laughing.

For a moment her energy quailed before the magnitude of his
imperturbability.

"Papa, now listen."

He pinched her cheek.

"Now listen. I want to ask you something. Terribly."

"*Und so weiter.*"

"I sometimes get to thinking, Father. I sometimes get to thinking what this town must think of me."

"This town?"

"Yes. The men around it and the men who come to it from other
towns."

"What should they think?"

"Well, what would you think, Pa, say if you were MacQuirk or
Prothero or just any one of a dozen boys who hang around the Stag
a lot? What would you think if you were one of those fellows, and
I was a girl like me? Just a regular Cincinnati girl, born and raised
here, Lutheran, going to school here, living at home with my folks,
going down to the business since my second year High and—well,
running around the way I do. What would you think?"

"Think?" he said, and leaned over to enclose each cheek in a
pinch of his chubby thumb and forefinger. "I'd think I was a lucky
man to get the company of Ray Schmidt."

"What else would you think?"

"I'd think I'd never seen a girl I think so fine and pretty."

"Papa, try not to be yourself when you think. Just think as if you
were Mac or Prothero or a fellow loafing outside the Stag."

"That is nonsense. How can I think what I would think, if it was
not me thinking?"

"Would you think I was a bad girl, Pa? Fly, or dirty?"

He looked at her for the first time with something like a shocked
attention and paused in the act of biting down into pumpernickel.

"*Was sagst du?*"

"You know. That I wasn't—good?"

His face fell into pleats of helplessness, his jaw loosened, his eyes became the mute pleading ones of a spaniel.

"You want to make me talk nonsense?"

"But, Pa, did it ever occur to you that perhaps, as Tagenhorst says, you trust me too much?"

"A woman trying to make a good stepmother of herself don't dare to trust for fear it will look careless."

"Doesn't it occur to you, Pa, that all these fellows who take me out—Over-the-Rhine—Hayden's—races—that some of them, most of them, maybe all, except home boys like Kurt, look at me as if I were—just so much flesh, Papa? Flesh that perhaps they can sleep with. . . ."

He made a noise of strangulation and began to twist his neck in its low halter of a collar like a turtle giving evidence of distress in its shell.

"What are you talking about? You want to make me crazy? Has anything happened that makes you want to make me crazy?" He began to make small crying sounds in a manner she had never beheld except on a day she dimly remembered, when the oblong shadow of her mother's bier had lain down the center of the very room in which they were sitting. Soft bleats of sound that some-how corresponded with the falling of his face into the loose laps of flesh. She wanted to hush him, at any price, back into his unassailed complacency.

"Can't you take a joke, Father?"

"Don't ever," he said to her in almost the first admonition she could remember, "don't ever let me hear you talk like that again. Don't ever."

"I was only foolish, Papa," she repeated, against the flash of something she had seen dart in among the pleats of his face. "For goodness' sakes, don't have a conniption fit over nothing."

Ugly joking. What had got into this girl who was his daughter and yet at the same time reminded him of his mother, who had died forty years before in Mainz? What in the world had got into her? Women got nerves. . . .

"Drink this coffee, Father, and forget it."

Funny thing had happened to him. Felt as if he had just had a chill. Perhaps he had.

"I think maybe I've caught a cold."

"Tagenhorst ought not to bank the fire before she goes up to bed. She ought to know you mustn't sit around in the cold. You tell her, Pa. She won't take it from me."

"Don't ever talk ugly like this to me again, Ray."

"Papa dear, I won't," she said, and crossed over and stood behind his chair and placed her lips to the smooth dome of his head, feeling all over again her impulse to cry over him. "Come up to bed."

He creaked out of his chair, still unable to be certain that his curious unease had been chill.

"I forgot to tell you Fred Hecker was here after supper to know if you will ride with him on his tandem out to the zoo Sunday morning."

"I can't. I promised Kurt I'd go over to the shop with him Sunday morning and balance his books. Did I tell you Kurt and Eddie Winton are trying to rent a store in Poorman's Block, and sell bicycles as well as repair them? Sounds good, doesn't it, Pa?"

"That is sound. Like Kurt. There's a big future in bicycles, the way everybody has got the bug for running around quick, as if almost everything in life wouldn't keep until a little later."

"I wonder how many in this town would believe, Pa, that Kurt Shendler is the only fellow who has ever, in my whole life, asked me to marry him. . . ."

He turned to regard her, as he limped his great overweight body out of that dining room of gaslit murk, into which swam greasily a black-oak sideboard freighted with pressed glass, a wire flowerpot stand of half-asphyxiated geraniums, a flock of ten black-oak chairs around a table still spread with a supper cloth upon which there were stains.

"Don't fiddle around waiting for something better than Kurt, when it's just like life to hand you something worse. I'm right, daughter?"

She leaned over to kiss him, as he grasped the newel post for the first slow hoist of his vast body up the stairway.

"Good night, *Schnucke,*" she said, giving him a boost for the first step, which seemed too hard for him.

That was the night, peacefully, without so much as a rattle of breathing loud enough to awaken Tagenhorst, that Adolph Schmidt, dearly beloved husband of Cora Tagenhorst Schmidt, father of Ray Schmidt, stepfather of Freda and Marshall Tagen-horst, died in his sleep.

4

"Papa wouldn't have wanted it this way, if he could have foreseen how things would turn out," was the sole comment Ray was ever to make on her predicament of sharing so little in her father's leavings.

The transaction of making over the homestead to Tagenhorst had seemed fair enough when it happened. She had put her savings of twenty-five hundred dollars into the business at a time when the advance in rental was embarrassing Schmidt acutely. That, then, was right and fair; and Ray herself had been instrument to running back and forth to the lawyer in Sixth Street with deed and document, and there had been two journeys with Tagenhorst to the offices to sign the transferal of the deeds.

It was what happened subsequently that made the division galling, because, after the house, the estate of Adolph Schmidt resolved itself into something like this: five hundred dollars benefit from a local Turnverein society; household effects too negligible for listing; a considerable array of business debts, amounting to well over three thousand dollars; a practically new rubber-tired surrey which he had taken over in lieu of a debt five years previous and kept stored in the loft of a neighbor against the day when he should feel in the position to append to it a good chestnut mare; gold lockets, rings, chains, and a watch that had been Lena Schmidt's; a business that proved to be worth precisely the life of its owner.

Legally, had it been thinkable to contest for them, there were rights for Ray lying about even among this rather barren débris of her father's estate; but the desire was not for the exercise of her prerogatives, but for peace.

"You're a fool, Ray," said the more intimate of the friends who were watching it happen. "Tagenhorst won't think any more of you for being so easygoing. Don't let her walk off with the situation."

"Let her have it. Papa would hate to see us squabbling over what little he left. Anyhow, now that he's gone—everything's gone. . . ."

"But your mother's bedroom set. That old-fashioned stuff is worth a lot."

"Let her have it."

"But she thinks you don't know any better."

"Let her think."

"Well, in your mother's lifetime she always gave me to understand that some day she wanted me to have that hand-painted piano scarf I notice the widow has whisked out of sight."

"Let her have it. . . ."

No, Papa wouldn't have wanted it that way, if ever it had even occurred to him to make a will.

"You are welcome to make this your home as long as you like," had been Tagenhorst's retort to this sole observation of Ray's.

As long as you like! As long as you like in the house in which you have been born. Why, in that narrow wooden house on Baymiller Street, with its two plane-trees out along the whitened coping, its long parlor windows opening onto the porch, the front yard the shape of an oblong bedspread, fenced off from the sidewalk in iron scrollwork, the elephant-ear bed in that front yard and the hydrant to which you attached the hose, Ray had first opened her eyes.

Lena Schmidt had borne her in that house, and sickened in that house, and died in it while Ray was still playing with the big-sized doll that even now sat stiffly in one of Ray's little-girl chairs in the parlor. She could remember this mother in two outstanding ovals of memory chiefly because every portrait of her mother extant—a brooch painted on porcelain, a crayon enlargement that had once hung in the dining room—had been in the shape of a mournful sort of "O." Another memory with an oval etched bitingly into it, was that of her mother sitting in a cane rocker in the bedroom later to be occupied by Schmidt and Tagenhorst, coughing with her handkerchief to her lips, and then holding it away to regard, with her dark ruby-colored mouth opened to the shape of an appalled oval, the bright-red stain upon it.

It was not only the oval, appalled mouth that lay etched in Ray's memory, it was the way in which the round, stretched eyes had traveled to Ray, the child, sitting there in her little rocker, with the bisque doll clasped in her arms.

It was Lena Schmidt's first agonized look of realization that she must part from this child.

To be told in such a house that you were welcome to make it your home as long as you liked! Even in the years when Adolph rented the house to Tagenhorst, and he and his daughter had continued on as boarders, it had seemed to remain primarily the house of the Schmidts. The name chiseled into the little square hitching-stone at the curb had never been changed. "SCHMIDT." After the marriage of Schmidt and Tagenhorst, even the small restraints of the years of tenancy under Tagenhorst, the landlady, were minimized still more under her régime as Mrs. Schmidt the second. Once more, now, she kept her towels and toothbrush in the bathroom instead of carrying them back each time into her room. There was no longer need for tying up the small bundle of her and her father's clothes every Monday morning to be called for by Libby, a colored washerwoman. Family washing was once more done in the Schmidt kitchen, Ray's and her father's along with Tagenhorst's and Freda's.

To be told in half a dozen subtle ways, as they sat around the dining-room table the Sunday morning after the funeral of Schmidt—Ray, Freda, Tagenhorst, and a son Marshall, a Tagenhorst offspring of her former marriage who had suddenly materialized from Youngstown—that she was welcome to remain in a home that had suddenly and surely slipped from under her!

Papa would be turning in his grave, could he behold Tagenhorst, sitting there in curlpapers and the blue challis wrapper which she had dyed black, hurting her so!

Not that it really mattered so devastatingly, as she put it bitterly to herself, that, as things were working out, practically everything became his widow's. Rather, it was the principle of the thing.

Come right down to it, one could not call this much of a dilemma. On one of her recent buying trips to New York, she had been offered out-and-out, right there on the spot, a position with the firm of Ledbetter and Scape, a well-known concern on Greene Street, from which she had bought passementeries. For that matter, right there at home she had been given to understand, by no other than the head of the department who was her friend and liked to buy her steaks at the Burnet House, that should she ever decide to leave her father's business, a position at Pogue's could be arranged.

No, it was not her failure to come in for any share of patrimony that mattered so much, there were various avenues of livelihood open, but it was this sense of somehow being alien to his death. This Tagenhorst sitting there had the rights. The widow, who had only had the last years of his darling life, sitting there in black challis and curlpapers, vested with first place!

Not first place in grief. But first in her right to sit there, this Sunday morning, checking off, with the heretofore hearsay Marshall, who had never showed himself in Cincinnati, the furniture, and even the large gold watch and chain that Schmidt had for thirty years worn spanning the great girth of his vest. There had once been a small photograph of Lena Schmidt, in bangs and basque, with the cheek of Ray crushed up to hers, in the back of that watch. And now the watch was Tagenhorst's, and the dining-room table, about which they were sitting and which had been coveted, chosen, and purchased by Lena Schmidt, was Tagenhorst's, and the usurped right to dispose of everything pertaining or appertaining to the dear figure of Adolph, who had lived and died so snugly within the small orb of his Cincinnati home and business, was Tagenhorst's.

"Papa would not have wanted it like this," Ray could not help blurting out. "He told me once, just before his remarriage, that he intended to make a will."

"You are welcome to make this your home for as long as you like. . . ."

Underneath her little bosom, with the barrage of starched ruffles

worn to bolster it up, something must have stirred and given pang
to the blonde Freda, who placed her hand, with its turquoise ring,
on top of Ray's tannish one.

"It's more your home than mine, Ray."

That was true; yet the mere saying of it by Freda was sufficient
to assuage the hurting of some of her resentments.

After all, Tagenhorst was within some of her rights, and Adolph
had been her husband; and a widow, at sixty, with the blonde, flaccid problem of Freda, under whose pasty prettiness ran vexatious
problems, and now this heavy-necked son by a former marriage
turning up, was not fit to cope with trials that to Ray, nineteen,
were not even trials.

Whether Adolph had made a will or not—what did it matter?
The *Schnucke* in Adolph had failed to make it. The heartbreaking,
good-natured complacency for which lay a perpetual little pool of
tears in the heart of Ray, had failed . . . not Adolph. . . .

Let come what might! Suppose Tagenhorst did have the house.
And just for argument, suppose then that some day Freda, and this
big bull here, did inherit it. Terrible of course, in a way. Terrible!
And yet, obviously, this big-headed bull, to whom Tagenhorst was
forever sending small sums, could never be more than just what he
was. Truck-driver for a coal firm in Youngstown. Nothing to hope
for from that direction. As for Freda, little, horrid-minded Freda,
she was always creeping into her bed of a Sunday morning with
intimate soiled questions on her cherry-colored lips that made her
seem to need every ounce of the meticulous protection Tagenhorst
could afford for her.

One had to be philosophical to keep from succumbing to an
impulse to cry one's body into a veritable pool of tears. It would
have helped to be able to scourge these people here around the
table—her table—with anger. But somehow, even in the act of taking from you what was rightfully part yours at least, it was difficult
not to feel compassion for Tagenhorst, sixty, widowed, acquisitive,
and tired.

Let them have it. Likely as not, Freda, whose rabid little appetite for answers to the soiled questions was insatiable, might sink to

this lowest level of herself. Without it, Tagenhorst was fairly sure to become an object of Ray's perpetual financial responsibility. So it was just as well. One had to look at it that way to be able to bear it at all. Adolph's watch and chain, for instance, lying on the thick pad of Marshall's appraising palm.

The bull Marshall, whose nostrils were distended as if he smelled meat, was all for immediate disposition of the holdings. Well, let them haggle; they had yet to learn to what extent the holding of the store, lacking the personality of its founder, was defunct.

The business must go for debts and good will. No one, not even those who had held for years that the firm was going into decline, knew to what extent the little old trimming-business was sinking in its tracks. Bradstreet knew. Certain creditors suspected. Adolph Schmidt, fumbling hours on end, days, months, years on end, among the rear boxes of chenilles, tassels, jets, bindings, jabots, fancy buttons, and buckles, had known.

But not even he had known, as Ray from her angle of salesman, buyer, and accountant knew, that the "one-hoss shay" of the concern "Adolph Schmidt—Trimmings and Findings" was going to pieces.

A natural demise. The younger generations of the petty genteels who had been content to purchase their dressmaking-findings of Adolph Schmidt, now either drifted around to Vine Street or West Fourth, to Le Boutillier's, Alms and Doepke's, Caldwell's, Mabley and Carew's, or Shillito's, more elaborate emporiums, where the selection was wider, and, by virtue of quantity buying, the prices actually lower.

Poor old Adolph's leavings had been lean. "There are just a few personal things I would like to have. My mother's sewing table."

"That's a shame now. I crated it to Youngstown yesterday!"

"Papa's walking stick with the ivory horsehead from Frankfurt. He loved that."

"Now where could I have packed that?"

Ray wanted to add: "And his gold watch and chain too. I could always hear it ticking when I was little and he lifted me up on his lap." But she did not. All three of Adolph Schmidt's little personal jewelry appointments, the watch and chain, a small gold clasp for holding necktie in place against the front pleat of the shirt, and a fob engraved with the seal of a Turnverein Society, had disappeared from his top dresser drawer. Even that could be borne, if only the watch, Papa's own, were not now reposing against the heavy breathing of Marshall.

"Any little things you want, Ray, you can have," said Tagenhorst, at her perpetual business of picking up from the breakfast table and nibbling with her front teeth small particles of crumb and caraway seed that had dropped from the large loaf of rye bread lying beside its long steel knife, on a wooden board. She was like an untidy blonde old crow, pecking up what she coveted.

It was the first Sunday morning in all Ray's life that had not been crammed with the doings of her father. He pedicured that morning, he shaved at greater length than usual before a hand mirror tacked to the upper sash of the bathroom window, he dug up around the elephant ears in the front yard in summer, and in winter among the geraniums on the wire rack in the dining room. He tinkered around the tandems of the young men who came to take her bicycling, he rattled among the German newspapers, and at eleven o'clock he attended the Lutheran services, alone or with whatever member of the family he could muster.

It struck Ray with a pang, that for the past year she had either gone bicycling every fair Sunday morning, or down to Kurt Shendler's shop to balance his books. Except for the eagerness with which Adolph accepted her occasional company, you would never have known that he minded, particularly in the years when Freda or Tagenhorst, upholstered as any piece of furniture their parlor boasted, had accompanied him.

It was just that death, somehow, gave you hindsight. Papa would have loved for her, looking bright and stylish, to walk in to services with him. He had been content with Tagenhorst and Freda, never crossing Ray or expressing what must have been his wish for the Sunday-morning companionship of his daughter, who was busy always, cruising with the boys.

What would Papa, so indulgent, think now, lying out there

beside Mama under earth that was still broken from the spade? What would he think if he could see her sitting there amid the strangers—Tagenhorst, Marshall, who had turned up for the first time in all the years, as if scenting carrion, and Freda acquiescent, placid, flaccid, and yet her glance, as it curved mamaward, tightening the Tagenhorsts.

"The thing to do," said Tagenhorst, pecking up the caraway seeds, "is to let things drift until we see what is best. 'Dolph wasn't orderly."

The eyes of Marshall, which were set into pleats of whitish flesh, shot down toward his mustache, which shot upward.

"Sell!"

To think that Papa's watch was ticking against that bulk!

"What time is it, Marshall?"

At her question, his hand moved toward the speckled waistcoat and hung there cautious.

"About eleven, I guess."

That she could be made sufficiently snide over Father's watch to have caused her to employ that device, caused the tears to spout.

"Are you going bicycling this morning, Ray?" asked Freda brightly.

She hoped so, although none of the boys had said anything, owing, no doubt, to deference for the Sunday morning following her father's death.

The glance which Tagenhorst, blonde crow, hooked onto her from above lips careful not to interfere, said its usual volumes.

"It's time to dress for church, Freda," she said to her daughter, with her eyes on her stepdaughter.

Well, no matter! She would no more have carried the ache that lay in her heart for Adolph into the pew that became stuffy and without God, once Tagenhorst set foot into it.

"Mama, can't I ever go bicycling on Sunday?"

"No, you can't ever."

And yet, strangely, even as the baby treble in Freda's voice struck her to derision, she would not have wanted Freda to go. You were fly if you did things like that. Why, even so much as take a

ride with the average young fellow, out toward Sedamsville, where
the gravel road began, and you could almost tell, to the mile, under
what shade tree along the roadside he would want to pause and
throw himself down on the grass beside you, so that your knees
touched, and surreptitious spooning became the order.

"But Ray goes, Ma."

This invariable little pouting remark drew from Tagenhorst four
small explosives.

"Yes—but—you—don't!"

"Could I go if Hugo asked me?" When Freda asked this question,
sitting there with her scooped-out eggshell which she had eaten so
neatly and cleanly in two careful halves on the table before her, the
small pearls of her teeth immaculate of stain, her blue eyes floated
upward as if they had been soap bubbles.

"Hugo would not ask you to do such a thing."

Was it possible, after all, that Hugo Hanck was serious-minded
in his growing attentions to her stepsister? Freda might look it, but
she was nobody's fool, anyway, where Freda was concerned. The girl
who married the meter-reader for the Cincinnati Gas, Light and
Coke Company also married the only nephew and heir apparent of
Herman Hanck, wealthy retired brewer and bachelor. The girl who
married Hugo, married prospects.

It would be good to think of Freda, who could be sweet after a
fashion, and at the same time so unbelievably horrid-minded, married to Hugo who had inherited, and snug as a bug in a rug. She
would be that way. A small round little bug in a cozy rug. Freda
needed to be married. The trend of her questions made it imperative for Freda to be married. Why, some of the questions she asked,
on those mornings she climbed into Ray's bed—it would never do
to admit it, but Ray had never even heard the phraseology of some
of the thoughts that hopped, toadlike, from the cherry-colored sills
of Freda's lips.

"There's Kurt outside whistling for you now, Ray."

Yes, there it was! Two long and a short. Kurt was one of the
few boys who called for Ray who had the habit of venturing into
the house. But now, since the passing of Adolph, to whom he had

invariably brought an El Merito cigar on the occasions of these visits, there seemed something strange to Ray about having him enter this house—of strangers.

"So you're going," said Tagenhorst, with her medium-blue eyes focused in the center of their rigid, stone-blue whites.

"Yes. I promised Kurt I'd look over his books with him this morning."

"I read in the *Enquirer* yesterday," said Freda, in her treble, "that a girl in South Bend, Indiana, went up in a bicycle-repair shop a fellow kept over a feed-store, and was found dead with her head off in a gunny sack two weeks later. Case of assault. What is assault, Ray?"

"It's enough for you to know it's a word you shouldn't ever use. I hope you don't ever answer the child's foolish questions, Ray."

"But I don't see why I can't go bicycling if Ray—"

"Ray's ways are her own ways," said Tagenhorst, still at the caraways. "I guess she knows what she is doing. Always has."

The sentence fell down like a portcullis, shutting her off on her separate side of the moat from the mother and daughter.

"I'll be going. . . ."

Outside on the front lawn, his bicycle standing wrongside up on its handle bars, Kurt Shendler, as he waited, was spinning a pedal and tinkering with it.

It seemed to Ray, as she hurried out, snatching her natty straw sailor hat from the rack and pinning it onto her pompadour, that the only person in the world to whom she could turn, while the pools of misery lay in her heart, was Kurt.

5

The repair shop smelled of graphite, lubricating-oil, and inner tubing. In one corner of the disarray, against a bare brick wall and beside a rusty stove, was backed the flat-topped desk at which Kurt and Ray were in the habit of spending an occasional Sunday morning.

It was a desktop of an unsavory confusion of bicycle-parts, wrenches, bolts, sample tins of grease, cotton waste, adhesive tape, tubes of tire cement, and, tucked away into pigeonholes, a further miscellany of worn-looking account-books that contained what story there was to tell of the financial status of "Kurt Shendler— Bicycle Repair Shop."

There was something, each time she laid aside her hat, slid into Kurt's sleeve-protectors, swirled the stool higher, that never failed to appal Ray, as she lifted these grime-coated books from their compartments.

There was lack of tidiness, lack of system, lack of law and order in Kurt's bookkeeping. True, he seemed to have some sort of order to his own methods, could tell to a penny and without reference to his books the status of accounts paid and unpaid, but this period of auditing with the astute Miss Schmidt was of a paramount importance to him, quite apart from the red and black columns of his ledgers.

The fact that she had sat at that desk, her hat laid aside, her large sleeves ballooning against her sides like wings, her hair in a thick soft "horse's tail" against the back of her neck, and that soft golden glow off her flesh, almost as if you could feel the heat radiate, was to leave for Kurt, weeks after, a flavor that was stronger than the lasting smell of the graphite and the blur of dust off the wooden floors.

In the sense that his predilection for mechanics, his aversion for salt meat, his talent for organization, and his inborn interest in ways and means of moving about this earth, were part and parcel of his personality, so was his consciousness that in Ray was his woman.

He saw her as wife in a home of his making. Her hands were in the clay of which his life was to be molded. She was the woman to be in and out among his days, in and out of his doorways, of his bed, and her sweet curved waist and the acquiescing eyes, kind beyond any telling, and the generosity that seemed to envelop her in an ebullience, were the very grain and texture of his future which contained her.

And now this passing of her father, who had sort of died in his tracks, of placid routine, and over whose daughter was powdered some of his benign personality, was sure to have the effect of drawing her more surely into the web of his life.

He wanted to take her, as she sat there beside his desk, poring over his slovenly accountings, and bend back her head until he could feel the warmth of the golden glow off her face onto the flesh of his own, and let her tears, which he knew were in a knot beneath her smile, run warm against his flesh.

He had, it is true, held her close and long, one twilight hour, in a sequestered glen at Eden Park, where they had bicycled for a picnic supper. Passion had raced in him, and his lips had dragged her cheek, and his breathing had fanned the glow that he felt emanating from her. He explained to her later, when his lips would carry words, that it had been the overwhelming passion of a man for the woman he would make his wife. She had been acquiescent in a way that had puzzled him. It was as if he had left her untouched by his vigor, unimpressed by his force, but pleased with the knowledge that she had given him pleasure. He had the feeling, watching her, that she was regarding his lips, as they coined the phrase of his proposal of marriage to her, with the fascinated attention of a child.

He had not, somehow, even with her large indulgence, dared to follow it up. In fact, he could not be quite sure that she had heard. Now, in her new loneliness, there was that which gave him courage. There was a droop to coveted, stylish Ray Schmidt this day, as he sat beside her, hearing with mock humility the storm of her mock reproaches for his untidy bookkeeping.

"What in the world is this six dollars and twenty cents? Is it against Eddy Slayback or the Eddy Steam Fittings Company? Honestly now, Kurt, I ask to know! Who could tell from the way you've made this entry?"

"Don't potter over the books today, Ray."

"Say, Beanpole, I'se goin' to lay you across my knee if you doan behaive. . . ."

At twenty-seven, before he had filled out to what astonishingly was to be mild corpulency, Kurt was six feet tall and weighed one hundred and eighteen pounds. It was the lankiness of early overgrowth, because he had been that six feet back in the days when his parents had still lived and conducted their small tobacconist shop on Sixth Street, and he had run his first errands as boy-of-all-work for Miller's Carriage and Coach Company, at Sixth and Sycamore streets.

"Let those books go, Ray."

"But, Kurt—"

"I want to talk to you. Haven't had much chance since—since your old man went out. You must know how I feel about anything that hits you. . . ."

"Don't make me cry, Kurt," she said, looking away from him. "I cry easy—yet."

"It's a funny thing to say, but I'd like it if you cried, Ray."

She sat swallowing.

"Papa was everything I had."

"Don't say that!"

"I mean—I can never be as all right to anybody as I was to him. He just—liked me—terribly for what I was or wasn't. Didn't matter. And nobody knows better than I do what I wasn't."

"You can have consolation, Ray, that you never gave the old gentleman a day's worry in your life. You've got no regrets."

"I know better," she said, and began to mark crosses on a piece of blotting paper. "But anyway, it helps to know that Pa never felt troubled enough about me to sit down and try and figure me out."

"I've figured you out, Ray, but I don't care why you do things. I just know that if you do them, they're right. For me, anyhow."

"If I could figure out for myself why I do things, maybe I'd have enough sense not to do them."

"You're gay by nature, Ray."

"Gay? Gay as my Aunt Hanna's black bonnet. I'm not gay, Kurt. I'm an old sick cat at heart."

"Ray, I just hate to hear you say that."

"I've got a hurt in me as big as a hen's egg. Always had it. Born with it. Don't know what it's about, but it's in me."

"Marry me, Ray."

"Remember the last time you said that to me?"

"Yes, but I didn't think you even listened."

"Will it surprise you, Kurt, if I tell you that no man has ever asked me to do that before?"

"You're so head-and-shoulders above every one of them. I'm the only one who has the conceited nerve."

"'Tisn't that, Kurt, and you know it."

"Well, then, every fellow in this town, or that ever comes to it, is crazy—except me."

"Every man in this town, or that ever comes to it, figures he can have me anyway, Kurt."

"I wish—I wish you hadn't said that, Ray."

"It's true."

"Well, anyway, I wish it like the very devil, that you hadn't said that."

"You know it's true."

He rose abruptly and walked over to the grimy window and stood looking down on a sooty agglomeration of old bicycle junk, while she sat with her clasped hands held motionless.

He came back presently and stood with his feet planted far apart.

"It isn't true, is it, that they—can have you?"

"No."

He swung her into his arms then, and kissed her again and again on the mouth.

"You mustn't do that, Kurt."

"Why?"

No reason, except that she usually said that.

"Aren't you mine?"

"You mustn't do that."

"You made me feel sick just now. Just as sick as a man can feel."

"I know I did, Kurt. It hurt me to say it."

"Then why did you?"

"It's true."

"Didn't you just say it wasn't?"

"I mean it's true that they think those things."

"The man who thinks them from now on has me to contend with."

"Funny thing, Kurt, but I've always been like that."

"Like what?"

"Too free—easygoing—"

"You're too big-minded always to be sniffing around the p's and q's of every little thing you do."

"There's not a nice girl in this town would be sitting up here in this deserted loft with you of a Sunday morning, Kurt."

"Shows you're big-minded!"

"Shows I don't watch out for my own good."

"You certainly don't do that, Ray."

"I am what I am. I simply cannot always be figuring out what I do, as if I was too good to be doing this or that. I can't feel I'm that important, Kurt. I guess I have no dignity."

"You won't feel that way about things when you've a home of your own, Ray."

"Reckon not, Kurt?"

"I know not," he said, and kissed her again.

"The way I feel now, Kurt—so confused—I don't know how I feel."

"Is it any wonder? Guess the old woman up at the house doesn't make things any easier for you."

"She's all right."

"According to how you look at things."

"She's his widow. A woman may not ever have been much more to a man than his widow, even during his lifetime, but after his death there can be dignity and profit in being his widow."

"I guess they're hogging everything."

"Not much to hog; and what there is, they're welcome to."

"That's about the way I look at it. Makes me feel more as if you belonged to me, Ray. I want to take you, now that you're kind of stunned and hurt, and baby you, and get myself in some sort of a position to marry you."

"That's wonderful, Kurt," she said, and placed her hand on his knee and regarded him with the gray eyes that were washed in what to him was to remain indescribable sweetness.

"The shop isn't yielding yet, Ray. Won't be until I've cleared the debt to Osterlitz for backing me. But next year I expect to begin drawing out. This is the makings of a real going concern, Ray, and our future is ahead of us. The bicycle is here to stay! I'll be riding you around in a landaulet, one of these days, on bicycle-money, Mrs. Shendler."

"Me married?"

"Why not?"

"Kurt, will you feel hurt if I tell you something?"

"The only way you can hurt me, Ray, is to break my heart with a two-letter word. Don't say that word to me."

"Kurt, no man has ever kissed me so that it really mattered."

"You haven't been waked up."

"Go along, Kurt. I've been about more than most."

"The other will come."

"That's what I am afraid of."

"I'll love you into making it come."

"What if it should come after I'd married you? The caring for someone, I mean. I know myself so well, Kurt. I'm all the way or zero. God help the man I fall in love with."

"You can't frighten me off that way. Living and loving and building as we go, maybe I won't have time to patronize the same tailors those salesmen and brokers around town do, but I'm going to make you money, honey, one of these days, big money, mark my word, and I'm not caring if you love me little, just so you love me long."

"You're sure, Kurt, it's not because I'm down? What would you say if I told you I've got good reason to believe there's a place for me in the trimming department at Pogue's? I don't know that I told you that on my last trip to New York I had quite an offer from a firm we've been buying from for years. . . . If things happen so that the business goes on the sandbar, I know where to turn, Kurt."

"There's not a doubt in my mind that, let alone, you'll go down in the history of this town as one of its first crack business girls. But you're going to quit it and go down in the history of my life instead."

"We'll let it ride for a while, Kurt. You're not ready. I'm shot to pieces. I need to get my bearings. Meanwhile, you're free. I'm free. How's that? Fair enough."

"Not for long though, Ray. I'll be on my own, before you can say cock robin."

"I'd be a fool to let it be for long."

"I love you," he said, and kissed her again and again on the mouth that had been kissed again and again.

"Now what about that six-dollar-and-twenty-cent entry, Kurt, was it against Eddy Slayback or the Eddy Steam Fittings Company?"

6

It was strange and difficult and often heartbreaking, after a meeting of creditors had averted receivership, and one Heyman Heymann, formerly of Middletown, who held two notes that practically plastered the entire holding, had stepped in to recruit what he could of the assets.

The arrangement with Ray was one which provided that she remain only long enough to acquaint the new owner with the multitude of small intricacies of a new business. But there was something pathetic about his dread of being left alone with this little white elephant which he suddenly found on his hands. He seemed to have a horror of being left alone with it. His way of seeming to make sure that Ray would not desert and leave him to the strange mercies of this strange phenomenon, his new business, was to manage to be about as little as possible, leaving responsibility of decision and transaction to her.

The affiliation with Heymann was in the main pleasant. He was a corpulent middle-aged Hebrew of twenty years' excellent business standing in Middletown, who had succumbed, when this opportunity to take over a Cincinnati business presented itself, to the pressure of a wife and marriageable daughter and migrated to the opportunities of the larger city.

His financial dependence upon the business was negligible. He owned the building in Middletown that had housed his button

factory before he had retired from it actively, and was reputed to
have further real-estate holdings in Hamilton. Be that as it may,
he was a less generous man than Adolph had been, imposing, from
the very first day of his taking-over, small new restrictions that were
prohibitive to Ray.

For instance, the long narrow old store, lined with boxes to its
ceiling and flanked by counters stacked with more boxes, was at best
but dingy lure to either wholesale or retail trade.

Heymann's habit was to follow the departure of each customer
by jerking the chain dangling from the Welsbach lights over the
counters, and reduce the store to a kind of gloom, which could
flow over and in turn reduce Ray to a depression that soaked her
into disinterestedness. Heymann saved the backs of old envelopes
for scratch paper, curtailed what he regarded as waste of twine
and wrapping papers, cut down in minor and enlarged in major
ways that doubtless attested to his astuteness over and above old
Adolph's; but somehow the new little economies, so unpracticed by
her father, filled her with nostalgia, kept the hurt in her stirring and
seeming to move about behind her bosom.

The old habits of routine went on just as before. Willie Meyer,
ancient nitwit about town, still did the chores of scrubbing up and
deliveries. The same old stream of traveling salesmen dropped in,
and, to a large extent, so did the same, if diminishing, clientele.

Heymann was not the man to inject "new blood"; but rather,
new conservatisms. Same old "Schmidt's," the stylish Ray, handsome in mourning, still dominating the old establishment, moving
among the dusty boxes, each one of them identified, as to content,
by a button or tassel or bit of jet or braid pasted on one end.

You dropped in to see Ray Schmidt when you checked into
town, at the Burnet House, St. Nicholas, Stag, or the Grand Hotel,
just as naturally as you delved into Over-the-Rhine for a bock of
Moerlein, Hauck, or Hudepohl. It did not matter whether you dealt
in dry goods, wet goods, implements, luxuries, or commodities, you
knew Ray for the town's tony girl.

Curious, but to Kurt, who except for the line of graphite under
his fingernails wore his blue serge with almost the nattiness of a

drummer, all this was a source of pride. Her desirability, now, somehow, that the close and homely truth of her had been revealed to him that morning in his repair-loft, was emphasized by the class of men who were eager to be seen out with Ray.

A tony girl who had them all guessing, but who could be relied upon to take care of herself.

If sometimes beneath his gay acquiescence to their suspended sort of relationship, fear smote Kurt, it was laid by the practical streak that dominated everything he said and thought.

"There isn't a marrying man in the lot of them."

Ray knew that too, and used to smile a lot about it to Kurt.

"Mark Steinberg and several other New York stockbrokers are on for the races. Dollar looks like a dime to them, Mark's Silver Boy is running at Latonia. Look for the handsome brunette in black surah silk and a yellow chrysanthemum, sitting beside Mark in his black-and-yellow wire-wheeled trap with the tandem horses. That'll be me, Kurt, helping Mark forget he's a grandpap."

And so it went, after the death of Adolph, for the most part as it had gone before, except, after a dreadful fashion, in no wise as it had gone before.

No matter how right eventually, things could never now quite have their flavor back. Never.

It was usually around the low-ebb hour of dawn that, awakening after a habit that had become troublesome to her, realization would pounce upon Ray, causing her to lie trembling and miserable while day climbed slowly over the roofs of Baymiller Street. Early-morning depressions which, as she lay there on the bed in which her mother had died, could make rising to face another day almost more than she could bear. To find that the death of Adolph was not a nightmare, and that she was lying there on the wedding-bed of her parents, now loaned to her through the largesse of Tagenhorst, was to make it a touch of bitter pain. To be sure, she paid her board, twenty out of the fifty dollars a month she now earned in the store, where by the same devastation of death she had become an outsider; but her universe had slipped suddenly, like land, sliding into a sea of bewilderment.

To think! Papa, sitting there so normally over coffee boiled with milk and sugar in it! And then, two evenings later, lying boxed, his face that had always been swept by heavy breathing, lying covered by a wooden lid, like merchandise on a store-shelf.

Elementary wonder at death's impartiality was out over Ray. Adolph could conceivably be dead to Tagenhorst or Freda, but to have left her like that. Without a word! Without a look back. With the passing of her mother, there had been only the rather terrified awe of the child. But Adolph had come so far into life with her. And she had not even closed his eyes in death, or seen to it what kind of socks he wore in his coffin. He had been borne, horizontal, bobbing, on the six broadcloth shoulders of six Turnverein members, out of the front door, carried tilted, down the front steps and along the red-painted brick walk, to a hearse with wooden plumes on its four corners. Adolph had gone to God without so much as a backward glance at his daughter left alone among the strangers— Tagenhorst, Heymann, Freda, and Marshall.

As she lay on her bed in the dark hours before dawn, half awake and half submerged under the depression that made these slow awakenings her horror, it required all her energy to force herself to rise to face the days.

Risen, and with the normal circumstances of the morning taking shape, she found that depression, in a large measure, lifted, and life became a matter of rushing ahead of who was sure to monopolize it, into the bathroom, buttoning into your shoes, buckling into your corset, looping and swirling at your pompadour, hooking, hitching into your petticoats, corset-cover, shirtwaist, and skirt, boiling your egg, and usually eating it standing beside the kitchen stove, and then bolting for the car if the weather was bad, or, if it was fine, leading your bicycle out from under the hall stairs.

Usually on Sunday morning, these indeterminate months following the death of Adolph, when the house was plastered with a "For Sale" sign and Marshall appeared now every fortnight or so from Youngstown in the capacity of advisor to his mother, Freda stole into bed beside Ray.

There was talk of moving to Youngstown, where, it developed,

Marshall had an eye to a coal business of his own, everything of course subservient to the disposal of the house, so that it might be a comfortable widow who could one of these days turn her face toward setting herself and her son up in business in the nearby town.

The prospect, however, was clouded somewhat for both Tagen-horst and her daughter by the uncertainty into which matters were further thrown by the failure of Hugo Hanck to precipitate his attentions to Freda by an offer of marriage.

"Ray," trebled Freda, one of those Sunday mornings when she had climbed from her mother's bed and padded across the hall into Ray's, "what is adultery?"

"Why, Freda Tagenhorst, what's on your mind?"

"What is adultery?"

"You know as well as I do."

"Honestly, Ray, I don't. Of course I know it is something bad, but I don't know what."

"You know your Commandments, don't you? You've gone to Sunday school all your life."

"Yes, but I don't mean the thou-shalt-not kind of adultery they talk about in the Bible. I mean real adultery right here in Cincinnati."

After all, what a child she was, lying there pink and soft and strangely kitten-like, her flaxen braids across the pillow and her softy young breasts breathing of the little excitement her question seemed to inspire.

"Adultery, Freda, is not being true to the person to whom you are married."

"Oh, then it isn't just something that any man can commit against a girl?"

"Yes, any man who is not true to his wife commits it."

"I mean if he isn't married. . . ."

"Why, no, Baby. What a silly you are."

"Ray?"

"Yes."

"Do you know that nuns are awful bad?"

"No."

"Well, they are. There's a girl in my class named Katy Schwa-baker, who went to a convent-school. She says . . . Oh, you ought to hear what she says about—"

"Stop filling your ears with such. It's all talk made up by dirty-minded girls with nothing on their minds but nastiness."

"And you know what she says, Ray? She says you can make a man marry you by pretending you're going to have a baby."

"Freda, you deserve to have your mouth washed with lye and soap."

"But you have to be bad before you can pretend that, don't you?"

"Why do you think such things?"

"*You* think them, only you don't say them."

"I do not."

"You do so! With all the men running after you, how can you help thinking about what makes them do it?"

There was something to that, only Freda's foul-mouthed little manner of suggesting it made it loathsome. Naturally her thoughts sometimes turned to the riddle of the unanimity of the male reac-tion toward her. Yet who would believe, Freda least of all, how sel-dom, considering, such scuttling little rats of sex-thoughts as her stepsister's darted through her own brain? There was something latent and fearful and wonderful—something dangerous and shot with the glory of being alive—in this constant teasing sense of the mystery of sex. Ray sensed that, of course. What girl didn't? You couldn't help thinking sometimes of the something in you that you knew was there latent, but which up to now had never been really stirred by the touch of a man. With Freda, now, it was different. She was a seething hotbed of forbidden flickers of passion. Darts of desire, in the form of the ugly questions, were constantly on her lips. How in the world expect to make Freda, lying there beside her, believe that she, Ray, did not harbor the same secret and forbidden thoughts that had been bandied among the girls in the locker room at Freda's parochial school?

What good did it do to try to make her understand that some

of her lascivious questions were couched in a phraseology that was absolutely ununderstandable to Ray?

"Don't know what I mean? Oh no, you don't know. If I know as much as I do—how much must you know!"

How much must Ray know! The question tormented Freda. How good was Ray? How bad? How did she handle men? Had she ever . . . ? How fly was she really? Except on her trips to New York and the visit to the St. Louis annual exposition that she had once made with her father, there had never been a night which Ray had not spent in the house on Baymiller Street. Staying out all night was part of it when girls were supposed to be bad. Probably, as Tagenhorst said, "Ray had it behind her ears." What was it kept the toniest men hotfooting after Ray, if it wasn't—that? What was it, but that, gave a girl the name of being fly? Girls didn't let themselves get that reputation just for the good dinners and shows that were in it. Why, most of the men Ray ran with were married men and would cut her dead if they met her with their wives or daughters. Just how fly was Ray? Where did it get her? Kurt Shendler, a bicycle-mechanic, was the only fellow in town on the level with her. A tony girl like Ray having to wind up and marry a domestic product like Kurt! What was the mystery of Ray? Was it possible that she had no realization of the importance of sitting herself pretty? Or was it that she had some bee in her bonnet that would fool them all? Or would she be content to become the mistress of one of the town's big men or one of those New York traveling fellows or brokers who were always after her? Not for Freda. Marriage. Security. Freedom from the bickering thraldom of Tagenhorst, and now, with the few dollars from the sale of the house in the offing, the threat of having Marshall and his family within range. Marriage.

"Ray, would you like to be married?"

"Of course I would, to Mr. Right."

"How do you get Mr. Right?"

"How do I know, not having got him?"

"Why not Kurt? Or are you out for a big gun, or if you had a good chance would you just—just—live—"

"Freda!"

"I want to be married more than anything, and I'm not ashamed to say it."

"And so you should, honey. If you are as sweet on Hugo as he seems to be on you. . . ."

"Last night he took Sadie Kisterwell to the Music Festival. He can't get away from me that way. He can't get away from me a-tall."

The flaxen little Freda, lying there beside her, sent a quiver through the bed then, of the movement of her body. The quiver of a woman whose fury is beginning to be stirred. . . .

7

One Sunday evening during this same month, which was a humid May of premature heat, Ray, who had dined with a drummer at Mecklenburg's Summer Garden, a popular family resort out on Highland Avenue, found herself being importuned to accompany him to the station where he was to take a C. H. and D. train for Dayton.

"Come as far as the depot with me, Ray. It will cheer me on my way."

"But, Bakeless, it's so hot, and I hate the smell of train smoke."

"Yes, but think what you will be doing for a poor wretch who has to take the trip in this heat."

As a matter of fact, there was an additional reason for Ray's disinclination to accompany Bakeless to the station. Kurt, who had been away in Peoria for the greater part of a week, on a matter that had to do with going into partnership with a pair of brothers who had a patent on a gasoline-driven bicycle, was due at the house that evening at eight. Bakeless's train left at eight-fifteen, so there would be nobody at home to receive Kurt. Tagenhorst had hired a surrey for the afternoon, and with Freda and Marshall and Hugo Hanck had driven up to Hamilton to visit a crony there. A deserted house would greet Kurt.

"I have to get home, Bakeless."

"You're the darnedest! You know a man wants to be with you

more than anything, and then you make him sit up on his hind legs and beg for every little thing."

They were standing on the sidewalk outside of Mecklenburg's during this debate. In the heliotrope dusk, even the brick sidewalks gave off a faint heat-glow, and under her black sailor hat there was a film of moisture that not even the prepared chalk she used as face powder could keep under.

True, as she had realized as she put it on, her black-and-white-check coat-suit was too warm for the day. But its nattiness was simply not to be withstood. She had made it herself at dressmaking-school. The skirt, shirred up slightly along a front gore, was the new smart suit-length of one inch from the ground in front and slight drag behind. The coat, tapering into a faultless eighteen inches at the waist, flared at the hips just sufficiently to reveal a gleam of red sateen lining. A high stock, held with a gold horseshoe, completed the stylish effect. Sporty, but not horsy, had been her estimate before her mirror.

When she and Bakeless, who represented a New York buggy concern, had walked into Mecklenburg's, along its gravel-floored garden to a table under an ailanthus-tree, the crowd of Sunday-evening patrons had noted her to the tips of her scalloped-topped shoes.

The tony Ray Schmidt. Style.

It had been worth the scratching sense of discomfort the heavy cloth entailed; but now, out on the heated sidewalk, it seemed to Ray she could scarcely wait to be home and free of the unseasonable weight of her clothing.

"This weather takes it out of me, Bakeless."

"So you won't come along as far as the depot?"

He was a middle-aged, slightly rotund fellow, shiningly, too shiningly, groomed, from the tips of his toothpick shoes to the dyed mustache which he frequently attended with a pocket-comb. A val-ued territory man, of twenty-five years' standing with his firm, and an established clientele in Ohio, Indiana, Missouri, and Kansas.

"It isn't exactly that I won't go, Bakeless. Don't put it that way."

"I'll even go you one better, Ray. What say to coming all the way along? You and me could have Monday and Tuesday in Dayton. There's an idea. . . ."

"I'll go with you one year from today."

"There you go again. Darnedest girl for letting a man know where he's at. Well, anyway, it isn't going to hurt you to take me as far as the depot. Come, here's a couple going to dismiss a hansom. Hey, cabby, how much to C. H. and D.?"

She sighed her acquiescence, her eyes smiling, but troubled with the thought of Kurt smoking an impatient pipe, as he waited on the deserted porch.

It was cooler driving, bobbing along over cobblestones that flung them together and apart. Warmed with Rhine wine, conscious of her nearness, he became immediately amorous.

"Every time I come to this town, I say to myself, the one thing that gives it tone is Ray Schmidt."

"Nit."

"True as I'm sitting here. I've good Cincinnati accounts, but the best account of them all, Ray Schmidt!" Under the wooden apron of the hansom cab, his hand, a dimpled one with an island of black hair on it, poked a forefinger into the hole of her kid glove.

"If I wasn't a married man . . ."

Here it was again!

"But the way people like you and me look at these things is broad-minded. I'm not a small man. The nicest little flat in the world would be none too good for a girl like you. What say?"

The way to retort, as Tagenhorst would put it, was to haul off and slap his bluish jowl. Well, she wasn't built that way. This traveling man sitting there making illicit proposal to her, his heavy hand sliding off and on her knee, was just part of the pitiable sordidness of so much of life. He was trying to squeeze his joy out of the none too joyful business of being drummer for a firm which dealt in surreys, traps, runabouts, cabs, and coaches. Of course he was being disloyal to vows and decencies and to his wife. But the fault seemed not so much his as it was the routinized scheme which permitted a man's life to become a matter of surrey-upholstery, aging wives, Pullman cars, forbidden desires, and receding ideals.

There was something vaster and more reprehensible and more soul-sickening than this lascivious-looking drummer who needed his face slapped. It was the scheme of things to which, bobbing along in the hansom cab, they were both more or less helpless parties. There were those, of course, who triumphed, and they became the great, good, wise ones of the earth. But that did not mean that somehow, terribly, the story of the mortalness of clay was any the less poignant. If only she were not sorry for Bakeless.

"My life's been all a compromise between what I wanted and what I got, Ray. You would be one thing I wanted—and got."

"Why," she wanted to shout at him, "why do you dare to put to me a proposition that you would not broach to a single girl in this town except those who live on George Street? What is there about me makes a man feel I'm the kind a man can ask to be his mistress? An old dodo grandpap like you! Tell me. I want to know, in order that I may know this strange poor me, myself!"

She did nothing of the sort, but withdrew her hand gently, and made a move at him.

"That's the way you feel now."

He caught her cheeks between his thumb and forefinger.

"Don't make those girl-I-left-behind-me eyes! I don't want to leave you behind me. If you escape me once more, I'm going to advertise in *The Cincinnati Enquirer* personal column: 'Will brunette in black sailor hat and checkered suit who ate supper at Mecklenburg's last Sunday night please let me know where I get off with her?'"

Ray (to herself): "Where do I get off? Where do I get off?"

"Look! I want to give you something, Miss Ray. Little present I picked up yesterday at Hershey's. Bought it for my oldest girl. You know, I'd kind of like to give it to you."

"No, no, Bakeless!"

Men did not usually refer to their daughters. . . .

"I'd kind of like for you to have it, Ray."

He produced from a waistcoat-pocket a box containing a small silver human foot, meant to dangle from a fob or neck-chain.

"Why, Bakeless, you take that right along back to New York to your—to her."

"I'll get her something in Dayton. Take it."

"You're a dear!"

"What do I get?" he said, and puckered his lips.

She kissed him, as they bobbed along in the gathering darkness.

"That's right. Pay Papa."

"That wasn't pay."

"You're right. That's what I like about you. Never feel you're bleeding a man. Give me another."

"Not here, Bakeless, right in front of the Burnet House."

"Think over my little proposition, Miss Ray. I'll be back in three months. New York is a big town and I'll tuck you away in it as snug as you please. I'm telling you, Ray, I'm not small."

Now was the time to slap him resoundingly across that blue jowl.

"Put your arms around me, honey, for I've got a lot of money, love me little, love me long."

"Let me out here too, Bakeless! You don't need to send me home in this cab. I'll take the Colerain Avenue car."

It was there, at the curb of the C. H. and D. depot, that she met for the first time Walter Saxel, who, with satchel in hand, was making for the hansom cab which she and Bakeless were vacating.

"Hello, there, Bakeless. Don't mind if I take your cab, do you?"

"Honored, as they say in the classics. Saxel, want you to meet a tony little friend of mine. Ray Schmidt. Ever met, you two? Might ride her up a ways, Saxel," called Bakeless over one shoulder, as he dashed for his train.

"Your way is my way," said Saxel, and stood aside for her to mount back into the cab.

It was to occur to her countless times in later years that the first words he ever said to her, five of them, reversed, so as to apply to her, were to become the slogan for the rest of her life.

"Your way is my way, Walter," was born into her subconsciousness that hot May evening toward the close of a century, as she stood at the curb in front of the C. H. and D. station, looking for the first time into the face of a young man whose heavy black eyebrows were the shape of Mercury-wings.

8

"Why do you want to go home?" he said, after an introductory argument as to destination. "You can always go there."

She laughed the first laugh of what was to be her perpetual delight in his smallest saying. Kurt lay on her mind, but remotely now.

"I'll have to telephone. The store at our corner has a Kincloch. One of the boys there will take a message across to the house for me to somebody waiting on the porch and tell him I can't be home."

"That is precisely what corner stores are for."

"Do you always get what you want this easily?" She usually said that, when responding to the importunings for the many favors she had to yield.

"I have never wanted anything this badly, so I don't know."

There was a sticky, pleasant quality about his voice, as if it wanted to cling.

"Tell you how we are going to do it. I'm going to break my supper engagement too, only I'll have to write a note and send it out by messenger. We'll drop off here at the Burnet House, and get ourselves fed. Hungry?"

Time and time again in later years she was to recall to him this evening, when she followed up, within the hour, a meal at Mecklenburg's which had more than satiated her, with double sirloin steak, accordion potatoes, and tutti-frutti ice cream at the Burnet House.

"Funny that I've never seen you around town," she said to him across a table in a dining room of heavy drape and crystal chandelier. A candle burned under a pink shade, and women in dolmans, with bare shoulders rising broadly from their eighteen-inch waists, and aigrets waving in their high psyches, arrived and departed across the heavily carpeted floors. The men were a miscellaneous lot. A few of them in black broadcloth and white planks of shirt front, but most of them like Saxel, in their sack suits and derby hats.

"Fact of the matter is, Ray—you don't mind if I call you Ray, do you?—I live in Hamilton. Ever been to Hamilton?"

Had she ever been to Hamilton? Ask Nat Paisley over at Niles Tool Works if she had ever been to Hamilton. Or Otto Kugel, or Phil Dinninger. Ever been to Hamilton? How's Stengel's? And the St. Charles, and Mosler Safe Works? Where did he buy the necktie he was wearing? Strauss's. Ever been to Lindenwood Grove? Did she know Hamilton?

"Well, that's fine. I live there alone with my mother in the same house I was born."

She was right. The thought had struck her from the very first that he might be Jewish. Yessir, he was one of those high-class Jewish boys. The mother determined it. They lived at home, those Jewish fellows did. They stuck. Catch one of those high-class Jewish boys behaving like Marshall and never showing up around his mother, years on end, until there was something in it for him. Those gray eyes and that nice shiny black hair and the little mustache were what gave the hint, although he might just as easily have been Italian.

"So you live in Hamilton?"

"Guess that's the way you'd put it, but I work down in the city. Clerk in the First National."

The thought trailed through her mind: "First bank clerk I've ever known. Nice. Clean."

"Takes me a full hour coming and going. About the only man out of Hamilton who does that. My next move, I guess, will be to try and pry my mother out of the old house and move her down to the city. Girl like you makes a man realize what he's missing in a small town."

"Oh yes, I know all about you fellows and what you miss!" Those high-class Jewish boys were all of a stripe. Ray had known one. Arthur Metzger, lived on Richmond Street where so many of the high-class ones dwelt. Father owned Metzger Jewelry Store on Vine. Arthur one of the best fellows in the world. Not a suave, good-looking type like this one. Beaky. But a good spender. Kind of boy who gave a girl the best of everything. Best seats, best shows. Drove his own phaeton, and, in Ray's case, always deplored the fact that she did not drink the champagnes and other wines he was eager to provide for her.

But one night, in a burst of confidence, he told her what she had long suspected. With the Jewish fellows of his class, girls were divided into two classes—"shiksas" and the girls they would marry. Ray was a "shiksa." Out of his class and out of his faith and out of his reckoning, except as the kind of girl on whom you could sow a wild oat. He taught her a few phrases like "shiksa." Goy. *Batsimer.* It was his great joke to make her repeat these words that sat so oddly on her lips.

"What are you, Ray? Go on, say it again. It sounds cute."

"I'm a goy."

But something leaden as anything she had ever felt in her life dropped heavily into her conscience, as she sat there in the Burnet House opposite Walter Saxel.

"I ran down to the city this evening after spending Sunday up in Hamilton with my mother, in order to visit a friend of mine on Richmond Street."

"A girl?"

"A young lady."

Of course. One of those well-to-do Jews in the stone fronts on Richmond Street. If a fellow like Saxel called on one of those girls, you just bet it was a "young lady." Ray classified as "goy."

"Don't let me detain you."

"Now, Ray, was that nice?"

"It wasn't. I'm sorry. Funny, now. Known you about forty minutes and feel jealous because you're not spending the evening with me."

"Well, sir, you'll think I'm talking through my hat, but I'm going to do something I never did in my life before. Call up a girl like Corinne Trauer at the last minute and tell her I can't come along until later."

"Corinne Trauer! I know her! She's been in our store. Blonde. Pretty. Kind of fat. She and her mother buy trimmings from us."

"That's Corinne. Her uncle is Felix-Arnold Friedlander, of Friedlander-Kunz, the New York bankers. Her mother was a Friedlander."

There was that solid thing again.

"What if she were to find out you were wasting your time sitting around the Burnet House with a shiksa?"

He threw back his head and laughed. "Where did you get that?"

"Oh, I may be a goy, but I know what shiksa means."

"You're a darling. But I didn't know the map of Jerusalem was on my face."

"It isn't. You might be Eyetalian." She knew better than that! Italian, of course, but everyone around her pronounced it as if it were spelled Eyetalian.

"Then how did you know?"

"The way you talk about living up in Hamilton with your mother."

"Do you have to belong to the Plum Street Temple in order to live at home with your mother?"

"No, but you boys are almost all that way. I even knew a boxer once, Butch Horowitz, rough as anything, who used to have a special place at all the armory-bouts for his mother, and used to take her traveling with a special cooking outfit for her special foods. It's nice. I like it."

"Ray, I want to see a lot of you."

"You've a funny way of showing it."

"Why? You mean because I have to show up at the Trauers' later in the evening?"

"Not saying."

"You're a sensible girl. You ought to understand a thing like that."

"I do. It's just—I don't know what's come over me."

"It's because you like me, Ray. I like you. If you don't want me to go to the Trauers', I am not going to the Trauers'."

"But I do."

"But I thought you just said—"

"Never mind what I just said. I live just three blocks from Richmond Street where the Trauers live. You can take a Colerain car with me."

"But I am all ready to telephone that I can't make it at all tonight."

"You don't do things that way."

"Why do you say that?" he said half querulously.

"Because you don't. You're solid. I like it."

"Too deep for me," he said, and ran his hand over the thatch of his smooth black hair and took up the waiter's check. High-class Jewish fellows did things well. A good substantial dinner, for which unfortunately she had no appetite. The offer of Sauterne, which she declined, and then light Moerlein's beer for him. Not a foolish spender. Those boys weren't. He added up the dinner check and picked up a ten-cent piece off the plate when the change came, leaving a twenty-five-cent tip. Plenty, but not too much. Just right. A boy couldn't afford many Burnet House dinners on a bank-clerk's salary. Poor fellow, and she had forced her dinner too. Well, it wouldn't happen again. Plenty of excellent eating-places Over-the-Rhine, less than half the price. She had seen the check with the worried tip of an eye. Cassolette of lobster, forty cents; double sirloin steak, sixty cents; tutti-frutti ice cream, twenty cents. One dollar and twenty cents for dinner for two. Ruinous!

He suggested a cab. She would not hear of it.

"Colerain car goes by my door and right by your corner."

"All right, then, if it makes you feel any better. . . ."

"It does. I don't believe in throwing away."

"If you aren't the mightiest nicest girl! I'm going to see a lot of you. Only you haven't told me much about yourself. Guess you live at home and all that?"

He did not guess anything of the sort. It was his way of finding out that she did not live at home. Thank goodness, though, the truth of it was that she lived at home as much as any Trauer, Moss, Strauss, or Littauer girl of Richmond Street. She knew them all. They came into the store, usually with their mothers. Good dressers. Good but cautious spenders. Knew values. On summer evenings you could see them sitting out on their stoops, talking from house to house. Well-kept, secure homes, with immaculate whitened copings and the shoulders of upholstered furniture in summer covers showing through the open windows. Well-kept, secure families, with surreys or smart little traps at the curb.

"I live at home with my stepmother and stepsister. 'Schmidt's—Trimmings and Findings' used to be my father's. I am still in the store."

"Seems to me I've heard of you. Ray—Schmidt."

"Probably." It smote her with a sense of unutterable depression that she hoped not.

"Well, anyway, we've met!"

The conductor on the Colerain car pulled his cap at her and grinned as they entered.

"The boys on the line all know me," she said, by way of explanation, as they seated themselves. "Lived on the line all my life"—and then could have bitten back the words. Nothing to be ashamed of.

"What is the procedure? Does one come to call on you, or I'm wondering wouldn't you like to go Over-the-Rhine one of these evenings? I stay in town one or two nights a week, when I know my mother has one of her friends spending the night with her."

There it came! He would not even ask, much less take, Corinne Trauer Over-the-Rhine, unchaperoned. Or for that matter, chances were he would not have asked Freda at all.

Well, no use crying over that. You were what you were. Besides, just suppose he had asked to call. That would be nice, wouldn't it, with Tagenhorst having all sorts of people in and out, over the project of selling the house, and, more likely than not, Freda monopolizing the parlor, with the door left open a discreet six inches, but an unwritten law against entering it. Not what you would call a home to the queen's taste! Anyway, these high-class Jewish boys were not given to calling at the homes of shiksas. Della Garfunkel, a girlfriend across the river, in Covington, Kentucky, had married one, Max Victorius, of the family of bankers in Muncie, Indiana, without his ever having laid eyes on her folks. Jewish boys were funny that way.

"You can telephone me at the store some day. We haven't a telephone, but the cigar store next door, Fink's, will call me. We'll see."

"We won't do anything of the sort. Some day! We'll see now. Look here, Ray, wasn't it agreed I am going to see a lot of you?"

They sat in the rumbling streetcar, washed in dirty lamplight, their bodies touching softly to the jerkings and the short stops, and now, more completely than ever, there was no such thing as her ability to say no.

"Suppose we meet at your store on Thursday about six and we'll decide then where to go."

Monday—Tuesday—Wednesday—Thursday. The waiting was already begun.

"I guess that will be all right."

"Not disappointed about anything, are you? Would Friday be better? Mentioned Thursday because it is one of the evenings my mother's card club meets, and it's easy for me to be away."

"Thursday is all right. I don't like the boys to call for me at the store. Meet you at the Burnet House."

Why had she said that! What was it made her do the common thing? Catch Corinne Trauer meeting him at the Burnet House!

"That will be fine," he said, with what seemed to her a new ease.

Rumble, rumble along, their bodies giving slightly to the motion, the sultry breeze causing him to lift off his derby hat. An elation laid hold of her that was absurdly out of proportion to the act of riding home with a nice young fellow who might have been one of a half-dozen she was apt to meet in the course of the month.

The elation continued until she was home and in bed, when, presto, it turned into depression.

9

Later, when Ray, who was clumsy at evasion, explained to Kurt, in what terms she could muster, that a "certain party's" turning up unexpectedly from out of town had made it necessary for her to send the telephone message of Sunday evening, he interrupted her in a matter-of-fact voice that was surprising most of all to himself, considering the pounding against his temples.

"Surest thing ever, Ray," he said, "it was exactly as if somebody had tapped me on the shoulder when I was sitting there waiting for you to show up, and said to me, 'Kurt, watch out!'"

"Why, Kurt Shendler, what are you talking about?"

"I don't know just beyond what I'm saying, but I'm watching out for all I'm worth."

What did he suspect? What was there to suspect? What did she herself suspect? Acting guilty when there was no cause to be guilty, and acting that guilt toward Kurt to whom she was not pledged!

"Oh, I'm not saying you owe me an explanation," he said, as if in answer to her thoughts. "What satisfies you, Ray, has to satisfy me. I'm just saying I had the feeling, sitting there Sunday night waiting, as if someone was looting my life or my repair-shop of the contract I signed up at Peoria on the gasoline-driven bike."

"You're talking nonsense, pure and simple."

They were walking along Richmond Street in the twilight of

the Tuesday following, Ray having suggested what was rare for her—a neighborhood walk.

Burning, the desire to pass the Trauer residence lay against her consciousness. She knew the house, had known it for years by sight, but now she felt the need to refurbish the slipshod impressions that lay palely in her mind.

Suddenly that house on Richmond Street, just three blocks from her own, which up to now had been as commonplace to her as any house on Dayton Street, West Ninth, or Freeman, had become of peculiar, almost hypnotic, interest. The blonde Corinne Trauer, whom it now seemed to Ray she could remember as an overplump little girl, two or three grades beneath her in the Eighth District school, dwelt in this shrine to which came Walter Saxel on the twenty-five-mile trainride from Hamilton the one day in the week, Sunday, when he might have been free of the journey.

What was the relationship of these two? What thoughts did Corinne Trauer, laying her slightly kinky blonde head nightly on her pillow in the house just three blocks removed from Baymiller Street, carry of Walter Saxel into the secret watches of the night?

Ray wanted to pass and repass the house, constructing what picture she could. But she did not, until Tuesday evening, when it seemed natural to stroll by with Kurt.

There it was, third from the corner, one of the narrower and more unpretentious of the block's dwellings, set back nicely on a lit-tle terrace with a white-stone coping. It was a smallish snug house, which a young man of this tight, solid race would only dare visit with such regular periodicity on the basis of intentions or promise of them.

It was still precocious May, stuffy and of unseasonable heat, and Richmond Street, fed, was disporting itself, in its family way, along the rows of well-scrubbed front stoops.

There was no one before the Trauer home, but the front door stood open, and there was a small gaslight burning in red glass in the hallway, and you could see beyond that the dining room was lighted. Trauers at supper. There was a hatrack, with antler pegs, and a china umbrella-stand in the hallway. Walter's hat had hung there! A light-tan runabout, on wire wheels, stood at the curb, its overfat little tan-and-white mare hitched to a black iron boy. There was something about the small horse, with its pretty cream-colored mane, and tail that had been braided and brushed out, that suggested Corinne Trauer. Its plump sides breathed evenly; its pale-brown eyes, in blinkers, knew no fear. It was a cared-about little horse. Perhaps Walter had driven it. Or would drive it.

"Wait until I give you a ride on our gasoline-bicycle, Ray, then you'll know what real motion is," said Kurt, his eyes all for the picture she made stroking the well-curried flank of the plump little horse. "Come, it will be cool in Lincoln Park, let's go there."

He wanted, before this evening was over, to have cast out the unease in his heart. The thought even smote him of trying to get Ray to elope with him to Covington. Right off. He had a chum, Tom Buzzel, and his wife, who would go along. Trouble with talking about a thing too much was talking too much about it. Two could live as cheaply as one. Always a way. The longer they hemmed and hawed, the more difficulties would present themselves. There was money ahead in this new partnership with the inventor of a device to attach a motor to an ordinary bicycle. Ray was not the girl to risk getting into lean times, dear darling, and yet on the other hand, she was the one girl with the stamina to buck them. Any way you looked at it, there was going to be disapproval over a marriage with Ray on the part of the stepaunt with whom he made his home. Dang it all, just fool woman-stuff. Never willing to let one another live.

"Ray, if you only would?"

"Would what?"

"Your mind is a thousand miles away."

The Trauers kept tony hours. Seven-o'clock supper, and still at table, with the whole of the rest of Richmond Street already out on stoops. After all, the New York Friedlanders were among the world's largest banking firms. She knew. She had looked them up. Aaron Trauer might be only in the life-insurance business, but he had these enormously wealthy connections of his wife to lend prestige. Catch a rich Jew like Felix-Arnold Friedlander seeing his sister or his sister's children want for anything. Plain as the nose on your face that a mere life-insurance agent could not unaided afford that house and the smart little horse and buggy in front of it. Chances were, the eastern connections would take a clean, bright young fellow like Walter into the New York banking house. For all she knew, that might be the secret of his position in the Cincinnati bank. Who knows? The sense of misery began to crawl around her heart again, and roost there.

"Come, let's go into the park, Ray. I can talk better there."

She lifted her skirts to cross the street, conscious that along the stoops heads were turning after her.

"That's that Ray Schmidt. Stylish, isn't she? Those *batsimers* wear their clothes well. The boys don't exactly come out and say she is n. g., but my guess is that she's fast. That's a pretty idea, isn't it? Gored skirt with a Spanish flounce. They say she makes every stitch she wears over at Alvin Sewing School. Those shiksas have a knack."

It was pleasant to feel the heads turn after her dotted-swiss dress over its blue sateen slip and caught in at the waspish waist with a wide blue satin girdle from which depended a chatelaine of silver knickknacks. The big balloon elbow sleeves, with the black lace gloves tucked up under them, and the large leghorn hat with the wired bow, completed an ensemble that was an eyeful for Richmond Street. Couldn't help knowing that. Despising yourself a bit for the knowing and the glowing that went with it, but glowing and knowing just the same.

At Freeman Avenue the little park loomed softly in the dusk, pairs of figures strolling about beneath the trees along the ordered walks.

They sat down on a bench, and she unpinned her hat and placed it carefully on her lap; and then Kurt, by way of preamble, took up one of her hands in its black lace glove and began to bend back the fingers softly, one by one.

"This is the way I have figured it all out, Ray. The longer you wait to make up your mind, the more reasons you are going to find for not making it up. To my way of thinking, the way to reach an important decision, in business or out of it, is not to think about a thing so long that you lose your point of view. Ever keep saying a word over and over to yourself until it lost its meaning? Well, that's my experience on a decision. In business I think for all I'm worthwhile I'm thinking, and then I act! That's the way I bought Ed Rokehauser's patent in Peoria the other day. If I had stopped to turn that matter over in my mind as long as I wanted to, seeing how I had to scratch for money, I'd be turning it over yet, and somebody else would have the patent."

"And if I don't make up my mind, somebody else will have Kurt?"

"Now, Ray, I'd sooner cut off my tongue than have you think I meant it that way."

"I know you didn't, goose!" She wished he had meant it that way. She wished she was anybody except herself, sitting there in Lincoln Park with the heartbreaking task of letting Kurt know she had already reached her decision.

Fool that she was! She knew, sitting there pecking at the wired bow, and trying to find a way to tell him, what had decided her. A chance meeting with a man to whom, nine chances out of ten, she would never be more than shiksa, had decided her. And even supposing things were different. A bank clerk in a town like Cincinnati, unless he had the unusual opportunity of a Friedlander for a relative, could live and die a bank clerk. Now, Kurt here, crude as he might seem, had a future. A girl would be crazy to choose between them. Kurt already had a dandy business head on him. Kurt was her own kind. Why, for all she knew, Walter Saxel was engaged this very minute to Corinne Trauer. Of course, he had said to her . . . Pah—they all said! A Jewish boy talking to a shiksa said anything that came into his head. For a girl like herself, without anything to fall back upon, her home about to break up, no relatives, Kurt was a godsend, that's what he was. Men weren't so quick on the trigger to talk marriage to a girl if she had the reputation for being fly; and, no getting around it, men did think that about her. Kurt was a godsend, and yet, just as surely as she was sitting there, her decision persisted. Pity smote her—for Kurt, who must now hear this decision, and for herself, because she was making it.

"Kurt, there is a great deal in what you say about the way to make up your mind to a thing. I'm a chickenhearted old coward, or I would have made up my mind long ago about us, for your sake, Kurt."

"Ray, you're not going to—"

"Honey, you going to be terribly upset if I tell you something? I'm the biggest fool ever walked in shoe-leather, but I can't marry you, Kurt. Feel like—well, I just feel something terrible, putting it to you that way, but I know that's the way you would want me to do it."

He sat quite still, with his hands hanging loosely between his spread knees, and the light from a gaslight throwing pallor against his pallor.

"It's you, Kurt, ought to be turning me down, not me you," she said, closing her eyes on the spectacle of him sitting there in the fallen-forward attitude.

"I knew it," he said, without moving, and his voice sounding to her, as she sat there with her eyes squeezed shut, like a buggy rumbling over an old wooden corduroy bridge. "Something decided you Sunday night, when you never showed up."

"Why, Kurt . . ."

"Something decided you that night, Ray. I don't say it would ever have been different in the long run; but the next time I heard your voice, when I called Monday early to take your bike down to the shop, something had dropped out of it. For me. Tell me, Ray!"

"I can't, Kurt," she gasped. "I can't."

"Why?"

"Because there's just nothing—to tell."

10

It was happening, and the marvel of it to Ray was that the part of her life which had not contained it seemed never to have existed. Terrible, in a way, because even that part of her life which had so recently held the darling figure of Adolph was part of the unreality of those yesterdays which did not contain Walter.

The years that did not contain him were so many dead segments of time, to be counted off rapidly, as you would count days off your fingers. Curiously unrelated yesterdays, through which you must have moved simulating eagerness, when it transpired you had never known eagerness before it began for you that warm Sunday evening on the curbstone in front of the C. H. and D.

It was happening with more completeness every day. The waiting for the telephone message. The waiting on the corner of Sixth and Race, to meet him to go to lunch. The waiting with him at the C. H. and D. for the tiny hurried good-bys as he caught the five-forty-five for Hamilton.

Precisely nothing else mattered. The days were punctuated by how much you could be together, how these meetings could be arranged, where to meet, when to meet, and how not to be too conspicuous about it.

Curious, but from the first, this need to be furtive established itself on an undiscussed basis.

"It won't be easy for me to stay in tonight, Babe. That would make three Wednesdays in succession, and the first thing I know, Mother will begin bothering her head about why I stay down-city so often."

That sent the bottom scuttling out of Wednesday evening, leaving it simply something to be endured through until Thursday luncheon, assuming that luncheon could be arranged.

Luncheons were simpler, but not always possible.

On Tuesdays the Dutch Treat Club met, an organization of fifteen or so of the town's young Jewish men, who assembled for luncheon at the Stag. The town's best, Ray noted with pride, as realization of young Saxel's connections began to impress her. Walter's father, a Hamilton businessman who had died twenty years before, had been first cousin to Stanley Hoffheimer, of the Hoffheimer Avondale Promotion Company, with whom Walter had lived during the three years he attended Woodward High School. Members of the Dutch Treat Club comprised such names as Milton Freiberg, Walter Seasongood, Jr., Stephen Straus (Straus and Mindlin), Junior Sonnenfeld, Mark Wise, Lester Wormser, and the Bowman boys. You walked on Wormser-laid sidewalks in Freiberg shoes. The huge Straus Clothing advertisement was as regular a feature in the *Enquirer* as the death-notices.

It was a matter of pride to relinquish Walter to these upstanding occasions, even when secretly it seemed to her he should at least have made the offer to relinquish them in favor of lunching with her, around at a place called Hayden's, famous for potato pancakes.

Had the situation, she often told herself, been reversed, nothing could have taken precedence over the possibility of an hour with Walter. Indeed, always on the supposition that such an hour might unexpectedly offer itself, it soon became her technique to accept only tentatively whatever invitations presented themselves.

"I think I can go, but I can't let you know definitely." (Must ask Walter if there is any chance of his staying in the city Tuesday evening.)

"Don't count on me for certain; I'll come if I can." (Two or three times, lately, Walter's mother had developed sudden euchre games, making it unexpectedly possible for him to remain in the city.)

These little matters were scarcely sacrifices, because nothing mattered very much relatively, except being with him, therefore you lied, prevaricated, maneuvered. A man was different somehow. Walter, now, for instance, was always talking about justice and being fair to the other fellow. As if that mattered. Of course, if he cared for Tom, Dick, and Harry more than he cared for you! That was scarcely the point, and she knew it, and yet somewhere, deeply imbedded in each of them, was a different set of ethics. Walter cared, all right. But if he had told a party he would meet him at the Burnet House at five o'clock, and desperately she wanted to see Walter at five o'clock before he caught his train, Walter was sorry, as sorry as could be, and she must know how much seeing her mattered to him, but there was that arrangement to see that certain party at the Burnet House at five, and nothing was farther from his makeup than to lie or prevaricate his way out of it.

"Of course, if any mere appointment is more important—"

"It's not that, Ray!"

"Tell him you have to stay at the bank and catch up on your work. You know you do, lots of times."

"Yes, but not today. I'm no good at lying in these little ways, Ray. You girls don't seem to mind it. Bill Cook is an old friend of mine, Babe. Wants to see me on a little matter of business."

"If the situation were reversed—"

"I know that, Ray. But it's just not in me. Besides, we have tomorrow evening—"

Tomorrow evening! Hours of minutes, minutes of seconds, to be got through somehow.

Saturday was the evening to be lived through with the heart in her feeling pinched to the hardness of a pebble. Saturday, it now transpired, to the convenience of everybody concerned, was Walter's evening at the Trauers'. There was never any discussion about it. There it stood, isolated by silence into strange portentousness, the sense of the impending beginning when Walter cut short his noon-hour at Hayden's to hurry to the St. Nicholas to his barber.

From then on, the shadow of the evening began to reach a long finger across her day. Any drummer in town could have her

Saturday night for the asking. Dinner at Kissel's Atlantic Garden if he wanted it, where, along about eleven, Johnnie Carrol or Emma Carus would have the entire crowd to its feet singing "Little Annie Rooney" or "Down Went McGinty to the Bottom of the Sea." Or, as an alternative, Heuck's Ten-Twenty-Thirty, or Weber and Fields, at People's. Wielert's Pavilion; Shackling's Opera House, Music Hall, and Promenade Garden, where you could hear a forty-piece reed band, or behold twenty celebrated European performers in spectacular and startling specialties.

To be sitting in Kissel's, listening to Emma Kissel play the fiddle in her father's garden Over-the-Rhine, or dining on the veranda of the Lookout House, at the top of the Inclined Plane, with the basin of the city spread dramatically below, or playing hazard in the rear of Chick and George's with Fred Niemeyer, a malt man out of Philadelphia, or George Bader, whose father was a large stockholder in Latonia racetrack, while Corinne and Walter were tucked away in the well-nigh unbearable propinquity of that parlor in Richmond Street, was just about the cruelest refinement of punishment.

What were they saying and doing, and, more important still, what were they feeling? Walter and Corinne alone together and exposed to the lure of their young bodies and their young hearts and their young lips, while she, helpless in the face of a condition and a danger that were crazing to her, sat in the midst of scenes and people that seemed separated from her consciousness by a film, as if they moved in submarine gardens.

What, seated in the secure bright parlor of that home on Richmond Street, was Walter saying to Corinne, who, as Ray had so painfully reconstructed her from the memory of casual glimpses, had the plump white flesh, on her short neck and high little bosom, of a tender young fowl?

It was as if, there in a world that had suddenly become about as glamorous to her as an old shoe, she were asleep and dreaming of Walter, seated in that brightly lighted parlor on Richmond Street, making highly proper overtures to a personable and marriageable young girl whose innocence he reverenced.

Fool, fool, to have let him taste her lips, when the sweetmeat of what must be the desirable mouth of a girl like Corinne Trauer had surely been denied him. That is, unless they were already his, by the sacred right of an engagement between them.

Not on again, off again.

Jews were like that. A Jewish fellow began to prepare for being a steady husband from the very first moment of his engagement.

Sometimes the pressure of the picture against her brain was almost more than she could bear. Headache began to be almost a regular Saturday-night plea to terminate an evening that along around eleven o'clock became almost beyond endurance.

"What's the matter with Ray Schmidt, these days? Dead cat! Look here, sister, is it my company gives you the headache? This is the second time you've left me high and dry with an evening just beginning. Tell you what! I know a nice quiet little place that don't give you a headache. If I felt right sure how you would take it, I'd say come along with me—"

Here came the proposition again. How soon before Walter would make it? How soon before he dared? She had already, in the dubious privacy of a lovely dell in Burnet Woods, lain in his arms. Where so often before her sole pleasure had been the giving of pleasure, why not this supreme moment of her compensation? She had lain in his arms, a shiksa, who, so far as he took the trouble to judge, was without innocence or the impeccable purities he demanded of the woman of his own race who would bear his children. A shiksa whose lips were desirable.

He had told her as much. Not then, but later, when her body was no longer touching his, and they were walking toward the car.

"You're a wonderful girl, Ray. I haven't the right to be telling you such things, but you're a wonderful girl."

What had he meant by that? Hadn't the right. She could not bear the thought of parting from him that evening without knowing what he meant.

"I'm not wonderful, Walter, except in a way I have always known I could like a person, once I—like him—I think I could be wonderful to someone I liked terribly— I know I could!"

"It must be wonderful to be loved by a girl who has it in her to love like you, Ray."

What had he meant by that? Must be. Must be wonderful for a man who wasn't already engaged, or about to be?

Was this thing that was happening to her—had been happening to her ever since that day at the curb of the C. H. and D. depot—going to mean birth of pain that was entirely uncorrelated to any previous suffering she had ever known? Unless one had the power to sweep one of those boys off his feet, like the case of Della Garfunkel, of Covington, a shiksa was hopelessly outside the marriage pale of a boy like Walter.

Even with all the implications that went with it, there were advantages to marrying a good Jewish boy. These boys had by instinct the qualities that could make life sweet for a woman. Fidelity. Stability. Generosity. Reverence for the unit of the family.

As a child, along with the youngsters of Baymiller Street, Ray had used to shout at the children over on Ninth Street and Richmond Street, "Christ-Killer! Sheeny!" without much realization of what they meant. Later, however, even before she met Walter, it was to become abominable to her even to hear Tagenhorst blurt out against the "Ikeys" who were beginning to "run the town."

Adolph had always liked them as customers. They were good pay and large accounts. "Jew boys," as Ray had often put it before she met Walter, were usually good spenders, good company, but too cautious to so much as get on a tintype with you.

How horrid of her to ever have been capable of the phrase "Jew boy"! And here, now, one of them was a prince! That became her favorite way of trying to be casual when referring to Saxel. "Do you know Walter Saxel? Prince of a fellow, isn't he?" Well, he was! One who now made her despise, after a fashion, the traveling salesmen with whom she shared big juicy sirloin steaks at the expensive pleasure resorts of the town, enduring their pawings and petty liberties in payment.

And for what? True, the world of the large hotels, Latonia racetrack, Over-the-Rhine, and the occasional glimpses of Chicago and

New York, were immeasurably more to her liking than the small Rhinish one of Baymiller Street. No use pretending that she didn't enjoy the sporty pastimes that were not considered admirable. Neither fish nor flesh nor fowl was the stylish Ray Schmidt, but gyrating somewhere between the dull and respectable little orb of Baymiller Street and the sportier realm in which she loved to strut.

To invade that sportier world as the wife of a man like Walter! The secret of his ability to do the handsome things that were so obviously outside the limitations of the bank clerk had been revealed in a chance remark which he let fall. There was an income from his father's estate which he shared with his mother. Emanuel Saxel had been one of three partners in the small Hamilton jewelry firm of Dreyfous, Saxel and Kahn, now defunct. There was something of the odor of success about Walter. His manner of calling all waiters George. His manner of tipping them. Every time he took the train for Hamilton there was a delicacy under his arm. Hothouse peaches from Peebles'. A sugar *Kranz* from Doerr's. Bissinger's candied nuts. New dill pickles. A bottle of *kümmel* from Levi & Ottenheimer's.

He would be a man with whom to keep young—with whom to love the good things of life. His manner of ordering a dinner, with the proper touch of wine, which he drank so conservatively and she drank not at all, his epicureanism and love of sophisticated foods, his way of buying a bunch of violets off a vendor's tray and giving her carte blanche to go shop his mother a silk shirtwaist for her birthday, were worldly little aspects of him to strike delight to the heart.

Not that you could judge a man by the trifles of these externals; but the worldly stripe in a man, as Ray used to designate it to amused New York salesmen, made life so much gayer than life in the sauerkraut belt, where money was something to be earned solemnly and spent reverently—if at all.

Funny thing, but Walter the bank clerk came to epitomize for Ray, from the moment she clapped eyes into his gray ones, a diversified worldly world of which he was not really a part. There was something portentous about him, suggestive of the hotel lobby, the racetrack, and even the Music Festival, where the Longworths, the Tafts, the Emerys, the Hannas, and the Warringtons could be seen in close-up through one's opera glasses.

Then, too, Walter had been to Europe. He had taken the trip with Myron Hoffheimer, a cousin his age, as a gift from his aunt Hoffheimer, during his second-year vacation at Woodward High. He had been to Hamburg, Carlsbad, Frankfurt, Berlin, and London.

Was it any wonder, Ray used to ask herself, as she sat in public places with the picture branded against her brain, or moved through her days at the trimmings-and-findings store, or entered a house so preempted by Tagenhorst that the last vestige of Adolph was already fading out, that the new and twisting unease she was experiencing on all sides was causing her constantly to feel like crying?

Sometimes in the weeks and then the months that followed her meeting with Walter Saxel, the wish that she had never laid eyes on him would mingle with her torment.

11

Many the year, after it happened, Ray, with her lips twisted until they were pale snarls in her face, was to repeat over and over again to herself: What is to be, will be. It was in the cards that it should turn out this way.

The incident that justifiably or not she was always to feel had such vital bearing upon the trend of her entire life, was brought about by a remark from Walter that caused her head to spin and her legs to feel as if they had turned to water and were flowing away from her support.

It was the day of the week that she had come to dread. Saturday, which meant Walter's evening at the Trauers'. They had lunched together at Hayden's and there still remained time for them to make a few rounds of the oval esplanade of Fountain Square. It was a noisy promenade, set within the heart of the city's din, every carline in town passing within a block of it, and the Tyler fountain rather futilely lifting the thin clear voice of its ornamental waters against commotion.

Presently, at Fifth Street, they would separate and go their ways, Saxel to the bank, Ray to the "Findings and Trimmings." Would the day ever come when they would not be perpetually in the act of separating? How short those noonday periods! He had been quiet at lunch. Unusually so. What was on his mind? Something concerning her? He regarded her at times as if he would cleave with his glance the curtain of the unspoken between them. What did he suspect? What did he know? What did he want? He wanted his cake, no doubt, like all the others, and to eat it too. The rigid right-ness and conventionality of the procedure with Corinne Trauer was one thing; the freedom of passing the time with a shiksa on the side, another.

If that were true, one should despise him for it. Once a local fellow, named Willie Stamm, had said to her, "If you're so darned nice to all us boys without caring a whoop about us, God help the one you really do fall in love with!" And here, living between Ham-ilton and Cincinnati all these years, had been that one. Why, he had actually attended Woodward High just three years before her cursory course there. There must have been times, think of that, when they had sat at the zoo listening to the same band-concerts on the same evenings. Perhaps, who knows, they had mingled in the same Music Hall crowds during Festival Week or ridden up and down the Ohio on the same excursion boat. And all the time, all the time, everything latent in her had been waiting. For this. For just the half-furtive act of walking with him around the esplanade of Fountain Square—of sharing him with the stoutish, blonde, secure Corinne Trauer, who on Saturday mornings was taking her piano lesson at Clara Baur's Conservatory of Music. She would play to Walter, evenings, "Alice, Where Art Thou?" "Traumerei," "Hungarian Rhapsody," "Scarf Dance," "Dance of the Fireflies," in a bright parlor of lamps, bric-a-brac, and Honiton lace, and a sofa where the young husband of the young Corinne could relax with his head in her lap. . . . Thoughts like these spotted the bright day with anguish. . . .

And then suddenly, walking beside her, Walter said this:

"I'm staying in town tonight, Ray, and my mother is coming to the city on the eight-forty-five tomorrow. We're having Sunday dinner at the Trauers'."

Oh, God, then, here it came.

He had never been out-and-out frank with her. What right, he might have flared in retort to such a statement, had she to expect it? But in his way he had tried, constantly and consistently, to make her understand how things stood. There was the feeling that conscientiously he was trying to place himself in a position where one day he could say to her, "I never concealed anything from you."

"I see," she said finally, in response to this statement about his mother, and looking away, because she could feel, as always, her lips crawl into a tight, ugly shape when she made retort to any one of his strained remarks about the Trauers.

Well, after all, it was high time. Strange that the Trauers had permitted it to drag on this long without demanding from him a declaration of intentions. Unless one had been made long ago. Well, what of it? One lived. One lived through such things as this. One did. One must.

"Ray, I've been thinking. Funny thing, but I've got my heart set on it. Before my mother and I go to the Trauers' tomorrow for dinner, I'd like mighty much for my mother to meet you, Ray."

That was when it seemed to her the very capacity to stand on her legs was flowing away from her. What was going on in this boy's head that he was daring to confront his mother with her? Was he contemplating, as the shades of what might be a formal engagement began to close him in, the rash act of coming out in the open with his declaration of preference for Ray Schmidt? Jewish boys did not present goy girls to their parents unless . . . What could Ray Schmidt be to Mrs. Saxel, and vice versa, unless it was that Walter knew that their two remote orbs were about to swim together in an intermarriage?

Could it mean that happiness, actually beyond computing, lay in store?

"Walter, do you mean that?"

"Certainly. My mother likes to meet my friends. She's nice that way, and interested. I thought I'd take her to spend tomorrow morning at the Zoo. She loves to see the animals there. Do you suppose you could manage, Ray, to meet us around the lion cages about eleven? Mother likes cubs. Suppose you just seem to happen into us. Know what I mean? No use making it seem like a set engagement."

If, where he was concerned, she could have found it within herself to have pride, this would have been terrible.

You didn't confront your mother all at once with a shiksa. And yet—yet it showed what forces must be at work in his brain. Walter was trying to maneuver the most delicate situation of his life. She had won in her tactics with Walter! The puzzled look in his eye, time after time, as he left her at the gate to the house on Baymiller Street! Oh, she had known what lurked there, all right. How far dared he go with this *batsimer?* She had seen the question play across his face, linger there, fade out into uncertainty. Once he, too, had walked her down Elm to the corner of George Street, pausing there apparently for the effect the propinquity of this neighborhood of elaborate women and drawn blinds might have on her. His hand at her elbow had trembled. She knew what was at him. Desire, and the impulse to dare to suggest to her what sooner or later they all suggested. She actually prayed to herself a little. Fear was on her that he would not have suggested in vain. Before his wishes, all things went down. But, somehow, she had staved it off, and the wrinkle of puzzlement between his eyes was to recur again and again. How far dared he go?

The answer lay triumphantly in his suggesting to her now that she meet his mother. She was the kind of girl to whom one introduced one's mother.

"I'll be there at eleven, Walter, strolling around just as if I were looking at the cubs."

"You understand about the pretending, don't you, Ray? In some ways my mother is more like a baby than she is my mother. I want her to know all my friends, but, at the same time, there are some things—there are always certain things, with a mother, have to be handled with kid gloves, or they can be spoiled from the start."

Walter was being cautious with her and trying not to let her know how desperate his dilemma between her and the little fragrant pincushion of a creature out on Richmond Street. It was his last desperate move before the machinery of the Trauer-Saxel marriage began to stitch the pattern.

It struck her all in the midst of an agitation of blowing hot and cold that she must show this old woman. Oh, la, la, she would wear her gray voile over pink; with the pink velvet-ribbon borders on the gray ruffling and the leghorn hat faced in pink and loaded with rib-bon. This old lady, darling because she was his mother, would learn a thing or two about who could do most for her son. A snug, pretty little blonde, who used to be called fat-sock at school, with her rich connections, or a goy.

That old lady, down for the day from Hamilton, had a surprise coming to her.

Old lady, don't you worry. I don't know anything about this little Jew girl you've got your heart set on. She may be good as gold. So'm I, old lady, where your son is concerned, and all the things you think are going to give you conniption-fits about me aren't going to give you them at all. I only wish you Jews baptized, because I'd be baptized. I'll sit with you fasting on fast days, in your pew in the Plum Street Temple, and love it. I'll love him and honor him in his own religion; and if you'll give me half a chance, old woman, I'll do the same for you. . . .

It was October, and there were leaves flying, and along the esplanade women's skirts were blowing sharply forward, and so were the waters of the fountain, but the face she turned toward him, because of the hot flashes across it, was spangled with a tiny sweat.

"I'll be at the lion cubs, tomorrow morning, Walter, at eleven on the dot."

"Make it seem accidental."

How constrained he was.

"Walter."

"Yes?"

She wanted to say to him something like this: "I'm your hap-piness, Walter. I wouldn't harm a hair on the head of that girl up there, or of your mother's; but I'm your happiness, and don't you ever forget it." Of course, she said nothing of the kind. "Good-by, dear, the lion cubs at eleven."

12

That Ray did not turn up at the lion cubs on Sunday morning at eleven was to mean a lifetime of reiteration of a phrase that was to grind down a groove into her heart. What is to be, will be.

Would it have made any difference? Had her failure to appear at the lion-cub cage that Sunday morning changed, in some mysterious way, the ebb and flow of her life? What if she had appeared at the cage of the lion cubs . . . would it have made any ultimate difference? Had there been in Walter's heart, when he suggested her meeting his mother, anything but a casual and perhaps unexplainable desire to have her look upon the tinfoil glory of the goy he was about to renounce?

What had been in his heart, that noonday, as, dark and troubled, he paced her around the esplanade? What?

And strangely, although she was to ask, she was never to know. Chiefly, she concluded, because he himself did not know. Well, be that as it may—

On the five o'clock of the Sunday morning that she was to meet him and his mother at the lion cubs, she was awakened out of a sound sleep which it had taken her long hours of wakefulness to woo, by a noise that sounded like a small dog scratching.

At first leap of her mind into wakefulness, she thought it must be the adorable pug puppy that Walter had brought her from a street vendor two days before; but when she shot out her hand to feel for him, there he was curled up at the foot of the bed, snoring away as fast as his tiny sides could expand.

It was Freda, crouched across the pale streak of dawn that slanted into the room like a pencil held in proper Spencerian position, who had made the sounds. What in the world? At this hour! And what a Freda!

Something terrible was wrong with that specter sitting on its knees at the foot of Ray's bed. Here was no little Freda, cuddling up for the surreptitious talk in which she so delighted. Five o'clock in the morning meant something different. What?

"Freda, how you frightened me! Come in under the covers! What's wrong?"

She just sat shivering in the shaft of the dawn.

"Freda, come here."

She drew herself with a sort of bleat from the touch of Ray, who was on her feet by now, long, narrow, indefinably taller in her ruffled nightgown, her brown hair waving along her shoulders and giving her five years more of youth than the edifice of pompadour.

"What is it, child?"

Without more than the second's preparation for it, she knew.

"Sister, come here!"

This bleating, shuddering, chattering creature, smeared with pallor, grimacing with terror, had fallen out of the cradle of her blonde and flaccid girlhood into this horrible dawn. Freda was in terrible trouble.

"Sister, come to bed. Don't be afraid."

"What'll I do, Ray? What will I do?"

"You'll come to bed and get warm."

"Don't. I can't bear to be touched. I think I must be going crazy."

"Put this blanket over you. Let me hold you."

"What'll I do, Ray?"

"Ray will make him do right, Freda."

Why, this was like one of the plays at Heuck's. Life was a ten-twenty-thirty!

"Go to him fast, Ray. You can't wait a minute."

"Oh, Freda, little baby, how could you!"

"I told him last night, Ray. I had to tell him. . . ."

"Hugo?"

"I had to tell him, didn't I, Ray? I waited so and prayed—that it wasn't true. But then, when I saw that it was—I had to tell him that when she found out—if he didn't make it all right quick, Mama would kill him. You know Mama. I had to tell him."

"What did he say, Freda?"

"He got so funny then. It was as if his face, right there in front of me, turned into a fish's face. I thought I'd die."

"Tell me quickly, darling, everything he said."

"He looked at me, Ray, he looked at me kind of funny—I couldn't ever tell you what it was—that look—that look—"

"Shh-h-h-h, honey, crying won't help. You must tell Ray everything."

"You know how we've been going together."

"Yes."

"He got to hate to come here. Our parlor windows open so plainly onto the porch, and everybody that passes can gape, and then—Mother, sitting and sitting out there rocking—all the time—"

"Yes, I know."

"He wanted me to go around places with him—the way you do. . . ."

"No, no, no."

"He began to get mad. Said I thought more of everybody else than I did of him. Kept saying that, every time I had to say 'no' to something he asked me to do. Kept saying and saying it until I got scared."

"You should have explained to him right from the start, Freda, that you are not the sort to go gadding—"

"I did. I did. But he said—he said—"

"What did he say, dear?"

"He said, if—if you were the sort, why was I any better than my—sister?"

"If I was?"

"Yes. If you were fly, how could I expect him to think I wasn't—"

Was this flaxen child, huddling there in her arms, challenging her aid? Was there something of steel beneath this hysteria? . . . It did not matter.

"And so?"

"And so, what was I to do, Ray? He kept thinking I was the kind would do it if I wanted to, just as—you would— He got to acting so mad with me, Ray."

"Oh, Freda, what did it matter? Hugo is just a little pimply fellow you wouldn't look at twice, if it wasn't for his uncle. For all you know, the old gentleman may not even leave him a penny. Then where would you be?"

"Herman Hanck has made his will. Hugo told me. Hugo will be rich some day. Ray, what'll I do?"

"You haven't told me, Freda, just how it happened. He got to acting angry with you, and then?"

"And then—you remember that Sunday evening you wore your new checked suit and went out about six to meet some fellow at Mecklenburg's and you passed by the parlor and looked in and said to Hugo and me sitting there, 'Ta-ta, be good.'"

"Well?"

"Well that sent him off. Said there wasn't any more reason why I had to spend my time sitting him around in a dark parlor on a slippery sofa than there was for you. Said he hated our parlor, hated sitting around in it. Didn't intend to. That evening—we didn't go over to the Young People's Forum at the church. We went down to a place on Fifth Street where—they gave us a room. I don't know how it happened that way. I said, 'Let me out,' when I saw the place—the room—the bed—I yelled so that he had to put his hand over my mouth. I never would have, Ray, only he wanted it so. He kissed me so and said every girl was a booby in the eyes of every boy until she did. Said, anyway—as soon as his uncle got finished with the rubbishy idea that a fellow should strike out on his own, he was going to set him up, and we'd get married. I can't tell you any more. Isn't that enough? Ray, hurry. If Mama knows, I'll kill myself, because she'll kill me first if I don't. Hurry, Ray, and tell him he's got to make it right."

Ten-twenty-thirty. Ten-twenty-thirty. It was impossible to feel any reality about it. Freda in her nightdress, her flaxen braids plaited too tightly and hanging stiff as clothespins down her shoulders, crying her bitter salt tears into the dawn, the clock on the mantel ticking loudly against her sobs.

"Why, darling, it's dark yet. I can't go to him now."

"If you don't—he may get away somewhere. He acted so funny. Said he'd pay—if I'd do something about it—go to one of those terrible doctors that kill girls with illegal operations—"

"Freda!"

"He said it would be a terrible come-off to spoil things for us by letting this happen now—he—he— If you don't hurry, Ray, he may get away somewheres."

"What is it you want, Freda? What must Ray do?"

"Get him. Tell him something terrible will happen to him if he doesn't see me through. He doesn't think I know it, but there is a girl over in Covington named Kate Shray. He's been going with her on the side. You may have to hunt for him, Ray. He's scared. Maybe he didn't sleep at home last night. Then you must try his uncle out on Burnet Avenue. You know the big red house. Take a Zoo-Eden car, and change. Don't let him slip away, Ray. Tell him if—well, just tell him what I'll do. Tell him it will be the most scandalous thing ever happened in Cincinnati. And it will. If Mama finds out, she'll kill me, if I don't kill myself first. So will Marshall kill him. Get him quick, for God's sake."

"But, Freda, these things can't be done in a day. Give me until tomorrow—this is Sunday, I've got an engag—"

"If you don't get him now," said Freda, sitting up and dragging her hair back off her forehead with two palms until her eyes seemed to jut, "if you don't get him now—this morning—sure as my name is Freda Tagenhorst, I'll shoot myself. I've got Marshall's gun and I won't tell you where! I can't live—"

"Oh, my little girl. . . ."

"Oh, no. No, no, no. Don't my-little-girl me. That won't help. You've got to get him. I wouldn't ever be in this fix if he hadn't seen shady goings-on all around me— You, for instance—"

"Freda!"

"When he saw you gallivanting off night after night, what was there left for me to do but—what he wanted?"

"Freda!"

"It's true, and you know it! I don't know whether you sleep with boys or not, but that's the way it looks to lots of people in this town, whether you do or not."

"Freda, sit up! Look up! You're a horrid lying little scorpion!"

"I'm not. I'm not. I'm not!"

"I say you are," cried Ray, and shook her until her blonde plaits flew.

"You're for sale, and you know it!"

In the silence that followed, as they sat there in the brightening shaft of dawn, Ray reached out then, and grasping the shoulders of Freda with her two hands, shook her until her head rattled against the baseboard of the bed, and her row of small white lower teeth banged against the uppers.

"Liar! Nasty, mean, scheming little liar!" And shook and shook again, and the bed rattled, and the chandelier rattled, and finally it seemed the room and the universe rattled. "Liar. Liar. Liar." And shook and shook until the blonde pulp of Freda lay breathless across the bed-top, and, breathless, sobbed:

"I'm done now. I'm finished. This is the end. Go away. I— wonder—what—to—do— I'm done now."

"Oh, my little darling. Poor Freda. Dear Freda. I must have gone crazy. I'll do for you anything you want. My poor little sweet. Ray won't let anything happen to you—oh, my poor sweet."

"Then hurry, Ray. Go to him. Find him. Tell him that Freda won't live if he don't. Every day it makes it more terrible. Mama will find out. I can feel myself getting big. God would strike me dead for getting rid of a baby that's so far on its way. Tell him I won't do that. I'll die before."

And so it came about that while Walter, puzzled, dallied with his mother around the lion cubs, Ray, on fire with her predicament, was racing from Hugo's rooming house in Race Street, where he was not, to his uncle's address on Burnet Avenue, where he might be.

13

The meeting with Hugo was one that was to bite in permanent and ugly etching against her memory. As luck would have it, he was seated on the steps of the side porch of his uncle's large horrific red-brick house of ell, millwork verandas, architectural excrescences, wallowing a fox terrier.

He was a pale-eyed, pasty fellow, with an Adam's apple straining against the wall of his long, thin throat, and wrists that shot out like turtle necks. There was about him a manner of one born to the denim, of Monday morning's overalls, which not even Sunday's black-and-white pin-striped suit, with its padded shoulders, peg-top trousers, stiff detachable cuffs, and tan toothpick shoes could dissipate.

At sight of Ray, suddenly standing there in the side yard, a wave of red poured along the pimpled plane of his forehead. Apparently his first instinct was to bolt, but since his sole choice of direction away from Ray was through a door that led into a dining room, he seemed to think better of this as an initial tactic, and resumed with the dog.

She stood on the grass plot, watching him begin making false and highly self-conscious feints at the terrier, who wanted to tussle.

"You know why I'm here, Hugo."

"Not asking, am I?"

"But you do."

"Maybe I do and maybe I don't."

"No maybes."

He was no good at concealing unease, and began ambling in long-legged fashion down the porch steps.

"If you've come to start anything, you're up the wrong tree. My uncle keeps big dogs. You're trespassing."

Well, anyway, here was mere silliness to combat, not viciousness, as she had feared.

"Hugo, all I ask is that you come for a little walk with me where we can talk without interruption."

"And suppose I say naw?"

"You won't."

"I will."

"Hugo, there is nothing to keep me from walking up these sideporch steps and into that dining room where I can see the top of your uncle's head at the table and have the talk I need to have with you, with him."

The manner in which the pallor and color flew alternately across his pimples was horrible. He was a horrid boy. A narrow fellow, with whom it seemed almost pathetically easy to cope.

"If you think you can come around here trying to scare up a rumpus—"

"Very well, then I—"

"Take your foot off that step."

"You can't frighten me, Hugo, from doing my duty."

"This is private property."

What a little fool he was!

"Hugo, hadn't you better agree to talk this thing—this terrible thing out quietly with me?"

"I don't know what thing you mean."

"Come along, then; I will tell you as we walk."

"Well—not because you're scaring me into it."

"I don't want to scare you into anything, Hugo."

Their walk petered out from the start, because halfway down the block, in front of a vacant lot, she spun and faced him.

"What you have to do is plain as the nose on your face."

Procrastination gone to the winds, he thrust his lean features angrily toward her.

"She's lying!"

"How dare you say that of my little sister!"

"She is, and you know it. I've got her ticket. She's molasses that only pours the way it wants to pour."

"You've done the most terrible thing to her that a man can do. You've got to right it the only way a man can."

"If that was the case, pretty nearly every man in this town would be righting you!"

She stood her ground, feeling for a frightened moment as if she had congealed into something too rigid to enable her ever to move her lips again.

"It's vile of you to say that, and untrue. But that doesn't change the one thing I'm out here for. You are going to marry Freda. Immediately."

He threw back his head, as if to laugh off an absurdity, but his lips did not complete the gesture. They began to tremble.

"You're crazy."

"At heart, Hugo, you are the kind of boy who would want to right a terrible thing like this. Don't make things more unbearable by forcing us to force you."

"Not a chance. I know that baby. She's trying to trap me. She's molasses that pours the way it wants to pour, and she's pouring toward me because she thinks she sees money ahead. Well, she don't need to. His nibs is after a gal in this town himself, and the money she thinks she sees may go into that gal's pocket for all I know."

"Hugo."

"Tell her for me, she's pretty slick, but she don't quite slide!"

"You—"

"Tell her for me, little Willie is wiser than he looks. Tell her for me, I pretended I didn't know what was going on in her and her mama's head, but that a blind man could have seen it. Tell her for me, I was willing to do the right thing, and get a doctor, even if I suspected her of lying all the time, but now I've changed my mind.

What that little gal don't know about how to take care of herself, there's other members of her family can learn her."

"Are you finished?"

"Yeh, unless you want me to repeat anything."

"Now, Hugo, you listen to me. I can stand your insults to me, chiefly because deep down inside of me, where none of you can get at it, I know it's not true; but we're here to talk about Freda, and I am free to say to you that, if I had it in me to act the way you are acting, then I'd take the gun Freda says she has hidden away, point it to myself, and say here goes good riddance."

Alternating pallor and crimson raced under his skin, and he began to roll himself the fifth cigarette of the interview, cramming the tobacco pouch back into his pocket, and making little snorkling sounds, as he ran tongue along the paper.

"'Fraid she'll have to shoot."

"Is that what I am to tell her?"

"'Fraid so."

"Hugo, as God is my judge, I'm afraid she'll do it."

"Not a chance," he said, along lips that were wavering like the stripes of a flag in a breeze.

"If it was me, there wouldn't be enough money in the world to make me marry you. But it's Freda, a little thing who hasn't got the nerve to face it out; and nothing in the world can save you from marrying her. Let me say that to you over again, Hugo, slowly: Nothing—in—the—world—can—save—you—from—marrying her."

"Find me."

"Running away won't help. If anything terrible happens to Freda Tagenhorst because of you, this town will find you. I'll find you. Your uncle, one of the respected businessmen of this town, will find you. Oh, Hugo, be a man."

"That talk don't scare me."

But he was frightened, no doubt of that, the bravado seeming to ooze through his fingers, leaving them dry and inclined to pluck at one another.

"I told her that I'd help pay a doctor—and that's more than most would do, considering I don't believe I'm the one got her into it. . . ."

"You're even lower, Hugo, than I thought. My little sister isn't going sneaking around town risking her life and soul in the horrible kind of place where they do that horrible illegal thing. She's going to be the kind of respectable married woman in this town that she—"

"Yah—that's what she's after. Smells money, somewhere. Sees a chance for sitting pretty. Using me. Well, I won't be used. If she's caught the way she says she is, then she's caught. I'm willing to find the doctor. . . ."

"Hugo, you're caught. Not Freda."

"That ten-twenty-thirty talk don't scare me."

Ten-twenty-thirty. The phrase spun around like a pinwheel. Even he, horrid pimply boy, saw the snideness of this predicament. But that did not change matters. Life and death and all the ingredients mixed up here, passion and vice and childbirth and sin, were melodrama. . . .

"Trying to make small of things won't get you anywhere, Hugo. They are not small. They are the very stuff life's made of. You're going to marry my sister, right away."

"You're crazy."

"Don't make me go on threatening. Can't you see there is no way out? You're going to marry my sister. You're going to lead decent respectable lives together and have decent respectable children. If you try to dodge doing the honorable and upright thing now, your life is going to end, before it's begun, in scandal, notoriety, and disgrace. And worse! I know the kind of man your uncle will be, when it comes to funny business from you. I know the kind of woman my stepmother is, when it comes to protecting Freda. I know the kind of deal you can expect from me if you let anything worse happen to my sister than has happened to her already. Come, Hugo, you're the kind of fellow was made to walk in step—and like it."

"You can't scare me—"

"Maybe not. I wish I didn't need to try, and that Freda had the stuff in her to tell you to go straight where you belong, but she hasn't; and so, scared or no scared, you're coming right down to Baymiller Street with me now, and tell her you're going to marry her. It's costing me the most expensive engagement I ever had in my life, to see to it that you go through with what you started; but there is not five minutes between now and the time you are married that you can expect to be free of my company. See?"

Somehow he did. The gray pimpled mask of pallor that faced Ray in the sun-slashed eleven o'clock of that bright Sunday morning, did see.

14

The same edition of the *Enquirer* that carried the small item of the marriage of Freda Tagenhorst to Hugo Hanck, also carried, more prominently, a paragraph announcing the betrothal of Corinne, daughter of Mr. and Mrs. Aaron Trauer, of Richmond Street, to Walter D. Saxel, son of Mrs. Emanuel Saxel, of Hamilton, Ohio.

Clad for the store in her modish shirtwaist and five-gored skirt, Ray read both announcements over her self-spread breakfast, the morning *Enquirer* propped up against the vinegar cruet, as she drank her coffee.

It was a wet day, filled with the dripping sounds of water running off tin gutters pouring into rainbarrels, and beating in fast, steady hiss against windowpanes. The streetlights were still burning, the Welsbach over the dining table making the daylight a gray rag. A soaked October morning, filled with the pulp of sodden leaves and blackening lawns. From the dining-room window, the side yard presented a spectacle of raked leaves, becoming pulp, and Tagenhorst's washline, which, despite Ray's remonstrances, she would not remove after Monday morning's wash, crisscrossing the scene from week to week.

Tagenhorst, exhausted by a Monday which had swept her off her feet with the quick sequence of desirable events, was oversleeping. Spiciness of dead carnations lay on the air. The young couple, on a leave of six days' absence, allowed without pay by the gas

company, and seventy-five dollars from Tagenhorst, were just about
arriving at French Lick Springs, where a remotely related Tagenhorst conducted a boardinghouse within half a mile of the French
Lick Springs Hotel.

A pair of adorably naughty children, cheating Tagenhorst of a
wedding celebration that might easily have cost a pretty and unnecessary penny, had expedited matters by eloping! Oversleeping, a
smile lay sunken into the mouth of Tagenhorst, who had removed
her teeth.

Curiously, as she sat there at the breakfast table, while rain
tapped, sipping her coffee and gazing over the cup-rim at the newspaper which bore the two tidings in such ironic propinquity, a smile
also dragged itself along Ray's dark-red lips.

Well, what was there to knock you skywise about that? You had
known it all along. On the very evening you had first met him at
the C. H. and D., he had been neatly and rightly on his way to this.
It was as it should be. Now was the time to be grand about it all. It
had happened. It would happen again. Worse things had been lived
through. It was for the best, all her trumped-up evidence to the
contrary notwithstanding. Intermarriages were a risk. Just as easy
for a man to make up his mind to fall in love with the right girl as
with the wrong. On the other hand, why should anybody not born
a Jew elect to be a Jew? People born Jews turned Gentile, but who
ever heard of a Gentile turning Jew? All for the best. Probably best
thing that could have happened. All for the best. Certainly for Walter's best. But why—why always Walter? What about herself? Well,
perhaps, who knows—as good fish in the ocean as ever came out of
it. Perhaps some day— But to get back to Walter. Best, no doubt,
for him. There was about Walter the aura of a man who would some
day be rich. There would be perfectly matched pearls in the creases
of Corinne's fair neck. There would be well-dressed children and a
home in Avondale, or perhaps New York. The banking Friedlanders
would establish him there. Solidly right, as it should be. Madness of
her to have even attempted to tinker at the gate of this mammoth
tower of race. Fool! Just as good fish in the sea as ever came out of
it. Buckle down now to good old common sense. Life would go on.

Rather! Today would be a crowded day at the store, due to having missed two days getting Freda and Hugo married. Oh, there was plenty to do. Plenty to fill life. What is to be, will be. Pouf!

And pouf it remained for a period long enough to sustain her over such subsequent excitements as marriage in the house, an important bid for the homestead from the owner of a small sausage factory, and Marshall's determination to transplant his mother's interests, such as they were, to Youngstown.

Life to be lived, and just as good fish in the sea as ever came out of it. Better! Why make life more difficult than need be? Funny thing, but in all innocence a drummer had just told her that Jews were not tolerated in certain of the better hotels along the board-walk at Atlantic City. That was almost as bad as being black. Nothing so bad but what it could be worse. Hard enough to be born a Jew, but why break your heart because you had missed—had lost—had failed—oh, God—pouf!

There was plenty to do. She volunteered, of course, in all the high-pressure excitement, to give up her room to the young couple and move into the sewing room—the move not so simple as it sounded, considering it had been so privately her own for practically a lifetime. Then, too, Heyman Heymann, hard-pressed, had taken it into his head to clear out the jets and passementeries, and make room for a larger line of dressmaker findings. That meant clearance sales and quite a general readjustment. Then, as luck would have it, the Music Festival was on, and a drummer for a Boston sheet-music firm had planned with her, a whole year in advance, to be present in Cincinnati to attend at least two concerts with her. She had purchased seats in response to a reminding telegram from him, and there was a violet plush bell-skirt, already cut and planned, which had been lying at sewing school for weeks, waiting to be completed for this occasion, along with one of those extremely stylish little shoulder capes edged in ball chenille which were all the rage. A subdued half-mourning color combination, sniffed at by Tagenhorst in black, but the only outward manifestation Ray could endure to wear for Adolph.

Oh, there was plenty to do to keep the mind occupied! But

beneath the doings there persisted, there persisted, the lurking, hurting hope—surely he would come. He must come. It was not possible that there remained not a word to be said between them. Just some decent sort of obituary over days that were gone; some decent sort of good-bys to be said between them. But meanwhile, it was good that there was that violet plush to be finished, and the move to be made, and the confusion of the return of the bridal pair, and so many of the drummers coming to town—fall trade— anything, to keep the mind moving.

He did not come. Perhaps it was for the best. That was doubt-less how he was putting it to himself. A man would make it simple for himself that way! Of course he wouldn't come. Of course he shouldn't come. There was already something legalized about his allegiance to the plump little girl on Richmond Street who would some day wear his pearls in the crevices of her short white neck. Life wasn't like that, in neat closed chapters. The thing to do, loose ends to the contrary notwithstanding, was to begin another chap-ter. Plenty to do. What was there to the whole business, after all, except living and loving and helping? If you couldn't love again, ever, the next thing was to help. Help Freda. Help Tagenhorst. Yes, help the bull, Marshall. Help in that absurd struggle out there, of the people to whom things blessedly mattered. . . .

It was strange that Kurt, who neither knew nor suspected any-thing of all this, should call for her that evening at closing. And it was stranger still, that as he walked home with her through the rain-washed air, and along the drying sidewalks, she should find herself telling him, gently, and in all the merciful words she could muster, that her decision not to marry him was final.

15

The trip to New York, buying dressmaking findings on the strength of Heymann's sudden determination to enhance that section of the stock, accomplished more than just tide over the precariousness of days that had flattened out into the formation of rows of numbers on a calendar.

Buying dressmaking findings on the strength of Heymann's determination to attempt a last resort, brought about the renewal of the old offer from the Greene Street firm of "Ledbetter and Scape—Ribbons, Veilings, Linings, and Dressmakers' Findings."

"Ever think about that offer we made you three years ago, Miss Schmidt? Still holds good."

The salary, especially considering the more complicated living procedure the move to New York would immediately entail, was none too interesting. Fifteen dollars a week in Cincinnati, even with the weekly stipend of eight which she was now paying Tagenhorst, was one matter. Twenty dollars a week in New York, another. Nevertheless, while she contemplated nothing so drastic as even entertaining the idea of the move to a city which baffled and terrified, reiteration of the offer gave her a gratifying sense of security in the face of the unmistakable conditions in her late father's business.

Heyman Heymann, in spite of this outward gesture of trying to resuscitate the neglected department of dressmakers' findings, was contemplating, Ray had good reason to know, the dissolution of the old firm with which he found himself saddled, into the name and prestige of one of the largest concerns of the kind in the Middle West, the Acme Dress Findings Company of St. Louis.

Should materialization of this incipient plan take place, what then? Would Acme take her over? St. Louis seemed a good live town, judging from the drummers from Rosenthal and Sloane, Rice Stix and Eli Walker, who occasionally dropped in. Not likely, because, with an old conservative firm like Acme, women employees were an innovation yet to be made.

Plans, it seemed, were afoot not only for dissolution of the business, but it had begun to seem apparent that the house on Baymiller Street was not, after all, to go to the owner of the small sausage factory, who had finally forfeited the option twice extended to him; but a "swap" was being eventuated for a two-family house in Youngstown, one-half of which had heretofore been occupied by Marshall and a wife who was reputed to have been cook for the Tafts.

Plans for dissolution all about, just as, with every ounce of resolution at her command, she was struggling to fit into a world that no longer seemed to interest her enough to screw up desire to face the days.

Where was her old vitality for the small fry of activities? Where the old flare for the day unto itself, the eagerness with which she met the issues of business, the next new proffered form of entertainment, the vivacity that had always been hers to expend upon the delights of modish regalia, the energy, after a day at the store, to hasten to sewing school, there to spread out her patterns, snip, stitch, and chalk until as late as midnight? And for what? The snide and now, in the nausea of realization, vulgar compensation of the drummer's stare as she tripped past the Stag; the chuck under the chin from the escort who liked to shine in the inexpensive and reflected glory of the attention her modishness attracted?

Where were those old days, old only in the sense that they lay moldering in her memory, now that her vitality for them had dimmed?

It was difficult to drag the lids awake upon the new régime of a

life suddenly devitalized of practically every former desire. It penetrated, this vast inertia, to such literal appetites as desire for food.
Breakfast became a matter of forcing down coffee against a throat
closed to it; boxes of sweets (and it was a rare week that several of
these easy tributes of the passing drummer did not find their way to
her) lay moldering in her desk or dresser drawers. It was mysterious, the way in which the flavor had been whisked out of a manner
of life that she had heretofore accepted as unquestioningly as she
accepted the color of her eyes or the height of her body.

In a way, her every day reminded her of her recovery from a
severe siege of typhoid fever during her father's widowerhood, when
she was about ten. Tagenhorst, with whom they had been boarding
at the time, had nursed her through it, and memories of those long,
ministering hours had mitigated against many a subsequent impulse
to harsh judgments against her stepmother. It seemed to Ray that
her feeling now was something akin to those first feeble days of
her convalescence. The world without was something that flowed
normally and eagerly about a body too tired and spent to lift a hand
toward its maelstrom. It was desirable, and above all peaceful, to lie
away from it, face to wall and spent body relaxed. If only one did
not ever have to rise or face the wear and tear. One's spirit lay like
a stone fallen to the bottom of a pool, and one's heart was the pool.

A difficult hour was the one before dawn, when, half awake,
the pug nestling its warm body against the coverlet, and the eyes
squeezed closed, you tried to shut out the impending inevitability
of the rising hour. Then the dash down the hall to the bathroom,
rigmarole of buttoning and hooking into the day's armor, breakfast standing beside the kitchen stove, or with the *Enquirer* propped
against the cruet on the dining-room table. The bicycle ride, or the
Colerain car, to work. The musty Welsbach-lighted interior of the
trimming store, gray as a moth, the walls lined with boxes tagged
at each end with a sample of their content. Gold tassel. Silver button. Lace medallion. Velvet violet. Heyman Heymann puttering
around what had once been her father's desk. The trickle of customers. Trickle of talk. The business day through which she could have
made her way blindfolded, so versed was she in the stock, the trade,

and the technique of buying and selling the contents of the gray boxes that lined the shelves. The wholesale trade, fingering bolts of tulles and veilings; the retail trade, concerned with yards and, too often, the half yard; the dressmaking trade, sometimes Madame Dimonson herself, who dressed the Tafts, the Emerys, and the Longworths, plunging nearsightedly into bins and boxes. The drummer on his rounds, or, more frequently, the drummer in to see Ray. Rendezvous for lunch, dinner, Music Hall, river excursions, buggy ride. The boys. The joys. And now, suddenly, that abysmal heartache of one who is loath, upon awakening mornings, to turn away from facing the wall for the purpose of rising to face the day.

Oh, it was right that Walter did not come. Right and loyal and part of the solidity that to her was always to seem fearful and wonderful in its immensity. The solidity which had practically destroyed her, and yet which was something to admire and about which she felt fascinated.

Catch what the Jewish boys called a *batsimer* standing up to his sense of obligation in that fashion. Catch Marshall Tagenhorst, for instance, who had married a loud and irate cook, against every family wish, caring a rap what his mother, or his religion, or his responsibility required of him. Why, even Kurt, whose old parents had gone to live at Simmons Corner, confessed to not having been home but twice, the last two years of their lives. Twice in two years, mind you, and Simmons Corner not forty miles away. Catch a Jewish boy treating his folks that way. Oh, it was right that Walter did not come. In fact, after the first few weeks, it seemed to Ray that to encounter him anywhere along the way where his habits were apt to take him, would be more than she could bear. Her trip to New York, which had consumed only eight days, made the time that had elapsed since the morning she had read the news in the *Enquirer* seem somehow longer than it actually was. That, and the sudden cataclysmic change in the household brought about by Freda's precipitate marriage, had packed a brief period with a dazzling allotment of events that seemed to throw sense of time out of plumb.

The young couple had returned from French Lick Springs and were installed in what had been Ray's bedroom, a second-story rear one, with two exposures overlooking side and backyards. Ray had given them the use of her brass bedstead and bird's-eye maple set, assisting Tagenhorst in seaming, ruffling, and hanging new transom and window curtains, and in scrubbing the Axminster rug with soap and water. Before the return, she managed, too, to complete a burnt-wood toilet set for the dressing table, etching with a hot needle point Freda's wedded initials onto the backs of hairbrush, hand mirror, shoehorn, and pin tray. The old habit of pottering about at the doing of chores for others, matching a sample of embroidery silk for a neighbor, racing around town on a quest for a wire hairbrush for Marshall's wife, whom she had never seen, survived through her inertia. There had been a fierce kind of joy in decking out the room for the return of the bridal pair.

It was extraordinary, the quality of submission Hugo had brought to his marriage. Once the words of sacrament were spoken, there had descended upon him, like rays of sun penetrating fog, the demeanor of bridegroom triumphant. The flaxen Freda, doll-eyed, but as rigid-looking in her pretty, bisque way as if she were still concentrating on achieving what she had already accomplished, returned from her brief honeymoon, the lovely and surrendering bride of an absurdly pretentious young husband.

Herman Hanck had resisted at first, coming out with a statement which he made to a reporter that he washed his hands of his nephew's elopement; but after overtures from the young couple, there had come along a wedding check for five hundred dollars, and a supper at the house on Burnet Avenue, from which Freda and Tagenhorst had returned in delirium of enthusiasm for the elderly brewer, who had sent them home from his fine brick house, in Avondale, in a carriage.

Now, however, was not the time to press matters. Herman Hanck was a conservative, if ever there was one; but that he had plans was manifest.

He as much as told his nephew, after pinching Freda's cheek and running his heavy reddish hands along the flank of her young body, that whether or not he decided to bring them into his home, depended on certain developments. That, of course, was his way of refusing to make matters too easy for the youngsters. Obviously, the clever strategy was for Hugo to continue his position with the gas company, while Tagenhorst adopted the temporary policy of acting hostess to the young couple. No use trying to force a Hanck. Hugo knew the wisdom of biding his time with his uncle.

It was vicariously reassuring somehow to be around the enormous complacency of the mother hen Tagenhorst, whose chick was about to sit pretty, and also to behold the phenomenon of Hugo, doltish fellow, seeming to fall in love with his wife. In a dozen secret ways he was solicitous of her, and although she wore, as yet, no badge of the growing period of her pregnancy, he was at her elbow for every step, concerned about the slightest strain upon her little dollie body, so much so, in fact, that it seemed to Ray that the eye of Tagenhorst, with its constantly narrowing pupil, like a parrot's, might one day flash in quick suspicion. But nothing of the sort. Freda's quality of immaturity, now that you thought of her as wife and mother, was more and more a striking and quite a lovely thing about her. Her whiteness made her seem flesh of the pearl; and the way in which she wrapped her head in yellow flaxen braids kept her childish looking in a manner that seemed just to have dawned, in delight, upon the heavy-handed, pelican-faced Hugo.

And how she fitted into marriage! As if it were an old dressing-sack which she donned comfortably. Scarcely two weeks after the return from the honeymoon, she began to appear at the breakfast table uncorseted, her heavy creamy breasts loose in a dressing-sack, her feet slouching about in slippers she would have scorned as a girl. A newly economical, purring little Freda, who followed her husband mornings to the porch, holding her dressing-sack from falling open as far down as her breasts, waving him good-by as he swung aboard a car, and then slouching back into the house on the shoes that shuffled, and, likely as not, spending her morning at making their bed, exploring her face for blackheads, sewing buttons on Hugo's cheaply flashy shirts, and, if the autumn days permitted, sitting on the front porch, riding a darning needle in an up-and-down motion through his cheaply flashy socks.

To think that Freda was going to have a baby! Sometimes, lying awake, it seemed to Ray nothing short of incredible that beyond the thin partition that divided her room from that of Hugo and Freda, the miracle of the making of a baby was taking place. Well, what of that? Millions of babies were on their way into the world, but not somehow in this kind of precious propinquity. She had never lived so intimately around a woman who was going to have a baby. And Freda made it seem fastidious and lacking in all the revolting physical aspects that had been part of the childbearing of many of the girls she knew. Freda took her breakfast with gusto, bright was her morning eye, and her body, no plumper than usual, kept its normal, pretty curves. As such things go, she had been a bad girl, no doubt of that; but just the same, now that she was in the midst of the making of a baby and that baby was assured of a father awaiting it, everything dropped into the category of the beatific.

It was fine to plan for the baby. As she lay wakeful, night after night, when misery threatened to come down like scythes slashing through and through her, and her toes climbed in a pain that had no name, it helped to concentrate on that baby. "Fleischer Brothers— Infants' Wear," on Fourth Street, would allow ten percent off on purchases in the name of the firm of Adolph Schmidt. They always carried things in the window like pink-wool coverlets and jackets and white-celluloid rattles with pink forget-me-nots on them.

If only one had the time, all those things could be made at home, and so much more cheaply. How Tagenhorst, who had her days to herself, would begin to crochet and knit when she knew. When she knew! Freda would not hear to that, yet. Meanwhile it was lovely to have the secret for a little while longer, of that life in the making.

How lucky, after all, was Freda! Life was going to be right and normal for her after its terrifying beginning based on a silly mistake. From now on, particularly after Hanck took them into the fold of his wealth, it would be safe. Secure. She would have more babies. Hugo would mature and fill out and become less silly.

Corinne would have babies, too. His. Well, she was not the only girl in the history of the world to have a baby by a man loved by some other woman. The kibosh on such thoughts. But what if you could not help thinking them? What if they kept the night a feverish horror? Lying a few blocks away, asleep no doubt, care-less of her blessedness, lay the girl who would be wife to him, and mother to his children, and recipient of the touch of his hand and the caresses of his eyes and the intimacy of his bed and the security of his home. That was as it should be. It would be a firm, tight, protected home, where Walter would prosper, and his children would be born and thrive and study and learn music and science and the arts, and become accomplished, after the fashion of Jewish children. They had always been smart in school. Sometimes you hated them, with their hooky, eager faces and curious pretenses of inferiority that were crowned with secret convictions of superiority. Walter's children—it was as it should be. Like to like. Walter to his kind. Ray to hers. What was her kind? The married drummers who liked to slide their hands along her flanks under the tables of pub-lic eating houses. The elderly men, with the moist lips that always reminded her of liver, who sooner or later directed their eyes or remarks toward George Street. Kurt? Ah, why not Kurt? . . .

The thought rolled over Ray, troubled night after troubled night, that if only she had never clapped eyes on Walter Saxel, life would still be something to be lived up to its hilt, instead of some-thing to lie broken and huddled over in bed, whole nights through.

I've had a crash. I must get over it. Thousands of girls do. But I won't ever. Because I can't. I am like that.

16

One snow-decked day, about two weeks before Christmas, this happened: There walked into Schmidt's, with flakes on her shoulders and caught charmingly into the mesh of her veil, Corinne Trauer and her mother.

There she was, the fair, plump Corinne, in a short sealskin jacket, its peplum spreading from her slim waist as it tilted off her bustle, hat that rose with that same gesture of a boost from the rear, and hands thrust into a round sealskin ball of a muff upon which were pinned fresh violets. A fashionable little person, lovely smell of cold violets all about her. Mrs. Trauer, a sealskin cape of fitted shoulders and a bonnet of sprays of swinging jet, looking the animated and well-fed rôle of any Richmond Street matron. Their good mornings were the polite toneless ones that fell just short of the added intonation that would have gone with "Good morning, Miss Schmidt." Vaguely, to their shopping memories, she was just that stylish-looking girl who had been for years at Schmidt's. One went so seldom to Schmidt's these days—but their veilings were still the best in town.

"White net, please. Point d'esprit. Finest mesh." And then, with the air of oh-if-you-must-know "—wedding veiling."

Here it came, crash at her. Wedding veiling. And there she was, Ray, tilting the great bolts of net off the shelves and ballooning before them the tulles that rose in soufflés.

And then, presently, sure enough, there, oh, it was funny, considering that her impulse right along had been to seize and unwind one of the bolts and wrap it around the busy little body fingering at the textures, were the three of them, with Corinne standing posed before a pier glass, and Ray holding the tulle so that it might cascade from the crown of Corinne's head.

What a busy, canny little pair they were, these Trauers, rubbing the sheerness of bridal veiling between fingers, holding it against a sample of ivory-colored satin, ordering Ray, in their agreeable manners, to again and again commit the experiment of showing Corinne with different varieties of the raiments of the bride.

"Mama this. Corinne that. You see, miss, her dress is to be out of my own wedding dress. A little more ivory in the veiling—oh, daughter, stop fidgeting. How can the young lady manage? It's to be a Plum Street Temple wedding."

"Oh, Mama, wouldn't it be heavenly if I could have orange blossoms on the hem? Walter says he's sure to trip over it, hurrying."

The impulse to throttle her with the veiling became more and more absurd. Down underneath her shoulders another and hidden pair of shoulders kept shaking and shaking with the submerged silent laughter. What high little hillocks of breasts she had. Creamy deep, lovely and tender. His head would lie there. . . .

"Four yards—let veil cover face just enough to make it a simple matter to lift it after the ceremony—please, Mama, don't get me nervous again. I'm going to have my veil that way if it's never been done before in the history of the whole religion!"

Walter would lift the veil after the ceremony, to kiss those pale roses of lips. Those lips were there now, close enough for her to touch. To twist!

"Don't you think some of that pretty little Valenciennes edging will be nice for corsetcovers and dressing-sacks, daughter, to wear around the house?"

While she was having her babies, Corinne would wear dressing-sacks, sheer white ones with Valenciennes or crocheted edgings. They would be part of the intimacy of her life with Walter. They would reveal to him loveliness of soft breasts.

"But Walter's mother is crocheting so much lace for me!"

"So she is! Then come, daughter, we'll be late at Madame Dimonson's for your fitting. You'll send the things promptly, won't you, miss? You see, they're for a wedding."

"Indeed I will. Oh, Miss Trauer, here, you are forgetting your muff! The pretty violets!"

The—pretty—violets-the-pretty-violets-the-pretty-violets! His to her. The pretty violets that were on the grave of the day.

What happened subsequently, after the two had passed out into a world lit with swirling snowflakes, was what kept her stiffly to her feet instead of permitting her to obey an impulse to huddle down hidden behind a counter and just crouch hurt there, until somehow this day wore on. Heyman Heymann, as if he had only been waiting for the lull between customers, was at her side, cracking his knuckles and trying to be kind.

"Schmidt—Trimmings and Findings" was sold. Even the name was to be absorbed into that of the St. Louis firm. Day of little business was gone. Fortunate to break even. Of course, had already put in an excellent word for Ray, but ways of big business stereotyped. General reorganization. No women had ever been employed by the St. Louis firm. Y'know! Conservative town. Of course, always glad to put in a good word for her. Mighty glad. But ways of big business stereotyped. Never tell how the big fellows might jump.

In this instance Ray could.

She knew, just as surely as she stood there staring into the pier glass that had so recently reflected Corinne, that her days at Schmidt's, where she had spent so many years of her life, were over, beginning January first, when the new firm took over the old.

So much was over! There was a member of the Cincinnati ball team, Jack Shrier, coming to take her to dinner that evening at Lookout House, at the top of the Incline, and then on later to Atlantic Garden, Over-the-Rhine, where it was coming to be the fashion to slum after eleven. That kind of thing, the ability to spend hours with a lout of a fellow who, when out of training, drank himself, before eleven, into an amorous stupor, apparently was over too, because she sent him a message around to the Stag Hotel, stating, without troubling to offer reason, her inability to meet him that evening in the lobby of the Grand Hotel.

On Baymiller Street, the Tagenhorsts were already at table when she arrived, bearing a dozen links of a local brand of blood sausages as peace offering for appearing unexpectedly upon the supper-scene against her announced intentions. There they were, the three of them. Tagenhorst, in a black flannelette wrapper printed all over in the design of tiny anchors, Freda and Hugo, seated around the table over a meal of a ham-end that had been boiled in stringbeans, fried eggs, cold soda biscuits over which you poured sorghum for dessert, and a pitcher of pale brew which Hugo had "rushed" from Bader's corner saloon. There were various food knickknacks and leavings from other meals on the table. A snack of boiled beef, cloying under cold horseradish sauce. A saucer of animal crackers. A warmed-over dish of kohlrabi and a bowl of weatherbeaten-looking *schmierkäse*. Tagenhorst prided herself upon a copious table, a sort of nibble of this and leftover of that, detested by Ray.

There was never an occasion when she showed herself for an evening meal that Tagenhorst's lips did not fold themselves back for the identical remark: "Well, to what do we owe this treat?"

"To the fact," said Ray, tossing down her offering of blood sausage, and drawing up a chair, "that I'm dead on my feet."

"Should think you would be," said Tagenhorst, who chewed rapidly on her front teeth. "Can't burn the candle at both ends and not look like the wrath of God."

"I suppose I do look the part," she said, and smoothed her hair as if it felt tired along with her bones, and began hacking herself a piece of the end of the ham.

There was a small blueprint spread beside Hugo's plate, which he perused through nearsighted eyes as he bolted his food. How rutted they were! How irredeemably committed and destined to commonness! How committed the entire world, in which she, Ray, moved, to the snide happiness to be derived from just the doing of things. Races. Ham-ends. Buggy rides. He sez 'n' she sez. What must it be like to know someone like Della Fox or Eugene Field or President Cleveland? Commonness here. Bread stabbed up off the center plate by Hugo's fork. Tagenhorst's red-fringed napkin with egg stain. Freda's high little bust always half exposed. Not even ensconced in the red-brick house on Burnet Avenue would Freda ever rise to anything above her little rhinestone commonness. Indeed, on the contrary, her little pasty gleam would run, with the years, into dinginess.

For Hugo there was simply no redemption. His huge feet would always sprawl on the floor, pointing inward. There would be that tiny tuft of hair at the tip of his rather foolish-looking nose, and the habit of hunching himself over his food until his elbows sprang out like the legs of a grasshopper.

The Tagenhorsts, and Ray with them, even Freda and Hugo, after they achieved the house on Burnet Avenue, would go through life on the plane of the unglamorous people who wore black flannelette with anchor designs and hacked at ham-ends on littered supper tables. The rutted horror of life in a house that smelled perpetually of the suds of family washing, the boiling of potatoes, and the gilt on a parlor chair that had a pink moire bow on its left shoulder.

The Trauers, who were nobodies—Jews always were sort of nobodies, except in a rich way—would never live that trashily, even though their old man was nothing much more than an insurance agent. And he wasn't their "old man" either. You didn't refer to Mr. Trauer as "old man." He was listened to respectfully whenever he spoke, and helped at street corners, and reverenced in his home. It was trashy here. Marshall's attitude toward his mother was trashy. This house was trashy—and yet Hugo's next words, leveled at her with the sly cruelty of a small boy about to pull the tail of his cat, made it seem suddenly and surpassingly dear here.

"Marshall has swapped this house for what looks to me like a pair of twin packing cases in Youngstown," he said, and shoved the blueprint toward her.

She had been prepared for this. The negotiation was one of long duration and endless discussion, and now here it was, and suddenly this house on Baymiller Street became unbearably precious. She had been born in this house. The mother whom she scarcely remembered by feature had lain in a box the shape of the sole of a shoe, down the center of the room adjoining the one in which they were now seated. She had boarded in this house when Tagenhorst had become landlady of it, and when the father whose memory she loved had taken for a wife the big-boned Tagenhorst, who had ministered to him in a fashion that was snide, but which was apparently sufficient for her nondemanding father. This was a square frame little house, crammed with the memories of her lifetime. She had lain in her cradle here, toddled through its halls, felt the first pangs and joys of adolescence moving up against her body like grass tips against spring soil. Stirrings had taken place in the buds of her consciousness here; she had become aware here, within these trashy, paper-covered walls, of so much that was strange and new and mysterious about herself—about her body—about faint stirrings of dreams, desire, love, beauty, that for want of something better were classified as soul. And now, suddenly, the last vestiges of those days were to end.

Tagenhorst, smitten evidently with some of that same sense of eruption, snatched at the blueprint.

"Nothing is settled yet."

"Good as."

"Nothing is signed yet."

"But you've got to sign, Mama," piped Freda. "Marshall put the cross right there, where you must write your name on the dotted line."

"It's hard to know what to do, in this tormenting world," said Tagenhorst, defensive, nervous, ready to be easily irritated where she and her stepdaughter were concerned in this matter of the property leavings of Adolph Schmidt. Or, rather, where Ray was not concerned. Out from under her, months ago, had slid the anchorage of her father's business. Out from under her, now, was about to go his home.

"It's all right with me," said Ray, and drank her coffee in quick, nervous gulps.

"Where will you go, Ray?" queried Freda, in her treble.

"I'll board."

"We will too—won't we, Hugo, until—"

"I'll go right on to Youngstown and help Marshall rent the other half of the house. No use my hanging around Cincinnati, now that the children will be going to live at the Hanck house. . . ."

"Down went McGinty to the bottom of the sea," was Hugo's retort to his mother-in-law.

"Why, Hugo, we will be at Uncle Hanck's soon. Mama's right."

"Down went McGinty to the bottom of the sea. We will; but why not now? What's he waiting on?"

"I wish I knew," sighed Freda. "It's hard living this way from day to day—on hopes—"

Whenever she discussed life in the big brick house on Burnet Avenue, and the brick stable with its two rubber-tired carriages, surrey, tan trap, and storm buggy, her blue eyes began to burn as if someone had set a match to two laid grates. How they leaped with the flames of desire!

Well, it was right to desire. It was necessary to desire. Tagenhorst, popping forkfuls of food into her mouth, was desiring. She desired profit. She desired well-being and improvement for her children. She desired much for herself. It was not inconceivable that she could marry again.

Only Ray lacked desire. It was borne in upon her, crumbling her bread into pellets, that among those sitting there, filled with intent and purpose over the pattern of their lives, only she alone of them found herself in the predicament of not even desiring to desire.

Let the eruption that was about to happen all about her take place. What then? Life would flow on—new interests perhaps. . . . Pogue's might give her a position in their trimmings—she would find a boarding place— Why feel so seriously about anything? . . . Life would flow on—Freda would have her baby—

There was a present for baby that moment in her muff out on the hatrack. A tiny knitted jacket and cap, with a pair of pink bootees to match, making an adorable set. She had purchased it that morning on her way to the store; and there it reposed, waiting to be given, in secrecy, to the flaccid little mother-to-be who sat tilting her dessert dish of canned peaches for the last bit of syrup.

Almost immediately after the meal was cleared, she snatched

Freda into her bedroom, closing the door, locking it, and springing the knitted set full upon her by spreading it across the bed.

"If it's a boy, Freda, you can exchange it for blue!"

"If what's a boy?" cried Freda, and then stood with her telltale eyes stretched with realization of the heaviness of her blunder.

Strange, but in that instant each knew her separate truth. Ray with a sense of being taken in and a sense of sickening impotency the like of which she had never known before. Freda with the thoroughly aroused realization that it was futile to try any longer to postpone the hour of her inevitable reckoning with Ray.

"I thought I was going to have a kid at first, Ray. Honestly I did."

"You lied from the first."

"I didn't. I thought—"

"You lied from the first."

"I didn't."

"If you stand there saying that," cried Ray, and caught and shook her shoulders until the fair white teeth of fair white Freda rattled, "if you say that again, I—I'll hurt you!"

Freda began to whimper, letting her body droop with the sudden inertia of a sack being emptied.

"You won't tell Hugo, Ray, that it was anything but a miscarriage?"

"I won't tell him anything," said Ray, in the lusterless monotone of a voice too tired for inflection. "I won't tell anything to anybody—ever—because I don't ever want to see anybody again, least of all you!"

"Ray, it was this way—"

"Leave me alone. I want terribly to be—left alone. I promise anything—but if you don't go, Freda—there's no telling— I feel so kind of desperate—if you don't get out of my sight—I—I might even hurt you— Go!"

Left alone, she began to laugh and sob along her twisted lips at the first of a series of pictures that were to stalk her mind that night through: Eleven o'clock of a chiming Sunday morning. Walter and his mother dallying before the lion-cub cage at the Zoo. Herself and Hugo Hanck, standing face-to-face in front of a vacant lot on Burnet Avenue—

17

The precipitate kind of haste with which events proceeded struck Ray as being just as well.

By the time the Christmas wreaths in the windows had begun to accumulate the dust of the last days of the year, Ray, to her complete lack of surprise, had received her notification that the scheme of the absorption of "Schmidt—Findings and Trimmings" into Acme Dress Findings Company of St. Louis did not include the taking over of the Schmidt employees.

Freda, by the simple device of remaining in bed for a day, looking waxen and flaxen, had succeeded in conveying to Hugo whatever it was necessary to convey, because now, beatitude unpunctured, his husbandlike concern seemed switched to his wife's return to an unimpaired state of health.

Christmas in the house on Baymiller Street had been spent among packing cases, trunks, and dismantled rooms. The Youngstown deal had gone through; and Tagenhorst, on the strength of her renewed relations with her son and his wife, was about to embark to Youngstown for a visit, pending certain decisions of Freda's and Hugo's, which, of course, had to do with Herman Hanck.

It was all precipitate, and yet an ordered kind of dissolution that seemed to have pattern. Things had been moving toward this culmination since the death of Adolph, to say nothing of the fact that, while to all intents and purposes the situation with Freda had closed that night in the bedroom, it was hateful almost beyond endurance to have access to the knowledge of the intricate and ruthless little mechanism concealed somewhere behind the docility of Freda. It was more than that. It was frightening.

Freda and Hugo had rented a furnished room over a grocery store on Goodman Street, near Burnet Avenue. The desperately hoped-for invitation to share the redbrick house had not yet come from Herman Hanck, but he had eaten his Christmas dinner in the house on Baymiller Street, was apparently enormously taken of the *Mädchen* Freda, whose cheeks he was constantly pinching, and had sent around, on the eve of Christmas, by carriage-and-two, a bushel basket of walnuts and forty-eight bottles of the brew of beer which, long after he had withdrawn from the concern, continued to be manufactured in his name.

This had thrown Tagenhorst and the young people into a state of excitement, because, at first, disappointment had been keen that the invitation for Christmas dinner had not come from Hanck. In fact, the laboriously composed little note from Freda and Hugo, asking him to holiday meal in the house on Baymiller Street, had been sent only as a reminder where lay his duty.

But the old man, apparently unplumbed, had accepted with alacrity. For three days, in the midst of a move that was as difficult as it was complicated, Tagenhorst had been obliged to lay aside everything and concentrate on this feast. And feast it was! For three hours and a half, on Christmas Day, the groaning board of Tagenhorst offered up its viands—its noodle soup, its roast pig, its boiled beef in kraut, its drop dumplings, its hot biscuit, its seasoned gravies, its suet pudding, lemon pie, Edam cheese, its nuts and raisins, popcorn, sweets, and fruits—to Hanck who, with napkin spread, legs spread, and face spread, as it were, partook with a sustained vigor worthy of his great girth.

It was after the dinner, warmed, it is true, with a bottle of the late Adolph's long-hoarded Rhine wine, that Hanck, apprehending Ray alone in the hall under the stairs, grasped her with both his pudgy arms about the waist.

"You're a fine girl," he whispered to her. "Would you like to have a good time some night at my house? Or maybe Atlantic Garden? Say quick!"

Here it was again. Damnably. Mysteriously. Sickeningly. This piece of old rubber ballooning, bloated, piggy eyed, daring such a procedure, and in her own home! His little gesture of pinching Freda's cheeks had been the gesture you reserve for children. He had even remained on his dignity, such as it was, with Tagenhorst, who had goaded him, as the Rhine wine and Hanck beer began to blend. But with Ray, who had scarcely spoken a brace of words during the long and votive meal, he had dared to run swinish.

Lecherous, naughty old man! True, doubtless, were the rumors of his liaison with the notorious madame of one of the houses on George Street.

That he should have dared, made her lips tighten for days of a compression that kept them jammed and rigid-looking against her clear white teeth.

If Tagenhorst noticed, she was noncommittal.

"I cannot make up my mind if what I am doing is for the best," she kept saying. "For a penny I'd back out. I half wish Marshall had kept out of my affairs, the way he did before I had any to attract him. Then those children boarding out that-a-way! The old man says he is going to take them in, but meanwhile we can all die in our tracks waiting. I only hope what I am doing is for the best. Marshall's wife is trying to do her part, writing me that letter to come to Youngstown, but once a slut always a slut. . . . I only hope what I'm doing is for the best. . . ."

For Ray it was; of that much she felt sure. Her heart might twist and hurt at what was about to befall her, as she lived for weeks in the center of the disintegration of the house in which she had been born; but somehow, with consistency, the hand of change was upon her.

She had taken a room at the Auths', a house two blocks away, on Baymiller, one of the oldest houses on the street, but of immaculate upkeep by Bertha Auth, who was reported to scour the roof every morning. The Auths were an elderly pair who had borne the four daughters, all married, and out of the nest, not one of whom had ever learned English. He was a master builder from Stuttgart, by trade, and reputed wealthy, which in no way mitigated against Bertha's constant effort to keep the rooms hitherto occupied by daughters, rented out to lodgers.

The Auth girls, rigidly reared, had played through the years of childhood in the Schmidt backyard, but, as they grew into maturity, had not been allowed to "go" with the fly Schmidt girl.

It was easy for Bertha Auth, however, who found her third-floor front difficult to heat and therefore difficult to rent, to forget. It was easier for Ray.

What did it all matter? Perhaps she had been right about her daughters. At least they were all married to good substantial cabinetmakers, carpenters, men in line for the building trades. By now, practically every girl with whom Ray had grown up, was married. What future was there in clerking at Pogue's and rooming at the Auths'? Idiot. Idiot. Idiot. The way to security lay in Kurt. He would go far, and in a line of business that had to do with transportation, and that meant his interests would be close to the sporting world. That meant much to Ray. Well, what of it? No harm in loving the excitement of the races and baseball, or the thrill of playing hazard on bets the drummers staked you to at Chick and George's after eleven. Kurt could be trained to do the gay thing like races and occasional trips to New York. Some day, with Kurt, she might even be driving around town with her own tandem! Idiot. Idiot. A Jewish boy with gray eyes and black lashes and a black mustache over square white teeth, and a gentleness of manner and easy-spending way, and an inherent regard for the things that make for respectability and stability, had taken the heart out of every other desire.

One went on trying to pretend that the days were worth rising to meet, or the nights, except for the blessed oblivion of sleep, worth any of the recreations that had once mattered. Was this the Ray who loved clothes, races, hotel meals, smart tilted-looking traps in which you could see and be seen, and who was not above parading, on fine Saturday afternoons, past the Stag Hotel in costume calculated to stun?

"Ray is losing interest in herself," Tagenhorst confided one

morning to Freda. "Came down in the kitchen this morning, looking like a dead one, to press out a shirtwaist she wouldn't have worn
to a dogfight a year ago. I always did say, the flashy kind peter out
first. I'm not so sure Kurt is going to ask her but, if he does, my
advice to her is to grab him and grab fast."

"I wonder," said Freda, standing at the kitchen window and
pulling at her lower lip—a lifetime habit of hers—"I wonder what's
the matter with her."

"Nothing would surprise me," said Tagenhorst, spreading a
clothesline in the kitchen because the icy wind out-of-doors stiff-
ened the drying clothes. "She'll get caught one of these days,
mark my word. You can go on just so far, getting off scot-free, and
then . . ."

"What do you mean?"

"Thank God, even if you are a married woman, you're too innocent to know!"

"If you want to know it," cried Freda, on a sudden high note, "I
don't believe Ray has ever gone the limit with a man."

"What I don't know, I'm not saying," said Tagenhorst, beginning to soap the washboard, "but nobody on God's earth can keep
me from thinking . . ."

"Well, I guess Ray thinks too when it comes to that. I guess she
thinks plenty at what's going on around here."

Ray did. Generous to a fault, she found it next to unbearable to
sit silent to the spectacle of the square piano being crated for ship-
ment to Youngstown, and the small square horsehair stool, upon
which she could remember her mother sitting perched in the dusk,
playing slender little airs like "Listen to the Mocking Bird."

Almost equally unbearable, however, was the packing of her own
belongings and such of those household objects to which she was
unquestionably heir. Her father's old rolltop desk, with the smell of
his tobacco deep in its timbers, the gilt chair which her mother had
painted, her own bird's-eye maple bedroom suite, enlarged crayon
portraits of her parents, the doll in the rocking chair that had stood
in the parlor for fifteen years. One of the boys, Jim Wohlgemuth,
whose father owned warehouses along the riverfront, and where

later these possessions were to go up like so much timber in a wharf fire, agreed to store all this for her, until such time as her plans should take shape. It was a heart-sickening business, breaking up the house on Baymiller. All this, notwithstanding the fact that not for worlds would she have had it otherwise.

The position at Pogue's did not come off. After the first douse, it struck her that this was neither as important nor as significant as it had seemed at first shock. Wasn't an army of the unemployed marching on to Washington at the very minute? Papers full of it. Bad times. Well, that was not her immediate worry. With nine hundred dollars in the bank, and the knowledge that there were several good contacts still in the offing, she could afford to take her time. As a matter of fact, Alms and Doepke, hearing of her availability, had made an advance to her during the period she had considered her negotiation with Pogue's practically closed.

She never entered into the matter of employment, however, with them, or any other Cincinnati firm, because one morning, seated at breakfast, and reading the announcement of the wedding date of Corinne Trauer and Walter Saxel, the thought flowed calmly over her: Why should I stay around here? I think I'll wire Eddie Ledbetter and ask him if the job he offered me in New York three months ago is still open. Funny I never thought of that before. Why should I stay around here? . . .

BOOK TWO

18

She was always to say, even when her residence in New York had lengthened out into years, that to her it was never more than a resting-place between trains. A Cincinnati girl visiting New York she was to remain, with the feel of every bone in her body. Even after five years, when the large front parlor which she occupied in a boardinghouse on West Twenty-third Street had gradually come to be furnished in practically all of her own private objects, she was still using such allusions as, "When I go back home—"

Strange, too, because from the first, roots of a sort had gone down into the new asphalt soil. Her business affiliations with Ledbetter and Scape, of Greene Street, started off being a success, because at the conclusion of her second year she was drawing ninety-five dollars a month, the next-highest salary of any woman in the house where she boarded. With the exception of the first few months, when she changed address frequently—for such homely reasons as cockroaches, inebriate neighbors, lack of heat, lack of cleanliness— she had found permanent residence at "Mrs. Blamey's," two red-brick houses joined by bridges and giving the combined effect of a small hotel.

There had been little time for the alleged loneliness of the big city. The work at Ledbetter and Scape, mere stock supervision in the veiling and artificial-flower department, which she regarded as child's play after the more responsible combination of buying- and selling-rôles she had been accustomed to assume, was nevertheless confining. You arrived at Ledbetter and Scape at eight-thirty and you signed out at five. Supper at six-thirty in the basement dining room of Blamey's was a gaslit, noisy, highly gregarious affair, where you made social connections, such as they were. At least, such as they were to Ray. Middle-aged businesswomen in "McKinley for President" or "Bryan for President" celluloid buttons, who came down to meals bearing copies of *She, Robert Elsmere, Ramona, Ben Hur, Under Two Flags*, or *A Forbidden Marriage*. The married men, most of whom looked as if they were insurance- or bond-salesmen, with typical boardinghouse wives, and children who were being reared in the miscellaneous but respectable atmosphere of Mrs. Blamey's. The single men at Blamey's always seemed to Ray to belong to an uncannily consistent species, with extremely long noses and colds in all of them. From the swivel chairs of small offices which they usually shared with two or three other concerns, they represented lumber firms in the Northwest, or constituted the New York agency of a child's patent high-chair corporation that manufactured in Grand Rapids. Not a few of them held desk positions in freight offices or with the big wholesale-merchandise firms along lower Broadway and Fifth Avenue. There were two claim agents for streetcar systems boarded at Blamey's, and a ticket man at the box office of Tony Pastor's.

A credit man at Lord and Taylor's fine store at Broadway and Twentieth Street had boarded at Blamey's with his wife and two children for eleven years. Also a head bookkeeper for one of the New York offices of the Singer Sewing Machine Company, and his wife, a deaf-mute of arresting beauty, were among those whose long residence attested to the stability of Blamey's. As a matter of fact, the original Mrs. Blamey had died during the second year of her proprietorship, and two middle-aged bachelors, Ragland and Stooey, had carried it on ever since.

One of the popular witticisms in which everyone indulged on every possible occasion was to refer to old lady Ragland and Miss Stooey. Even Mrs. Levantine, the deaf-mute, never failed to lip-read the phrase, if it were used at table, and her lovely face break into smile.

A Miss Taddie Selcox, of Blamey's, said to be one of the fastest court-stenographers in New York, and recipient of many competitive awards, had once suggested to Ray that they pool their resources and rent a pair of rooms where they could arrange for kitchen-privileges and feel in a position to entertain, but the idea stirred her not at all.

Curious, but to the Ray Schmidt to whom the constant public excitements of hotel lobbies, racetracks, variety theaters had once been staff of life, the need for recreational and social contacts in the big new city scarcely troubled her. There were always men to be met, through business contacts, the boardinghouse, through the girls with whom she almost unavoidably established acquaintanceship in washrooms, office and boardinghouse, but gone was much of the old zest that had once given her the vitality to rig herself in the most extreme accouterments of fashion and sail past the Stag Hotel on Vine Street for the paradoxical emotions of resentment and thrill as the comments flew.

Still given to the vagaries of fashion, the zest for parade, however, was gone. Once or twice, in something spick-and-span off her dressmaker's-form, she had sailed down that aisle of a thousand eyes known as the Peacock Alley of the Waldorf Astoria Hotel, and, as of old, heads had swung. Once on a Fifth Avenue, Easter morning, as she sailed past St. Thomas's Church, attired in a brand-new navy-blue bolero suit with a freely gored skirt whose brush binding swept the ground, and a bolero jacket trimmed with brass buttons off the uniform of a United States Army officer, whom she had met at a public charity euchre, newspaper-cameras had clicked after her. But while she followed the vagaries of fashion, and thought little of stitching away until past midnight on tomorrow's newest thingum-bob in millinery, the real zest was gone. You dressed well because you had a figure, needed to look well at business, and because, well, because you were that kind of person. You had style!

A couple of stockbrokers in Wall Street, whom she had come

to meet, never mind how, were fond of taking her out on this score. To boxing bouts at Madison Square Garden; to Tony Pastor's or to Parker's or Shanley's. Even for New York, here was a girl who knew how to carry herself! One of these brokers, Alan Butler, who already had laid the first foundation of what was to be the fabulous Butler fortune, was fond of driving Ray, of a Sunday morning, along Fifth Avenue, past the reservoir at Forty-second Street, and on as far as Central Park, where an ordinance barred those alluring driveways to the danger of his horseless vehicle.

Owning one of the few motorcars in town, a curved-dash Duryea, which rattled unevenly over the cobblestones, these weekly excursions of Alan's, which kept him perspiring over a complexity of pedals and levers to be operated simultaneously, were at best in the nature of adventure.

"Get a horse!" rose in ribaldry along the more or less harassed route of the itinerant motorist of those days.

"Alan, do you think it's right to scare all the horses so?"

"It's not my machine that is stopping traffic, it's the girl I've got beside me!"

One Sunday evening, as Butler was driving her along the city streets, this conspicuous performance almost threatened to achieve her notoriety—in fact, did so, to the extent of her seeing herself in a news-item that appeared in the *New York Herald* the morning after the event: "Unknown Young Woman Leaps from Horseless Carriage of Wealthy Broker."

They had been rumbling along late one evening in Butler's Duryea, when suddenly the plump-faced youngish man turned into Sixteenth Street and drew up before a house as brown and as narrow as a prim-looking spinster.

There was something about this house, to Ray who had never seen it before, which struck at her consciousness as if cymbals had been hit, causing her to ring all over with quick apprehensions.

"Why are we stopping here, Butler?" she asked, and moved sharply to the far side of the seat, clutching the leather tufting as if she did not mean to be pried off.

"Ask me no questions, sweet, and I'll tell you no lies."

"But I do ask. What do you want me to get out here for? It's twelve o'clock. Take me home."

They had been dining in what Butler called his club, a handsome house near the reservoir, where men and women in smart street and evening attire dined in a room brilliantly lighted with crystal chandeliers and frescoed in scenes of men with faunal feet and women wound chiefly in grapeleaves. Afterward the guests could repair to an equally brilliant and frescoed room, where there were tables for vingt-et-un, poker, baccarat, and a roulette wheel. Ray, who loved a game of chance, had won eighty dollars at roulette, on Butler's stake of five. There had been wine, but chiefly out of deference to the house. Butler, already at forty under his physician's orders, drank his allotment of one glass; Ray, with a characteristic lack of appetite for it, scarcely that. So he was not drunk, except that suddenly there was about Butler an air of intoxication that was frightening.

"Don't you want a good time?"

"Take me home."

"Come now, you've known your Uncle Fuller long enough to stop trying to pull his whiskers. One of the finest gals in this town runs things here. Ever been to this one?"

For answer she grasped the clutch, throwing it, and with a forward leap over the cobblestones the car began to rattle and quiver.

"Here you, are you crazy?" shouted Butler. "Take your hands off! Let go!"

"Then you take me home," she said, pressing her foot on the first pedal within reach, and sending the car careening unevenly along the deserted street.

"That will be about enough of that four-flushing," he said, red with rage, easily forcing her fingers free of the control and throwing her sharply to the opposite side of the seat. "You're going to do as I say tonight, and without pretending or trying to make a ninny out of me." And he began the precarious business of trying to turn his car in the middle of the block.

"I am, am I?" cried Ray, crazed, not so much by any sense of fear or inability to outwit him, but rather by an overwhelming flood of dreariness that made sitting there beside him an instant longer, in the sordid pool of her predicament, out of the question. "I am, am I?" And then, just as the vehicle completed its turn and began its return rumble down the street, she jumped over its dashboard and down on the cobblestones.

It was one of those little midnight episodes common enough to city streets.

Plainly a man and a girl in a row; and while the girl picked herself up, the rotter, a swell, no doubt, rumbled away in his horseless carriage. Luckily the woman was unhurt, so it was unnecessary to pursue the horseless carriage, although one of the small group that seemed to spring out of nowhere, identified the disappearing conveyance as Alan Butler's. A policeman jotted down the name she gave him in his notebook, just as if he did not know it to be a fictitious one, and told her she ought to be ashamed, a nice-appearing girl like her, and to hurry along home and behave herself.

Time and time again, subsequently helping her to realize what a poor thing her old vigorous zest had become, she was to find herself wishing that, miraculously, the girl who jumped from the horseless carriage that midnight had been lucky enough never to have bothered to rise again.

Once, in a poor inchoate way, she tried to convey some of this lusterlessness of her spirit to Miss Taddie Selcox, the only feminine connection she had formed during the years in New York. Their rooms, old-fashioned parlors in a defunct mansion, were separated only by folding doors. It was characteristic of their relationship that they never intruded upon each other by way of these doors, going, instead, the more formal way, around the hall.

Miss Selcox was a small girl with brown hair so kinky that it might have been removed from a mattress. This, added to the fact that she wore it in the elaborate fashion of the day, gave the top of her head somewhat the appearance of the elaborate layout of a summer-resort hotel. The great center-puff was the hotel proper, the lesser puffs outlying bungalows and stables, the hills and dales and waving meadows formed by a process of apparently trying to wave the kinks.

There was little about her to indicate her stunning speed as a stenographer. On the contrary, she was the sort of girl who liked to curl up in a nest of the hand-worked pillows with which her room was strewn, and pick a string or two of a mandolin.

> *I've a secret in my heart, Sweet Marie,*
> *A tale I would impart, love, to thee.*
> *Every daisy in the dell*
> *Knows my secret, knows it well,*
> *And yet I dare not tell, Sweet Marie.*

Other favorites that must have been lodged firmly in the timbers of the room occupied by Miss Selcox were, "I Don't Want to Play in Your Yard," "The Picture That Was Turned to the Wall," "Two Little Girls in Blue," "The Golden Hair Was Hanging Down Her Back," and one of wailing persistency, called "My Sweetheart's the Man in the Moon."

This last, so far as anyone was able to determine, applied literally where Miss Selcox was concerned. She was twenty-two, willing, personable, eager, but given to fits of depression.

"Too eager," was Ray's laconic summing-up of Miss Selcox.

"I wish I had some of your ginger about life," Ray told her one evening, as she too lounged in the pillow nest of Taddie's hot, gas-lighted room.

"Goodness knows what keeps me that way. It doesn't get me anywhere. You have ten times the fun I do."

"What makes you say that?" asked Ray, trying to keep down her general sense of nervousness—the terrible growing feeling that everything, including talk with this frizzed stenographer, was too futile to be endured. Was this the beginning of a nervous breakdown? Was nervous breakdown another phrase for crazy? A girl in Cincinnati had been obliged to stop high school and had been in a sanatorium ever since. They said she stuck pins in her wrists. Sometimes—even back there in high school—the thought of the beauty of putting oneself to death had entered one's head! Stop such terrible thoughts! One must pull oneself together. Young people were often in love with death, but not when you reached an age! Taddie was chattering—talking—

"I say it because it is true. In lots of ways you're like my married sister," pursued Taddie, making careful stitches along a small kidney-shaped bit of batiste. "My sister Carrie only needed to enter the room, to have every boy there behave like a black cat meowing on a back fence."

"Why, Taddie, that's not a nice thing to say!"

"Isn't it?" she said, raising her unluminous eyes to Ray. "Now isn't it funny? That's just what's the trouble with me. I don't know enough to know why that's not nice, but I can see that it's not. It isn't as if I'd said any cat, Ray. I said black, and that makes it kind of funny. Why isn't it nice?"

"I don't know, except that it isn't!"

"You ought to know, because you're just like Carrie, only more so."

"What did it get her?"

"A husband, and a good one. Frank's one of the finest. A steady good boy in his father's cooperage business in Fredericktown. Carrie's expecting. This is the sleeve of a baby-dress I'm making."

"That's more than it has got me."

"Ray, this is a funny question for one girl to be asking another; and, in a way, rooming next to you, and hearing you come home to sleep every night, I guess I hadn't ought to ask. But it's some of the old hens around here. They think you're fly. I know you think I'm a kind of silly, anyway, so I might as well out and ask what's on my mind. Are you fly, Ray? Have you ever—would you ever—oh, you know what I mean— I know you're not bad, or I'd never have been asking you to take rooms with me, but—would you—if a man—I just like to know things, Ray. I've been in this town five years now, but I've met fewer folks than I would have if I had stayed home in Fredericktown. How do you meet the kind of fellows who take you out to Parker's for lunch, and riding around in horseless carriages? I just can't seem to meet any men, except the deadheads who board here, and I wouldn't waste time on them, even if they asked me."

"The way I meet men, Taddie, is because most of them want to
meet me. I can't tell you why, since you're just as good-looking as
I am, perhaps better, any more than I can tell you just why it is my
eyes are one color and yours are another."

"You've got magnetism, that's what it is."

"Fudge, I've got something pretty cheap, whatever it is. I could
go out and earn my living with it on the streets, I guess."

"Why, Ray Schmidt!"

"Oh, I'm on to myself, Tad, and don't you forget it. There is
something cheap or snide or fifth-rate about me, or I wouldn't find
myself in the predicament that comes my way every once in a while.
No, I've never slept with a man, if that's what's on your mind—"

"Ray—"

"I'm as much of a virgin as you are, if you call it being a virgin to
arouse everything that is low and horrid in a man without meaning
to. I don't know what it is about me. I'm kind of common, I guess,
Tad. Like good times. Like to gamble. Enjoy a horse race and can't
help it. Like clothes. Loud ones. That must be what misleads them.
But what would you say if I was to say to you, Tad, that there is only
one thing that ever happened to me in my life that really mattered
to me much one way or the other, and that thing went the other?"

"You mean—a man—an affair?"

It was impossible not to think Tad silly-eyed, as her hands, with
the bit of sewing, curved inward toward her breast and her gaze flew
extreme northeast. Silly-eyed. Futile. Empty. Futile like everything.
Like everybody. She must fight against this inertia. The desire never
to have to lift her head off a pillow again. To sleep—sleep—sleep—
Scat! There they came again, the thoughts that, sure as fate, would
send you crazy if you did not throttle them down!

All around, as you sat in Taddie's frilled-up back parlor, there
were being lived in Blamey's boardinghouse lives that seemed part
of the general pattern of futility that was bearing down your spirit
and your will to live. Where was the old mysterious impulse that
gave even the doing of little things the illusion of being worthwhile? One now began the day with almost the feeling that to so

much as lift the hand required an initiative that was beyond you.
One began the day wondering at the mysterious stream of vitality
that impelled the futile boarders, in the futile city, to begin their
lusterless rounds of routine. The self-deception was beyond the
reach of your vitality. The deception that it mattered—mattered
whether your egg lay cloyed and cold on your plate before you could
muster up desire to lift a forkful—mattered whether you arrived
among the dotted veilings and the cotton pansies of Ledbetter
and Scape, or kept your appointment with Tom, the bookkeeper,
Dick, the stockbroker, or Harry, the middle-aged of no known
occupation—mattered whether you lunched at Parker's, dined at
the Astor House, or sat through what entertainment Tony Pastor's had to offer. Opportunities that in the old days, when it was
just the transient salesman or local fry, would have inflamed the
anticipation.

In a way, New York had enhanced the size of the "fry." Miraculously, the salesmen to whom she had been a girl in port, had fallen
away since she had moved to the city of their headquarters; but in
their places, one contact leading to another, the easier-spending
procession of the broker, the bookmaker, the white-haired playboy,
made the days of Over-the-Rhine seem as if, back in her memory,
they had been played on a stage no larger than a postage stamp.

And yet—ugh—this present—how did one go through with it?
How did one refrain from shaking the fuzzy-headed Taddie by her
lean shoulders to realization that all her yearnings, all her sense of
frustration, were phony? Silly little sex-hungry fool, sitting there
feeling herself cheated, denied, when there wasn't anything worth
feeling that way over. Nothing matters, idiot! Take what you can
get, only don't bother much about getting it, because it doesn't matter when you do get it. Get to care less and less. Make life a waiting
room for death and then it can't hurt you so terribly much, as if you
let it matter. . . .

You could not very well voice those loathsome lusterless senti-
ments to the rather ridiculous Taddie in her frizzes, as she sat there
shirring the sleeve of a dress for her sister's unborn baby.

"Tell me some things—oh, about—the kind of things you

must know, Ray—knowing men—knowing life—the way you get around—"

"Give me that other sleeve, and I'll hem it for you."

Until three in the morning they sat stitching away on the small batiste dress for the unborn baby of the sister of Taddie who lived in Fredericktown.

19

Ray used to say about herself, scrutinizing her face in the mirror, that she was one of those cheviot people who did not show wear and tear.

This was not true, in the sense that it was understatement. Like many who mature at a precocious age, at twenty-four she had caught up with herself, so to speak, and could, as a matter of fact, be said to look younger than she did at twenty. A certain over-ripeness was gone, slimmer her figure, steadier and even slower her smile. On those rare occasions when she met someone out of the old Cincinnati days, the outburst of comment was almost identical:

"Why, Ray, you're getting better looking every day!"

The boys in general seemed to think this. It was all she could do to manage an evening or two a week now, in which to remain home and catch up on her sewing, or keep her growing hobby of souvenir spoons polished and arranged alphabetically, according to towns. Amityville, Boston, Chicago, Duluth. There was quite a collection. Just went to show what a cosmopolitan town New York was, compared to Cincinnati. Why, in Cincinnati it would have been impossible to round out such a collection. Here it had been a simple matter to almost fill in the alphabet between Albuquerque and Zanesville within a few months.

The boys came flocking to New York like flies to sticky paper. Memphis. Altoona. Cleveland. Dallas. Seattle. And scarcely one of them failed, after his return home, to remember her request for a souvenir spoon. All pretty much alike, these fellows; but, just the same, they kept one from having time to let tastelessness lie along the tongue in bitterness.

One kept them at arm's length, sometimes almost breaking the arm to do it, and during the repetitive days, one succeeded apparently in making the pansies and dotted veilings matter, because at the end of the second year there had been a ten-dollar-a-month raise.

This ten dollars, from the beginning, went regularly to Freda. There were two children by now, and affairs had not gone well in Youngstown. The appalling had happened not six weeks after Ray's departure for New York. Herman Hanck had married the big, furiously corseted woman known all over town as Cora, proprietor of one of the most successful of the dark, narrow houses on Longworth Street. A public display of an old man's licentiousness that was resented by the community at-large.

In the wake of the disaster, and Herman Hanck's gesture of final dismissal of his nephew by way of a check for five hundred dollars, the three, Tagenhorst, daughter, and son-in-law, had departed for Youngstown.

From the first it seemed obvious that Marshall had steered his mother into rough sailing, because the house which had partially been traded for the one on Baymiller Street turned out damp and unrentable, to say nothing of the fact that, once established in Youngstown, it seemed consistently impossible for Hugo to hold a position for more than two weeks. The array of those he had held and lost was appalling. Gas-meter inspector. Cable-car conductor. Handbill distributor. Bicycle-agent. Brush-and-broom vender. Paper-hanger. Clerk in a local agency for Yucatan chewing gum.

Freda's desultory letters dwelt lightly upon her mother's predicament, her particular tussle seeming to center about the relentlessness of the succession of her babies—three miscarriages—and the fact that Hugo, although possessed of what can often be the pathetic willingness of the inefficient, could not even hold the trivial positions that matched his caliber.

The souvenir spoons were for Emma, Freda's eldest, when she should grow up. Every once in a while, this three-year-old tot, her hand obviously guided, wrote in some such vein as this: "Dear Aunt Ray, Thank you for the pretty bunny blanket. We are well and hope you are the same." Or: "Dear Aunt Ray, Thank you for the one dollar. We are well and hope you are the same."

There was a photograph of Freda's two flaxen babies on Ray's dresser. The little boy was puny and in the string-bean image of his father. Emma, over-fat, with creases for wrists, and her mother's blondness out all over her, was Ray's idea of a really beautiful baby. The little gold pin which the child wore in the photograph, engraved "Baby," was also Ray's gift. "Dear Aunt Ray, Thank you for this," and for that, the guided little fingers had occasion to write with considerable frequency.

It was fine about Emma. It gave one something to shop for. Even when the regrettable need arose for spectacles for Emma, when she was only four, it was a warming chore to be able to have the prescription for the lenses filled by an expert New York optician. Ray, who loved to spend money, could gratify that instinct ever so cheaply by browsing around Stewart's, Lord and Taylor's, Hearn's, or the novelty stores, in search of some trifle she could wrap into a tiny parcel and send to Youngstown. It gave her destination, in the hour between the completion of her own working day and the closing of the department stores. Shopping for Emma. Incidentally there was that eye of hers always peeled for the remnant, the bit of braid, the odd-and-end of taffeta or buckram, to be put by for future use. She still designed and made her own clothes, attending a dressmaker's college for the heavier or tailored garments, or basting, stitching, or pressing away her rare and rarer evenings at home, sometimes going upstairs to run up seams on Mrs. Levantine's sewing machine.

The old indictments, even as it had been back in the Cincinnati days, persisted against her. "Needn't tell me she can dress the way she does on what she earns." All this, notwithstanding the fact that it was well-known around Mrs. Blamey's that she did much of her stitching on Mrs. Levantine's sewing machine, and that the yardage out of which she made her garments was, often as not, lying about her room.

"She is a mystery to me!" Or: "Why are you always harping on the fact that she is in to sleep every night? That doesn't prove any-thing, these days. Watch out, I say, for the girl who never brings her escorts to the doorstep. Beware of 'meeters.'"

Not that, in the last analysis, it mattered. Ragland and Stooey, meticulous in their policy to keep their brace of boardinghouses within the neat pale of respectability, apparently found no evidence for complaint. On the contrary, exhibited regard for their front-parlor tenant of House Number Two.

Evidently they looked upon the comings and goings of Miss Schmidt as matters strictly within the realm of her private affairs, so long as her habits continued within the ethical standards of a house "strictly first-class."

Speculating on what might have happened, if the rueful inci-dent of Butler and the horseless carriage had ever made its way in full to the newspapers, Ray found herself confronted with the odd conclusion that after all it would not have mattered much. By virtue of habit she preferred Blamey's as a place to live. Her room there, including breakfast and supper, was still more reasonable than she could hope to find again, now that prices, due to post-panic period, were advancing. But eviction, for one reason or another, would not have mattered. How to care! How once more to feel as if the sur-face of her body were something more than a callous surface insu-lating her from delight in doing. The knowledge that there was a little Emma helped. Going about with spending men helped. But chiefly her sole motive was to while away time. It occurred to her frequently, and with a sense of sickness, that what she was doing was to while away life. And life was supposed to be so precious. The struggle for it all around her indicated that. While Adolph had lived, there had been the meaning of the sweetness of mattering to him. For a while, the sense of Kurt needing her had been part of the argument she had brought to bear upon herself in the days when she was weighing his proposals. Of course, Emma needed her! The child had weak eyes! But how trivial her services there!

Occasionally, of a Sunday morning, she ventured to the Third Presbyterian Church, on Twenty-third Street. Of rather a mystical nature, inherited from a deeply religious mother who had not lived long enough to pass her outward observances along to her daughter, it was easy for Ray, who had never had a church affiliation beyond desultory appearances with her father at Lutheran services, to conjure a sense of God—to give herself over, as to a warm bath, to the ministrations of ritual. Adolph had not been a godly man in the churchly sense of the word. She had accompanied him to this or that neighborhood church on Sunday mornings. Usually Lutheran. But that sense of God dwelt in any church house! She went there to stir it awake. God was a bosom toward which you turned a tired face that ached to cry, and somehow seldom did or could, except in church. There, during prayer, during responses, during hymn and rolling organ, the tears could course unrestrained against hands clasped to eyes, behind which she was trying to pray. Most of the time, sitting on a bench in hat and wrap, reading from a book, repeating litany, and twisting open the clasp of her purse for money, it was hard to feel intimate with God. But in the language of tears she could cry her heart out to Him, even in church.

So it went.

One night, in the Eden Musée, of all places, there came to her, from a widower named Russel Loemen, of Chattanooga, her second experience of a proposal of marriage.

A city salesman named Edward Macrin, said to be the highest-priced man employed by a large wholesale dry-goods house, had organized, with an eye to entertaining the trade, a dinner-and-theater party, composed of Ray, Loemen, head of the large Chattanooga firm which bore his name, and another young woman buyer from Altoona.

There had been dinner at the Waldorf Astoria, first-row seats at Weber and Fields' and, afterward, champagne and rarebit at Rector's. Loemen, plainly smitten, had invited Ray, in his southern drawl, for dinner the following evening, and for want of something more diverting they had wandered from Lüchow's to the Eden Musée.

"You know, Miss Ray," he said, as they were standing beside a menacing wax Svengali, "believe it or not, Ah caint somehow make myself belong to this sporty town. Ah'm a family man, Miss Ray."

She took this at first for the usual explanation of the married man, being cautious.

"To tell you the truth, Mr. Loemen," she replied, in what was her stock phrase to remarks of this genre, "I never thought much one way or another." As a matter of fact, she had, wondering from time to time if he were married.

He was a tall florid fellow, fifty, in loosely spun clothes, handsome scarfpin, and strong tan-and-gray hair growing on his head like bristles.

"Look here, Miss Ray, you're going to think me plumb crazy, Ah know that, but Ah'm the kind of man thinks fast when he starts thinkin' a-tall. Once Ah know a thing, Ah know it. Ah haven't thought about much else since Ah clapped eyes on you last night. Ah want to take you back home as Mrs. Loemen. Ah can afford to. Ah'd mighty well like to, and what's more, Ah intend to."

Instinct told her that this was real. Loemen had the sheepish look of a man meaning what he says.

"Mah first wife died thirteen year ago, Miss Ray. Fust time Ah've so much as looked at the same woman twice since. She was a good woman, but Ah believe at last Ah've met her equal. . . ."

Thinking it over later, again and again she was to marvel that never once had she hesitated in the definiteness of her reply. Folly lay in that reply, wilful renunciation of most of the things her loneliness craved, and a chance to redeem what looked perilously like a life in danger of slipping away into nonentity. Folly, yet the reply was on her lips almost before his words were off his.

There were the makings of a prosperous, well-ordered life with Loemen, who was a young fifty, childless, eager. In dismissing him, consciousness of all this trooped through her mind. The volition of her will seemed something outside of herself. "No" to Loemen was inability to keep from walking down the steep depression that had become her life.

Repeatedly she said to herself during these years of the aching

void of days: People pass through phases like this. Common, everyday thing for people to pass through phases like this. Especially
women. Unmarried girls, she had heard time and time again, sometimes have nervous and queer years of adjustment. Shock, such as
the advent and exit of Walter Saxel, in her life, could easily be
expected to temporarily unseat one's frame of mind for over a period
of years. That was as near as she ever came to admitting to what
extent he continued to dominate her brooding.

That curious external self of hers, which had so casually dismissed a man like Loemen, was the one with which she had now
entirely to reckon. It was the self she carried with her to the business
of Ledbetter and Scape; it was the self that lunched at Shanley's on
Saturdays, danced at the Haymarket, played euchre at public card
parties, drove once in a hired tally-ho with a group of eight to Saratoga over a big Saturday racing event, or went walking on Sunday
afternoons in the nattiest of the moment's modes, her skirts plucked
high with the twist of a wrist that helped give her style.

It was that external self made the men with whom she now
came in contact in growing numbers delight in her free-and-easy
companionship, up to that inevitable time when the demand was
sure to be for more than that, and then each and every one of them,
feeling somehow cheated and led-on, resented her.

In appearance she was at her best. "Dressy and good-looking,"
the glances of people in public places and on the streets voted her.
A swell-looking girl, with whom you were proud to be seen about.

"You're the kind of girl who misrepresents and won't go
through," a broker once told her, when he was sufficiently in his
cups to say what he was thinking, rather than to think what he was
saying. "That kind of leading a man on is dishonest. I'm not out
buying virtue. When I want that I go home for it."

That was being pretty plain. That was being plain enough to
start the misery crawling. . . .

In a way, it sometimes seemed to her rank immorality not to
have wormed her way into the security of a life with Kurt or Loemen. The alternatives she chose—the life of the hotel luncheon,
the Albany night boat over Sunday, provided there was the saving

decency of another girl in the party, Fifth Avenue of a Sunday morning, to the buckshot of remarks as she passed, Shanley's of a midnight—were pretenses just as dishonest as one of these marriages would have been.

At least, it would have been easier to give for value received. There was, at any rate, the decency of honest barter in giving yourself to a man for home and keep. Your game was to buy without paying. Good times, recreation, gaieties, food and drink. The fact that she did not drink, far from reducing her sense of obligation, heightened it. The anomalous position of playing around with men who, as the broker said, could go home when they wanted virtue, was one that began to weigh, as more and more the spirits flagged, and as more and more the ability to care receded.

It was well along in the seventh year of what was becoming the unutterable staleness of the days and nights, that, walking along Wall Street one May evening, toward the office of a friend with whom she was to dine, she encountered Walter Saxel.

20

"This is a surprise, Ray," he said, taking her hand slowly, regarding her slowly, and in anything but the key of surprise.

She would have supposed of herself, had she visualized this meeting, anything except what was happening.

It might have been Vine Street, after they had not met for twenty or thirty hours, instead of six and one-half years. It might have been almost anybody she was encountering there in the narrow din of Wall Street, except the one capable of bringing to her this surge of an almost unbearable excitement.

"Well, of all people!" she said, just as she would have said it to any number of others from home. "What are you doing here?"

"What am I doing here? Why, we've lived here for almost two years now."

"You don't say so," she said, with the usual polite surprise. But inside of her, tumbling, was the chaos of the thought that for two years of days they had trod this same city, and she had not known it! Strange that her old intuition to his nearness had not taken care of that! They had been walking the same streets, breathing the same air, and, for all she knew, ridden the same streetcars, sat inside the same theaters, at least if not at the same time, within the day, the week, the month. And she had not had the miracle of understanding to sense it. Seeing him was to stir into pain again the mortal sickness at her heart. So long as he had been out there at arm's length—eight-hundred-miles'-length—from her pain, her predicament was something she could keep as unreal as the memory of a dream. . . . Now here he was, and the pains were tumbling about like acrobats.

They stepped into the shadow of the Sub-Treasury Building, and, for an hour, while the tides flowed past, talked in the tempo of those who have little time and much to say.

"I felt bad, your leaving Cincinnati as you did, Ray. Without a word."

She was suddenly, after the six quiescent years, so hurt and bitter that she did not trust her lips to try to frame the words of a reply.

"You knew I was here, Walter?"

"Well, yes, in a way."

"You look well, Walter. A little stouter."

"Getting along in years. I'm the father of two."

Without a thought for her, without a sensibility for her, without even a suggestion of awareness of the silent scream of terror she could feel dart through her as he said this, he took out a small leather case and showed her the two, their small faces bunched together. She did not look long, because all she saw was a spinning pinwheel the size of the picture.

"Fine, Walter," she said, and returned it. "Your family here?"

He seemed to regard her in a sort of mild incredulity that she could be so unaware of the momentous.

"You didn't know? I'm a junior partner, Friedlander-Kunz!"

It had come so soon, then! Rightly, normally, as it should. He was a young banker now. Looked it, in the well-made gray sack suit that fitted his slightly stouter figure. He was almost imperceptibly gray at the temples too, giving him somehow, to her, the artificial look of age achieved by an actor who whitens his hair.

"Oh, Walter, I'm glad!" She was. She was, even if miseries that had for so long lain half-frozen in her were suddenly rushing in quickly released streams.

"My mother died last April, Ray."

He had suffered, and not even that had got through to her.

"Walter, dear Walter."

"Curious thing about that, Ray. I always wanted you to know Mother."

He could actually say that, apparently without knowledge that he was twisting her pain.

"I wanted to know her, Walter."

"My wife's parents died within two weeks of each other two years ago."

So he had been through death and birth, and by now was in the sinew of settled manhood! They, he and Corinne, had the ropy, fibrous tightening-bond between them of private sorrows and the private ecstasies. Life, death, birth. Maturity was part of his general thickening. His fingers with the square tips. His polished, squared-toed shoes. His face, now that the cheeks were heavier, seeming more four-square than of old. Solid, substantial. A banker. The un-Jewish-looking Jew, already something moneyed about him. The acceptance and solidity with which he said "my wife." Even while it smote her, and excluded her, the solidity, as always, wrung her admiration.

"You have been through a great deal, Walter."

"Good and bad, Ray. And you?"

Her lips began to slip away from their firm tension, and she hauled them, with all her strength, back to where she could feel them smile.

"Same old Ray, I guess, Walter. Working along, living along, playing along best I can."

Something of tenderness came out in his face, in a way she knew by heart, almost as if she could have touched each lineament of expression, before it lighted up.

"I've missed you, Ray," he said, as if realizing it as they stood there.

She was conscious of her lips again and her will to keep them firm.

"And I've missed you, Walter. I mean—missed the way we used to have of talking over every little thing that happened. I'm like that. I like to listen to every little thing about a person—in his business—in general."

What nonsense this, and yet her lips talked on.

"That's true, Ray. You were always a good listener. Flatters a fellow like the dickens to be listened to. Remember the day I thought they were going to bounce me at the bank because I honored a power-of-attorney check for eleven hundred dollars after the power had lapsed?"

Did she! They had sat four hours in the C. H. and D. waiting room, while he let the last Hamilton train pull out, discussing his dilemma. She had gone home at three in the morning, leaving him to snatch sleep on the hard bench of the smoky station, and they had met again at breakfast to devise a way to cover up his predicament. Did she remember!

They stood for an hour, tearing apart the obscuring years, and Walter reconstructing, step-by-step, the processes that had brought him east.

"My wife's mother's brother is Felix-Arnold Friedlander, of the firm of Friedlander-Kunz, you know that of course?"

Oh no, she didn't know that! But what she said was, "Is that so?"

"Reason they never took Aaron Trauer into the banking house was because he not only preferred his own town and his own little business, but he just out-and-out wasn't cut out for anything else. They look on me as young blood, you see."

Her eyes ached with the years of seeing.

"Well, anyway, seems there has always been an agreement between Felix-Arnold Friedlander and his partner Kunz, never to force an issue in order to favor a relative. Most conservative pair of fellows you ever saw! But when one of the junior partners was sent to Berlin to open a branch there, that seemed to constitute an opening that was part of the ordinary course of events, and so they sent for me."

"Walter, you will go far."

He would! There might be nothing of the genius of industry or high finance about Walter, but he would carry on, with munificence and a certain oriental magnificence, the traditions of so stately a house as Friedlander-Kunz. He would be a banker in whom were vested trust and respect. He would further stabilize the solidity and stolidity of the house of Friedlander-Kunz with faithful and imitative purpose. Friedlander-Kunz had long been conspicuous in foreign loans of one nature and another. Who knows? He, Walter, might even come to have an occasional finger in the international pie and consort with diplomats upon the spending money of empires!

Walter, with his charming, gregarious manner, his inborn unction, his rather shrewd capacity to withhold a decision until just the inevitably right moment—his well-oiled mathematical bent of mind—coupled with all the ready-made power of banking paraphernalia behind him, would, in the eventuality of succession, carry firmly forward.

This much, without her being able to formulate it in words, she knew irrevocably about Walter. As they stood in the violet-and-mauve dusk that began to wind itself against the doors and windows of Wall Street, his talk with her grew lambent, more revealing, more confidentially a résumé of the past since they had met. The business ramifications of his life, since marriage. The crucial occasion of the summons to New York. The present delicate and difficult years of adjustments. The complicated fabric of international banking.

Her own elementary mathematical instinct made his talk comprehensible. Her self-taught facility in bookkeeping was the result of a talent. For years she had kept her father's books, and Kurt's, and part of the neighborly willingness to accommodate her with the telephone service during the Baymiller days, had been her reciprocal willingness to balance the corner grocer's books for him every month. Even where she could not fully comprehend, she could be intelligently interested, and Walter, feeling himself heeded, let expansion take place that carried him back to the days when, for hours on end, with her capacity for interest in his affairs, she could listen without interruption.

"It's getting chilly standing here this way, Ray. Couldn't we, for old time's sake, step into Procter's for a bite of dinner?"

That she was being waited for, in an office of one of Wall Street's new fifteen-story skyscrapers, by a broker who was to take her to

Lüchow's, did not even occur to her. What did occur to her must have flashed into her face, because he said hastily:

"I often telephone home not to wait dinner when I am detained. Will you come? It's been so long since we have had a talk. I feel the need of it, Ray."

Standing there, it came over her with finality what she knew to be her inability to deny him.

21

The coming together of Ray Schmidt and Walter Saxel was something so gradual, so innocent of scheme or plan, that its course was unmarked by the concrete incident of reaching their conclusion.

It was impossible, looking back, for Ray to determine exactly when she reached her decision to leave Blamey's, where she had spent six years of her life in New York. More than that, it was even difficult to go back over those conversations with Walter that had dwelt upon the feasibility of a flat.

Certainly there was in Ray, the day, some two months following the encounter, as she rode in a cab, holding on to hatboxes and minor baggage, consciousness that, in traversing the short distance from West Twenty-third Street to the redbrick apartment house on Broadway near Fifty-third Street, she was crossing the vast steppes which separate respectability from démodé. But not in the sense of any overpowering realization that she was burning bridges after her.

There had never been an instant, in the years intervening between that first meeting in front of the C. H. and D. and this sharp transition in her life brought about by the step she was now taking, that subconsciously she had not been prepared to do, not necessarily this, but whatever was wanted or desired by the one human being in the world whose wish was her law.

Even back in the Cincinnati days, Walter, she now realized, could have had this for the asking. This, or less, or more: everything, or, as he had chosen to decide, nothing. As he would; then, as now. In fact, she caught herself thinking, one day, in the solitude to which she was to become so inured, "It is sweeter this way." In almost any other relationship, she would have given him less. Her isolation into a corner of his life was to become more complete as affairs between them became more and more clandestine. This way, it was all or nothing. Yes, it was sweeter. . . .

Here was a situation that unfolded itself not by machination, but as naturally as a flower unfolds itself.

The talk about the flat had been scrappy, and chiefly, when he began to find it difficult to determine upon places for them to meet or dine, in order that their presence would not seem repetitious or conspicuous, as a means to an end. Indecision, doubts of her which had so characterized their early days, seemed to have vanished, because he said to her so simply that her heart did not even quicken by a beat: "Ray, this can't go on. The time has come for us to have a place of our own, where I can come without all this scheming."

"Yes, Walter."

"We need a flat. Some place where I know we can be quiet and alone. This kind of thing cannot go on without becoming conspicuous, even in a city like this."

"I've thought of that. You have so much to consider."

"I want you to feel about all this, Ray, as a Frenchwoman would feel about it. The time has come for us to call a spade a spade. My feeling for you and my feeling for my wife and children are things separate and apart. I can be loyal to both these feelings, because they are so different."

Should she despise him for that? The thought rushed to her that now was the last instant of her last opportunity to keep her life her intact own. To refuse to become part of an active disloyalty to the wife of a man who coveted and was coveted in return. To refuse to become the mistress of a man who took pains to establish this wife's footing, on the very eve of her surrender to his convenience.

There was yet time; but so fleeting was the hesitancy that her next question was acquiescence.

"Shall you find the—place—the flat—Walter?"

"Yes."

It was better that way. The talk of money would have been abominable to her. What he could afford, or what he could not afford, was sure to be equally right.

What he chose was a three-room apartment on the third floor of a large, five-story, redbrick building on Broadway, not remote from the beginnings of Central Park. It was a rear flat, and the bathroom and bedroom, looking into a narrow airshaft, required gaslight burning in them all day. But the large living room and full-sized kitchen facing the backs of buildings of a parallel street, Seventh Avenue, were filled with morning sunshine and remained bright into late afternoon. Offhand, it was the sort of apartment house that, externally at least, seemed far too pretentious for the modest rear flats that were tucked into it. But apparently those facing Broadway justified the heavily embossed pressed-leather foyer-walls, solemn walnut stairways with a plaster Nubian slave on the newel post thrusting up a gas torch in a red glass globe. They were of ten and twelve rooms, built railroad-fashion along a narrow hallway that shot the entire length of the flat, and rented for as high as sixty dollars a month.

Into her small rear one, furnished in what Walter had apparently chosen *en suite*, Ray fitted with the close adjustment of a bit of fungus to its wall. Snugly and immediately it became home to her, the first premises that had ever allowed her the full privacy of a kitchen in which to putter unrestrictedly. There was a parlor set, consisting of five pieces, mahogany with freckled cinnamon-plush upholstery edged in ball-fringe, a substantial five-piece mission bedroom set, of walnut, with a fine clear mirror in the wardrobe-door, taboret, dresser and washstand and Walter's cunning afterthought of a "whatnot," to say nothing of a Verni Martin curio-cabinet for the living room, into which would cram the tiny ivory carvings, filigree objects, porcelain dogs, cats, marsupials, carnivora, and minutiae of a sort that had always delighted her heart.

It was dear of Walter to have remembered that Verni Martin cabinet. Bless him, he had stocked one of its mirror shelves with a tiny porcelain barnyard. Cow. Hen sitting in a nest of porcelain straw.

Pig, all porcelain, with two suckling piggies. She had exclaimed first of all over these, on beholding her flat.

Then, too, it had always been her desire to attach small gay tassels to the ends of the strings of window shades, and somehow in the house on Baymiller it might have incited people to laugh. Within a week, however, there they were, dangling from the end of every window shade in the flat; and such a litter of silver-framed photographs, fringed scarves, crocheted tidies on the backs of chairs, bisque and porcelain objects, hassocks, and the like, from her store of personal possessions, that mantels, tables, dresser, whatnot, and every conceivable plane surface, were promptly covered.

There was a small bisque angel, attached by a bit of ribbon to the center chandelier of the living room, which was to dangle there in swimming position until, from proximity to the gas jet, its pale little thighs took on a sootiness that would not scrub off.

Immediately this flat became to Ray her kennel; her business days little more than long, chilly intervals between leaving and returning, evenings, laden with foods, commodities, thumbtacks, screening, meat grinder, toothbrush-rack, cushion tops, tidies, and luxuries for the larder.

At once there developed in her, full-blown, out of the Zeus of past experiences, a talent for cookery, garnered from long years of memories of the house on Baymiller Street, abetted by the many times she herself had assisted her father or Tagenhorst at the huge old range; and, strangely enough, memories of the many succulent German and Austrian dishes that had been served to her in Vine Street food-palaces, lingered so poignantly against her palate, that she was able to reproduce them. *Gedämpfte Rindbrust.* Nothing more than the right cut of pot roast, eye-of-the-round, properly managed in a Dutch oven. The Dutch oven to be bought at Macy's for six dollars. Cheese *Kuchen.* A matter of obtaining the proper pot cheese (a journey to the Jewish district would ensure that) and baking with a proper degree of oven heat. Walter's capacity for cheese Kuchen, she used to joke him, was beyond the output of so small a kitchen as theirs. Lamb stew with spätzle. A matter of dropping the dough from the spoon with just the proper turn of the wrist. Dill pickles. Soaking the green cucumbers in a stone crock under vine-leaves that you journeyed to Spuyten Duyvil to gather. No housewife on Baymiller ever brewed tastier.

Homey foods that her hand had the knack of keeping delicate for Walter, whose tendency to overindulge in certain dishes to his liking, had not diminished with the years.

Their very first dinner in her flat, the table was spread with a completeness that was more and more to characterize it. Polished silver and well-filled cruets. Heavy silence cloth, covered with a weighty damask that had been among her possessions from home. Lace mats and tidies. She could crochet rapidly, as she talked, loved the small addenda of the doily and the tidy, using them in profusion against the backs of chairs and beneath small objects.

And so, almost overnight as it were, this abode took on a lived-in aspect, even in that early period when the place stood dead silent all day long during her absence at business; and the evenings, except the one or possibly two in the week he managed to spend there, were solitary, except for the incredible number of the chores of house-primping she could cram into them.

And Walter liked it. Immediately it assumed for him something of a Hamilton interior. Its smell of good spiced foods lurking in portieres and plushes was part of the lived-in atmosphere, where cookery was sure to be of the best ingredients, and where you could stretch yourself out in a Morris chair that was designed according to the most relaxed lines of the human body, and where you could be a little gross in the things you wanted. If you happened to want, without employing any of the finesse necessary to coax down inhibitions in Corinne, in whom sex impulses were languid, to take Ray, she came as if the latent ecstasy pressing against the warm walls of her being were only awaiting release which he could make exquisite. She came to one on the high tide, relaxed and indescribably pliant. Supple, almost overpowering in the completeness of her surrender.

Funny thing about this Ray. A sweetheart strung like a harp that plays to the wind, and withal a woman so slightly and rightly gross! Amenable, even though not always amused, to the slightly soiled story; a woman not easy to offend, who could lie in his arms, her eyes drugged with his nearness, and yet, the next instant, turn around and prepare a dish of pig-knuckles and sauerkraut to what Walter described as the queen's taste, provided the queen be of delicate taste. One could dare be himself in that flat.

It was the same with Ray. Almost incredible, to herself most of all, was the rapidity with which her interests narrowed to the interests of this flat. Even on those evenings she did not see Walter—and these were sometimes five and six, had been known to be seven in the week—there was not only occasion and obligation to be home, there was desire.

Walter had installed a telephone. That was lovely. It hung against the wall in the entrance foyer, and on one or two occasions had been ringing as she unlocked her door. It was like a voice screaming for her presence, and she liked it.

It seemed to her that somehow the men she had been in the habit of meeting after work hours for the divertissements of the evenings must have sensed what was what. Actually they did not, but what they did sense, with the quick antennae of ego, was her new and inner indifference. It was easy to drop out of the rigmarole of being a business girl who was not averse to the attentions of men who could show her a good time. One refusal, two, almost surely three, were sufficient to scratch her off lists that were as washable as the little silver-and-celluloid memorandum pad she wore jangling from her belt along with a chatelaine of other trinkets.

One or two of the older men with whom she had been in the habit of going to comic operas and cafés looked askance at her second and third refusals, and a stockbroker on Nassau Street asked her outright, over the telephone, if her sailor lover had come home. But within the month that tempest in the demitasse of her affairs had died down. Without comment, even from the office force or the men and girls with whom she was thrown in close contact at Ledbetter and Scape, she was free to go home, to walls that enclosed her like the grateful folds of a shawl, there to putter, there to adjust, and, most of all, there to wait. If, during the long, quiet evening, the telephone against the wall crowed, there was the invariable thrill of jumping to its mouthpiece. If it did not, well, you knew that it was one of those evenings devoted to Corinne or social interests, and that there was tomorrow, and if not tomorrow then the day following, or the day following that. Even when a week elapsed and he did not come, there was seldom more than a day or two that he let pass without telephoning.

Once, when she was unlocking her door at evening, frantic, what with her hands filled with small packages, to get to the telephone before it stopped ringing, there was no one at the other end of the wire when she finally did reach the instrument, and a despondency, out of all proportion to the mishap, flooded her.

She would never have ventured the misdemeanor of telephoning him, either at his business during or after hours, or at his home— one of a row of new brownstone houses on Lexington Avenue. So that it was with a sick sense of disappointment, finally overflowing into tears, that for two hours thereafter she sat moping beside an instrument that would not ring again.

About eleven, Walter, equally disgruntled and off even keel, put in an appearance at the flat.

That was the evening, what with her tears and his own sense of disharmony induced by the trifling event, that Walter suggested she give up her position at Ledbetter and Scape.

"I want to feel that you are here when I want you. It helps me to talk things out with you. That's why it upset me this evening, when you didn't answer the telephone. Needed to talk over that project of the Jersey City Trust Company with you. Helps me. I need you, dear, on call."

There was never any more to it than that. It came as a shock to her; it came as something more than that. It meant the cutting loose of the last tie that bound her to a busy outside world, of which she had always been a gay part. It meant—sitting there opposite Walter that evening, pouring him cup after cup of coffee of rich brew she knew how to prepare in a pot to which she applied a cheesecloth drip-bag—it meant—well, it meant cutting away from under her the business ground upon which her feet had so long stood.

"I've been a business girl for fifteen years, Walter."

"And now your business is me, Ray. I need you."

The suffusing sweetness of that was almost more than she could bear.

22

It had always seemed, in the days when she had dared to let her mind wander to the possibility of life with Walter, that nothing of a character that was not part and parcel of ecstasy could ever get at her again. With him, even the dull day would be lived on a singing plane.

Nothing of the sort. The ecstasy was there, all right. She would dawdle through her morning chores, singing and pausing to smile back to herself in the large gilt mirror, or sit sewing with her lips lifted. The incredible change had come so credibly. It had all been so quiet. No doubts, fears, sense of the forbidden. Not even the pang of terror where thoughts of Corinne were concerned, or much awareness of that sure passing over into a world admittedly demimondaine.

The first night with him was like feeling her body become the life stream upon the secure bosom of which he could lie blessedly safe and secure. They were elements bound tightly in the wonder of blending so perfectly. With his head at her bare breast, there could never be anything so extraneous and unintimate as modesty or shyness or doubt or unfulfilment again. There were no words now needed to be spoken. The light of the perfection of the under-standing between them had been kindled at the altar of that first night.

But a few nights following, drawing down her stocking to

minister to a large, throbbing water blister on her heel, rubbed there by a badly fitting shoe, she said to him:

"It is wonderful that I never need be afraid anymore of ever revealing to you an ugliness about me. We are one, Walter."

He looked at her without flushing. "One," he repeated, after a pause so imperceptible as to be perceptible only to her.

The thought of Corinne was to begin to lie at the bottom of a pool of silence between them, seldom stirred, seldom causing turgid waters.

Trifles happened from the very first. The iceman, calling up the dumbwaiter, demanded to know if she wished her weekly bill made out to Miss or Mrs. "To Miss—no, no, Mrs.!" Mrs., of course! The vacillation had been a slip, causing the iceman to grunt his laugh in a way that was pretty bad to have to hear. "Mrs." it must be from now on. Mrs. What? Mrs. Schmidt. What did it matter, so long as indubitably, past redemption, past change, past anything that could ever happen, she was Mrs. to him? And so, "Mrs. Schmidt" read the name on the bell plate. He laughed when he saw it, without self-consciousness or sensitiveness.

"That will make it easier," he said.

She wanted him to be tender over it and hold her closely when the precious implication of the "Mrs." sank in. When he did not, her tenderness flowed out just the same. She was "Mrs." all right. To him.

And so, rapidly, the trifles grew that cemented the newness of the situation into accepted fact. Before she realized it, life had taken on its new routine—a slow-paced routine, which, far from keeping her pitched to the state that would have seemed to coincide with her heart's delight, kept her somehow a little doused, as it were. Humbly quiet. Content to sit at sedentary tasks, while the great slow tick of a cuckoo clock she had coveted and bought herself, interspersed with the ticks of smaller clocks, made little dins against the silence. Content to sit looking out over the back roofs and the back windows and windowsill milk bottles, while rain drizzled or sunlight slid along the sooty walls. The days were each like a warm bath from which she was reluctant to emerge, lying back in them, as if, with the eyes closed, and the mind and body relaxed, it were enough just to wait. To wait for the ringing of the telephone in the entrance hall.

Even on the days when he did not come at all, or on those rarer ones when the telephone did not even ring, there was no disappointment connected with the waiting. The pattern of Walter's time was fairly well-defined. He came on those evenings when to absent himself from home seemed most natural. Sometimes, because of conditions into which she never pried, it was nine o'clock before he arrived for dinner. She had a self-devised system for keeping the food hot, by means of immersing the pots and pans in boiling water. But always on the eve of a pending banking problem, Walter came. Strange too. She said relatively little as he talked—thought out loud, as he was fond of putting it—listening as always with an adoring attention, but slow to advise. He liked that. The word or two, the phrase from her that might steer his course just as surely as if she had spoken her thoughts, did not seem advice to him.

A woman across the hall, named Hattie Dixon (and it is strange how under such circumstances there almost invariably develops a blonde woman across the hall), used to visit in and out during the long days; nor was Ray above a dash or two a day across the hall to the poisonously gilt-and-saffron flat of Hattie Dixon. Hattie, who was forty, but still striking in a bold Spanish sort of way, used openly to quiz Ray about the financial status of Walter.

"Is your friend well-off?"

"I guess he is."

"You guess? Don't you know?"

As a matter of fact Ray did not. It was a subject that had never come up for discussion between them. But more and more, it was being borne in upon Ray that, despite a modest, highly conservative hand to the purse strings where she was concerned, Walter, while his position in the banking house was still the rather nonclassifiable one of junior partner, was not only permitted, but expected to sit in on various types of negotiation which it was assumed he would ultimately have to meet as official.

Obviously, already, Walter had begun to lay the foundations, in a small way, of a fortune. The quite handsome house in Lexington Avenue testified to that. Ray would still walk out of her way to look at a house occupied by Corinne. This was a narrow brownstone structure, with a high stoop, windows handsomely crisscrossed in net curtains, with small iron balconies across the sills. Once again, the shoulder of handsome upholstery showed between the curtains; and, on one occasion, as she had been passing on the opposite side of the street, there descended the stoop the slightly heavier but still blondely pretty figure of Corinne herself. It was winter, and her hands were tucked primly into a rug-shaped moleskin muff, and the rear of her handsome moleskin dolman, fringed in chenille, fitted her to perfection. Mounted on her face veil, just at the edge of her lip, a large black chenille dot, the size of a dime, enhanced her fairness. A pretty little peafowl of a matron. Snug. Right. Tight. Curious that, viewing her, little of the anomaly of her position smote Ray. Corinne was someone to regard wistfully, from a distance.

No great sense of social misdemeanor smote Ray. She would have given much, of course, to feel free of the furtive poaching sense of theft on another's preserves, but Corinne's was the place in the sun of the victor. She had him in the secure, normal, protected fashion that she would always have everything. Ray's position on the edge did not intrude into that security, except in the sense of—that was the part you did not permit yourself to think about! No denying that in literal interpretation Walter was being unfaithful. That was terrible. That was wrong—of them both. And yet, if the edge that you shaved off the pie before you put it into the oven were sufficient to keep another spirit alive! That spirit was Ray, living on leavings; on crumbs from the rich Corinne's table, exulting on leavings, with no point of view except the makeshift one engendered by her yearnings and her spiritual and bodily hunger.

That busy little matron, hurrying along Lexington Avenue in her modish furs, her children, her servants, her household, her security, back in the brownstone-front, was being cheated with every step she took. There was no argument against that, just the sickening knowledge that it was true, and that perhaps that very evening, liaison with her husband would take place in a homely little flat on Broadway. And yet for the life of her, admitting all this self-loathingly, it seemed to Ray so indubitable, so indubitable, that what Walter gave to Corinne was in no way lessened by what Walter gave to Ray. Shameful self-justification, of course, but a man could care for two women at the same time. The husband and father in Walter was Corinne's. His first loyalties were hers. There would be no hesitancy in his choice between them. The mother of his children, the banner-bearer of his respectability, his success, his stability. That handsome moleskin wrap was a banner to his success. Every aspect of his polite life was bound up in Corinne. She had rights—property rights, legal rights, moral rights, ethical rights. The woman in the flat, content with the leavings, walking surreptitiously behind the moleskin wrap, was not a menace to this security. Not even to the well-being.

According to certain established precedent it was the woman in the flat should have been shrouded in mole, instead of in the plain home-tailored jacket. Not Walter! No lavish hand where Ray was concerned. Even while often she wondered and sometimes resented, it was the way she preferred, helping somewhat to alleviate the out-and-out sting of the anomaly of her position as mistress.

It was imperative to find some sort of philosophy to help reason out to herself her lack of sense of horror at what was happening. Spiritually, a woman must be a poor thing not to feel revolted at the predicament of being mistress to another woman's husband—and that husband the father of small children. She wanted to experience spiritual nausea at her dilemma, and yet, all the while, it was next to impossible not to go through the days to a singing of the heart such as she had never known. Never known? Why, never even conceived! That was how the days, those first few years, spread themselves out in a fan of delight. The delight of that first little clearing of its throat, before the telephone rang. The delight of filling her flat with the kind of small inexpensive objects in which she reveled. The delight of shopping for the kinds of food that were warming to Walter's palate. Even the delight of the long hours indoors, while sunshine and the comings and goings of people who were not living surreptitiously, flooded the street scene.

This, then, the old Ray, with her gaiety undiminished, but her desire for its more palpable forms of the theater, the racetrack, the restaurant, practically vanished. On a few occasions, such as Walter's absence from the city on a business trip or on a sojourn with his family, she had lunched at the large hotels, attended horse races, or an occasional theater with Hattie Dixon; but the fact remained that, over a period of three years, she had not ventured out of her flat for more than two or three consecutive hours, and then only at long intervals. The ever-impending contingency of that telephone bell!

The appearance of a slight but persistent bronchial cough that threatened to become chronic, precipitated the rigor of this régime. The old physician who occupied a neighboring apartment diagnosed her complaint as one induced, partially at least, by lack of fresh air and exercise, and prescribed at least four hours daily out-of-doors.

To Ray, who had a horror of even a slight indisposition, and who had never permitted Walter to suspect the sleepless nights occasioned by the cough, there was something peremptory in the old doctor's dictate. A sickly woman would be an abomination to Walter!

When she suggested to him that he try and arrange his telephone calls and visits in some sort of pattern, so as to allow her more freedom of action, there was such genuine bewilderment and rueful surprise in his face that she caught his cheeks in her hands, and declared, between kisses, that she did not mean one word of it.

"Why, good Lord, Ray, I never thought of that. You've been tied down here like a slave."

"I have loved it, Walter. It's just that I'm beginning to think that if I don't get out a little bit more I'll turn into a fat bronchial old lady and you'll hate me."

"I never want you to stay in on my account again," he said, and lied.

"Why, Walter, I wish I hadn't mentioned it, if you're going to take it like that."

"I'm glad you mentioned it. Trouble is, I can never tell ahead just what days I can get here for lunch. Uncle Felix is getting so that he likes to have me sit in on lunch-conferences. As for the other, well, you know the situation on Lexington Avenue."

Did she! She knew it by heart, by rote, by day, by night. The holidays of Pesach and Rosh Hashanah, when the family foregathered. The days Corinne lunched at the Bankers' Club with her husband and Uncle Felix. The Saturday-afternoon drives Walter took with his children in a large basket-phaeton drawn by Shetlands. The birthday celebrations of each and every member of the family. Corinne's birthday dinner. Walter's. Little Richard's. Baby Irma's.

On Felix-Arnold Friedlander's birthday, the family dined at the Harmonie Club. On Yom Kippur they dined at his Fifth Avenue home. There were certain calendar dates like these that could be definitely foreseen. Those were the days of matinée, theater, or races, with Hattie Dixon, or if Hattie's "friend" happened to be in town, there were one or two of the other "girls," in the building, whom she had come to know.

"Tell you what I'm going to do, Ray! I'm going to make it my business to try and let you know by eleven every morning what my plans are for the day. No use your sitting here like a bump on a log all day long, waiting. Funny thing now, I never thought of that, and you goose," he said, and kissed her, "wouldn't speak up if it killed you."

The thought that flooded her as she sat there with the constricting bronchial pains in her chest, was how unselfish, after all, he was; and if possible her tenderness to him became tenderer, and she began her favorite habit of kissing his fingers, one by one, and then beginning all over again, and placing each finger that had been kissed, against his lips, and without ever seeming to feel foolish, he would kiss off her kisses.

"Walter, have you any idea how much I love you?"

"Now why do you ask that?"

"Oh, I know you like me a lot, darling, but what I mean is, well, I mean it's on the principle that you can't pour two tumblers of water into one. I sometimes think I love you more than you're built to hold, Walter."

"I'm a one-tumbler-capacity man, is that it? Well, I don't know just what you mean, but it sounds to me like you're saying something I mighty much like to hear."

Once he was out-and-out frank with her, in a way that she was to hoard as something precious. For the first time he referred to Corinne in other than such indirect phrasing as: "You know the Lexington Avenue situation; I must be home for a euchre-party tonight." Or: "There is no use my doing anything on Lexington Avenue that may make it more difficult for us. I won't see you tomorrow night. It's Hallowe'en. Look strange for me not to be at home with the children."

They had been sitting on the cinnamon-plush sofa in the overheated and by now overcrowded parlor–living room, Ray in a flowing wrapper of stripe of embroidery and blue ribbon, which she had fagoted together by hand, Walter in a dark-green housejacket, which she had made for him and kept hanging on a hook on the bathroom door. His head was on her lap. It was evening, and they had just dined, too well, off a table that had been dragged to one corner of the room and covered with a spotless cloth to conceal used dishes.

There were two Welsbach lamps burning, and the chandelier that dangled the bisque angel was going at each of its four brackets. Walter liked light and plenty of it. It helped embalm the smell of recent foods, the somewhat coarse foods which he preferred in this atmosphere of Ray, and which she prepared with a really incomparable kind of delicacy.

He had been telling her, his head back against her lap, and her fingertips moving lightly through his hair and along his cheeks, stirring the down in a way that drew occasional delighted little shudders from him, of a pending loan in contemplation by the house of Friedlander-Kunz, to one of the small principalities of Southern Europe, which, if consummated, would create an international deal of many millions. While his position in the firm was, at the time, little more than that of bystander, it struck Ray, as she sat there, that vast affairs hung closely in Walter's offing—affairs so vast and so close, that their imminence frightened her and made her possessive.

"Walter, some day you will be a great international banker and forget all about me."

It was not like her to project herself; but the fear that smote her was stronger than she was, and she let her hands rest suddenly upon his head, as if she felt him slipping away.

"Never do that, Walter. It would be like throwing me out of a boat into the ocean."

"Why, Ray, what's got into you?"

"I don't know. Silly of me to say that, wasn't it? Now what do you suppose made me say that? Go on, I didn't mean to interrupt."

"But I want to," he said, kissing her palms, "when you feel like that. But I'm surprised at you, Ray."

"I'm surprised at myself, Walter. Don't pay any attention to me. Go on. I'm a fool."

"You know how indispensable you are to me."

"I think I do, Walter. But I just wish you'd say it more often."

"I'll try to. I keep thinking you take it for granted."

"I know. Men are that way. It's their great sex-error."

"I know things aren't easy for you, Ray. As a matter of fact, neither are they for me—this arrangement, I mean."

"I realize that, boy, with every breath I breathe."

"Life is a complicated enough arrangement—without this—this—"

"Don't I know it?"

"Guess I shouldn't have said that, now, should I?"

He shouldn't. He shouldn't.

"But I figure you know where I stand, Ray—between you and Corinne, I mean."

She sat for a moment without breathing.

"I'm in love with my wife, Ray. You know that."

"Yes," she said, trying to make the word audible.

"What makes you so wonderful, Ray, is that you're not the kind of person to go flying off at a tangent at a remark like that. You understand."

"I do, Walter," she said, feeling as if there were ropes around her heart, trying to haul it from its moorings.

"I love Corinne, Ray."

God, God, God, if he would only quit saying it!

"Whatever doubts I may have had back there in the beginning—"

Then he had had doubts! Damn Freda! Damn life—no, no, no—as if that morning at the zoo would have made any difference!

"Whatever doubts I may have had, back there when we both were free, are gone now, Ray. I did the only thing there was to do. Corinne has been a good wife, a good mother, and I owe much to her—connections—"

Cad, you. No, no; darling, you. Life is like that. Nobody is all good, all bad—

"And I love you too, Ray. Lots of women could never understand that. The French do. Corinne couldn't. It is a strange thing, Ray, this loving two women at the same time in a totally different way. Sometimes I feel so puzzled with myself that I marvel I keep quite sane."

(Himself. Himself.)

"Strange, take that little woman in the house on Lexington Avenue. She has not got your mind, Ray. I can't talk to Corinne for five minutes at a time that the same thing doesn't happen. Trifles. Gets off the main issue to the personal. Can't pin her down. One of those skidding woman-minds. Ambitious for all sorts of things that shouldn't matter, but do. Stewing over the children. Worrying over cooks and fur coats, stair carpets and winter apples. Financial affairs of our friends and how to outdo them. Most loyal little creature you ever did see. Go through fire for me. Wonderful mother, good housekeeper, fine appearance, great connections, good as a glass of fresh cream, go through fire for me."

(You've said that once.)

"Knows how to wheedle her uncle where my interests are concerned. Great little diplomat. Big spender, where it is necessary, but conservative where it is not. Kind of woman who will head a home in as fine a fashion as a man could wish it."

(Go on, maybe it will help me to hate you!)

"I'm telling you all this, Ray, because I feel I owe it to you, and because you understand. If I seem nervous sometimes and jumpy, it is because I'm in the devilish position of wanting to be two places at the same time. Here, and there with her and the children."

"Better if you'd never clapped eyes on me!"

"Yes, if you look at it in a certain way. It is a dangerous position for a man like me, and yet, take my word for it, I wouldn't change things. I couldn't give you up, Ray. You're just the Rock of Gibraltar to me. You're more than that. You're the only person in the world to whom I am myself. That's a fact. The one minute in the day that I really become myself is when I enter this door. You're the reason, Ray. Always the same. Selfless. You're a woman that can satisfy a man completely. You're tolerant of a man because you understand him. When you love a person you love him more than you love yourself."

(You don't! You don't! You don't!)

"Often when I've gone away from here and get to realizing the way I've sat for hours talking about myself and my affairs and my interests, I get ashamed. I like to think out loud to you, Ray. I'm myself, here. Corinne is all ambition for the children, for the home, and for me, and that is as it should be. You're ambitious too, but in another way. I can talk to you about my work. I need that, Ray. Just between you and me, I'm in deep waters most of the time; in the midst of affairs that offhand seem over the head of a man like me. That's why I need encouragement and understanding, on my way up the scale. Sometimes it seems to me that if I don't get here to talk things over with you, that I can't go on. My wife's Uncle Felix is a hard man, Ray, in the sense that he expects his kind of efficiency, plus, out of the man who is to carry on his work. Corinne doesn't realize that. I firmly believe I am qualifying every day for my work, but half the time I'm panting, Ray. With fear."

"My poor boy, my darling boy. You have it in you to accomplish what you set out to accomplish."

"I have, haven't I, Ray? Say that again."

"You have a good, strong, receptive mind, Walter. You have cool judgment, caution, and solid reasoning power. You are a splendid mixer. You have personality. You observe and you remember what you observe."

"By God, I do. Now, take this case of the Fulton Mortgage and Trust Company. Remember my telling you about our firm and the Mississippi Valley loan. . . ."

"The time you went out to St. Louis?"

"Yes, remember you looked up some data on the Mississippi Valley matter at the library for me to study out on the train."

"Yes, I love looking up data for you, Walter."

"Now, I couldn't have talked that Mississippi Valley any place in the world the way I did right here in this flat, Ray. That's what I mean. I needed to think out loud."

(You needed me to think out loud!)

"I needed your sympathetic understanding. You've got that, Ray, sympathy and understanding and patience and sweetness, and I love you."

"And I love you, Walter, so terribly that sometimes it frightens me."

"Tush! Nothing to be frightened about. So long as you are the dear, sweet, patient girl you are, nothing can go wrong. Temperance in this thing, and seeing each other only as often as it is easily possible, rather than as often as we wish to, is all we need to keep everything sweet as new cream. If I had my way, Ray, I'd be here twice as much as I am. Remember that and be content."

"I am content."

"And more than content?"

"More than content."

"How much more?"

"So much more, Walter, that if I were to go to sleep tonight, and never wake, I would have died the happiest person in the world."

He could have cried. . . .

23

One day, seated before her writing desk, which by night became a folding-bed, and going over her household accounts, which for her own edification she kept in immaculate order, it occurred to Ray that it might be a good idea, now that more of her time was her own, to "take up something."

Money matters, where Walter was concerned, had from the very start been a source of peculiar strain and self-consciousness between them. It was not that he was exactly penurious; it was never to analyze that simply. It was just that the subject of money seemed to embarrass him, as if it were something too gross to bear discussion, even while his conservative disbursements, to her at least, indicated a preconceived scheme.

His way of evading was to leave, the first of every month, five new twenty-dollar bills stuck into the bisque basket on the back of the bisque figure of a fish peddler on the crowded shelf of the crowded sideboard. That apparently was the monthly sum he had figured could cover the expenses of the little ménage.

In a way it did. Thirty dollars rent left, if cleverly managed, a sufficient margin for gas, telephone, ice, food, clothing, and incidentals, particularly if you were as handy with the needle, as canny a shopper and cook, as Ray. But barely more than sufficient. Walter abominated a tough or inferior cut of meat, and what with sirloin-steak fourteen cents the pound and chicken sixteen, it required the unerring hand of the calculating buyer. He was a great one for fruit, too, stretching out on the sofa after one of the full and satisfying meals, with a cut-glass bowl of apples, oranges, and bananas on the table beside him, and making the peeling of an apple with unbroken rind quite a function. Wines he usually sent himself, either clarets or ports, and, as his taste became more precious, Moselles, Sauternes, Cointreau, and dry and fine champagnes. But often while shopping on her own budget, it was more than Ray could do to resist for him the lure of a cobwebby bottle of Chianti in its crib, or the rows of translucent violet, crystal, and brown liqueurs that the liquor stores mounted in their show windows.

It meant managing a bit, hunting around for remnants where her own clothes were concerned, and watching such items as gaslight, laundry, carfares, and cookery, when Walter was not about. Once or twice she had run beyond her allotment, but there had been her own small nest egg of several hundred dollars. When that petered out, as it did to her surprise, due chiefly to the troubled problem of little Emma Hanck's eyes, there were a few occasions, such as the imperative need for a new kitchen-range, a large dentist-bill, a music box for which she hankered, when it became necessary to raise the vexed question of money.

"Walter, I hate to have to mention it, but really, that is such a bad bare spot on the wall between the doors! Those newfangled cuckoo clocks are darling. I don't suppose you'd feel like affording one for eighteen dollars?" Or: "Walter, I just can't bake you pie-crust that's fit to eat in that old oven. What do you say to one of those new Pet ranges? They're forty dollars, but worth it." Or: "Walter, would you think I was nervy if I wanted one of those six-dollar Dutch ovens for pot roasts?"

There had never been any demurring. The money had been forthcoming, not out with it and down with it then and there; but after his departure, there it would be, tucked into the basket of the bisque fishmonger.

Strangely, this seeming delicacy on the part of Walter was secretly the source of much hurt pride to Ray. When you were as close as she to Walter—as close as Walter to her—there was no place for a reservation such as this one. The strange guarded manner with which he withdrew into himself on the subject of money, kept a distance between them that was mystifying. Again and again she told herself that it could not be penury. When in his middle thirties, Walter was already in the ranks of a man reputed to be wealthy. Not that he ever permitted Ray, who understood most of his financial affairs so intimately, to know just what he was actually drawing from the banking house. But what she did know was the amount of Walter's life insurance, the nature of certain of his private holdings, the growing values of at least three of his small parcels of city property; and one wintry day he had sent her to Brooklyn for the purpose of "sizing up" the lay of a fifty-foot lot on Joralemon Street. "Just kind of see how it looks, Ray. You've good judgment."

It was wrong of Walter to place her in the rigid vise of an allowance. Dear knows that she spent his money with far more conservation than she would her own, and with sole aim to conserve for him, whose every interest was infinitely more to her than her own. It was not nice of Walter, to say nothing of the fact that, what with his growing epicureanism and delight in the table, his desire to see her at least always nicely dressed, it kept her pinched.

His expenditures on family, although he was constantly complaining of the increased demands upon him, were beginning to approach the magnificent. There were two nurses for the children now. A closed carriage, closed coupé, landaulet, and the children's phaeton and Shetlands.

Within four years, Corinne had refurnished the house on Lexington Avenue from top to bottom, and Walter had recently purchased a fine old Georgian mansion set in three acres, at Deal Beach, for the summer home.

Not but all this was as it should be. Imagine the life-giving sun and salt air and open space flowing into the bone and sinew of growing babies. Besides, a man owed it to his prestige. But it seemed a shame that along with his increasing munificence of scale of living the thought never seemed to enter Walter's head that it might be equally within his power to lighten things materially for Ray.

It was quite one thing to have to count hopefully on a small

killing at the races in order to be able to send along a money order
to Freda (nothing could have induced her to divert Walter's funds
into her family-channel, certainly not to little Emma's); but it was
quite another matter to be obliged to confess to a woman like Hattie Dixon that balcony seats were all she could afford for a matinée,
or that tea or a drink at Martin's afterward was too much a stretch
of the purse.

"You're a fool! Ask! Catch me not asking George for what I
don't see!"

That must have been true, because Hattie was usually well-
supplied with money, to say nothing of a collection of quite valuable
jewelry, by the big bluff Buffalo broker whose occasional weekends
in New York were the source of noisy parties in the Dixon flat.
"Ask! Them as asks, gets."

Perhaps. But even when the allowance was running low, solely
because of her expenditures on Walter's behalf, the words would
not come. Guilty of the very reticence she resented in Walter, she
tightened her purse strings for a series of small private denials until
the next appearance of the banknotes in the bisque basket.

Curious that Walter should subject her to this. But even while
at times her blood boiled, particularly after an enforced humiliat-
ing revelation to Hattie, who was always willing enough with the
proffer of a small loan, she would invariably melt into a state of
idealization of his shortcomings.

What a small boy he was! Probably if she were to call his attention to these occasional lapses, his chagrin and repentance would be
of the same dear brand he displayed when she occasionally ventured
to tell him he had kept her needlessly waiting, hours on end, for a
telephone message which had been agreed upon between them and
which he had meanwhile forgotten. One did not take the chance,
though, where money-matters were concerned. It was a subject sure
to make him look harassed.

Hattie had suggested an explanation that was as peculiar as it
was possible.

"He don't care for the money. I know those Jewish boys. Look
the way he throws it around every other way. Didn't you tell me

yourself he keeps three carriages? He don't care for the money, Ray.
He wants to keep you little. I used to have one like that. Birds-of-
paradise and diamond bowknots for some little chippie he didn't
care a tinker's dam about. But ruching at the neck instead of diamonds and sapolio-perfume for me. He figures if he dikes you out
too flashy, and other fellows begin throwing eyes your way, that will
take away his feeling of security about having you here when he
wants you. Don't tell me! What I don't know about the male profession you could write on a postage stamp."

There might be something in that. Something subconsciously
at work in Walter. He frequently praised her ability to look so stylish in homemade clothes. Hattie, who in her parlance had feath-
ered her own nest, was forever warning Ray of the importance of
putting by a few jewels, a few furs, a few expensive trinkets, for
the proverbial rainy day. Walter's gifts of jewels to her had been so
inconsequential that they verged on the childish. A turquoise ring.
A watch to pin to her waist with a garnet fleur-de-lis brooch. A pair
of gold link bracelets for which she collected heart bangles. Occasionally a gold or silver spoon, for Emma's collection.

It was not improbable, after all, that this might be Walter's way
of keeping their relationship on a plane far and safely away from
the calculating one that was so horrible to her in the women with
whom Ray realized she was now classed.

She might shop with them, lunch with them, attend races
with them, as so often she did when tedium was upon her, but
secretly she regarded her alliance as something special. Not in the
class with the sometimes promiscuous, always mercenary basis of
most of "the girls."

That was why the idea of "taking up" something smote her
pleasantly. It would not only help with the problem of idle hours,
sitting around in one flat or another, with Hattie or one or two
other friends whose chatter was not edifying, but it would enable
her to earn "pin money" and at the same time improve herself.

The desire to improve herself was one that flashed intermittently over Ray; had done so since the days subsequent to Woodward High, when she had made sporadic attempts at elocution,

burnt wood, and Delsarte. Piano lessons had entered her head since her new inheritance of leisure, but Walter had laughed that off. A Professor Ederlee, advertising in the *Times* a course of ten lectures at Beethoven Hall on "How to Improve Your Mind," at five dollars the series, had caught her fancy; and, paying in advance, she had attended three. But, poor Ray, the overheated lecture-hall, the reference to names, books, and places with which she was not familiar, and the atmosphere of upholstered middle-aged ladies with adenoids, had been too much for her concentration.

How could you improve your mind, she asked herself, in half-humorous disgust at her inability for sustained effort, if you haven't any to improve? Old duck of a professor! Come right down to it, he didn't seem to know any too much. He pronounced Cincinnati, "Cincinnatus," the one and only time he had occasion to use it from the platform. Besides, she could have sworn his body nudged hers too closely one day while poring over a book list with her.

Music was another matter. The purchase of a small music box she felt to be a step in the right direction, morning after morning, moving along to its unrelenting repertoire, sweeping, dusting, mending, cooking, to "Listen to the Mocking Bird," "'Tis the Last Rose of Summer," "Turkish Patrol," "Alice, Where Art Thou?".

All about town, if you ventured near park or popular concerts, Sousa's marches were raging—"The Washington Post," "Liberty Bell," "High-School Cadets," "Stars and Stripes Forever." Over in Hattie's flat, where there was an upright piano strewn with every conceivable song of the moment, it was lazy fun to while away an afternoon picking them out with one finger, or singing in duets, trios, or foursomes. "Sunshine of Paradise Alley," "She Was Bred in Old Kentucky," "Just Tell Them That You Saw Me."

Of course, the kind of music that really improved you was grand opera, or the concert hall, where you heard Calvé, Pachmann, Ysaye and Paderewski. Somehow, with the best intentions in the world, she never achieved the recital hall. How she did love, though, the lilting pathos of "Sweet Marie, Come to Me," "You Made Me What I Am Today," "The Pardon Came Too Late," "Darling Sue, Dear"! Tears glittered along her gray eyes, and she lay back on the couch in an orgy of sweet soul-sickness, while Hattie sang in a deep-voiced contralto, and a girl named Jessie Isman, who was later to figure in a notorious breach-of-promise case, splashed ringed fingers along the piano keys.

And yet it was consciousness of these long hours of flabby inertia, combined with a need to meet certain of the pressing demands that were coming from Youngstown, that prompted her determination to "take up" something.

What could a person do? It must be something that could be accomplished at home. Gone were the days when she even felt the urge to leave the house of a morning for a day among the moving marts of men. Gone, and strangely there was no desire for their return. The flat was so snug. It fitted like a warm cape. The ease of sleeping late was pleasant. The sweet delights of waiting, unquenched.

There had been a woman in Cincinnati, wife of the organist of First Lutheran Church, who had made quite a living in ceramics and had finally procured a position in the Rookwood Pottery because of her proficiency with glaze. China painting was fashionable, lucrative, and genteel.

There was a sign in one of the windows of a ground-floor apartment of the building in which Ray lived. "China Painting Taught. Fifty Cents a Lesson." Even Walter was receptive to that idea when she broached it, lying one evening in his arms while this time he bent back her fingers one by one.

"You girls are always wanting to mess around in one thing or another," he said. "Never saw the like with women nowadays. Restless, that's what you are. But go ahead. China-paint to your heart's content."

The following day she began learning to outline pink and yellow rose petals on teacups, with a green leaf lying on the saucer.

24

"You would be surprised," Ray was fond of remarking to "the girls" during their periods of more or less protracted visits to one another, "how much my work has done for my nerves. Quieted them down like anything."

A vigorous, high-busted blonde, a Mrs. Saperlee, had recently moved into the building. Her flat was one of the elaborate, front ones. The life-size plaster-of-Paris Negro boy who stood at the entrance to receive visiting cards, but never drew more than cigar butts, was indicative of the interior. Mrs. Saperlee's flat, which she had formerly conducted on the top floor of an old house in Fifteenth Street, was elaborate with everything, from an upright piano with plush flanks, to gold furniture and pale rugs that were splashed with full-blown pink roses. Men and women in evening-dress met there over card tables covered in green felt; and until four and five o'clock in the morning, the two Rastuses, Mrs. Saperlee's pair of gray-headed Negro servants, both of whom answered to the same name, served bowl and weal.

During the day she was generous with her premises, passing around leftover sandwiches and half-emptied bottles of good vintage with a generosity that came to establish her flat as favorite headquarters for afternoon gatherings of girls with time on their hands. Euchre and poker games flourished there among them, usually for indifferent stakes, Saperlee not being particularly receptive to that type of trade.

She was one of Ray's best customers. "I know just how you feel, dearest, about the china painting quieting your nerves. It does for you what a bit of snuff in private does for me. Gets your mind off yourself. I think I could use another dozen of those sweet little ash-receivers with the forget-me-nots and pansies."

The girls kept quite a flow of orders coming in. Dresser sets, consisting of comb-and-brush tray, hair-receiver, small stand on which to hang finger rings, hairpin tray, powder-box. Breakfast sets, tea sets, even luncheon and dinner sets were in demand too, and scarcely a day that Ray was not busy at turning out the souvenir cup and saucer, inscribed with the recipient's name. Shaving-mugs too came to be a specialty, "Pet, to Fred." "Love Me Little, Love Me Long." "Tom's Cup." It was pleasant work, leaving no evidence in the flat, except a small table laid out with objects that had not yet gone to be baked.

It is doubtful if Walter, after the first little while, when the arrival of each new piece from the ovens was an event, was ever even conscious of the considerable traffic in china painting that occupied part of Ray's days. That she executed pieces and small sets was known to him. There were his own porcelain cuff links monogrammed; and every once in a while she pointed out that a salad-dish done in yellow daisies was new, or the china globe on a lamp, elaborately designed in full-blown roses. What he did not realize was to what extent the sideline took care of such matters as little Emma, certain table delicacies that found their way to the fulsome meals, or the hassocks, sofa-pillows, slippers, and lounging robes that were constantly making appearance for the purpose of aiding and abetting his comfort.

It was easier to concentrate on the china painting than it had been on the lectures. Here, the mind had free play. Etching the outline of petals onto a china pickle dish was a different matter from trying to clutch on to abstractions of thought. Three volumes of the prescribed reading of the course stood quite showily on the cellarette, giving an "effect." "Highlights in English Prose." "Highlights in American Prose." "Highlights in English and American Poetry." You still wanted terribly to improve yourself; but, while you read, somehow the mind skidded.

China painting, now, was another matter. You could think, for instance, and plan the evening meal in case Walter were coming, or ruminate among languid, pleasant thoughts of a general nature. Then too, unlike the lectures, which were held in a formal hall, going for a china-painting lesson was simply a matter of throwing on a cape over one's wrapper and going downstairs, and the indoors was something from which by now you had become almost inseparable.

It was easy to learn to become a homebody. Strangely, except for occasional parties to the races, or marketing, or a stroll down the avenue, Hattie and Mrs. Saperlee and one or two other girls in the building were just as disposed toward the indoors. For a while, Ray, to combat this, determined upon a daily walk, but that petered out. After her chore of marketing, it was good to be home again. There was something big and exposed and unfriendly about the old street-scenes in which she had reveled for so many years of her life. The ogling of a male frightened her; the close voice of someone passing her. Traffic seemed somehow to have quickened in the years since she had been daily part of it.

There were many of these hateful automobiles by now, and electric cars with the habit of clanging right upon her, and something disconcerting even about the eye of the casual passerby. Eyes that stole her privacy—hard small eyes and probing eyes that roved and roved all over her until the flesh felt dessicated.

One day something happened that discomfited her so, that she trembled for hours after it had occurred. Whom should she encounter on the corner of Sixth Avenue and Thirtieth Street, where she had gone to purchase tarragon vinegar from an importer's shop for Walter's salad-dressing, but a Cincinnati girl whose name had been Retta Spiegel before marriage. Retta and Ray had attended one year at High together, immediately after which Retta had married and moved away.

"Ray!"

"Retta!"

"Well, if this don't beat anything. You living in New York, Ray?"

"I certainly am."

"Well, if this don't beat anything."

Retta was a matron. She was the sort of woman you saw walking her small children to school in the morning, carrying their books and pausing every so often to twist her handkerchief against their noses. Retta, who had been slim, and, as Ray remembered so well, had worn ruffles on the inside of her shirtwaists to give her contour, was filled out now, wearing her corsetcovers tight, to produce an opposite effect. She was the kind of woman whose husband would call her "Mother."

"I married a Toledo boy, Ray. We moved East three years ago, when he got transferred to the eastern headquarters. He's a draftsman. We live in West Orange. Nice little home out there. My oldest boy is eleven."

"My, my," lied Ray, a victim of the silly trembling that had hold of her, "you certainly don't look it, Retta."

"And you—honestly! The same old tony Ray. Remember the time Will Cupples was so sweet on you that his mother took him out of Woodward High before Easter? You married, Ray?"

"No. I came East after my father died. I—I'm just going along about as usual."

"I see," said Retta, her eyes suddenly, to Ray at least, roving and roving until she could have screamed of their burn—"I see. Well, it's mighty nice to have seen you. Give my love to old Cincinnati when you write out there. Good-by."

Such a trifling incident to cause her to go scurrying fast as her feet would carry her back to the security, the overheated privacy, the snug, safe retreat of her flat.

That night, in one of her elaborate wrappers, and her hair down her back, and an air of general exhaustion about her, she told Walter the incident, plucking imaginary threads off his coat-lapel as she talked.

"I can't begin to tell you, Walter, what I suffered. I thought—I thought I'd die."

"Thought you'd die? Why? That's not like you."

"I know it, Walter. Just seems like I hate to meet people anymore."

"Now, that's nonsense."

"I know it is. I'm not ashamed of anything. . . ."

"Of course you're not."

"If I had to do it all over again I wouldn't change things. It's just that I'm getting right sensitive about silly nothings. I'd rather stick right here at home, Walter, where even if you're not here, your things are hanging on pegs. Here, where you eat. Here, where your chair stands beside the table."

He was moved at that, and pinched her cheek. "Goosie."

"I guess I am." She wanted to cry. But she would no more have given way before him! She knew his masculine dread and susceptibility to tears. Corinne cried. Walter was not sympathetic to tears. He always said, "Bawl." Besides, it needed only one glance at him to know that he was bristling with something to tell. That was why his glance half slid as she talked. He was not so much listening as waiting. He was like a small boy, she thought, her indulgence flowing over her sense of hurt. He is waiting for me to ask what is on his mind.

"There's a girl," he said, when she sprang back from his arms, grasped him by the shoulders, and said:

"What's on your mind, darling?"

He felt for a cigar. She was before him, bounding over to his humidor, withdrawing one, lighting it, and passing it from her lips to his.

"You smoke too," he said, and lighted her a cigarette. It amused him to see her pull awkwardly and feel with the tip of her tongue for tobacco crumbs.

It burned in her sullenly upon occasion that smoking was something he not only would not tolerate in his wife, but would be proud to be reactionary where her preciousness was concerned. Queer mysterious differentiation that she was apparently always to suffer in the minds of men. Even in the mind of this one.

"Ready now for a good long listen?"

"In a second."

She had been peeling him a huge yellow apple, removing the rind in one long curlicue. This she whisked out of sight.

"Now," she said, and wound her arms around his neck and lay with her ear to his heart. "Now what?"

How safe it was there. How good. How warming. "Tell me what is on your mind, darling."

"Ray," he said, and withdrew his cigar, regarding its moist end for a full half-minute before resuming, "something mighty important is about to happen to me."

"You mean the Guaranty Loan is going through?"

"Now, either let me or you do the talking."

"I'm sorry."

He continued to regard the end of his cigar. There was gray in his hair by now, and she wanted to reach up and stroke it, but, not quite daring, lay tense and waiting.

"Looks to me, Ray, as if my wife's uncle, Felix-Arnold Friedlander, is getting ready to put his house in order. He's a sick man. Diabetes and complications. Wouldn't be surprised if he isn't beginning to make up his mind that his active days are numbered. He sent for me today to have lunch with him. Important things are about to happen in the firm, Ray."

"Walter, you don't mean . . ."

"I do."

"But Mr. Kunz . . ."

"That's just the point. Kunz is no spring chicken, either. Ultimately he plans to retire, too. Oh, not today, or tomorrow; but, looking ahead, from what I was able to understand, that seems to be the picture."

"Then you mean . . ."

"I don't mean anything that isn't as plain as the nose on your face. It looks to me as if I'm directly in line. In fact, from what was said in that office today, without coming right out in so many words, and from what I understand was said at last directors' meeting, I don't see how I'm going to escape it."

"I just don't know what to say, Walter."

"Don't say anything until it happens. There are alive and kicking men in between me and the post at the minute, but I am giving you an idea of what may happen."

"I always knew some day—of course. But to think there is out-and-out talk about it already."

"Not exactly. Don't misunderstand. It is just the nearest the old gentleman has ever come to putting a card on the table. Talked and beat around the bush at that. Kept harping on the two foreign loans I've been telling you about. That's not all. I'm going to France."

It seemed to her, lying there, that everything about her just stopped. Her heart, its beat. Her blood, its course in her veins. The noises and sounds of everyday life, including Walter's voice against her eardrums. This was vacuum. Lying there against Walter's heart, conscious that "I'm going to France" had been said, and yet not hearing it any more.

"Felix-Arnold Friedlander seems to think I'm the man to swing the deal from that end. And I—well, sir, Ray, I don't know whether I feel so set up, or so bowled over that my wits have deserted me. I came straight here from the bank. A man's got to think. Out loud. Anyway, that's what I need to do, if I can pull myself together."

Walter was frightened. She could feel him tremble. Walter needed to be bolstered.

"What this amounts to, Ray, is out-and-out international banking. If I go over there, I'm mixing myself up with the history of two small kingdoms. Pretty small ones, but nations on their own. Now, rather than tackle a thing like this if I don't feel up to it in experience, now is the time for me to come out like a man and say, 'Look here, Uncle Felix, this is all very fine, but I'm not ready!'"

(Yes. Yes. Yes. Stay with me, Walter. Don't outgrow me. Stay with me.) He was frightened of his life. She would have given everything to be able to reach out her hand and say to him: "Stay back with me, Walter. You will fail. In this snug, sure little nest of our enormous compatibility, be content."

But Walter would not fail. He would succeed in the way the slow, the plodding, the bitterly tenacious, and the unbrilliant can succeed. Properly guided, always properly guided with the well-established pattern of procedure of the house of Friedlander-Kunz within eye-and-mind grasp, he would succeed.

"You will succeed, Walter." (One did not add: "Properly guided, you will plod to achievement. But it will be your grim desire, rather than your talent, that will succeed.") "You will succeed, Walter."

He caught her wrists.

"Does it seem that way to you, Ray? Sometimes it seems to me you know me better than myself."

"I know you will succeed."

"To hear you say that is worth everything."

"You need not worry about your lack of experience. You are the one to make use of the experience of others. . . ."

"What do you mean by that?" he asked, a quick cloud chasing the satisfaction across his face.

"Why, darling, that you will climb higher on the underpinnings that others have already erected." (Neither did she add: "Because you are emulator, not creator.")

"I know how long my arm is. I will not try to stretch beyond its reach."

Exactly! Said better than she could have, even had she dared.

"Never make a move, on your way up, Walter, anyway until you get the knack of walking in a high place, without consulting someone who is wiser than you are. You'll get that knack, Walter. This is a high place compared to the old days, and see how gradually you have been climbing up the mountain almost without knowing it. Watch the other men who have succeeded before you, in your kind of work. Watch. Take their advice up to the point where you believe in it, and from there on use your brain as if you had two of them. One for and one against. May the best of your two brains win."

"I think you will have to be my other brain, Ray."

"You'll succeed, Walter."

He had never been so tender with her. Stamina revived in him, until he became cocksure, pretentious, and more than ever the small boy.

"I love you, Ray. Don't know what I'd do without you. You give me nerve. You give me confidence. I'll show them. I've never really let off steam. Ever observe that about me, Ray? I'm the sort who goes slowly until the right moment, and then bingo!"

(Who goes slowly until the right moment! What about the Guaranty Trust case? It was like holding back horses to keep him from plunging into what would have been that terrible mistake. Oh, Walter!) Of course, though, one said nothing of the sort.

"You saw the way I handled the Guaranty case. Another temperament would have snapped up the first offer and made the mistake of his young life. Did I? Not me!"

(How she had prevailed and even forced upon him the policy of watchful waiting! Had caused him, in fact, to reverse, by wire, an important decision of impulse.)

"I'm going to be a force in the banking world, Ray. Governments will have to reckon with me. Why, if you look at it in a certain way, an entire little principality depends on the way my mind works in the next few weeks. That's the way my wife's uncle put it. 'Handle this thing your own way, my boy.' I've a level head, Ray, if I do say so myself, and I know how to keep it square on my shoulders." (Her phrase, this last.)

"Corinne, now, doesn't quite understand. She's all impulse, ambitious for the children, ambitious for me, for the home, and naturally she only sees the immediate result. That's what I love in you, Ray. Your level head. Sometimes, after I've talked with you and got my bearings, I see myself as I am. Now, take today; came here scared out of my wits, admit it, but feel now as if I could go over there across the Atlantic and make terms with high government moguls as if I were one of them myself. Kiss me, Ray. I love you."

"Oh, my dear. Oh, my dear, dear!" she said. "How terrible never to be able to find words to tell you how much I love you."

"Darling, what can there be sinful in loving you as much as I do, so long as no one else is really hurt by it?"

How they salved and salved themselves on this philosophy which she had concocted for them out of his and her darts of spiritual neuralgia.

"That is my credo. To live so as to hurt no one else. Otherwise all is fair." (Her phrase.) "I could stay here," he said, in the drugged way he had of talking when his creature-satisfaction was soon to demand completion in her arms, "and let life and international banking and success flow past me like so much water."

She knew that he could not; but thinking of the brownstone house on Lexington Avenue, with its two nurses in uniform, and the three carriages and phaeton, and the implacable stone front to the banking house, and the way his name stood already in tiny type in the extreme northeast corner of the letterhead stationery of Friedlander-Kunz, the miracle of having him there all to herself smote her simultaneously with both fear and ecstasy.

He would be going away, sailing away. The days would be each an empty dice-box out of which every cube of meaning had fallen. Days and days—her lips would not frame the words to ask how many of them; and, as was often the case between them, which invariably they fondly noted, he replied to her unspoken question.

"I know what is on your mind, dearest. It won't be long. I'll be back by the end of August."

This was only May! Even his short trips had been almost unbearable; and now this! She felt her lips twisting and hid them against his coat.

"If only it were possible to take you with me."

He was thinking that there would be Corinne, too, to please. And, strangely, it smote him that leaving his small tender young fowl of a wife would be a deep pang all its own. Two women from whom it would not be easy to be away. There was a prank of circumstance for you! Caring for two such different women in two such different ways. As if life were not already sufficiently complex. Corinne would cry and hang about his neck with those tender arms of hers that felt almost as if the soft flesh were stuffed with a loose mash of farina instead of bone and sinew. They were as relaxed-feeling, those arms, as the paws of a very young puppy. They gave you somehow the feeling of wanting to pinch them. Yes, Corinne would cry. Her Uncle Felix had at first suggested that she accompany him, and then had seemed to reconsider it on the basis of the brevity of the trip. Another time. It would have been pleasant having Corinne along. Corinne would be all right to have along, but Ray, now, would be a godsend! What joy she would take in making everything easier. . . .

"The time will fly, sweetheart, and next trip you shall come along."

She sat with her hands loose and dead-looking in her lap.

"Yes, of course."

"I want you to do some reading up for me while I'm away. Spend lots of time at the library, the way you did for me on the history of banking in Georgia, that time we were negotiating for the state loan. That will fill your time."

"Yes, of course."

"You won't get into mischief, my sweet?"

The question was rhetorical, and absurd, and he knew it and she knew it; and they laughed and came together in their constantly recurring embrace. Mischief! Mischief, when it was difficult for her even so much as to put foot into a world that flowed on the outside of their private happiness. Mischief! The mischief of counting the days. Dear, dear heart. Dear, dear darling. She was embarrassed at the rush of these terms of endearment to her lips, and half the time she restrained them. It was just enough to lie there and cry inwardly at what was about to befall her, and soak in the sweet moments that were at hand.

He continued to be so tender to her that night, that a sudden fear smote her that persons might intuitively act like that before a catastrophe or a death that was imminent. Walter's death, or hers! That was nonsense. His talk was of a future, which, if she was not to share publicly, she was at least to help create.

All night she lay in his arms, and the tide of their ecstasies rose to its peak and receded, leaving them bathed in something stranger and sweeter than peace. When dawn broke, it was he who lay in her arms, the small boy—asleep.

25

That was the year, coming on the heels of President Roosevelt's great journey through the States, which saw the beginning of the Russo-Japanese War, the opening of the Louisiana Purchase Exposition at St. Louis, rainy-day skirts, the Baltimore fire, Fletcherism, lingerie shirtwaists, cigarette coupons, the ratification of the Panama Canal Treaty, and Phoebe Snow.

Into the torrid summer months of that year Ray was to cram mental torment of a variety which, she always averred, but laughingly, endowed her with her first gray hair. Walter, too, always regarded this statement as a joke, when she related, only in part, some of her travail during the period of his absence abroad. But deep down inside her Ray knew how relentlessly she had aged during those lean waiting-months. The gray hairs were dyed out, but the scars were not dyed out. There were little pools of old terror deep in her heart which were never quite to dry.

It all happened so needlessly. The contemplated trip to France, to confer with a small group of petty plenipotentiaries, took form so rapidly that there was scarcely time to collect one's wits. At the last moment, a circumstance so devastating to Ray that she was scarcely able to bear it, Corinne did, after all, accompany her husband, causing a confusion, a hurry of events, that precipitated the period of time they had put apart for farewells into a series of jumbled telephone calls.

Practically before she realized it, certainly before she had time to pull herself together for the ordeal, Walter and Corinne, two children, and a nurse were aboard the steamship, bound for France.

It was in a soggy world of rain-soaked unseasonable wind, uddery clouds swollen with the threat of more rain, that Ray found herself sitting that morning when her clock told her the *Kaiser Wilhelm der Grosse* was just swinging from dock.

At nine o'clock Walter had telephoned her for the last time—contrite bothered messages, filled with obviously restrained endearments and necessarily cryptic explanations of his inability to come to her the evening previous. Their last evening. Their planned evening. No possible time. Sudden change in plans. Felix-Arnold Friedlander's last-minute decision that Corinne and children go too. All muddled. Out of the question to inconspicuously get away from the house. Dear, be patient. Not for long. Keep out of mischief. Get on with the china painting. Read books on banking. Best girl ever. Take care of self. Won't write. Conspicuous. Don't you write either. But thoughts always with you. See you again before you can say Jack Robinson. Wish me luck—Sweet!

He was gone. Step-by-step, sitting there in the rain-soaked morning behind the elaborate paraphernalia of her lace curtains, Ray visualized the procedure. Trunks. Bags. Passports. Carriage waiting at the curb to be stacked with luggage. Corinne in veils. Children. Did Corinne know that for ocean voyages young children should be fortified with extra-heavy clothing? There would be the business of choosing steamer-chairs on the sunny side of the boat; and did Corinne realize that Walter must not be permitted to indulge too heavily in the wide variety of exotic foods for which the steamship line was famous?

To Ray, who had never been on an ocean liner, it was all, nevertheless, so clear. The newspapers were forever describing the arrivals and departures of notables. Many of the men with whom she used to go about had been importers. There would be messages and flowers and gifts at the boat. There stood her own little tissue-paper-wrapped package on the mantelpiece. A pair of handpainted lotion-bottles and a new pair of handpainted porcelain cuff links.

But even had it been possible to deliver them, it would not have been feasible. Caution. Caution. One misstep and one trembled to think. For every precaution of Walter's, she had two in its place. It was better to accept the heartbreaking edict of no correspondence between them—he had shown her how to watch the newspapers for the arrivals and departures of ships. As Walter had assured her in one of those last stolen messages over the telephone, of course it would be possible to have letters from her sent to a secret address, but the unforeseen was so apt to happen. Letters during periods of travel were uncertain quantities. Never tell where or under what circumstances a forwarded letter might overtake. Best to eliminate correspondence altogether, as they invariably did upon his shorter trips. A letter from him to her might tempt her to write. Oh, it was better so. Everything was better so. The days would pass. The weeks would pass. The months . . .

It was a full week after the departure, with its reaction into all the moods against which she had tried to so strongly fortify herself, that her strange predicament first dawned upon her.

Walter had left her with no thought and no talk of money. At the time of his sailing, what with the slight additions of the china-painting income, there was about thirty-five dollars in the house. It was only when this little bankroll of notes began to dwindle that the situation dawned suddenly upon her. Walter, although there had been plenty of time for it their last evenings together, had left without provision for her. In the hurry of departure, and then the omission of that last evening which they had planned, the matter had slipped his mind. Of course he would write or wire her funds. If only he remembered. He was such a child in so many things. The prospect of her little dilemma developing into an acute situation was simply beyond the thinking. But just the same, she broke briskly into one of her ten-dollar bills for a good supply of china for painting.

"Funny feeling," was the way in which she described those first days of her realization of her state of funds. Gave you a funny feeling to have a little thing like this happen to you. Of course, Walter would remember and find some way to wire her money, but that could not possibly be within the next ten days; and what would Mr. Kinley, the agent, think on Thursday, when he came as usual for the rent and the cup of coffee and slice of cake which she always offered him on his monthly rounds. Not that he would mind, for the first time in all these years, being postponed for a few days, but just the same—gave one a funny feeling.

Thirty days later, with the sensation that a steel band was tightening her heart, Ray asked Mr. Kinley for a second postponement, which was still taken with a certain good-humor, but of a sort that seemed to chill that warm day to its core. Neither did he rest for his cup of coffee and slice of raisin-bun, which she baked to what Walter called perfection.

Then and there the summer began in earnest its nightmare. Horribly, as everything consistently seemed to have to be those days, Saperlee, to whom somehow she felt she might have turned in this extremity, had closed her flat, and with much of its trappings departed for Saratoga Springs, where she maintained a "summer flat" adjoining one of the popular hotels. Most of the girls, for that matter, were scattered for the heated months. Hattie, rigidly subject to the whims of her friend from Buffalo, remained on, but it had long since been apparent to Ray that much of Hattie's bravado front was pretense. Ray suspected that secretly she indulged in an abominable, yet somehow pathetic, practice of sharing her excess in funds with a pale, pimply youth who came with frequency to the flat. But the fact remained that with the words jamming on the end of her tongue Ray could not quite bring herself to ask a loan from Hattie.

As luck would have it too, the little group of her china-customers, dissipated by summer, were not within reach. Even her teacher, an enormous Spanish woman who had finally been asked to vacate her apartment because of her insistence to share it with six cats, had migrated to Thousand Islands, where she accepted summer pupils. It was as if suddenly Ray found herself in the midst of an appalling plateau of a summer, so alone that the days seemed motionless and devoid of population, frightening too, as she found herself actually confronted with the incredible exigency of need.

If anyone had told Ray Schmidt, the tony Ray Schmidt of

Cincinnati, that on a certain day in July, along about the turn of the century, she would be seated in her overstuffed, ornament-jammed flat, confronted with the actual problem of where the next meal was coming from, she would have repudiated the prophecy as fantastic. Yet there she sat in the midst of a summer's day that was as hot to the face as a going stove, experiencing hunger pangs for a luncheon that she had not the wherewithal to provide.

Curious that in these days of passionate waiting and hoping, she "had not the heart," as she put it to herself, to cast about for ways and means. She, the Ray Schmidt to whom many a business-man had declared that he "took off his hat" when it came to up and getting, simply sat there in the midst of her torrid misery and imagined that each step in the hallway was the step of a messenger, or that presently that horrid old silent crow of a telephone must ring and convey news to her. Must. Must. Must. There burned in her no sense of shame about thus sitting around. There should have, she reasoned to herself; but where Walter was concerned, none of one's ordinary yardsticks for measuring behavior applied. Not one. She was a different person; she was her obsessed self. Between them there existed neither right nor wrong. Only the oneness. That sense of intimacy with him that transcended one's intimacy with one's self. The way in which he could read the thoughts off her brain almost before they were formed into her own consciousness. . . . No shame between them. No pride. . . .

Sometimes it smote her with a full blast of grim satire, how usual, compared to the vast sweep of hers for him, must be his feel-ings toward her. There was so much, according to the very nature of things, that he could never understand, any more than you could pour a quart of affection into a pint.

Doubtless, even now, as she sat there in the midst of an arid desolation that scorched her spirit, he was innocent. How could he suffer, who did not first feel? He loved her according to the pint of measurement, while she, Heaven help her, as she was fond of saying to herself, was cursed with an absorption that was as blinding as it was blind.

Not much doubt about it, Walter was deep in affairs that

consumed him. Walter, with her memory perhaps lying snugly in his brain, sometimes no doubt even hankering for her, needing her, was innocent of his lapse of thus leaving her high and dry without funds. The capacity was not in him to reach out with his sensitiveness to her plight.

Never generous with her, he was, nonetheless, within his reach, considerate enough of her welfare. What was happening to her would have been terrible to him. Not so terrible though—that she knew—as it was to her, sitting there in the thin wrapper that she had thrust off her back to be free of its contact in the heat, her hands empty in her lap, her knees wide, eyes lusterless, and, most fantastic of all, larder and purse bare of wherewithal.

The need of action smote her dully, as through blanketed perceptions. The thing to do, of course, while she was gathering her senses for action, was to raise money by pawning what she had that was realizable. By that time, no doubt, consciousness of his oversight would strike Walter like a bolt. There would be cables. There must be cables. Even without the need for precaution which had been ground into her, it would never have occurred to her to write. His word was law. Once or twice she found herself passing the sealed and shuttered house on Lexington Avenue, but even that in some way suggested to her the forbidden, now that he was out of the country and away from knowledge of her movements. He would not like her skulking that way. It struck her that there might even be indiscretion in pawning the few negotiable gifts he had made her. That, she came to realize, was nonsense. At a broker's on Sixth Avenue she raised eighty dollars on a gold watch and fleur-de-lis brooch set in garnets, the souvenir spoons, and an opal ring, her birthstone. It seemed to her, with two months out of Walter's three passed by now, that she could manage on that until his return.

How appalled he would be when he knew! In a way, all this horror was, one of these days, going to be worth what she had gone through. His gray eyes would pour pain for the pain he had caused her. He would hold her in the long, silent way she loved, and his compassion would stamp itself against her own heartbeat. Meanwhile, one must live!

In August, despite a schedule of life that for her was frugal, the situation again threatened to become acute. Freda was once more with child. Hugo had lost his position with the gas company, and there was talk of moving back to Cincinnati, where his old situation as meter reader there might be regained. It cost Ray a pang of fear, reading that letter one morning as she lay too supine to rise to the heat of the day, to enclose a ten-dollar bill in an envelope. What if Walter should not return on schedule! The twelve dollars that remained in her purse was ample for the intervening week that lapsed until the estimated date of his landing, but then came the rent again, with the back months due, the eighty dollars depleted, and again there rose the specter of that flabby horror of an object, her flattened purse.

For the first time, lying there day after day, half prostrated from the gummy heat, the grinding noise of streetcars, the humidity of her overstuffed interior, the idea came to Ray, businesswoman, to venture back into that maelstrom from which years before she had so precipitately withdrawn.

Hattie, who, by the way, had bought ten souvenir cups and saucers of her, each with the name of a different friend painted in gold and baked in the china, had finally gone off on a Canadian holiday with her friend from Buffalo. With this last exodus, the flat building with its embalmed-smelling corridors, was as a tomb. The asphalt streets, when she ventured out into them, swam in the heat, and gave like rubber under her feet, adding to the vertiginous effect of August.

It was out into this world, what with Walter already weeks overdue, and Kinley so little the man he had been that when she once more asked for extension he had at last uttered the threat, that there ventured, in immaculate white duck suiting and short-backed sailor with a glass-eyed bird, the timorous figure of Miss Ray Schmidt.

Perhaps it was the timorousness that mitigated so mercilessly against her. Ledbetter and Scape, she learned at once, had gone out of existence; and a firm, in the same building, with which she had done business in the Cincinnati days, had changed entire personnel and gave her scant audience.

It seemed to her that she was like a typhoid patient trying to get back her strength. To think, that of this strange world out here she had once been a vigorous and interested part! She must get back her legs, learn to walk in these regions again. Back in this clanging, interested universe of comings and goings, lurked a Ray Schmidt who was as mysterious to her as if she were observing her own yesteryear's image embalmed in a mirror.

The first day almost exhausted her. To creep back to her flat that had his robe on the bathroom door and his slippers in the cretonne shoebag, was the grateful experience of a tired dog finding his kennel. Before the tomorrow of starting out again, there intervened the long, secure night. Perhaps, before that tomorrow broke, some ship, not scheduled, would bear him to dock.

The thought of telephoning the bank, which had for weeks been hitting her with recurring, hammering insistence, made the instrument hanging on the vestibule wall seem to dominate the flat. Wires emanating from that little yellow box connected her with a source of information. An anonymous voice asking, "When do you expect Mr. Walter Saxel?"

What possible harm? What possible danger? Or she might even creep out to a corner telephone. Like a drunkard restraining his thirst, she did not. Walter would hate it. Silly of him. As if there were watchful detective-like figures lurking to overhear that particular telephone call. And just suppose there were! Then what? What possible harm could come out of slaking her torment with a scrap of information concerning the date of his return? However, she did not.

The thought came to her one day that it might not be difficult to obtain a salesladyship at one of the large department stores like Wanamaker's, Stern's, or Lord and Taylor's. Time and time again, in the old days, she had helped out evenings during the Christmas rush of various Cincinnati stores, and on several Christmas Eves had gone up to Hamilton to assist in Felsenthal's shoe store. She was an efficient saleswoman, with a natural enthusiasm for merchandising. It is possible that the idea might have been more feasible at another time of year. But in August, the ebb tide of all four seasons, her applications were not even considered. Then there was another occupation that had always attracted her interest: that of the women cashiers at their desks in the smart hotel restaurants.

One day, all decked out in the white duck, which she had immaculately laundered, she applied at the Waldorf Astoria, without so much as the knowledge that for such a position she must put forward a bond, to say nothing of a type of reference to which, outside of Walter, she had not the slightest access. Fortunately the matter never even reached those stages of discussion, because from her first word with the assistant manager who interviewed her, it became apparent that the Waldorf Astoria was not in need of cashiers.

On her way out, as she passed Peacock Alley, an incident occurred that sent a quickened feeling rilling in her veins, and a flashing sense of the old days out over her. A robust, middle-aged man in an "ice cream suit" and flashy-looking shirt strolled over from where he had been lounging in one of the chairs, and held his straw cady in the crook of his arm as he spoke.

"Beg pardon, but didn't I meet you at a Knights of Columbus dance and clambake down Cape May last month?"

Knights of Columbus dance down Cape May? How well she recalled the device. Many a St. Nicholas and Burnet House dinner in the old days she had consumed on the acquaintanceship struck up on this sort of fake pretense.

She regarded him and the quivering little places on his moist temples, which somehow always suggested to her a man who liked his beefsteak red, and, with distrust and annoyance apparent in her manner, murmured and passed on.

Now why had she done that? What she needed was a bit of the old-time cheerio with someone as obviously innocuous as this traveling salesman. What was dead within her? What had come alive? Free of the obligation of wifehood, here she was scuttling away like an outraged matron. Besides, the phrase "clambake" had set the juices running along the sides of her mouth. A flashy, good-natured fellow like that would have been all for boarding a boat for Sheepshead Bay, a cooling ride to dinner by the sea. . . . Fool!

It was midafternoon when she reached home, tired, hot, and hungry. The amount of her carfare, breaking into a dollar bill, reduced her purse to a flat object of a few coins, that you could flip as you would an empty glove.

The incredible was happening again. Inevitably, it looked as if she were about face-to-face with what would this time amount to the crisic dilemma of another month's rent. Kinley had given her to understand that. Three nights later, with an appetite for the rich concocted foods that had been fostered on German cookery, she sat herself down at the cleared end of her china-painting table for a meal that represented the expenditure of the last odds and ends of change left from the broken dollar that remained in her purse.

She had read somewhere, probably in one of the *Munsey's* or all-story magazines that were always lying about the flat, of a young woman faced with starvation, who had spent her last fifty cents on a bunch of Parma violets off a vender's tray. It struck her as debonair. But she did not emulate the magazine young lady. With twenty out of her last twenty-five cents she purchased leberwurst, a loaf of rye bread, and a bottle of beer, sitting there alone in the hot dusk of her flat, munching her sausage sandwich, which she washed down with the beer, and staring with large wide-open dreaming eyes at the vast aura of silence around her telephone.

Well, here it was again in all its fantastic horror. The dilemma of actually being faced with need for food. For two days there remained odds and ends about the flat. Soda crackers, condensed milk, fourth of a canister of coffee, end of leberwurst, a jar of maraschino cherries, the loaf of rye bread, sugar, tea, sufficient flour for a dish of spätzle. The spätzle with sausage would have made a meal tasty to her, but she ate them separately, in two meals. Chewing coffee-beans was slightly nauseous, but helped keep down appetite.

Why, people were reduced to this on desert islands, but not within stone's throw of delicatessen windows, where the tilted platters of boiled ham, tongue, cherries, and berries pressed their edible pink meats against plate glass. There was something obscene and terrible and private about sitting hungry in the midst of all this. Not that you were faced with actual starvation, with the negotiable furnishings of a flat all around you, but there were people about whom it was unthinkable that life should slip off the sure cog of stability. Ray was one. Something like the slow fire of anger began to burn.

It was on Friday, cloudy, humid, lowering, after having passed twenty-four hours on tea, which she imbibed slowly and frequently through a lump of sugar held between the teeth, that she began to wrap into a neat bundle, with the intention of realizing upon it, if possible, at the same pawnshop which detained her watch, a silver-plated nut-bowl that had been her father's.

Strange, she afterward reiterated many times to herself, that what did happen should have come upon the moment of her doing this.

A bolt out of the blue, or rather out of the sodden gray of a hot, sticky afternoon! To a ring at her bell, which she answered according to her cautious habit of inserting a toe into the aperture of the slightly opened door, there, in the gaslight, with the reflection shining against the glass, was a figure she recognized on the instant.

"Why, Kurt Shendler!"

"The girl is always right."

She flung open the door, and flew, in her panties, corset-cover, and open dimity kimono, into her bedroom, calling back over her shoulder: "Don't look! I'll be with you in a moment. Well, if you couldn't knock me down with a feather!"

It struck her, as she fumbled into a lace-flounced petticoat, that what she said was literally true of herself. You could knock her down with a feather. Of weakness.

26

Kurt had filled out, with even a threat of rotundity, but there was, to Ray at least, so much of his old gangling self intact, that he might have stepped out of his bicycle-repair loft, except that there was no longer the rim of carbon underneath his square white-rimmed nails, and Kurt's serge suit, while not natty in the fashion that made Walter's hang so well, was cut along the acceptable lines of the well-dressed average.

It was difficult to hold back the tears that pressed at the back of her throat. Kurt, all agog with what to him was a visit, was in reality a visitation. He was succor from Heaven. Well, at least, if not directly from Heaven, from Cincinnati. It turned out not to be even that. Kurt, three years since, had moved to Detroit.

"I tried every way to get my wedge into the hometown, Ray. You know me and my soft spot for old Cin-Cin, but she wouldn't be receptive to the industry. Not an inducement for a factory to settle there. Mistake of the old town's life to let a city like Detroit get us all, hook and bait. I'm in the automobile-part business, Ray. Manufacturing on a small scale in Detroit. Making parts for a firm called Ford."

"You always were interested in the horseless carriage, Kurt."

"Ten years from now it will be one of the big industries in this country. That's what I think of it. Future all ahead of it."

"How in the world did you find me, Kurt?"

"Easy. Met Freda Hanck on the street, in Youngstown, when I

was there two weeks ago on business, and she gave me your address. She was taking her little girl to the clinic when I met her."

"Emma?"

"Guess so. Sore eyes."

(Little Emma! That was terrible. Oh, that was terrible. Sure as anything, a letter would come now in a day or two—a needing letter.)

"And Freda? Guess things aren't going so good for Hugo. He was going to try moving back to Cincinnati, but last I heard he had his job back with the Youngstown gas company."

"I surmised as much. Freda looks right faded out. But you! Ray, I don't believe you've changed a day."

She, upon whom time was resting like a pall, drew down her lids that her eyes might not reveal the desire for tears behind them. Changed a day! In the past months it seemed to her that each day had taken its toll from her vitality, precisely as it had taken its toll from her purse.

"You think I'm looking well, Kurt?"

"You're looking immense. I've had many an up and down since I saw you last, Ray."

"But you've pulled out."

"Happy to say, yes. Not what you'd call on Easy Street yet, as the saying goes, but it looks like I'm getting around the corner toward it."

She placed an impulsive hand upon his knee. "Kurt, I'm mighty glad to hear that."

"I know you mean that when you say it. Why, Ray, I'll wager with anybody in this town who will take me up, that in the next twenty-five years there will be almost as many automobiles in this country as horses."

"What ever became of that gasoline-bicycle patent you once bought up, Kurt?"

He made the mock deprecatory gesture of warding off a blow.

"Lost seventy-five hundred dollars on that in the end, Ray. But I wasn't so stung as it appears on the surface. I just didn't quite have the eyes to see that we had to skip that phase of development, because the automobile was already here. You mark my word, sister, fellows like this Ford, and Duryea, and Stearns, and Apperson, and that crowd, you mark my word, there's a row of fellows already setting pretty to make half a million dollars apiece. That's why I jumped from my little old boat out in Cincinnati, when I saw it sinking, and climbed aboard this here Detroit lugger. Not saying the horse won't always be the majority's pick, but you mark my word, what's coming in the way of big automobile business."

"I wish you everything good, Kurt."

"I know you do, Ray. That's why the warm spot in my heart for you just won't cool off."

"Married, Kurt?"

"No. Guess you know where I stand on that. Freda tells me you've stayed single too. Wouldn't exactly say that was bad news to me, but wasn't that a 'Mrs.' on your bell-plate, as I came up, Ray?"

What a lunk he continued to be! A matured lunk, with even some manner of prosperity and well-being to him, but a lunk he would remain, even if, as conceivable, he realized some of these dreams of business success.

"It's easier in New York, Kurt, to stick a 'Mrs.' on your bell-plate."

"I know what you mean. More security, eh?"

(He knows what I mean. Don't make me laugh. But he is nice, all right. Plain, decent, all-the-way-through nice.) His glasses left the same old bridge across his nose. That sore might open some day. And stay open. What an end for Kurt. He would go on and on in that nearsighted fashion of his, battling against the terrible odds of conditions so much bigger than he seemed to be, and perhaps out of his persistent flair for the mechanical and inventive, he might one day strike it! Quite conceivably Kurt would. And then one of these days that old bridge across his nose would turn into an open sore. Cancer! And eat slowly and terribly and greedily into Kurt and his prosperity and—oh, God, this was flightiness induced by heat—no, no, by hunger—it was the room swaying caused the mind to sway.

"—same old busy business girl?"

"—guess that's what you would call it."

"—your sister Freda says—wholesale millinery house—"

"—yes—now is my vacation—"

"—good—want to see a whole lot of you— What about a good beefsteak-supper at that place down on Fourteenth Street they call Lüchow's? Fellow took me there last night. And then a good show. Only here a week. Show me the town—"

Good beefsteak. GOOD BEEFSTEAK. GOOD BEEFSTEAK.

One didn't cry. One daren't cry. One mustn't cry. The thing to do was to sit quietly, smile quietly, and say quietly something like, "That will be nice." But what if one could not restrain the impulse to do something a little terribly insane? Grasp his hand and sink a tooth into one of his fingers. Oh, this madness! Heat-and-hunger madness. One must somehow trump up the clarity to say, "That would be nice."

"What do you say, Ray?"

"That—would—be—nice—"

And to think that sitting there in that stagnating afternoon— while heat moved into the room like slow pants from some crazed old dragon on a Chinese pagoda, and nothing but the wall of her flesh prevented her topsy-turvy sensation from spilling into shrieks and cries—he could sit there so insulated from her misery. The shock it was to even sit contemplating what it would have meant if Kurt had not come. To sit there another supperless, motionless evening, in a flat to which they had written her a third letter of threat of eviction, and turning off the gas. Dear Kurt. Good Kurt. Godsend Kurt.

"—getting back to my hotel now. The Belmont. Meeting a fellow at six. Call for you round about seven. Biggest treat I've had, seeing you. Now you've got to keep them from pulling the hayseeds out of your country friend's hair, and do a little seeing of this old New York with me. Seven is the hour. Me is the party, who will be on hand."

"Yes, Kurt."

Before she closed her hot eyelids, not three minutes after his departure, and fainted back onto the couch, it struck her how bliss-ful it would be to swoon away, instead of wait away, the hours that intervened between that hot mid-afternoon and beefsteak dinner at seven.

27

It was difficult, crossing streets, climbing stairs, and doing the up-and-down things that gave license, to crowd back the impulse to clutch on to the sleeve of Kurt. That was wrong, because once or twice, by now, Kurt had given back warm little pressures, and it was not his sleeve that one was clutching. It was any sleeve. It was a tangible something to grasp, in a world where everything seemed in the act of falling away, like the objects on a table when you pull the cloth from under it.

No question about it, something—after that first evening at Lüchow's when she had had to hold on to herself in order not to commit the social and gastronomic error of giving rein to her ravenous impulse to bolt the rich, warming "man's dinner"—had perched itself across Kurt's face just as surely as his glasses were perched there.

Heaven only knew, Kurt least of all, what had been in his mind when he looked her up. As he was to retell her, when the thing once more consciously had him in its clutch, it wasn't that she had been consistently to the fore in his mind all these years. No point to pretend that. It was rather that in the interval he had never consciously or unconsciously thought of another woman in connection with his own life, except in terms of Ray Schmidt. Hope had lain dormant for so long, and now that same hope, feeble, was lifting its head. That, to Ray, was the sin of it. And yet, by very virtue of a week of evenings, dining at this hotel or restaurant—Waldorf, Astor House, Knickerbocker, Martin's, Shanley's, Brown's Chop House, Jack's—she encouraged that look, which was as specific as his spectacles, to gleam across his face.

"Ray," he said to her one evening at Shanley's, where they were dining before going on to see Weber and Fields in a burlesque of "Du Barry" called "Du Hurry," "I think I was a fool to give up so easy back there in Cincinnati when you threw me over. I think if I had made a fight for you, I'd at least have got your respect. Women are like that."

She was looking well in a big-sleeved dimity dress with cerise baby ribbon run through insertion, but for the hundredth time she wondered if, more subtly than she gave him credit for, Kurt was not somehow suspecting her of being in some sort of extremity. But no, not even the fact that she, whose generosity was a badge, had not once, in all the week, offered him the hospitality of her table, had apparently penetrated the immaculate simplicity that was Kurt's.

He was precisely what he seemed to be, a man to whom the fascination of one particular woman was irresistible, and who was eagerly, almost pathetically, attempting to get some sort of footing in her affection. What Kurt did not see, he did not query; and what Kurt saw was a beautiful, slightly matured, good-natured Ray, who helped him shop gifts for his sisters in Bellefontaine, Ohio, as tirelessly as in the old days she had squandered her time and her vitality upon his bookkeeping. Saw in her the same Ray as of old, only sifted over now with the slightly mysterious diamond-dust of a metropolitan quality.

Same old good-natured, easygoing, up-and-ready Ray of the days of Over-the-Rhine, only older in a way that was strangely moving, and crammed to the very ends of her long narrow-tipped fingers with something that was everything to his desires.

No, only that which Kurt saw literally with his eyes, did he actually behold. Beneath the surface of a situation so alien to his understanding that he could not have grasped it anyway, it never occurred to him to scratch.

Ray, living in New York, enjoying her vacation from the

millinery-and-trimmings firm, at home in a flat that, so far as his judgment told him, was the flat of any clever New York business girl, was just Ray. Oh, a little bold, some folks might take it, living alone that way, but not if you knew Ray as the boys back in Cincinnati had known Ray. Not if you knew Ray.

Exposed once more to the aroma of a personality from which he had, in a measure, at least, been freed, it was a simple matter for the old headiness to return. After the third or fourth evening, the need of rescinding, in this nightly performance with Kurt—of withdrawing back into the terror of her predicament—impressed itself upon her.

The chicanery to which that prospect reduced her was, even in the retrospect of years, to scorch her memory.

There had been occasions, during these days with Kurt, when, against the prospect of the painful gnawing day ahead of her, she had slipped into the large beaded reticule she carried for the purpose, a roll off the dinner-table, a stalk of celery, a few olives, and, on one occasion, an orange and plum.

That, it seemed to her, must represent the bottom of the abyss of her plight. But as the situation with Kurt wore its way more and more perilously to its peak, she found herself resorting to this: One evening after a performance of the Four Cohens in "The Governor's Lady," as they were having oyster-loaf and beer at a restaurant noted for this specialty, she clapped hands to her brow in the manner of one suddenly recalling an oversight.

"Forget something, Ray?"

His quick and right reaction made it easier.

"I should say I did! Forgot to go down to the store after my money-envelope today, and tomorrow's a Sunday, and Labor Day after that!"

"Is that all?" he said, slapping his wallet-pocket. "Guess I can help you out on that, if you're right good."

"I hate like everything to ask it, Kurt. But I like to pay my rent on the dot. I'm afraid I'll have to strike you for a loan for over Sunday."

His kind, large-boned face broke with pleasure into a smile that revealed the long, yellowish teeth of his narrow jaws. He began pushing bills at her out of his well-filled wallet, his delight in this service so genuine that she could have cried for him.

"Kurt, Kurt, not so much!"

"Take plenty, Ray. It's not good to be short on money over a couple of holidays."

"Think I will, Kurt, if you don't mind. Fifty?"

"Nonsense, take a hundred. I'm not afraid you'll run away. Wish you would, with me!"

She lifted three twenty-dollar bills, pushing back the remaining ones.

"Please, Ray, take eighty dollars, at least."

She crowded back his banknotes, in her hurry and anxiety to terminate the hatefulness of what she was doing.

"This is plenty."

"Just doing a little old thing like this means a lot to me, Ray. Don't be mean."

"I know, Kurt. You're the best thing."

"Ray," he said, leaning across the table, and much red diffusing his face, "does what you told me back there in the old days still hold, or is there a chance? Now, with us both considerably older—life being so short—if I had you, Ray, I'd be twice the man I am, trying to be half good enough for you. Guess you're not of a mind to turn about-face on that turndown you gave me way back there?"

"You mean—"

"Ray, you're not going to make me out-and-ask you all over again, are you?"

"No, no, no."

"My sun just rises and sets in you, always has, always will. And there's all there is to it."

"No, no, no. Please, Kurt."

"That—the way you feel about it still, Ray?"

This, she said to herself, is the folly of unreal people in plays and books. This, she said to herself, is the equivalent of insanity. To sit here saying no, no, no, to Kurt, was to stamp herself with an act that, to one in her plight, bore no relation to rhyme or reason. To be incapable of any of the pride and resentments and outrage which Walter's behavior toward her should so legitimately have engendered, was to own herself stricken with a fatal kind of folly. Here, before her eyes, was the same kind of security that was Corinne's. Here it was! There it went!

"—all right with me, of course, Ray. Seeing you again must have gone to my old head as well as to my heart. All right with me. Forget it."

This was insanity all right. The insanity of being glad, what with Kurt well on his way back to Detroit, that there was a tomorrow to face, which would be filled with the folly of continuing to wait for Walter.

28

The second morning following, which was Labor Day, after Kurt had taken the train, Ray, in a gingham apron, and her hair in a long, loose braid, was making jelly out of two pounds of blue grapes she had purchased at Charles', her mind moving along, over the process of measuring sugar against grapejuice, almost as if someone outside herself were engaged in this small folly of making jelly.

Walter liked grape jelly spread on his bread, as a small boy likes it. She had a trick of adding a touch of the spice of clove and mint, thereby achieving a tartness that was enormously palatable to him. As she sat over the simmering pan, that first morning in a long month of heated ones that carried not even a hint of autumn, a slight smile, like a crescent about to indulge in a sardonic droop, hovered along her face. It did not, however, achieve its threat of curve. The act of doing this close homey chore for Walter was not to be doused by any of the more knowing slants of her mind dancing in the heat lightning of anger, or a realization of the ridiculousness of her plight. There was something impregnable about the comfort of this act of making blue-grape jelly. It kept her from the mad feeling of wanting to cry out loud. It kept her from experiencing impulses to rush, tearing and preventing, down the railroad tracks after the train that, minute by minute, was carrying the security and the safety and the rightness of Kurt away from her growing loneliness and her growing fear.

The *Lusitania* had docked at twelve the day before. She had not quite realized to what extent she had banked on the arrival of that boat. It had not seemed possible that sometime during the afternoon following the landing, the telephone would not crow to announce the voice of Walter.

The ship had arrived on schedule; the hours following had moved on schedule; the grapes were jelling on schedule. Presently she would buckle up into corsets and street-clothes, venture around the block for her tiny supper provisions, return, unbuckle, light the gas, fry herself an egg and strip of bacon, pour the grease over some chopped cabbage to make coleslaw, drink her coffee with her eyes gazing above the cup toward that inanimate crow on the wall—that devilish inanimate crow on the wall—that silent terrible crow on the wall—that damned menacing dead crow—

People went mad permitting black carrion-thoughts to wheel and circle thus in the brain.

"Hayfoot, strawfoot," she began to have a habit of saying to herself. "Hayfoot, strawfoot" was a rhythm to which you could make a bed, stir grape jelly, stitch a turnover to wear around the black-ribbon stock of shirtwaists. Hayfoot. Strawfoot.

To allow herself to worry more and more about Freda's little Emma helped too. Concentrating on the child, who must have watery, pale, astigmatic eyes, according to Kurt's description of her, was more rousing than anything she could think of. The thing to do was to get away, begin over, take up the thread of the workaday life. And—perhaps—adopt Emma! The thing to do was to throw this nightmare off. Take hold, like a person recovering from a sickness. Get out of hell.

Of course, in her heart, she knew that she could do nothing of the sort, and that just as surely as the blood was locked in her veins, so was her inertia to clear herself of this octopus of circumstance locked in her temperament.

How right it would be—how well-deserved for Walter—to walk back into a flat that bore no trace of her. No little personal thing of her own. Only his sticks of wood. All there, waiting, empty, eloquent.

As a matter of fact, after the pouring and the cooling and the sealing of the jelly, she did sit herself down to write to Freda. "Out of a position, for the time, but prospects. Eager to help with the problem of little Emma's eyes. Write, Freda, and tell me everything. I am sure to be on my feet again in no time. Enclosed is a dollar bill for Emma. Please have her write me a nice little note."

It was toward the end of this letter that, without the preamble of telephone or doorbell, in walked, with his derby hat in his hand and a few raindrops glistering on his shoulders, the figure around which, from the first moment she had clapped eyes on it, her emotions had thundered and lightened.

She had often, in contemplation, dreaded this moment for what she feared would happen. She would begin to cry terribly. Ugly, retching tears that should be reserved for privacy. He would dislike them and be cold toward them and no little repulsed, and whatever else she was to endure upon this return, it seemed to her that cold distaste at her exploding agony would be beyond her control to bear.

There were no plans against this return, no scheme for the marshaling of her restraints, just this fear. The fear to cry. The fear to feel her naked, exposed face become the bare and rocky cliff down which the avalanche must plunge. She might have spared herself this dread. She rose, glad with the thought that her dotted-swiss wrapper was crisp, and that there was a bottle of beer on the ice.

"Why, Walter," she said, as he kissed her, "you're wearing glasses!"

The thought struck her that they were unpleasant. An obstacle to his nearness. Just three months, a week, and two days since he had sailed, and yet to her, who had kissed his eyes a hundred-hundred times, how changed and fenced-off he seemed, for the moment, in the shining gold-rimmed spectacles.

He had the perspicacity to lift them off and embrace her again, holding her in a way that was dear to her, arm rigid against her waist, so that she could relax to the limit of the weight against it.

There must have been a ship about which she had known nothing!

"I came in on the *Lusitania*," he said.

A wave of the anger she had anticipated washed over her then. So he had come on the *Lusitania*, and now, almost twenty-four hours later, was the first she knew of it.

He felt her stiffen.

"I've thought of you every instant since, Ray, but it hasn't been possible sooner. Richard has measles. Luckily the ship's doctor didn't pronounce it, or we would have had quarantine to contend with. He was pretty sick for several days, and of course his mother was in a state. It's been serious."

"Oh, my poor boy—poor little Richard—my poor you!" The palms of her hands encased his cheeks while she held his face closer, pouring her sympathy into it. He looked tired, and already there was about his eyes the look of a man accustomed to glasses and deprived of them. She fitted them back. She dragged him to his chair. She began the routine of the countless small deeds that kept him clamped to the habit of needing her. He had been through bad times. Damn, damn, damn, that there should be suffering she had not shared with him. That was what made separation so cruel to bear. With all her sensitivity where he was concerned, Richard, apple of his eye, had sickened, and never once had her intuition telegraphed it to her. Silent months lay between them like a chasm. She wanted to leap them. She wanted the certainty, not the hope, that he was back into the enveloping security that had not budged with the months.

"It's good, Ray, to be back"—and he sighed out, like a man who means it.

She was at her tricks. Bolstering him, quick with refreshment, pouring his beer in a fashion that pleased and amused him, miraculously to its peak, with not a bubble of foam overflowing, and then, collapsible as a traveling-cup, down she went into an attitude on the couch beside him, that fitted him and made his relaxation complete, even if her elbow "went to sleep" with the strain of keeping him at ease, and her hand, against his back, began, after a while, to sting of pressure.

"Ray, you look well. A little peaked from this summer heat I hear you've been having, but you look beautiful to me."

He had always told her she was beautiful.

"Do I? It's because I'm happy you're back. And Walter, you look not only well—but, oh, what shall I say?—successful!"

"I have been, Ray," he said, with an intensity that seemed new to him, but which was abetted because his eyeglasses shone. "I have been, Ray, but more of that later."

"Oh, my dear, I knew you would be—but it has been so long—waiting."

"Successful beyond my dreams, Ray."

"And now—"

"And now—nothing, except these good old times with my good old Ray."

"Good old Ray." It was the first time those three words had been assembled for her. She was not sure that she liked them. Good—old—Ray.

"Bad old Walter," she said playfully.

His eyes widened as he looked at her.

"Bad?"

Now why had she said that? What good was it going to accomplish at this moment? There would be time to establish her self-respect, with herself, at least, by somehow bringing him to judgment for his incredible omissions, and the pain and danger and cruelty and mental anguish he had bequeathed to her during his absence. "Dear old Walter."

He had the look, all right, of a man with whom all is right in the world. His and Corinne's world. All of the squashed-down jealousies that had been pecking her for months came pushing now to the surface. Walter and Corinne and their children. The habit of solidarity must be upon him. Corinne, toward whom, with her mind, she entertained conscience and respect and deep humiliation, was nevertheless a scald across her heart. She and Walter had traveled together, gone into the same staterooms and hotel suites and closed the door after them—together. Signed hotel registers as Walter D. Saxel, wife, and children. All the lean, waiting, scorching months that she had been sitting there in the midst of her terrible embarrassment, the solidity had been solidifying. Unless you were of the stuff that heroines in plays are made of, it was impossible to yield him to that solidity. Yield him? It seemed to Ray, alive to his nearness, thawed to happiness in a way that made her feel as if all her veins were little ice-bound streams suddenly released by spring, that, as never before—that as never before—here lay perfection.

"Walter, Walter, life is so short. We must never again be apart."

"Never, Ray. I needed you terribly."

"Say that again."

"Terribly. Time and time again it seemed that I must cable for you. Just someone to talk to, Ray. Someone to whom I could think aloud. I've been in large affairs, Babe. Of course you read all about how everything went through."

She had not. It had never occurred to her that actually this matter of a state loan was of sufficiently large significance for press notification.

"And Walter, Walter, it was all your doing!"

"Naturally the papers did not treat it from that angle. I wasn't mentioned, but my wife's uncle is enormously pleased, and so is the firm, and of course it is known all over the banking circles."

His wife's uncle! If only he would stop putting it that way. He did it so unconsciously. So solidly. So satisfiedly. Sometimes, on those rare occasions when these forbidden rages crept out like poisonous little mice from their corners, one had to stamp them down and stamp them down. After all, one was there to take what one could get. The fringe of his life. The fringe of his time. If need be, the fringe of his affections. Beggars were not choosers. Thieving beggars who took what was not their right, were not choosers. Take what you can get. Have no conscience about it, because all that life holds for you lies in what you can get out of the fringe to his life. What she does not know, is not hurting her. She has the entire pudding and you are only asking an occasional currant. Take what you can get. Keep what you have, greedily.

"These have been the most strenuous, nerve-racking months of my life, Ray, but they have been worth it, the endless delays and all. I've my pace now. This game no longer has me frightened. I've been through hell, though, getting that pace. I've needed you, Ray."

"Oh, my dear boy!"

"And I've needed this part of my life, Babe. Needed it until it seemed to me I must fly my way across the ocean. Negotiating with men in fezzes who don't speak your language even when they speak Oxford English, and trying to swing big affairs of state with an international background the size of Cincinnati, Ohio, for equipment, is more of a strain than a fellow realizes until after it's over. Time and time again I'd have given the whole bunch of tan-skinned plenipotentiaries for a fifteen-minute look-in on this. I feel like a man who is all of a sudden out of a pair of tight boots into his carpet slippers."

"Never, never let it happen again, Walter," she said, with her lips against the back of his hand. "It has been terrible for me, Walter. Terrible."

"I'll tell you the entire story another day, when I'm not dead-beat, Babe; I'll tell it to you from my first step off the boat in France, when the general manager of the Paris branch met me with some secret diplomatic news that changed the whole affair at the very beginning. I'm tired with my brain and tired with my bones. Is it any wonder, girl?"

"No, dearest, no."

"Did you think about me a great deal, Babe?"

"You know I did. About nothing much else."

"I need to relax. I'll get to relax—here."

"My dear. My dear."

"I've been like a tightly wound clock, for months now. Rest me, Ray."

"My dear. My dear."

"I need to be rested, by you."

"Ray will rest you. Lie here, my love."

His eyes closed; but his lips, against her hand, opened intermittently to whisper. "Tired. Dog-tired. I'm tired. Rest me, Ray. I'm tired."

"My poor tired dear. Rest. Rest."

"I'm tired—tired—"

As he sat there, his weight relaxed more and more against her, and her arm, of pressure, began to grow numb, a tom-tom beating itself softly into her brain:

Hayfoot. Strawfoot.—"I'm tired. I need to relax.—I've been like a tightly wound clock.—I'm tired.—I need to relax.—"

I. I. I. I. I.—Me. Me. Me. Me. Me.—I. Me. I. Me. I. Me.—I. I. I. I. I.

"I've been so pressed, Ray. So pushed. So dazed by it all. I've been so dazed."

I. I. I.

"I like to feel your hand."

I. I.

"I could fall asleep like this. Only I must be going . . ."

I.

"I never knew how really tired I was . . ."

I. I.

"I'll need you, Babe, more than ever now."

"My dear."

"I will."

I.

"I'm so tired."

I.

While he slept, her arm, which she could not relax, took on the feeling of something disembodied from its socket, and the tom-tom in her brain became slow anger.

Not one word, not one question, apparently not one direct concern for the interminable weariness of her waiting months. The worse-than-weariness, the interminable torment, deprivation, yes, actual want. There were soft little paunches sagging slightly from his sleeping face. Indulgences. The soft nonalcoholic face of a man who dined too well. A face that had not been denied.

The planes of her own face, which he had described as a little peaked, were flat. A lean denied face. Not one question. Not one concern. Me. I. I. Me. Not one realization. And it would go on being like this. Trapped by the incredible quality of her folly; trapped there with her arm as numb as it ever would be in its grave, while he slept, relaxed against it. Soiled, sordid, three-cornered predicament. Prisoner to this infatuation which had no ending; prisoner to his happiness, his desires, his well-being. If only he had asked once, just once! It was anger's turn now; and as her eyes grew dry and hot, he stirred and reached up to stroke her cheek while his eyes remained closed.

"That five hundred dollars that I stuck in the bisque basket a night or two before I left—I hope it lasted out all right, Babe. Should have wired you more, but kept thinking every next boat would be mine, and didn't want to risk anything further by wire—"

Before she need reply, he had dropped off again, this time relaxing against the cushion, leaving her arm free of its weight.

What had happened flashed at once to her as clearly as a cameo. Even before she rose, to tiptoe over to the sideboard, where the bisque boy stood in his accustomed place, it was all clearly defined in her mind in its dreadful irony. There was the bisque boy all right! What had occurred was no more than a small incident that had happened to her once before. The bills, inserted by Walter into the fishboy's basket, must have slipped out and rolled down onto the ledge of an "X" of unfinished woodwork reenforcing the back of the sideboard.

There they were! A roll of greenbacks, with a rubber band around it, caught in the upper half of the crisscross of woodwork. Nothing to be surprised about. You pulled out the sideboard a little, and there they were! Things happened that way. She started to laugh. *Sh-h-h.* One must not wake Walter. What if one could not stop laughing. She began to mash her hand against her mouth, to mash back the growing laughter.

Finally, because she could not crowd back the growing, crowing laughter, she went into the clothes closet of the bedroom, and there, crouched in the darkness among such muffling objects as her hanging dresses, let laughter have its way. . . .

BOOK THREE

29

The year that Woodrow Wilson was elected President of the United States, Walter's eldest child, Richard, became fourteen. These events synchronized indelibly in the mind of Ray, because her plan for Walter's birthday gift to his son was a long, framed panel, containing the photographs or pictures of the full line of Presidents of the United States, with those of Taft, Roosevelt, and Wilson autographed.

At Ray's instigation Walter had written to ex-President Roosevelt, to President-elect Wilson, and had sent a messenger to Washington for the Taft signature.

The extent to which Ray had set her heart on Richard's having his birthday gift from his father set off with the finishing touch of that signed photograph of the new President, was little short of fanatical. The photograph was procured all right and, mounted in its frame, which Ray had designed so that it could be enlarged for the photographs of future Presidents, stood wrapped and waiting, on Richard's birthday, for Walter to deliver it to his son. The frame itself was a labor of infinitesimal detail, which had cost at least half a year of minute labor. Of embossed leather, with the names of the various states and territories tooled in it, each name was intertwined with its own official or unofficial flower, the four corners of the panel studded with goldenrod embalmed under crystal disks.

"It's the kind of gift, Walter, a boy can remember his father by all his life," Ray tried to impress upon him during the long period of its making. "Richard is getting to be old enough now for educational presents. Not just toys that cost a lot of money. That's why I was so anxious for you to get little Irma the 'Lilliputian Travel Series,' instead of that doll's house."

"Something in that, of course," Walter had conceded over and over again, but with impatience toward the end. "Her mother wanted her to have that doll's house because it won the prize at some exhibition or other. I'll get her the travel set. As to Richard, that's all very well. I agree. But what is the use putting your eyes out over the embroidery and all that fancy-work of flowers around the names? The boy won't appreciate the amount of work that went into it."

"I want him to know the flowers of the states."

"Rubbish. Leave that to his teachers."

"It's not rubbish for an American boy to know things like that."

"Well and good, but don't get that fagged look around your eyes. It makes you look cross-eyed. Ever know that, Ray? When you get tired nowadays, you take on a curious out-of-focus look."

"Why, Walter," she said, rising and crossing to the mirror, and coloring as she always did when he made reference to her personal appearance, "what in the world put that into your head?"

"Won't do you any good to look now. You're fed and rested. I'm talking about one of your fagged days, when I come in and find you cockeyed from bending over that blamed frame."

"Well, I never," she said. "You do get the funniest ideas, Walter. Here you've been wearing glasses for ages, and I don't even need specs for sewing."

They had just completed dinner in the fashion they had been completing these weekly and biweekly occasions year in and year out; and over in the corner, with the snowy cloth flung to conceal the remains of repast, was the table, which presently, after Walter's departure, she would clear away, in a manner so routinized and familiar to her.

There hung in the portieres and curtains and upholstery of her more-than-ever-overstuffed rooms the same old highly seasoned odors. A faint aroma from a jelled concoction of pig's-knuckles, which under her hand became delicacy. The rich smell of her inimitably brewed coffee. Walter's favorite fish dish of pike, under lemon sauce, from a recipe culled from the old Wielert's days. There seemed to be something of subconscious pride in Walter's attitude toward the inviolability of the changelessness of this flat. Even the two trips to Europe of these late years—Ray each time following discreetly, by another ship, in the wake of "Walter D. Saxel and family"—had not jarred the precious immutability of life in this flat.

Traipsing around Europe, with Ray in the uncertain offing, tucked into this pension or that, somewhere near his pretentious hotel, was one matter; snug here, aloof, insulated in these rooms that were security and relaxation to him, was another. A dear, indispensable another.

With practically every other pattern of his life moving, shifting, jutting off into new forms, and the past decade one that had brought pomp and circumstance into his life, here was the one permanence, the one stability, the one rock against which swift tides pulled in vain.

At least, this was how Ray, when nothing in his attitude or his actions seemed explicable, tried to explain to herself the inexplicable.

Why did Walter, in his forties, and already a vastly rich man— sitting securely, if not in the exact kind of chair that had been occupied by Felix-Arnold Friedlander during his lifetime, at least in one of high authority in the banking house—permit luxury to permeate every aspect of his life except that which he shared with Ray? The luxury of the new four-story home in Fifty-third Street, not a stone's throw from the Avenue. The luxury of a wife who wore chinchilla in her box at the opera. The luxury of a summer home called Castle View. The luxury of permitting himself philanthropy while still in his forties.

And yet, when it came to Ray, whom in the social scheme of things a man would ordinarily reckon as his luxury deluxe, the lack of indulgence that had been characteristic in the beginning, when conceivably his financial conservatism might have been the result of inability to afford, persisted.

But now: the two new one-hundred-dollar bills which he left monthly in the bisque basket on the sideboard did not mean what the sum would formerly have implied. The scale of the value of the dollar had been a diminishing one that decade, as the scale-price of living rose. There had been a thirty-three-and-one-third-percent increase in the rental of the flat; and, even before the World War, the low cost of living that had marked the turn of the century was a thing of the past.

Two hundred dollars a month still meant that an occasional bout at the races, usually in the company of women neighbors whom she met from time to time, or the sale, through the Women's Exchange, of embroidered sofa-pillows with which handiwork she had followed up the demise of the fad for painted china, was a considerable aid in such little side luxuries as the overelaboration of her menu, or a gift for Emma, who was twelve and whose father still read gas-meters.

It was ironically characteristic that Walter usually failed, through forgetfulness, to reimburse her for outlays such as the presidential picture-frame. Or, more than once on their trips to Europe, railroad tickets and steamship reservations had been sources of embarrassment to her, because up to almost the last minute he had failed to provide her with the necessary additional funds. Well, she told herself over and over again, there was only one reason. He wanted to keep intact that which had given him the most happiness. And what had given Walter the most happiness, of that she felt proudly sure, rightly sure, sure in a way that made the unendurable endurable, was the unwavering stability of his life with her. Here was stability without the complications of ambition, the unease of responsibility, the inevitable dilemmas of family. Here was surcease from those things which maddeningly and paradoxically he simultaneously both wanted and despised. It was as if those things which could matter so passionately in the growing complexities of his rôles of banker, philanthropist, member of the Mayor's

Citizens' Committee, Harmonie Club vice president, chairman United Jewish Charity Drive, parent, husband and, in small way, art collector, need matter not at all, here, in the fastness, except insofar as he was sure of avid and sympathetic interest and abetment of all his plans.

No strain here, no conflict. No struggling to get on. No children who, even while you doted on them, had a tendency to pull at tired nerves as if they were so many hurting ganglia. No Corinne, who had changed surprisingly little from the unnervous, prettily plump little person of Richmond Street, except in the elaborate paraphernalia of externals, which gave her life somewhat the aspect of a simple girl walking down a boulevard, attired in a pagoda.

Change, change, everywhere except here. And the way to keep change out of here was to keep small, intact, unnervous, unambitious, untempted and untempting, the unadorned changeless Ray, who, in her middle thirties, had she only had the acumen to realize it, had gained flavor with the curious deepening quality characteristic of the type of woman who matures too soon. As Kurt had exclaimed of her, "Why, Ray, you look younger than you did at eighteen." In a measure that was true, because at eighteen she had looked way and beyond her years.

Corinne, now, had ripened out of her swiftly transient girlhood into this little dowager who easily looked her rôle of mother, and whose lust for the position and power and wealth of her husband and children was the animating force of her life. That was right. That was what it should be. A man sat at the opposite end of his long and elaborate table from Corinne, as her hair began regally to gray, and her pearls, more than ever, were no creamier than her flesh, and gloried in this wife and mother who graced his board as fitting complement for the growing solidarity of his life.

If the persistence of her various pressures upon him made him nervous and even unnerved him, and her lack of playfulness, as she grew older, her almost insane indulgence of her children, her tiny snobberies, her limitless faithfulness, her impeccable motherhood, her unassailable righteousness and conspicuous virtue, continued to drive him more and more surely and more and more securely to the less exacting atmosphere of a woman who also fed him well and loved him not wisely but well, the fact remained that in the house on Fifty-third Street there resided, in virtue, the fitting complement for the growing solidarity of his life, his importance as a conspicuous citizen and high type of Jew, his success, his philanthropies, art-interests, and expanding ambitions.

It was difficult, indeed impossible, to explain, even to oneself, the tremendousness of trifles. Never, in this flat, "Ray, are you tired?" but, "Ray, I am tired." Never, "Is it convenient for you, Ray, to hold dinner until eight tonight?" but, "Ray, have dinner at eight." Never, "Are you depressed?" but, "I am depressed." Never, "Can you?" but, "I cannot." Never, "Do you prefer?" but, "I prefer."

As he repeatedly said to her—and for some reason it pained her to hear it—she fitted him like an old glove.

The nearest she ever came to voicing some of the unconscious bitterness that on occasion would surge against him, was once when she said to him, quite playfully, "That is because I guess always I must be content to walk skulking along the back streets of your life." And he, who was notoriously quick to take offense, had sulked days after this.

"Why, Walter, I meant what I said, but I'm not complaining. I like it. Suppose I do walk the back streets of your life. I love them because they are your life."

He could turn sulky with a suddenness that never ceased to terrify, past master that she was at placating.

"I despise veiled discontent. I would much rather you would come out with what you have to say."

"With what I have to say! Walter, silly, what in the world could I have to say in that respect?"

"That is precisely what I cannot understand. I cannot see much back street connected with all the comfort you need, a trip to Europe every couple of years. The fact that you cannot travel on the same ship with me or live in the same hotels, seems hardly to need discussion. I—"

"That is just sort of what I meant by back streets, Walter. Nothing more. Of course it is wonderful going to Europe, but I, being piggy, would so love it if things were different, so piggy could cross on the same ship with you and not live in pensions around the corner from her Walter's hotel. That's all I meant. . . ."

"I see. In order to make things more thoroughly impossible and even more dangerous than they are?"

"Silly. Did I say anything like that? I was just trying to imagine what it would be like if we didn't have to do it this way. That's all I meant, Walter."

He was difficult to placate; and, strangely enough, the tactics she employed to bring him round were precisely the ones he employed with Corinne when something petty had incurred her displeasure which, in its way, was as quick off the trigger with Walter, as his could be with Ray.

Often it occurred to him, as she sat humbled before him, coaxing, placating, how strange it was that his methods in coaxing his wife out of a mood of real or fancied wrong could be so identical with hers.

"Walter, I love you. Say that you love me."

"Just let me alone for a while, Ray. I need to be alone."

Rigidly he could withstand her importunings for a period of hours, submitting with averted face to her touch, to her pressure, to her chirpings and her pleadings. "Walter, if you really loved me you could not hold out against me this way."

His capacity to remain silent was eternally baffling to her.

"Walter, sometime I'm going to try and get angry with you and stay that way, if only I could. . . ."

"I am not angry."

"You are!"

"You are what you are, that's all, and nothing can change you."

"But, Walter, I only meant . . ."

"'Back streets of my life.' Do you think it's pleasant or easy for me? A man in my position? Lies. Evasions. Fears. My children growing up. My affairs more and more in the public eye. It is danger every instant, and now I suppose you want a pair of marble front stairs on which to air the situation."

Was this the Walter who could be so suave—the Walter who

practiced after-dinner speeches in this very room, after she had typed them on the machine she had recently acquired and mastered as a surprise to him? Was this the Walter she had seen ride up the avenue in high hat and a big Packard car, in the wake of some distinguished visiting personage who was being conducted to the mayor by the Citizens' Committee? This snarling petty boy with the angry tan darkening his face.

"Oh, Walter, how can you think such things?"

"If you had any conception of what it means to live day and night the kind of life that could ruin you!"

Why hadn't she the pride to throw his freedom in his lap? Hundreds of times that question had moved tormentingly in her breast, and each time her sole response had been to wind her arms about his neck, coax his reluctant eyes around to hers, placate him with every method at her command.

"Walter, isn't our love worth it?"

"I suppose it is, or I couldn't go on."

"You know it is."

"I don't know anything."

"Walter, darling, you know it is."

"All right, anything you say."

This mood was terrible to her. Impenetrable, sometimes for hours.

"I'll go now."

"Walter, not this way. I couldn't stand it. I couldn't sleep. Don't leave this way."

"Well," resignedly, "what do you want me to do?"

"Smile. Be bright. Be sweet."

"Oh, I see. Smile because you feel as you do about the back-st—"

"Walter, if you don't stop putting words into my mouth that I didn't say, I'm going to treat you the way you would treat your little Irma if she were naughty, and stand you right over there in the corner. Darling, don't you know that the back streets with you are more than Heaven would be with anybody else? I'm happier here than I would be sitting in the first row of your box at the opera. I've had lovelier times in my little pension in the rue Cambon in

Paris than anybody could have at the Crillon with you. I love the little ships I cross on and the flat I live in and everything about everything—Walter—darling—"

His resistance gave way, reluctantly, but surely. Reconciliation, when it did come, swept him, on a wave of contrition, into her arms.

"You shouldn't torture me, Ray."

"Oh, my darling, I'd cut off my right hand first."

"You are my everything."

"And you are mine."

"Everything I have the strength or the purpose to do dates right back to you. I wouldn't have the courage to face this terrible game called success, without you."

"Oh, Walter, one minute I'm way down in the cellar and a danger and drain on you, and the next minute you put me up there on a pedestal. I'd rather be somewhere in the middle. It's safer."

"I can't ever place you high enough. There is not an hour in the day that I am not leaning on you, even if it is one of the days we don't meet. It isn't only your advice about everything pertaining to my life, Ray. It's more than that. It's the knowledge that there is one person capable of something utterly selfless and unselfish where I am concerned. No children to come between, no social consider-ations, no worldly ambitions, no money-grabbing, no family poli-tics, no consideration but me. . . ."

(Me-Me-Me-Me-Me-Me-Me-Me-Me-Me.)

"I love you, Walter."

"I love you, Ray."

"Say it again."

"I love you, Ray."

"I love you, Walter, I love you."

30

It should be said for Walter that his part in a drama that was to be played against the background of economics, diplomacy, philanthropy, and ultimately the war, international affairs, arms, armistice, and finance of high and intricate order, was to lodge in his mind as nothing short of phenomenon and accident of circumstance.

Long before America made formal entry into the World War, the firm of Friedlander-Kunz had already established conspicuous precedent for what was consistently to remain its policy throughout the holocaust years.

On the other hand, even when Ray had occasion to sit in the vast, red, gold-filled mouth of the Metropolitan Opera House, and listen to Walter attempt to inflame an audience that had been gathered there in the name of affiliated charity, of which he was a vice president, or as in later years, when she was to behold him seated on a dais beside men upon whose judgment the destiny of America in world war was to be decided, there seemed nothing incongruous in this evidence of his place in the affairs of men.

Not once, upon the occasion of Walter's active part in one of the largest drives in the history of organized charities, did it strike Ray, that afternoon in the Metropolitan Opera House, that it might be a far cry from the remote, diminished-looking little citizen with the authority to plead from that immense stage for the financial cooperation of the nation, back to the black-haired, gray-eyed youth she had first encountered on the coping of the C. H. and D. railroad station in Cincinnati. His place seemed rightly here among men of weight in the affairs of state and finance.

From where Ray sat, these men of weight were specks, animated shirtfronts, dots for features, reminding her in formation, of Lew Dockstader's minstrels. Only Walter emerged for her, the lineaments of his face filled with clarity, his address of flowing lucidity to her, partly, it is true, because she had composed and rewritten it time over again, on her typewriter.

Even the detail of his small black tie was apparent to her across the vast depth of auditorium. She had retied it for him, finally removed it, pressed, and retied it to a nicety.

Walter's was not an impassioned speech. Mayor Mitchel, Otto Kahn, Felix Warburg, John Finley, had previously moved the audience to tears, cheers, and checks. Walter's, on the other hand, was a careful and studied compendium of statistics and laboriously accrued facts which he had placed in a sheaf on the typewriter in Ray's apartment just twenty-four hours previous. Infant mortality. Aged Blind. Crippled Catholic children. Protestant Big Sisters. Jewish Juvenile Delinquency. The paper he was reading was her careful compilation of statistics, reports, budgets, pertaining to the sectarian charities of the city.

She wished passionately, sitting there bending forward to lose no sound, that he need not have to read it. Part of the success of his predecessors lay in the gesture of conviction, the moist eye, the booming and diminuendo voice. Walter's voice almost droned through his material. Walter, who could not bear to see a thinly clad child shiver, or encounter an elderly beggar! In the flat before the mirror, there had seemed to her to be the forthright qualities of vigor and passion in his voice. And now here, suddenly, before the thousands, something in Walter failed to project itself.

"Read, Walter, as if the needy poor were standing in hordes behind you, egging you on. Read, Walter, as if your own babies were undernourished and thinly clad and you were pleading for them."

All very well and good within the well-warmed crowded little room that was so benign to him at all times. There, his voice did boom, and his eye command; but here, in the impersonal vastness, that voice became the recitative one of the statistician, his impassioned plea took on the key of faint harangue, and the audience began to squirm. There was no showmanship in Walter's manner of address, which by its very nature needed, in order to challenge response, to be shot out of the cannon of a personality.

With a sense of frenzied futility, sitting there in the balcony, her hands white at the knuckles, Ray felt his poorly projected fervor and yearned for the power to somehow divert it into ringing blasts against a slipping audience.

Years later, before a war audience, in that same auditorium where hundreds of thousands of dollars were to be raised in a Victory Drive, he was to fail her even more devastatingly than now; was to hold back the self, which before the mirror in her flat, could sometimes seem to rise to impassioned oratorical heights.

How innocent Corinne seemed of all of Ray's kind of raging travail at the parade of his inadequacies.

In the third box to the right of the first tier, as if they were sitting for a portrait of "Mrs. Walter D. Saxel and children," were Corinne, Richard, and Irma. Corinne in a small mink toque with aigrets, a handsome mink jacket thrown open, and a shower of lace flowing among her two strings of pearls on her small high bust. Every inch the prideful, secure wife, the impeccable mother, the entrenched, the chaste, the normal. Everything had happened right in its place and in its order and as it should be, to Corinne. It always would. Life would see to that. Walter would see to that. Even her children were already grouped about her in a small barricade. Richard, gawkier even than when last she had spied him at the occasion of Walter's helping to officiate at Flag Day exercises. A tall, supine young fellow, strangely unlike either Corinne or Walter, but said to resemble the Frankfurt-am-Main Friedlanders. Irma, in the plump fair image of her mother, a fan of lovely yellow curls, spread as if drying in the sun along her lace collar.

They were like a dream, down there in that box, so snugly partitioned by brass and red velvet, a warm fragrant dream of security and solidity, a dream tinctured with nightmare. There were, in addition, two distant cousins in that box. Strong, lean, aquiline maiden women, with strong dark hair mixed with gray, and heavily decked out in the beautiful twenty-two carat gold-scrolled jewelry of the period. They were Hanna and Jennie Friedlander, maidens of vast inheritances, and, according to many a humorous recital by Walter, pests in the Saxel household. But nonetheless they were part in the solidarity. The entrenchment of Corinne. The entrenchment of the Friedlanders. Of the Saxels. Of the race.

How different the falling away of her own family had been. It was more than a month after Tagenhorst's death that little Emma had written Ray, thanking her for a ten-dollar check for an Easter gift, and adding, almost by way of postscript, the serious accident to her grandmother of a fall over a porch-rail while shaking a rug, the indirect results of which were so ultimately cause of her death. Even though she sent money to her people, as she constantly did, with the gleanings of her racing, china painting, and sofa-pillow money, and kept what contacts with them she could, by way of letters, small gifts, the solidarity was lacking. The superb solidarity of clan, which, with a paradoxical insistency, was something to admire, even while it continued to crush and defeat her.

There was, to be sure, her pride in Emma. The never-ceasing thrill of "Aunt Ray" with which her lusterless little letters began. Emma, from her photograph in first-communion dress and veil, was blonde, pasty, terribly nearsighted behind thick lenses, but, withal, a source of pride to Ray that could reduce her to the impulse of tears. There was strange solace and inner satisfaction in standing before the cabinet photograph of Emma in her communion dress and bouquet of carnations, and letting unshed tears obscure her into Ray's dim idealization of what Emma should be. Not frail and pasty and weak-eyed, but, through the blessing of tears, lovelier than loveliness. But even this rather vicarious yearning of a stepaunt over a stepniece was not quite the thing which you could almost trace by a dotted line, as they did in comic strips, from the calm safe eyes of Corinne to the figure of Walter, framed in the huge proscenium.

Damn them. Curse them. Bless them. These solid Jews. These sticklers for one another. These tight units of kith and kin, which

are more ostracizing than ostracized. How they did for one another!
The charities of Jews in the name of Jews! Honor thy father and thy
mother and the old and the broken ones of the tribe. All denomina-
tions, of course, gave by way of charities, to their own; but, somehow, it seemed the Jews who, self-conscious with past pain, gave
more bountifully, to spare their own future pain. Already, before
he was fifty, Walter's name was well to the fore of practically every
large charity in the name of his people. By the time he was fifty,
the Corinne Saxel Wing in the Mount of Olives Hospital was
completed. By the time he was fifty-three, he would have given
away his first million. You could count them off, too, the Jews
who, like Walter, the country over, were giving in the name of the
solidarity.

Try to break in. Try to crash the gate of Jewishness. That dotted line from the eye of her there in the box, surrounded by the
indescribable wealth of his children, to the eye of him there in the
proscenium, no larger than a raisin, but filled with the mysterious
mucus of family solidity.

Yes, even defeated by it, ostracized by it, she could not look
upon the calm little-dowager prettiness of Corinne—whose hair,
whitening, made her lovelier—and not thrill, and at the same time,
paradoxically, maddeningly, not feel bitter, rankling, hurting, and
soiled.

That was the part, this last, this feeling of smirch, that one
never dared quite to meet.

Leaving the opera house, crushed into the crush, as so many
times she had grown accustomed to nestling herself in the anonymity of the throng, at piers, at theaters, in hotel lobbies, in various
public places, there they were! Corinne, the Misses Friedlander,
Richard, Irma, almost close enough to touch. She could in fact
have reached out and tapped Walter as he joined them. The crowd
milled and detained them. There was a bright flush on Walter's
cheekbones, and his children reached out to him, and his women
laid hands upon him, and there were handshakes from those who
knew him and from those who ventured to extend the stranger's
hand of congratulation.

More and more, as the public aspect of his life claimed him, he insisted upon Ray's presence in the throng. It made subsequent discussion so much more vitally their common interest if she had heard his address, witnessed the same play or opera, been present at the same ceremony, or attended the same art show or auction. She had learned to be clever about this last, comparing art catalogues, digging out the history of paintings at the public library, inspecting the collection at close range long before the day of sale.

Then, too, on occasions like the present one, it was part of her duty to keep her ear primed for comment. Helpful hints, as Walter called them, demanding of her the uncomplimentary along with the plaudits. She knew better than this last. "Oh, Walter, the elderly man sitting behind me thought your voice carried magnificently." Never: "Oh, Walter, I sat next to Mrs. Sparfeld, the wife of the senator, and she said that you had the most tiresome voice in the world, no delivery, and that you gave her a pain in the neck." Never: "As I was leaving the balcony of the One-Thousand-Dollar-a-Plate Charity Dinner, I heard a woman in the spectators' gallery say you were a wolf in lamb's clothing. Not only a wolf in Wall Street, but a wolf who prowled up forbidden lanes."

That remark was six months old. What had it meant? Their discretion was so perfect. Their rule, never to be seen in public together, so rigid. Was this figure of herself, Ray, still modish, slim, solitary, skulking the back streets of his life, becoming noticeable?

For three months in Paris she had lived within a stone's throw of the Crillon. An entire season at Aix-les-Bains she had occupied a room in a pension just a flight of hillside stairs below the hotel where Walter and Corinne had taken the cure. Nightly, she had skirted the tables at the Casino, sometimes standing elbow to elbow at the gaming-tables, or within easy eyeshot of Corinne, and yet never once had they appeared in public or even exchanged greetings.

What had it meant—a wolf who prowled up forbidden lanes? What secret prying eyes might be tunneling under the foundation of her phony security? Nonsense!

It was in the milling of the crowd around her, the day of the conclusion of the Charity Drive at the Metropolitan Opera House,

that Ray, her ear cocked for titbits for Walter, heard spoken, at her
elbow, a remark which, directed against herself, raced down her
spine like a mouse.

"There she is! The tall one in the broadcloth suit with the silver
buttons. Saxel's shadow. They say he's been keeping her for fifteen
years. . . ."

31

The year he became president of the Affiliated Charities, Walter turned the Cape May house, Castle View, into a temporary home for convalescent children. Later he was to bequeath this Georgian seventeen-room mansion, on its two hundred acres, to the township of Cape May as a permanent seaside vacation ground for children from the New York tenements.

During the summer of 1915, which was before his acquisition of the even more elaborate estate of Rye, this voluntary evacuation had the effect of throwing awry plans for a summer at Cape May which had been more meticulously laid than usual.

The reason for this was to come to Ray later in a shock so blasting that she fell into the habit of dating her life before and after the episode of Youngstown. Part of the repercussive effect of this shock was the fact that she could find herself unhorsed and thrown into indescribable confusion by an isolated circumstance which, after all, was only part and parcel of a general condition which she had learned from the start to endure.

The turning over of the Cape May house, coming as an eager impulse from both Walter and Corinne, exerted no small pull upon the affairs of Ray.

For several summers, at Walter's insistence, she had occupied, in the township proper of Cape May, the small furnished flat of a druggist and his wife who, eager for the summer income, moved into the quarters of a tent colony on the beach.

It was a pleasant little apartment over the drugstore, on a busy street, but within walk of the ocean. Electric lights flowed into her front windows at night, and in many respects there was less of the shrouded feeling of isolation there than in the flat in town. It seemed to Ray, all things considered, that her times there with Walter had been happiest of all. Away from the propinquity of his affairs, a pretty well-worn-down vein of playfulness was in the habit of asserting itself, carrying them back to the lighter moods of the old Cincinnati days. He was freer to be himself, there. And often, against their rigid precedent, they strolled out together of late evenings, down toward the moon-swept, breeze-swept, deserted end of the beach, where white sands, the color of casket-plush, sparkled, and magic stole out.

Ecstasy, of a kind that made everything disenchanting that was already written into the years seem not to matter, touched these moody tender evenings with Walter. Their hands stole together, and locked, as they walked; their feet shushed softly into the white sands; and sometimes they sat and built around themselves a mound of it, as children might have. Two human specks, filled with the immemorial lure of the flesh.

Even the long days alone in the flat over the drugstore on the shoddy little street, or of wandering alone on the unfrequented ends of the beach, sometimes directly past the two Saxel children, or even past Corinne herself, strolling the sands with her husband or friends, were tinged with some of the retrospective or anticipatory sublimity of those few evenings.

The decision to abandon the Cape May plans for the summer came as a combination of keen disappointment and yet strangely, with a certain relief. On the one hand, release from the propinquity of that scene of the pouter-pigeon little figure of Corinne entering the country club, driving her own little electric sedan along the high road, twirling her parasol as she strolled the hot sands, or sitting beside her husband in the large Pierce-Arrow! And then, on the other hand, the sweet and all-too-fugitive visits from Walter, the little chintz parlor over the drugstore, which she had aided and abetted with some of her own manifold small objects carted from town, the cretonne-covered chaise longue preferred by Walter, the late suppers and all-too-hurried dinners she prepared on the gas-range of the druggist's wife. The tender moods of Walter beneath moonlight on white sands. . . .

He explained his decision to her, one muggy May evening, as they sat on the divan, the remains of the recent repast dragged into its corner.

"It's the thing to do, Ray, and more than that, it is expected of a man in my position. I see where Felix Waldheim has given Waldheim Park to the Mothers' Fresh Air Association."

"Oh, it's right that you should, Walter."

"Certain things a man has to do. Besides, I want to do it."

She thought, sitting there in the crib his arms made for her, how unbearable life would be without him, and how much, after all, there was to be grateful for, in a life that contained him, and how ennobling the whitening hair was to his face, and how she must somehow, some way, find it possible to trump up within herself some of this urge for what to her sometimes seemed the machine-stitched methods of wholesale philanthropy. The passion of the springtime of their love, perhaps, had quieted, but the passion of her surrender to his every conviction, wish, desire, spoken and unspoken, continued to lash and dominate her unabated through the years—a slavery that was precious to her, a subservience that exalted while it abased.

Were the emotional experiences of women like Corinne or the "girls" with whom Ray spent the rim of her time, in any way akin to hers? There had been plain talk among the latter, much of it revealing. Women like Hattie—who had long since drifted out of her life, changing residence as she changed allegiance—had a give-and-take philosophy that placed this complex question on a plane almost as simple and tangible as bookkeeping. Debit. Credit. Give what you must. Take all you can get.

Even Corinne, viewed from the strange sidelines of Ray's position, trafficked in reciprocity and demanded of her husband in return for what she gave.

"Corinne feels I owe it to her and the children . . ." was not infrequently on Walter's lips. With acceptance.

Why was it that she alone seemed so dominated by an incalculable passion that was infinitely bigger than her resistance to it? A man thought no more of you for it; less, in fact. That was the slogan of the women.

How dear and tired and small-boyish he looked, sitting there beside her. Life was wrong for her, terribly wrong, and yet nothing it might ever have contained without him could equal the fugitive sweetness of these edges of his time. Pride was for those who knew not the perfection of complete giving. There were times when you almost gloried in lack of pride. Gloried in the fact, for instance, that during the summers at Cape May you could slink up the back streets of his beautiful lawns, for the private sense of his nearness which it gave you.

"Giving over your house means no summer at Cape May, Walter. What then? Will you rent a house?"

"No. Richard wants to tutor this summer. We thought we'd send Irma and Mademoiselle out to the Friedlander sisters at Long Branch, and go to Mount Clemens for six weeks to get some of this rheumatism baked out of my arm."

"Walter, I think that would do you good, if only you will watch your diet too."

"My intention was to go alone, but Corinne is feeling none too well herself."

His way of preparing her for the item that Mr. and Mrs. Walter D. Saxel would spend May and part of June at Mount Clemens, Michigan.

"We leave on the twelfth. Think you'd better come out about the following Sunday, Ray. We can manage the way we used to at Aix."

Yes. That meant that about a week following the arrival, at the resort's best and largest hostelry, of Mr. and Mrs. Walter D. Saxel

and maid, a Mrs. Schmidt, tailored, chic after a slightly horsy fashion, nicely caparisoned with rather sporty looking luggage, and the
slim, slightly lined look of a woman who ages slowly, would step off
a train and debark for one of the lesser hotels, where reservations
awaited her. Usually a small suite, near a bath. A private bath would
have meant much to Ray, who enjoyed lengthy ablutions. Not that
Walter would have noticeably observed the indulgence, but somehow it was out of key with the scale he allotted her. "Keeping me
small." A commodity. Not a luxury. Sometimes, in his own way of
facing it, and in a vernacular highly different, that was also Walter's
own way of explaining his sparseness with Ray.

The hotel at Mount Clemens where Walter had instructed her
to write for accommodation was a rambling redbrick structure situated on one of the central streets of the sulphuric-smelling little spa.
Big interurban trolley cars, which ran the twenty-five miles from
Detroit, passed its doors; and figures in hooded bathrobes hurried or
rode in invalid-chairs through the streets.

The Grove Hotel, situated on the edge of the town in a small
park that overlooked a canal-like vista of St. Clair River, boasted
wide verandas lined with rocking chairs, a pretentious rotunda with
a colored-glass dome, flower gardens, billiard rooms, grill rooms,
quite elaborate private suites, a private bathhouse where the curative waters were piped into large tiled rooms, and a cuisine for
which it was justly renowned. On the opposite corner, in a white
frame structure with perpetually drawn blinds, giving it the look of
a gentleman's residence closed during the family's absence, there
flourished, between intermittent tiffs with the law, the complement
of a Casino, where guests from the larger hotels gathered for games,
from lotto to faro.

After their two trips to Europe, with their sojourns at Monte
Carlo, Deauville, Vichy, Nice, Aix-les-Bains, there was something
about it all that offhand seemed shabby, insular, and provincial. And
yet, withal, there was thrill in this first return to the Middle West. It
struck her with a kind of strange excitement, as she changed trains
at Detroit for Mount Clemens, that just within a few hours of her,
in Youngstown, there dwelt the nearest of her kith and kin. Gave

one a sense of belonging. It was pleasant to think of "my people" in Youngstown, just as it would have been pleasant to drive openly to the Grove Hotel and register there—openly—

In Mount Clemens there was even more time to herself than usual. The routine of the mineral bath, the massage periods, the aftermath of relaxing, kept Walter, who suffered from a rheumatic right arm, confined to his room until noon. After lunch, what with the limited activities of the little spa, sailing or fishing or motor-boating on the narrow river, which opened out quite grandly into Lake St. Clair, cards at the Casino, buggy riding, automobiling, or gay trolley parties in chartered cars to Detroit, to say nothing of a surprising and new insistence on the part of Corinne for Walter's almost constant presence at her side, it was, as Walter put it, almost impossible to "break away" for the Medes Hotel or an assigned meeting place.

After the women had retired to their rooms for siesta, the men lingered over cards or billiards; and even to attempt to drop out was to incur the uninvited company of one or two of them for a walk. Usually it was six o'clock, and then not daily, before Walter man-aged to snatch an hour to visit Ray in the small brown sitting room of her suite.

Not that this was without precedent. Once, at Deauville, because of the fast complexities of the life there, a week had elapsed without Walter once communicating with her at her pension. Although never before so exacting as now, Corinne was wont, how-ever, to claim the bulk of her husband's time on those occasions when she was able to sojourn with him away from the demands of his banking-hours.

"I'm sorry, Ray, I'd no idea this town was going to be such a goldfish bowl. You had better arrange to be at your hotel every day between four and seven, but the rest of the time you'll have to rustle around and keep yourself entertained. Corinne has her heart set on that Detroit party for tomorrow, and it won't do for me to decline to go to that launch trip J. P. Terhune is planning for Thursday. Terhune, as you know, is an important connection in New York. I don't believe, if I were you, I would come around to the Casino again, Ray. It is not like Aix or Monte Carlo. The rooms are small and not always crowded."

"It's all right, Walter."

"These baths are doing me a powerful lot of good. Even this terrible ill wind of war has blown some good. I don't believe the Carlsbad waters are any better than these. Shows a fellow that America has got pretty nearly everything, if he knows where to find it. Feel my knuckles."

"Splendid."

"Funny thing, Ray, I'm not seeing a blessed thing of you, except once in a while up here in your sitting room, but I need you here. That's all there is to it, I need you just as much as I need the air I breathe."

She had meant to ask him something that secretly and even painfully was gnawing at her, particularly since the remark she had overheard at the Metropolitan Opera House some months before had sharpened her perception.

Why, suddenly, was Corinne demanding all the free little edges of his time that heretofore she had allowed him without question? Late evenings, when, once or twice, he had ventured out for a walk, she had demurred. Walter had admitted as much in explaining failures to arrive at her hotel. Even his noon hour was now greedily mortgaged. But for the whirlwind exception of the gala week at Deauville, where, by the way, in her spare time, Ray had managed to win five thousand francs, there had never been a time when Walter could not, without question, manage to be away for luncheon.

In Mount Clemens all that was different. Three meals a day Walter took in the company of his wife. After the Casino, where often Corinne took a seat at the lotto table while Walter played the wheel, for conservative stakes, it was straight back to the hotel with his wife.

Why?

What atoms in Corinne's mind had been set in motion? Why these tiny new tactics? One morning she had by chance encountered Walter on the main street of the town, shopping strawberries for Corinne, who had suddenly expressed a desire for them. Why

these tiny new tactics? The question, though, which had trembled on her lips for so long, once more remained unsaid. Why set
into motion disquieting fears? Besides, in his present conciliatory,
explanatory mood of trying to placate her for his enforced defaults,
all her ready tenderness flowed out to meet his dilemmas; and in a
sense it was sweet to suffer the waiting around, or sit out the long
evenings in the crammed lobby of the Medes, talking aches and
symptoms with the garrulous and the decrepit.

"Just make up your mind we are not going to see much of each
other this trip, Ray, and figure yourself out a good time. There are
races down at Detroit, go win yourself a pair of new shoes."

So conciliatory was his mood for having dragged her out there
for the chief purpose of sitting hour after hour around the Medes
lobby, and finally in desperation herself taking the cure, that when
he departed, one evening, he left a hundred-dollar bill on the table.

"Go to the races. Kill time."

Dear boy. The thought was infinitely sweeter than the hundred.

One day she did trolley to Detroit on a shopping-tour for a
little ruby lavaliere, Emma's birthstone, which she had long contemplated, and which the hundred dollars made suddenly possible.
Paying back to herself money she had expended for Walter out of
her china painting and Women's Exchange earnings was her way of
explaining to herself this defection in her rule that Emma's gifts be
paid for in special coins of her own earning.

In the jewelry section of the foremost department store in
Detroit she found a pretty lavaliere on a fine gold chain, set with a
good-sized ruby surrounded by tiny "chip" diamonds. Compared to
the cost of similar ornaments in New York, it was a bargain at thirty-
five dollars; and it pleased her to send it with the Detroit postmark.
"Souvenir from the Wolverine City," she wrote on the card; and for
days thereafter she could visualize Emma, fingering excitedly at the
gilt cord, clapping her hands with delight, exclaiming!

But, in all, the journey was a hurried one, because of the need
she felt to be back at the hotel in Mount Clemens from four to
seven. In case! He did not come, but, greatly contrary to custom,
there was a short note from him on her table.

"Corinne has taken it into her head to spend a few days at the Hotel Frontenac in Detroit, while she selects herself a new automobile. Be good." Unsigned.

It was practically the only letter she had ever received from him, barring even more cursory notes which he sometimes left in the flat on those very rare occasions when he dropped in at odd moments and found her absent.

"Be good." How dear of him. You did not say that kind of thing to just anyone. It somehow denoted the close concern of someone beloved for a beloved one. Be good! As if there existed lure outside him.

Summer that year came into the small Michigan town with a flurry of precocious floral finery. June roses bloomed against the white-frame flanks of the houses, private boardinghouses, and small sanatoriums that lined the quiet, tree-bordered streets. And along the St. Clair River, as you went motorboating out into the open lake, willows in full green flush hung like women drying their hair over the reflecting mirror of water; and the open fields along the banks looked and smelled to Ray, who sometimes took the river-lake ride in an excursion launch that made the trip every afternoon, redolent of the Ohio summers that were packed away in memory after memory.

The walks were pleasant too, along the roads that skirted these meadows, except for the rather new fact that on the highways automobile traffic had become sufficiently general to create dust and commotion.

But even that had its compensations. It was quite a game to learn the different makes on sight. Saxon. Cadillac. Kurt-Sussex. Moon. Corinne would probably choose hers from one of the many Detroit factories or showrooms. A Pierce-Arrow perhaps, a Cadillac, or a Kurt-Sussex. As she trudged along the road, it was interesting to speculate what make of car Corinne and Walter were purchasing, perhaps at that very moment. What a lavish husband he was. Heavy new pearls had gleamed on Corinne's throat that one night she had glimpsed her at the lotto table in the Casino; her hands had flashed with jewels that she wore well and with restraint, and there were diamond specks on the edges of the white aigrets in her beautiful, prematurely white hair. What a lavish husband and what a parsimonious lover. Horrid, when you put it like that. Lover. Seemed to lose all its connotation, used in that connection, and became just a soiled and horrid word. But, anyway, it was supposed to be the other way around. Women in her position were supposed to furnish a glamor that was expensively provided in the form of furs, jewels, and the gay accouterments of indiscretion. But here, in the fragrant, jeweled, and always superbly furred Corinne, was reflected the lavishness of an indulgent husband. Ray it was who coped with the unexciting mediocrity of scheming to make ends meet, remaking last year's blouse into this year's guimpe, and, for want of a jewel, following the current fad of link bracelets hung with small gilt and silver bangles.

As she killed time, these long days—walking, taking the motor-boat excursion trip out into the lake—thoughts like these flowed in ceaseless little runnels along their well-worn ruts in her mind.

He wants to keep me unglamorous. Safe. His. And even in that she found consolation. If he didn't care, he couldn't write me a thing like "Be good." The note containing the phrase lay tucked against her breast. Be good. How easy to be good.

Evenings she was now free to venture into the Casino. This she did against her better judgment, but drawn irresistibly, as the dull after-dinner periods of the Medes Hotel began to close her in, toward the frame house of drawn blinds and discreet Negro servitors.

There was camaraderie, and the hospitality of sandwiches, pretzels, wine-cup, and beer, and a sequence of green felt-covered tables that never failed to flick her with excitement. Even lotto, at a dollar the game, and played to the drone of a voice calling numbers off wooden disks picked from a cotton bag, was not beneath her intense concentration.

There was something about gaming. . . .

But, for the most part, poker, vingt-et-un, roulette and the slot machines claimed her evenings. The last were endlessly diverting. Sometimes your fifty-cent piece, dropped into the slot, would yield the delightful profit of three, four, five, even ten times your investment, clattering into the metal cup. Discipline herself as she would, it was difficult for her to get through an evening without at least one or two forays into the small vestibule where stood a row of these iron men of chance.

Occasionally, one of the guests, feeding coins into these metal maws, staked her. One night, on a run of luck, instigated by one of these chance stakes, she drew quite a crowd around her, because she succeeded in emptying in quick succession, out of three machines, the sum total of about thirty-nine dollars.

Oh, there was something about gaming. . . .

During Walter's absence, despite the fact that at one time she was well over four hundred dollars ahead of the combined games of slot machines, poker, vingt-et-un, her final winnings resulted in little over ninety dollars, which, however, enabled her to pay, as she put it to herself, for Emma's lavaliere.

With the trifling sum of her lotto winnings, she bought herself, in one of the poky little shops of the town, five yards of dotted swiss, and, mornings after her sulphur bath, sewed away in an attempt to copy a frock she had admired on one of the women at the Casino.

One evening, along with a Mr. De Lima, who had requested an introduction from the clerk at the Medes, she went to the Grove Hotel for dinner. De Lima, a theater-orchestra conductor from Kansas City, oleaginous of eye and with a serious rheumatic condition which impaired his gait, was only one more variation of species long familiar to her, but the warm floral atmosphere of the Grove, as contrasted with her own narrow drummer's-delight of a hotel lobby, with its chairs facing a plate-glass window, which in turn faced the street, was pleasantly exhilarating, bringing back the warm gay odors of days long past, when the tony Ray Schmidt had been habitué in the smartest lobbies of the smartest hotels in Cincinnati.

Heads no longer swung around now to her entrance. Years of practice in neutralizing her appearance to avoid attraction had toned her down to a quiet, well-dressed figure without dash, but still with the slim, trim appearance of a small sloop under sail. There were gray streaks in her hair to be coped with now. Not the white scallops of hair that fell along Corinne's brow, softening it, but streaks of fading hair which were hardening to the features and which she dyed out. The dyed effect was what brought out, most of all, the rather brittle aging look. Otherwise the figure, despite the sedentary years spent mostly indoors or at inactive occupations, had kept its striking slimness. A slender, quietly distinctive woman, presumably in middle thirties, effective in brown silk that left her still-good shoulders bare, and harmonized well with the swarthy clarity of her skin, dined at the Grove that night without attracting more than a glance from the women. It was the men who still, while they might not swing a head, threw out the glance that lingered.

"Can you make me acquainted wiz ze tall one, wiz ze sporty figure and the stay-by-me eyes?" had been De Lima's manner of request to the clerk for his introduction.

In a way, even though De Lima was to prove troublesome before she dismissed him that night, the surging recurrence of old excitements was pleasant. After dinner, there was dancing on the tiled floor of the lobby, De Lima, in spite of his impaired gait, initiating her into the curved enchantments of the tango. Men and women, out of a world that corresponded to the secure one of Walter and Corinne, danced or sat indulgently about the bright lobby, or gathered about the cigar-stand to shoot dice for souvenir inkstands, woolly bears, or dolls on small music boxes.

The easy, half-carnival atmosphere of the health resort, after aches and pains had been tucked out of sight and youth would be served, was faintly in the key of Aix, even Cannes. Later still, there were sandwiches and horse's-necks, and then a final fling into the Casino. That was the night she created a stir, on a fifty-cent piece handed her by an enormously fat, badly crippled Minneapolis banker, by once more practically depleting three of the row of slot machines.

"My lucky three! My three iron babies!" she said, as the excitement of gambling mounted.

In the end, however—and the end, to her, was the closing of the Casino—it was she who fed the last fifty-cent piece out of the contents of her purse to her iron babies, who not only gulped back what they had momentarily yielded, but more than twenty-five dollars of her own.

There was something about gaming. . . .

But wrenching herself free of the routine embrace of De Lima that night, when he took her home to her hotel—and she had, not without force, to literally push him from the door—it struck her drearily that even while the evening of gaming and dining had been a blessed relief in aridity, there was no longer any use at pretenses. That part of her life, as represented by the De Limas, was finished.

De Lima had sickened her of his tiresomeness, as all men had for years and were sure to now.

And yet, the very next day was to come an occurrence on a clap of small thunder, so unexpected, so sudden, and so genuinely exciting was her meeting, on the main street of Mount Clemens, with Kurt Shendler.

There had sped past her, too quickly for her to note its make, although true to habit she attempted it, an enormous red touring car, with a horn attachment that was louder and faster than any she had ever heard. It was a commotion in any street, that car, low, swift, and conspicuous.

Suddenly, as if it had raced around the block (which it had), this car bore down upon her again from the rear, coming to a quick stop at the curb beside her. It was a Kurt-Sussex, light dancing on its red-enamel and nickel fixings; and there, leaning from its steering wheel, with his goggles pushed back, Kurt!

"I knew it! By Jove, it seemed to me that I couldn't be right, and yet I am!"

"Kurt!"

"I saw that walk and that figure with not more than a pinch of the end of my eye as I shot by, and I said to myself, 'There is only one walk and one figure like that, or I'm crazy.' And back around the block I come, saying to myself: 'You've got water and Ray on the brain. You're seeing things.' And bless my soul—bless my soul—"

"Kurt!" Yes; and Kurt with flesh on his bones and a big linen duster having to balloon a little over embonpoint, and face shaven smooth of the old mustache, and looking as she had never dreamed he had it in him to look. Sturdy. Filled out. But Kurt all right. Every inch the old Kurt, plus the strange and unconscious authority of success.

They drove for three hours that afternoon along the roads she had trolleyed and trudged. He was at home here, masterful, prideful of every inch of the way, eager to cram into their first five minutes recital of years.

"Just goes to show, a man's mind leads him to what is on it. I don't know as I realize it all the time, Ray, a man dassent brood, and certainly I didn't today, but there aren't many days pass that you don't pop into my mind one way or another. Just funny you didn't happen to today, until I clapped eyes on you. Tell me what brings you here."

"Why, I came out here, Kurt—why, I came out, I guess, to pay you sixty dollars I've been owing you for some time back. I'm fooling, Kurt. Can't you take a joke!"

"Speaking of that, Ray, all jokes aside, it hurt me to have you send that money back to me at that time, as if a little loan from me burnt your fingers. Think I've got that sixty dollars tucked away in a collarbox for remembrance."

"I'm fooling, Kurt. I'm just here—for a change."

"Not ailing, are you, Ray?"

"Do I look it?"

He did not press her, breaking into new volubility at every turn.

"Great country around here. God's country, every inch of it."

"It's been good to you, Kurt."

"You bet your life it has, and I know it. You never thought I'd be vice president of the firm that manufactures the car you're sitting in, now did you, Ray?"

"Kurt," she said, slowly, turning toward him, "You—don't—mean—to—tell—me—you're—the—Kurt—of—the—Kurt-Sussex—"

"You—don't—mean—to—tell—me—you—never—knew—that!"

Her jaw fell, her face fell, as if they were disintegrating there before him, like the celebrated one-hoss shay.

"Why, I never knew—why, I never dreamed—I never put two and two together. Kurt-Sussex never meant anything to me except the make of a fine car, and to think all the time it—it was my Kurt."

"There is just no limit to this industry, Ray. Remember I used to tell you that. Well, then I didn't know the half of it. Remember the time down in New York I told you about a fellow named Henry Ford who was going to make a pile for himself one of these days? Bet you gave me the laugh on that many a time. Well, what's happened to Ford is happening, on a smaller scale, at present, to the rest of us. Ford is no mere millionaire now. He's many times a millionaire, and I'm here to tell you, Ray, that nothing short of that is going to satisfy me. I'm going to take you around and show you some of the fairy tales that are happening in this industry. How many cars do you think we turned out last month? Why, I tell you, girl, you've got a liberal education coming to you. If this war were already over, as, mark my word, it's going to be before this year is out, I'd show you things that would make your eyes bug out."

"Eyes bug out!" Why, she hadn't heard that since the Cincinnati days. Or, "dassent." And to think the Kurt-Sussex—our Cincinnati Kurt.

"I don't want to seem braggy, Ray, but I do kind of want you to know a lot of things that will surprise you. I own all this land as far back from both sides of the road as you can see, that we're passing now. It's the old Barcliff estate, and I'm just about going to quadruple my investment, and that day is not far off."

"Of course, you live in Detroit, Kurt."

"Just batching it, around the Frontenac Hotel. Lived there six years now. Next best thing to a home I've been able to work out."

The Frontenac! Chances were he had seen Walter there and Corinne. Chances were, too, that as she rode, swift and sure, along the bright roads, he was putting two and two together. If strangers in opera houses were wagging, wasn't it fair enough to assume that Cincinnati wagged too?

As a matter of fact, he had not run into Walter, whom he did not even know; and, strangely enough, while doubts, which he kept jammed down tightly in his mind throughout the years, did sometimes pop up, the name of Walter Saxel was never associated in his mind with her. Things were as they were, with Ray. Just no telling about a woman. About all there was to it.

It made things easier if you never permitted certain thoughts even to take shape. Not that anything mattered—she was what she was—her every act another turn in the spiral of her desirability.

"Let me drive you back to Mount Clemens now and go into the Grove Hotel to visit one of my associates on business. He is there, laid up with rheumatism, and I came down to talk over some little matters with him. And then you let me drive you down to the Frontenac for dinner, and anything you say afterward."

"Not the Frontenac tonight, Kurt. I've a reason for not wanting to be seen there this particular evening."

"All right, just as you say. Take you out to Belle Isle then, and treat you to a good old-fashioned fish dinner. You've got to stay around here for a while, Ray, and get acquainted with God's land."

How good it was to be sitting there securely beside this decent, effervescent Kurt, who, beyond her imaginings, had filled out into someone personable, and who, in his middle age, bore little resemblance to the gangling fellow of earlier years. Time, or success, or both, had mellowed Kurt; put firm, genial flesh on his bones; even corrected his eyesight. Behind pince-nez that sat firmly across the unirritated bridge of his nose, the eyes now looked clear and enlarged. A new, bluff, western kind of fellow, in good, gray, checked clothes beneath his linen duster, and gray in his tan hair. How good to be sitting there with this eager, catering friend, irrestrainable in his excitement and desire to impress and please her. It made her feel as if for years she had been unbearably tired—so tired that the very withes of her being were twisted nerves being relaxed, and her mouth, which sometimes felt like a tight hard snake's-nest, felt moist and young as a girl's. How good.

"You've got to give me a whole day to take you through our plant, Ray. I want to ride you out along Woodward Avenue, too, and show you some of the prettiest homes you ever saw in your life. As I recall it, you like horse races. I don't know much about them, but that's a great sport hereabouts. You're going to know there's such a state as Michigan on this old U. S. map before you leave it. We can show a thing or two, even to New York."

How good. How good. Presently, in one of her semi-evening-gowns—a brown lace she had dyed and made herself—and a brown lace hat with a brown motor-veil, which she tied under the chin, they were on the drive to Belle Isle, wind in their faces and the edge of the veil snapping backward in the breeze.

"Ray, as my soul is my own, if I had the pick of surprises the world over, this one today would be my choice."

"Kurt, I don't know but what it would have been mine too."

"You know, Ray—now don't think I'm stirring up old dust, it's going to lie just as flat as you want it to—but there is a mighty sad side to the lay of things between us. I don't know much about your life, except what you choose to tell me, and if you don't know by now that I'm not quizzing, you ought to; but, without asking you a single question, or caring a damn what has been, I certainly could make your life what you deserve it to be, Ray, without saying much about what I could do for myself."

"You're salt of the earth, Kurt, and don't think I don't know it."

"Well, we won't bury Jake tonight," he said, and struck off on a dissertation of the Detroit land-boom that, during this period of crucial world conditions, was being held off like a lion at bay.

"Why, there's no limit to what's ahead for this town. Has anything been able to stop it? Not on your life!"

They dined on crayfish, as they used to in Cincinnati, asparagus with hollandaise, and nothing would do but a quart of very dry champagne, which she scarcely touched to her lips and Kurt touched not at all, except in the same mime of toasting the occasion.

"I feel twenty tonight, Ray. Besides, from the look of the thing, this may be about the last glass of wine you and me will be able to drink above the table in your old U.S.A. Yes, sir, I feel twenty tonight."

"And I," she felt impelled to say, "feel filled with all the years there are"; but she would have cried had she said it. And so they touched glasses in silence, and she sipped the edge of hers, and he regarded her above the untouched edge of his.

That was the beginning of a round of times with Kurt that helped fill the strangely static days. Even after Walter and Corinne had returned to the Grove, where Walter immediately resumed a second series of the treatments, there was time galore left for Kurt. For drives. For dinners at the Frontenac. Theaters and late suppers. For an inspection tour of the vast automobile plants, and luncheon served from a private kitchen in a small dining room adjoining Kurt's fine mahogany offices.

She told Walter, one evening, during one of their rare hours from five to six, that she could get him a special-body Kurt-Sussex at cost price, through the offices of an old friend of hers, none other than Kurt Shendler himself.

"I heard he was a Cincinnatian. Then you must have known him when he was running a bicycle shop back there."

"I sure did. He took me through his plant today. It's incredible what he has built up for himself. Kurt is the power behind all those blocks of factories. He certainly has shown me a pleasant time."

He was all for that, and, somewhat to her surprise, continued to exhibit a concern, not quite characteristic, for what must be the tediousness of her hours alone.

"That's right, Ray. Don't mope. There are only two more weeks of it, but since we cannot be together as much as we want to, try to make the best of them. Get this fellow Shendler to show you around."

She did not know whether to be hurt or gratified at this concern. Usually, the long periods of her waiting were so taken for granted. It was one of the rutted conditions between them; exigencies of business affairs, home conditions, made the edges of Walter's time uncertainties which one took for granted, and you cut your leisure to fit that pattern.

These few weeks somehow had been different. It was as if Walter were a little grateful to whosoever would fill her time. It was not that suspicion smote her. It was just that, within her, something stirred and feared.

"Walter, you—you know I never ask you about certain things, and if I am offending you by doing so now, you need not answer.

Why is it suddenly necessary for you to be so—well, what I mean is, in New York, and usually in Europe, you are not so tied. Why is it that, all of a sudden, you are not free even for an occasional dinner with me?"

He flushed and started to look angry, in a way she dreaded, an oxblood red flooding his neck and rising to deploy across his face, and then, suddenly changing his tactics, crossed from the window where he had been leaning looking down at the street below, to stand beside her, where she sat on the stiff hotel sofa.

"Ray, I've been meaning to tell you something for weeks. Should have in the beginning, but somehow I didn't. I suppose you're not going to like it. That isn't going to change matters. It's over twelve or fourteen years since, y'see? Little accident, I suppose you might call it."

"Call what?"

"Fact is, Ray, one of those things that can happen, but, somehow, after so many years, don't usually—fact is—Corinne is going to have a baby."

"I see," she said finally, between a pair of wooden clothespins for lips. "I see," she repeated, and sat, wooden as her lips, upon the rigid sofa, toying with the tassel of a cushion.

He had the nicety not to attempt to touch or kiss her as he went out, although such a departure was without precedent. She was grateful for it, though, because there was something gathering within her that, had he approached, would have made talons of her fingers.

32

This was a terrible situation. In shape, a vicious circle. In substance, revolting beyond any telling.

What right had she, Ray Schmidt, to any ground whatsoever in this matter? Where did her sense of outrage, violation, smirch, come in? What was there in her relationship to this entire affair to defend her against being plunged into the mire of this predicament? "Nothing," she cried out to herself, nothing, nothing, nothing, except somewhere, deep within her, the inability to foresee anything so gross and violating happening.

There were decencies; there were unspoken fundamental decencies that were pillars of the human structure of body, soul, and spirit. While nothing had ever been spoken between them on a subject to which she readily allotted him privacy, surely, she cried out to herself, she had been justified in allowing herself to feel safe in certain sanctities.

How dared he! Either to herself, or to—her! How dared he! That had always been one of her synthetic, home-brewed justifications. Thank God, she had only run into him again in those years after the completion of his little family. At least that made it seem less—less what? Less patently the thing it was . . .

All those years, all those months of days, that he had been coming to her, she had assumed to herself certain things that now, in the mocking, shocking light of events, she should never have dared to take for granted.

Certainly these were not the things you discussed, they were not even the things you discussed with yourself; and now here, in the dreadful array of full proof, lay the ruins of her illusions, the collapse of her flimsy castle, the end of the last shred of her pretense of justification.

As she sat there, in the stuffy, sulphuric-smelling hotel room that had suddenly become to her as stripped of pretense as she herself, this much became evident: something too smirched and besmirching had happened to make the old status of things any longer endurable. How had she permitted him to tell her this thing without letting loose upon him the sense of her outrage that was almost past the bearing?

Kurt was calling for her at eight. One must climb out of the ruffled negligee and into clothing for the evening drive they had planned together, precisely as if something epochal in its pain had not hung itself onto her heart since, in a normal unassailed world of twenty-four hours ago, she had made that plan.

How had she refrained, when he said, "Corinne is going to have a baby," from striking him across the lips that had uttered the everything unspeakable that the statement implied? She would have liked, now in retrospect, to have seen those lips trickle with blood that she had struck from them. How had she refrained from doing something in the way of force, with her body, that would have hurt him, degraded, destroyed him? How was she ever to succeed now, after having sat passive there while he threw over what universe she had been able to construct out of scraps, in conveying to him the fathomless depths of her sense of outrage? Nothing between them was any longer tenable—horror was upon her. . . .

That night, on the spur of the moment, for which no amount of preparation would have prepared her, she did something for which, in all her experience, there was no precedent.

For the first time in the alone years of the peculiar isolation of her position, with an amount of unrestraint that astonished her every moment that she felt her lips in full recital, she unburdened the unabridged story of her relationship with Walter. Minutely, in detail, the narrative, being born, came rushing from her lips.

She had been driving with Kurt along the paved road that led to Detroit, when he turned to her kindly: "Not feeling so well tonight, Ray? You're so quiet."

They were spinning past the fenced meadowlands he had pointed out to her as his own, and she put out her hand suddenly on his arm.

"Kurt, could we turn off here and get the car under one of those big trees? I want to talk to you."

"I reckon we can, since those trees belong to me," he said, and immediately and without surprise, which she liked in him, began maneuvering the big car onto the shoulder of turf that edged the road.

A whitish July night flowed down over the meadow, moonless, but with an unusually crowded attendance of stars. One of those nights when the Milky Way and the Dipper and Vega and Arcturus are in their brightest coinage.

"Now, what is on your mind?" he said, as, with the car's back to the road, they sat facing an unrelieved vista of star-spangled meadow.

"Kurt, what do you think of me, anyway?"

"You know what I think of you, Ray," he said softly, almost too softly, as if against an emotion ready to rise.

"I mean, Kurt, what are your thoughts concerning my life? What have you thought of me since you saw me in New York? What do you think of me now? About my being here. How am I here? Why?"

"I don't let my mind dwell on the things you don't wish to tell me."

"Come now, Kurt, surely it must have occurred to you that there is a reason for my being out here. Surely you have heard things?"

"I have heard nothing, Ray, so help me God. This is a big world and a small world at the same time. It happens it has been a big world where you are concerned. As to what I have thought—if I have thought anything, Ray, it has had to do with a feeling of resentment that somehow, even from what little I know of it, life hasn't done the things for you that you deserve. The rest is none of my business. Nothing you can do, Ray, or have done, can change my opinion of you."

"You know that I am some man's mistress, don't you?"

"I suppose so," he said, looking straight ahead and frowning.

"Do you know what man's?"

"No."

"Shall I tell you?"

"No."

"It will help me, Kurt—to tell you."

"Then tell me."

"Walter Saxel. Say something, Kurt, don't just sit—like that."

"What is there for me to say? I remember him, of course. You went together for a while, back there. I always used to date your meeting with him from that Sunday night you stood me up with a message from the corner telephone. But that passed out of my mind. He's made a big record in banking, I understand."

"You never knew—more—"

"No."

"But you suspected there was someone?"

"Dear Ray, I have tried to explain to you that always, over and above what you do, I know what you are."

She pressed her fingers against her eyes, and for a time they sat in silence. She was not crying. Her voice came quite evenly.

"Not many women could boast having a more perfect thing than that said to them."

"Not many deserve it."

"Is it clear now that I'm out here with—him?"

"Yes."

"He and his wife—he married a Miss Trauer of Cincinnati—are at the Grove."

He sat with his lips straight, his eyes ahead, hands on the

steering wheel, the knuckles of them large and white as mushrooms in the starlight.

"We were just friends before that. It was six years after his marriage that we met again. Will it surprise you, Kurt, if I tell you that he—Walter—was the first—the last? I know—even remembering all that I once told you about myself back in the Cincinnati days— how it must sound for a woman like me to be saying this, but it's true, Kurt. Take my word for that."

"I do."

"Dear Kurt, how terrible I am being to you. That wasn't your voice. That was something squeaking up there in the tree. Say it over again in your own voice."

"I believe you, Ray."

"I know you do, or I wouldn't be telling you things that I've never even told myself. Let's see, where was I? You see, the thing that you probably like about me is the thing that has always made me my own enemy. It's so hard for me to dislike people or get huffy over the things that the right kind of people dislike in the wrong kind. God knows, it is me people should feel sorry for, but it's me that is always a little sorry for people. To me, we are such a pathetic lot. All born into a world we didn't ask to be born into. All struggling, hurting, scheming to get a little happiness out of it before we go to square ourselves with God, or whatever it is constitutes our here-after. It is as if we get born with more appetites than we need, just in order to spend our lives trying to curb them. I read where a doctor once said a human being can only hope to conserve his health by satisfying his appetite for food by less than one-half. Same with life. We all seem born desiring so much more than is good for us."

"Something in that."

"But to get back—feeling all this about people—about life— I've never learned to say no without its hurting me a whole lot more than the person I've said it to. Even the rotters, the low-downs and the no-goods I've met in my life, haven't disgusted me the way they should. I've felt sorry for them for being so third-rate and scummy. I swear to you, silly as it sounds, many a time I've felt sorry for a fellow while he was insulting me. Seemed to me all the time he was just a poor devil trying to make an escape of some kind or another. I'm funny that way, Kurt. It's been my undoing—You listening?"

"Go on."

"Well, that's the way I've always been, and one day back in the days—yes, the very day I sent you the telephone message to the house on Baymiller Street, I met Walter!"

"It *was* him—way back there, then?"

"From the second I clapped eyes on him, Kurt, it was as if I—I'm not very good at expressing myself, but it was as if life for me had just—just begun to be life. That doesn't say it, either. I guess what happened to me the day I met Walter was what might happen to any fool girl the day she falls in love at first sight. But with me, Kurt, I just never stopped falling. There never was a second after I clapped eyes on him that he couldn't have had me, Kurt. It wasn't any longer a question of good or bad, right or wrong. I had no pride. I wanted no rights. . . . Know what I mean, Kurt?"

"Yes."

"Oh, I'm not trying to call a spade a silver spoon. I'm the kept woman of a married man. Only nothing—nothing can ever make it seem quite like that to me. I won't go into what he's been to me, or what I think I've been to him. I won't dwell on the torment of knowing the part I have been playing in his relationship to his wife and family; but nothing, Kurt—I'd be lying if I said it—can ever make me believe that there was anything but sanctity of human relationship in what we brought each other. I've not been bad, in my relationship with Walter Saxel. I've loved him with a oneness that makes me at least as much his wife as—never mind that part. It's too terrible. But with all the pain and the sin and the wrongness that belong to that side of things, the husband of Corinne Saxel and Ray Schmidt—I will say it, I will—has been blessed with a perfect love. I gave him that love, Kurt. As perfect as a crystal. Do you hear that? As perfect as a crystal."

He shuddered, with his face down in his hands—shuddered in the mild night air and hunched his shoulders as if he would retreat into them.

"Is it that terrible? Is it that horrible? It doesn't sound that way to me. Isn't that incredible? It doesn't sound that way to me. It sounds almost beautiful. I know it is beautiful, as it exists within me. As for Corinne—I've thought about her and their children, until it has seemed to me that my head must break in halves—and perhaps it is wrong—I guess it is—but it seems to me that the greatest wrong lies in the possibility of her ever knowing. Everything about her life has been so normal. So right. So as it should be. I haven't even taken Walter from her. His love for her is something separate and apart. What she does not know is never going to make her unhappy. That is my prayer, Kurt—otherwise—even if his children should some day learn of it, this much I know. Nothing in his relationship with me has ever tarnished their father. I've helped Walter, Kurt."

"I know that," he said, still into his hands. "You don't need to tell me that. I know it."

She began to cry softly, without sobs.

"What would you say if I were to tell you, after all this, that this is the end? Something has happened—something that no longer makes anything possible. I'm leaving Walter, Kurt. Isn't that curious? I didn't know that, when I started out on this ride with you. I know it now."

He swung slowly and took hold of her wrist.

"What does that mean for me?"

"For you? Why, Kurt—you darling—you mean—"

"I mean what I said years and years ago out in Cincinnati; what I said to you years ago in New York, what I am saying to you now. . . ."

"Kurt, if I cry the way I want to cry, it will be terrible. Don't say anything else, I can't—stand—it—"

Her face in her palms, he could feel her tremble, and once more he sat with his hands on the wheel, the mushrooms large and white upon them, the sea of starlight, the sea of meadow, and the sea of silence flowing ahead of them. . . .

It was considerably later when he did speak; and her trembling had ceased, and her hands had dropped into her lap, and her eyes, dry, were fixed on the landscape.

"Tell you what you do, Ray. No use making this any harder than it is already. Pull yourself together and take this thing easy. I'm going to drive you back to your hotel now. My advice to you is, get yourself together and take a morning train over to Youngstown and visit Freda a bit."

"I've been thinking about that identical thing, sitting here, Kurt. I'd like to see Freda and the children. Particularly Emma. I'm just hungry to see Emma. There is just one reason I can't quite bring myself to go. You know the reason. Not on account of Freda, she doesn't know anything from what I've told her, but, of course, she must guess. It's little Emma. She—I don't know—I don't feel I ought to—"

"You go to Freda's, Ray. You'll never put anything in the way of that child, or any other, but the best. Get your bearings. Get quiet. Think. Work it all out. I'm not saying anything one way or another, except to tell you what you already know. My heart is like an open house, waiting for you. Pretty fancy speech for me, but I feel it like that. And it is a good strong fine house with all the doors and windows wide open. I want you in it this minute, more than I've ever wanted you in my life. Think and be quiet for a while, out there, and get your bearings on this thing. I'll be in Youngstown in exactly seven weeks, as a delegate from our Chamber of Commerce to the opening of theirs. Before, if you want me. If I could bring you back here on the twenty-eighth day of August, married to me, I—well, there's so many ways of saying it, but I don't seem to be able to find one. I love you, Ray. More tonight, I think, than I have in all the years of loving you. Now don't the idea of a few weeks' resting and thinking and clearing up your mind visiting your folks in Youngstown strike you as fair? Think it over. There's an idea!"

"I have thought it over, Kurt. I'm going."

33

After the first sharp bolt of decision, the gathering-together of the personal belongings might have been done by someone outside herself, so far as she was conscious of fatigue or the passing of the long night that led to the dawn of the day of her departure.

Even the note to Walter, addressed after some thought, care of the clerk at the Medes Hotel, was not a composition of travail. It wrote itself glibly with that external-feeling hand of hers: "Dear Walter, This decision of mine to go to my family you will understand. I will ask you to break up things at the New York end without communication with me. That part of my life is finished. In many ways it is strange it should end this way, but not so strange as that which has brought it about. Even so, I am grateful for so much that has been. I am more at peace in my decision than I ever could have believed possible. I wish you everything good."

That is a good letter, she thought, without tears, because it is a true letter, every word of it. She sealed the flap of the envelope along her tongue, and placed it on the top of her handbag, to be left with the clerk as she departed.

There were countless small chores. A dress at the dry cleaner's across the street, to be called for before taking the train. Tips to be left for certain of the hotel help who would be off duty and not know of her sudden departure. The hotel porter to be dispatched to the nearby station for railroad accommodation. Her bit of fortune at the Casino and races proved a great stroke of luck. In all, there was over four hundred dollars in her purse. Dressed in her traveling hat and suit of tan percale, she had breakfast in her room on the small table beside the windows that overlooked the street.

The sun had not yet climbed over the roofs, and a warmish furry fog hung over the scene. Dogs without collars ran along the streets. A boy with a tray of breakfast rolls balanced on his head whistled past. The Adelphi Hotel across the way was having its spittoons cleaned. The sulphuric smell of the hot curative waters came through the window screens. A rather depressing sunless morning, and yet, to the person who seemed handmaiden to Ray, that curious external self of hers, not unpleasant.

The matter of the note to Walter once behind her, the problem now presented itself whether or not to wire Freda. How dumfounded she would be. Kurt had suggested wiring. Perhaps it would be better. She filled in a blank from a pad of them on the small desk in her sitting room.

"Arrive three-twenty, Pittsburgh and Lake Erie, for a little visit. Ray."

By then it was time to go to the train. The incredible act of performing, without consideration or connection with the doings of Walter, was about to take place. No hampering tie-up with his plans, his time, his preferences. Free. Free to go, to come, to work out her own today, tomorrow, while he, his pride, his terrible pride, stunned, a few hours later would stand beside the counter of the Hotel Medes reading the unbelievable.

How hurt and angered and unrelenting he would be. Oh, she had taken her life into her own hands all right. Even should she weaken—and weaken she not only would not, but could not—his pride would do the rest. His terrible, relentless, wounded-unto-death pride.

The person outside of herself was riding in a train that cut through fertile meadows. There was the rather absurd reality of the trainmen being obsequious, as members of train and boat crews somehow always were to her. The porter brought her a pillow and settled a stool at the foot of her parlor-car chair. The conductor,

taking up her ticket, passed the time of day and smeared his eyes
over the little swell her breasts made against her shirtwaist. Grit
flew against the screened window, and again the porter was at her
elbow, dusting the sill and hoisting her luggage from the floor to the
wire shelf overhead. The gritty dust began to settle along her lips
and the backs of her gloved hands. The day rose to its noon and she
could feel the back of her waist becoming damp and wrinkled from
its pressure against the railroad plush. A drummer across the aisle,
with his coat removed and his large soft stomach heaving under a
silk shirt that showed dark splotches of perspiration, leaned over to
strike up a conversation about the heat, which ended with his invit-
ing her into the dining car for lunch. Just a few desultory remarks,
mostly questions that came off the moist shelves of his lips without
waiting for a reply.

"Traveling alone? Going to meet the hubby? Know anybody in
Youngstown? Good town. Ever been to Jack's Eating Place there?
Doing anything tonight? That's the second call for lunch. Feel like
opening a bottle of beer with me?"

Just the most desultory replies from her, and yet he felt impelled
to ask her to lunch. It struck her, as she politely refused, and lay
back against her chair with her eyes closed, that the men who swam
around and ogled her in public places were no longer the younger
ones with straight figures, but almost all, by now, had protuber-
ant stomachs, heavy necks, and skin that hung like the folds of an
elephant. Men with high-blood-pressure records in their doctors'
offices. The younger, unprotuberant, natty men were not troublesome any more.

Rattly-bang over the rails. As she lay back, with her eyes closed,
the curious, light, astonishing sense of her lack of relativity to what
Walter's plans for the day, the week, the month might be, persisted.

"I feel as if someone had died," she told herself, "and it is too
soon after for me to realize it."

Rattly-bang—

Freda and Emma and Freda's youngest, a boy aged nine, of such
pale pigmentation that he looked albino, were at the station. She
saw them from the car window, lined up along the platform, as the

train drew in, and, except for her being so nervously on the lookout, would never have recognized the little group. Whatever of change she was prepared to find in the person of her stepsister, nothing had prepared her for this. Freda was as round and as stubby as one of the Chinese-lily bulbs Ray was forever planting in bowls of pebbles. Round, after the fashion of women who let their bodies sag all day without corsets, until time to hoist them into stays for an occasion. The hoisted ridges of Freda's flesh hung over the top of her corsets. The Freda who had been pastily pretty in her teens was middle-aged now, with fallen arches, shabby graying hair, and the fusty manner with children of one who boxes their ears frequently. Just one more of the many shabby women who move about the aisles of the marketplaces buying "seconds" of wilted vegetables, and the cheaper gristly cuts of meat, to cram into market baskets.

At sight of Freda, a deep-rooted fear smote Ray. The years had been moths at the body and probably at the soul of Freda. The same years that must have eaten, in their different way, into her.

Freda's first remark was reassuring.

"I'd have known you anywhere. You haven't changed a bit, except I think you're even slimmer, and, of course—yes, a little older, but not much."

How broad and how white her voice was. It had not seemed like that in the old days, and yet here it was familiarly Freda's own.

"Emma, here is your Aunt Ray at last. The child has been making herself sick with excitement since your telegram came. Curtis, go kiss your Aunt Ray; she has sent you so many dollar bills. Thank her."

The boy hung back, but Emma, in a white dress that had laundered gray, came forward with her whitish eyes that almost had the look of the blind in them, lit in the same sweet way of the anticipatory blind.

Why, Freda's children were the whitest, palest, most albino children she had ever seen. Freda and Hugo were blond, of course, but these two, they were like pale visitors from another planet. And no gainsaying it, Emma was not pretty. There was something studious though, and round-shouldered, about the little figure, something about the pale eyes that seemed a pathetic straining; but the girl here was not even a prototype of the communion picture that Ray loved. No luster to her, not even the bright blue and white prettiness that had been her mother's. Poor little Emma, how sweet she was, kissing her so timidly. What an ache she lodged in your heart. For that matter, poor little Curtis too, a pale sniffling boy with pipestem legs, and some of Hugo's gangling quality to their length. Oh, the drab three dears, dulled as a looking glass dulls when you breathe on it.

"That figure, Ray! I'd have known it anywhere. You'll never lose it. Look at me, mealsack tied in the middle."

"Nonsense, Freda. None of us has escaped the years. Where are we going, dears? Take me to a hotel."

"I've fixed it so you can stop with us. That is, if you don't mind. Things will probably be a little different from what you're used to. Emma sleeps on the sofa in the front room, but she's given that up to you, and will sleep with one of her girlfriends, who lives down the street."

"Oh, no, I couldn't. . . ."

"But I like it, Aunt Ray. I love it. . . ."

A pang smote Ray. She had counted on the privacy of a room in a boardinghouse or hotel.

"Oh, please, Aunt Ray."

"Of course, if you don't think it is going to be comfortable enough, Ray—"

"Nonsense, Freda. I just don't want to inconvenience you."

That ended the discussion, and presently, although Ray had suggested a cab, which Freda disclaimed because of the distance, they were bobbing along on a trolley car, through the repetitious streets of Youngstown, Ray between Emma, on one side, whose hand was securely tucked into hers, and Freda on the other. Curtis on her lap, because at that hour the streetcars were packed.

Like-a-dream, like-a-dream, clattered the wheels. Sitting out here in this Middle West, Ohio town, clattering home with Freda and her children to a place that was sure to flow around her in the

warm, fetid waves of the semi-slum. Why was this grotesque circumstance taking place? What next?

Sure enough, the house, an unpainted frame, without a porch,
a shutter, or an ell to break its uncompromising resemblance to an
old weather-beaten packing case, was situated in a burnt and grass-
less yard on a street of just such houses. You entered from the side,
because the front door, with a piece of lace curtain stretched across
its pane, was only a sham, without hinges or lock.

So this was Freda's castle, the castle for which the ignominy of
her unspeakable maneuver of other days still lingered across the
memory. It was a cramped, mean house, meanly furnished, but with
certain valiant touches. Yellow-tissue roses in a cut-glass table vase.
Some Japanese wind-bells that swayed in an open window.

There were only two rooms on a floor, kitchen and adjoining
parlor, where Emma slept, two pockets of leftover space with slant-
ing ceilings and high little windows upstairs, shared by the remainder of the family. No dining room, but the table was spread in the
kitchen, obviously with more ado than usual.

Quick perceptions flashed over Ray as she entered. There was
her mother's silver cruet on the table. And the wooden shelf-clock
with the flowers painted on the oval glass door had stood in the
house on Baymiller Street ever since she could remember.

In the front room where she removed her wraps, the picture of
the black and white pair of horses rearing at a zig-zag of lightning
had been her father's favorite. And that carpet hassock with the
red wool button in its center, and the china plate with her father
and Tagenhorst, cheek to cheek, baked into its center, stood in a
rack on the mantelpiece, precisely as it had stood on the rack on
the mantelpiece of the house on Baymiller Street. Those old gilded
cattails—who in the world would have thought of carting them
here!

Some of the old gall at the confiscation rose, but only for the
passing moment. Curtis, once at home, became himself, thawing
out of his rigid unease and dragging her luggage with willing hands.
With the stiff bird's-nest hat removed, and a wide apron tied around

the titillating jelled movements of her hips, some of the horrid, rigid look of pretentious poverty fell from Freda. There was still yellow in the gray of her hair, and even in the glaring gaseous interior of this poor home, something of the old hint of prettiness.

The major difficulty with the front room was that the well of staircase to the two upper rooms occupied by Freda and Hugo, Curtis and his brother Kruger, rose from the parlor, thus cutting off all hope of privacy. Unpacking a few toilet articles before going out to join Freda and the children in the cozier, brighter kitchen, a sense of discomfort set her immediately to contemplating some way out—some legitimate excuse that would not offend Freda, for getting herself a room. Curtis, loaded with the assurance born of being once more on his own ground, became the showoff, popping his head now every few minutes into the room.

"I'm double-jointed!"

(Curtis, close the door and let your Aunt Ray alone.)

"Hurry, Aunt Ray, we're going to have chicken and rice."

(Curtis, don't let me have to speak to you again!)

"Aunt Ray, want to see my fox terrier?"

(What I go through with that boy! Smack! Now, will that hold you awhile?)

"Yoo-hoo, Aunt Ray, look! Jackknife. Pap lets me have it on Sundays."

Presently, before Hugo came home from his gas-meter inspections or the older boy from his work at the brickyards, and after a peppering of Freda's do's and don'ts to the boy and girl that were already nerve-racking in their repetitiousness, there was time, with the dinner simmering on the stove, to sit for a bit beside Freda on a bench in the side yard.

"Well, Ray, how does it feel to be back with plain folks once more?"

"Plain folks, why, I wasn't aware I had ever left them."

Freda laughed in a high artificial little scale. "Well, New York, Europe, Mount Clemens don't sound plain to me. Not if you've lived the plain drudging kind of life I have."

Every word veiled, provocative, and in a curious tone of grievance.

"Did I hear you say, coming out on the streetcar, Freda, that
Hugo hasn't been so well?"

"Curtis, stop dragging that dog around, and go indoors and tell
your sister not to let the oven get too hot for those biscuits. There's
nothing much the matter with Hugo, Ray, except what's been the
matter with him since the day he was born. Nothingness."

"What do you mean?"

"What I say. Curtis, let that dog alone. Hugo's got no force, no
nothing that a man's got to have in this day and age to get on. No
wonder his uncle died leaving everything to that hellion he married.
I'd rather a person would be a hellion than a nothing. That's Hugo.
Nothingness is his ailment, and there's no way to realize what that
sickness is until you're married to it. Curtis! What's brought you out
here, Ray? Could have knocked me over, when your telegram came
this morning. Funny thing, that is the first telegram has ever been
delivered to this house since Mama died and Marshall wired from
Toledo he couldn't come for the funeral."

"I just felt, Freda, as long as I was out this far Middle West, I
wanted to see some of my own again."

"M-m. Well, I'm sorry, Ray, there's nothing much to see."

"Why, you look all right, Freda. The children are nice. Emma's
right sweet."

"Cur—tis, if I wasn't sitting here talking to your Aunt Ray, I
wouldn't wait until tonight to use what is hanging on the cellar
door. Yes, my children are all right, but I don't wish it to my worst
enemy, Ray, to have to contend with what I have in sickness and
getting Emma's eyes even to the stage they are now. You helped a
lot there, Ray. Don't know what we would have done without you."

"I wish it could have been more."

She turned like a shot on that. "Why couldn't it? You've fixed
yourself pretty, haven't you?"

How much did Freda know? How much had she heard? What did
she suspect? In many ways this was going to be terrible. Why—why

had she come? On Emma's account her instinct had been against it. Yet where—else—

"I wouldn't say that, Freda. Life has never been very lavish with me, if that's what you mean. I'm just used to turning the trick of making a dollar go twice as far as it's supposed to."

"You don't expect with your traipsing around on trips to Europe and resorts, that we've been thinking you have kept on with the wholesale trimming concern all these years? Maybe you don't realize it, but you've never told us different."

She had not realized that. What they thought out here in Youngstown among her own, she had never been able to marshal even in imagination.

"I guess you're right, Freda. Things, though, have been pretty much for me what I suppose you've guessed."

"What you suppose I've guessed? We don't guess anything that we're not supposed to know."

(Tut, tut! How she and, during her lifetime, Tagenhorst must have tried to rend the veil of their ignorance concerning her.)

"Well, anyway, you can guess that there is nothing much I have to tell that would make it the occasion of a Roman holiday."

"Are you kept?"

The question deserved its equally direct reply.

"Yes."

The boy ran shouting down the yard with his fox terrier; behind them, in the kitchen, but well out of sound, the slender figure of Emma, at chores, moved every so often across the screened doorway. Imperceptibly it seemed to Ray there was something of tiny withdrawal in the apparently motionless figure of Freda.

"Well—I only hope that if you've made that kind of bed to lay on, you've made yourself a comfortable one." There was resentment and grievance and bitterness and frustration in Freda's voice. "I suppose you have had a great many er—a—er—friends. I'm not the one to cast a stone, but I suppose you've had—many?"

Was it possible that the privacy of her life with Walter had been as perfect as they had maneuvered it should be?

"I've had one, Freda, in all these years."

"One! And you mean to tell me that one a poor man?"

Then the anonymity was true! Thank God for that. Thank God for that.

"My life with him, Freda, has been as much that of a wife as—as yours out here has been. More, perhaps. I've shared with him more as a Mrs. than as a mistress."

"Well, if I went that way for a man, it would have to be for a reason, and a money reason at that. Cur—tis, stop that. What is the use taking on the shame of being a mistress if you've got to stand for being no more than a wife? . . ."

"I guess you're right, Freda. I am like that, is the only answer I have."

"Well, I never! So this is the bird of plumage, come home. From the fairy stories I've told Emma about her Aunt Ray, and her fine position in the business world, I've built up a mighty different picture about you. What is that address, anyway, in New York, where you receive your mail?"

"That's my—flat, Freda."

"Then all that you wrote about your flat is true?"

"I haven't lied to you, any more than I thought you would want me to, about—certain things—considering Emma, the children—"

"Who is the man, Ray?"

"Does that matter?"

"I suppose it don't, since I wouldn't know him anyway. Man of means?"

"Yes."

"Then why—"

"Please—I, please—"

"Well, I guess I'm old-fashioned, but it seems awful to me, Ray. It's living in sin. It's sin."

(This was priceless, and you had consciously to hold your lips tight and straight.)

"Mama always used to say you weren't the sort of girl it would ever pay to go bad. The only reason, as a rule, that a girl is ever bad, is for what she can get out of it, and you never were the kind to get anything out of it. Em—ma, push the potatoes to the back of the stove. You're what your father was, a *Schnucke*."

"I guess you're right. Only it's over now. I've left him. I'm going to start over."

The wife of Hugo swung her heavy face around, eying her with an air of positive alarm.

"You're coming to Youngstown to live?"

"No, silly. Just to get my bearings, decide my next move, and visit you and Emma and the family. Just you wait, Freda. I can't talk about it yet—it's all too vague in my mind. But something good may happen. Can't talk about it yet, but you wait. . . . Good things may happen to you through me."

"You've got someone to marry you. . . ."

"Don't make me talk about it any more, Freda. All in good time. It's not easy. I'm hit. Terribly hit with what's happened to me. Crushed, as the saying is; but I'll get my bearings. I've a little money. Don't worry. My coming won't make it harder for you, perhaps even a little easier. Much easier, if I should make up my mind to jump a certain way. But don't let's talk any more tonight. I don't think I can stand it. Please, Freda."

"Mama was right. You're a *Schnucke*, like your father."

She sat in her wide apron, with her knees spread, looking silly and befuddled, and yet, withal, a little drawn apart, as if of fastidiousness.

"I need to get my bearings, Freda. It's been a little awful. Let me rest here quietly, a little while. . . ."

"Why—sure—"

"Just quietly."

"And this," said Freda, lumbering to her feet toward the kitchen, as she saw her husband and son open the gate below, "this is the bird of plumage come home."

34

The plan of sleeping in the front room usually occupied by Emma proved not feasible. First, the lack of privacy occasioned by Hugo and the older boy, Kruger, tramping down the stairs mornings, through the parlor to the kitchen, made it objectionable, and then the idea of Emma, with her comb and brush and toothbrush and her little night dress and kimono thrown over her arm, having to dash across the street to share the bed of her friend Olga, was worrisome to Ray and, as Ray rightly suspected, to her mother. There were sons in the Werreneth family, burly drinking men, ten and twelve years the senior of Olga.

After a few days, without consulting anyone, Ray took it upon herself to go over and engage from Mrs. Werreneth, who rented rooms, her second-story back, which was adjoining the bath and had a southern exposure. It was a mean room of a wooden bed with a mosquito netting spread from a barrel-hoop over it, a chiffonier, and a strip of rug. Unnecessarily mean, it occurred to Ray, who had the four hundred dollars in her purse and would have preferred a room in a hotel. But it would have incurred the hurt and the haranguing of Freda, over her inability to provide sufficiently attractive surroundings, which haranguing invariably rebounded to Hugo and, besides, it was pleasant to be within easy accessibility to Emma, to say nothing of the fact that the revenue from her meals, which she insisted upon paying, was welcome in that pinched household.

The new arrangement made the ensuing days of the long hot July more bearable, although those of her meals which she was expected to take with the family could be trying almost beyond endurance, and for a reason which filled her with self-loathing. Freda's older son, Kruger, an almost grotesquely slender, tall, narrow, nice-mannered boy, had an affliction which had dogged him all through childhood. His face twitched in quick heat lightnings of muscular contortions. It was something apparently which the family took for granted, scarcely noticing it. Seated at the supper table in the kitchen, the spectacle of this poor torn face was almost more than Ray could bear. The contortions in themselves were so racking to her, that even when the face was in repose, dread mounted in her. Dread for the next spasm of contortions which was sure to come. Sometimes it seemed to Ray that Hugo, too, would lay down his knife and fork as if too oppressed by the continuous torture of this spectacle to go on; but somehow things in that household did go on, automatically.

The thing about Hugo that you noticed, if you noticed anything at all, was that he, least of all, had changed with the years. Here was perfect capacity for surrender to routine and circumstance that apparently gave him immunity to the ravages of disappointment, disillusionment, and affliction.

Just as in the old days, when his marriage to Freda, once effected, was something into which he had settled without backward glance, so now the imprisonment of the years in a routine of meter-reading was something that he wore as you would wear an old glove. Comfortable, and without consciousness and without even discernible satisfaction that his account with Freda had been squared.

He was a pale, yellowish, youngish-looking man for his years, impervious, apparently, to the burning bitterness of Freda, perhaps secretly exulted by it, and himself impervious to the disappointments that had ravaged her face.

A walker in the valley of routine, fond of his children, concerned, but not vastly disturbed by their plights. An extreme example of a man who must unconsciously have established as his unphilosophical acceptance of life, "What is, is."

Poor little Emma, in many ways she was of the pattern of her father, plodding her patient, nearsighted way at school, and often in spite of diligence falling behind, due to faulty eyes. A patient, unrebellious child, who up to her thirteenth year had known the threat of blindness, and who had accepted her release from that terror as humbly as she had endured under the shadow of darkness.

To think that one year previous to this July, she, Ray, had been living in her flat at Cape May, reveling in the preparation of fine suppers to be shared with Walter, reprimanding him lovingly for overindulgence in her cookery, walking and riding along the lovely ocean front, partaking of the forbidden fruit of late-evening strolls along the moonlit beach with Walter; and now this.

Where was Walter now? He and Corinne must be back East. What—what—what had been the outraged panorama of his mind that morning after reading her letter? She had hurt him, but not, she told herself, over and over again—lying on her wooden bed, while mosquitoes buzzed outside the netting—so outrageously, so revoltingly, as he had hurt her. His hurt to her had been more than that. It had knocked dead something within her. Hours on end, the morning through, sometimes the midday through, until Freda, or Emma, brought her over a bit of lunch on a tray under a napkin, she lay thus in gnawing retrospect.

"Something is eating you that you are not telling," Freda blurted out, one high noon, seated on the side of Ray's bed, watching her lift scrambled egg off the end of her fork and letting the tines click lightly against her teeth after the manner of one who eats absolutely without appetite. "You're in some kind of a fix."

"Why, Freda, what kind of a fix?"

"Oh, I don't mean what you mean. But something terrible is eating you."

Yes, something terrible, as Freda put it, was eating her. Eating her heart. Eating her will to live. Eating her will to rise to face each day. Now that the reaction following the first excitements of the new environment had set in, it was easier just to lie in the rickety room, with the hot sun sprawling all over the place, her accouterments, much too elaborate for their surroundings, spread about, and her face, for the most part, buried in the crook of her arm.

"I've told you about everything there is to tell at this stage, Freda."

"About everything?"

"Oh, except just the little things that aren't worth telling."

"I don't want to seem to be pressing you, Ray. Your being here is a boon to us, you know that, but—but what are your plans?"

What are my plans? *What are my plans?* WHAT ARE MY PLANS?

The words ran in hoops down the corridors of her mind. What—are—my—plans?

"I wish I knew, Freda. I'm just resting, relaxing. Drifting, as the saying goes, until about the twenty-eighth of August. I can't last at it very long, for money reasons, but it's all right for a while."

"God, what a fool you are. Another woman would have salted away. Why, you haven't even got a diamond ring."

That was true. Not a bauble. Not an object of value.

"If there is any reason for a woman doing with her life what you have done with yours, it is that. And to think you could have had both. Of course, you know what has happened to Kurt Shendler. You could have had millions."

"I do think, Freda, and think, and think, and think."

"My God, what fools women are! I threw away my life, but at least I've got my children out of it."

"I love little Emma, Freda."

Her face hardened into a bitter mask.

"If life does to her what it's done to her father and me, I'll be sorry that I didn't bear her stillborn."

"She's studious, Freda. Did you ever notice that about Emma?"

"Lots of good it will do her. I said to her father last night, as much to see what he would say as anything, I said, 'Well, Hugo, Emma's grown up now; way past working-paper age.' 'That's so,' he said. 'That will help.' And goes over and begins practicing on his flute. 'That's all you care,' I said to him. I said, 'Well, just for your own information, she is going to finish High if she does it over my dead body.' By that time he's playing his flute and I'm wasting my breath."

"Yes, Emma is studious, Freda. When I think that I could have had the advantages of education and didn't take them! That has always been one of my regrets. I'd like to see Emma have college, too."

"Yes, college," said Freda, with the mask clamping down again over her features, "about all the college she'll ever have, or my boys, is reading the college booklets she has strewn all over the house."

"You can't tell. I want to help Emma get an education. Curtis and Kruger don't seem cut out that way, but somehow Emma does. I haven't any plans now, but it wouldn't surprise me if, between now and the end of August, I didn't make up my mind either to do something that I'm considering at the minute, or go back into business."

"Say, Ray, you hold your own pretty well, but you're not such a spring chicken that you can think about supporting anyone besides yourself."

"I might marry, Freda. That's one of the things that is on my mind and making me crazy with the need to decide."

"You mean . . ."

"I've a chance to marry. A good chance."

"A good chance. You, at your time of life, and you thinking it over."

"I—you see—it's like this—I don't—it sounds funny, as you say, at this time of life, after what I've been through, but I don't care for this party that way, you see, Freda. I guess, as they say in books, I don't love him. You see?"

"Yes, I see," said Freda, on a gust of small icy laughter that blew off the edge of her lips. "I see that there are things in this world that are too much for me. Most of life and its way of cheating mortals of its goodies is too much for me; but you—well, you take the cake for being too much for me."

For a dreadful moment it seemed to Ray that Freda, whose laughter was splashed with a crazy high note, was going to be hysterical, but nothing of the sort. She snatched up the tray with its half-eaten omelet, and went sailing from the room, head up, and shaking her gelatinous hips in a manner calculated to emphasize the overwhelming enigma of life in general and Ray in particular.

Well, she was right. Rattle the entire situation about in the tired box of her brain as she would, hour after hour, day after day, sometimes without rising until it was time to go over to the Hancks' for supper, the enigma of her predicament grew in oppressiveness.

Just on the basis of what she might do for Emma, made it so doubly worth considering. Sweet girl, who harbored in her heart innocence of the aunt she was daily placing higher and higher upon the pedestal of her young adoration. On the score of the young Emma, and on the score of the open-and-above-board nature of life as it was lived on this straggly street in the dull outskirts of the town, it sometimes seemed to Ray that she even envied Freda. Freda, safe and snug as the wife of the gas-meter reader, and the mother of the children of the gas-meter reader, went about her life in the open fashion that for so many years had been denied Ray. She attended Lutheran Church in that rôle, lorded it over her tradespeople, who somehow did not have toward her the subtle insolence to which Ray was sometimes subjected, and met her children on the fierce possessive basis of motherhood.

To come out in the open like that, to emerge into the easy, sanctioned institution of marriage, was to come out of the deep recesses of a mine.

Mrs. Kurt Shendler. Every time she mentally mouthed it, a thrill raced in chill down her spine, and yet the dull, lethargic days of that long, hot summer, with its reminder of war percolating in occasionally shouted extras, even to the straggling street near the gasworks, marched on, as, with her face in the crook of her arm, she lay beneath the mosquito netting, crushed with inertia.

Emma, who, during the school vacation, tended, for seven hours each day the two small children of a family five blocks away, pale, albino-white, tidy, would come in at five and delight in the business of helping Ray dress. Her nightgowns, rather simple batiste ones which she had purchased in Paris, with their microscopic handwork and ribbon rosettes, were sources of delight. The lace-bordered corsets which Ray wore pulled in tightly at the waistline with heavy pink-silk strings. Ruffled panties, rather antedated now, but which she still wore, petticoats with lace flounces, and corsetcovers of all-over eyelet-embroidery—all to Emma part and parcel of the luxury of this tall, slender, well-formed, gray-eyed, supernally stylish relative, whose letters from time to time had borne such postmarks as New York, Paris, Aix-les-Bains, Nice, London, and Berlin.

"Aunt Ray, I think you're just beautiful. M-m-m, let me smell that sachet-bag."

"You can have it, child."

"Oh, that's the sixth present you've given me today. This lace petticoat by itself would be enough to make me too happy to stand it. You'll make it so I can't dare admire anything you have, Aunt Ray."

"You're a sweet child, Emma. I only wish I were in a position to give you more."

"Why, Aunt Ray, you won't have anything left, as it is, to pack in your trunk when you go. Only you're not going ever, are you, Aunt Ray?"

"Why, yes, child, of course. Only not—not right away."

Little spurts of affection were always cropping out in Emma.

"I just love to touch you, Aunt Ray. I wish every day was a hundred years long, while you are here. When I was blind, Aunt Ray, I used to dress you up all in white, and stand you right in the middle of the darkness, and then it wasn't so bad."

It broke her heart into flakes, the thought of those bright-blue eyes ever having been flooded with darkness. It made her so tender to her that no small wonder the child was filled with delight and adoration.

"My little dear, was it so bad?"

"I couldn't read. I wanted to study for getting into High Preparatory. That made it bad."

"Would you like to go to college, darling?"

"Would I! Would I! Of course, I mustn't. Papa can't afford it, but if only I could be a teacher. You could teach too, Aunt Ray, if you had gone in for a certificate. I'll bet anything you could teach in any college on art. All you know about Titians and Botticellis and Murillos."

All she knew! Their relative prices. Their relative value in the dealers' mart! Dear innocence.

"I'm not one of those exacting girls like Olga, for instance. She wants to be an opera singer. Most girls hate to teach. I wouldn't. I'd love it."

"Don't be so sure, Emma, that you won't be able to, one of these days. Things look bad for it now, but something may happen. . . ."

"Oh, Aunt Ray, you—you couldn't! Mama says you're too poor now—"

"Sh-h-h, darling. Why, you're trembling. No, I don't mean that I could now. I'm just saying—maybe some day—"

"If I could go to Ohio State University, or to Miami, I think I'd be the happiest girl—I think I'd be the happiest girl that ever lived."

She was almost pretty when her pastiness glowed like that. Why, at Emma's age, she, Ray, had never given a thought to the advantages of education. She had discontinued High School without any duress from her father, but because the quick tides of life outside had lapped her feet. Boys. Dances. Canal parties. That, it was true, would not be the case with Emma. Even the neighborhood boys, dances, and parties were already passing her by. Emma would most likely be a teacher, work her way through the state university, live in a dormitory, and the routine of classroom and examination-papers would be no bore to her. A girl whose perpetual virginity seemed written across her face. Emma must be fortified with education for what life was apparently to hold for her. . . .

"Aunt Ray, I don't want ever to get married. I want to be like you."

(If you followed your impulse to laugh, something would bruise this child.)

"Oh, no, Emma!"

"I do. I don't like boys very much, Aunt Ray, and they don't like me at all. I want to do like you. Be in business. Only I want my business to be teaching."

Zealously and well, Freda must have guarded this girl of hers against the sound of the rattle of the family skeleton. Thank God for that!

"Be good and do right, Emma. The rest will take care of itself. You're too young to know yet much about what you really want."

"I'm not too young to know I want to be like you, Aunt Ray."

This stifling, this embarrassing adoration. You wanted to laugh. You wanted to flee from its sweetness and its wrongness. Only where?

There was the crisic date of the coming of Kurt, approaching day by day, and there was the weight inside her of the death she had died at Mount Clemens, and there was the terrible inertia that scarcely gave her the strength to face the days. It took strength to plan and act, or flee. Strength that seemed to have solidified into a dead lump too heavy to drag.

Then, along in early August, came a cool spell; and in an attempt to defeat somehow this inertia, she ventured forth, with Freda and with Emma, on one of the latter's nursing days off, for the unprecedented event in their lives of lunch at the town's largest hotel.

"Ray, I declare, the drummers still stare at you the way they used to in Cincinnati. Never saw the like."

"Nonsense, Freda."

"But it's not nonsense." Around the lobby the heads did still turn, but the bald heads now, of men with embonpoint.

One of them strolled over to her as she stood waiting for Freda and Emma while they were across the street gathering up a pair of shoes for Curtis that had been half-soled.

"Didn't I meet you once in Dayton?" he asked, through a toothpick.

"You did not," she said, looking him full in the eyes, which were swimming with mucous film.

"Who was that?" asked Freda, returning.

"One of the boys I used to know in Cincinnati," she lied. Somehow the very quality in her which had made possible the incident, was something to be ashamed of before Emma.

35

One August afternoon, of inability to endure another moment of the lassitude of lying hour after hour on the bed, Ray dressed about four and took a walk around the rather straggling streets of the tag-end of the town.

The sun baked against the dust of the unmade roads, and the blinds of the shabby workingmen's frame houses were drawn against heat and glare. Goats nibbling in the side and backyards of many of these houses were practically the only signs of animate life at this ebbtide hour of a midsummer afternoon.

It seemed to Ray, walking along under a parasol which she twirled, that the depression of it all—the flat turfless yards, the smoke haze from the brickyards and factories, the inanimate reminders of the dreary routine of the lives lived within those packing-case houses, as evidenced by washtubs tilted against the sides of houses, rubbish heaps, oleanders in tubs—was in a way worse than the depression occasioned by agony of mind. Here, embalmed into the heat haze of this picture, were the sordid monotony, ugliness of vista, repetition of dirty chore, soiled discomfort of bodies, imprisoned defeat. To suffer actively was preferable to what must be the passive depression of the lives that swilled their growlers of beer, scrubbed their stained clothes, earned their meager factory wage, cohabited in unsavory beds, bore their puny children, and had their day-by-day being in these avenues of unrelieved poverty.

It threw her into a mood of revolt and live-while-you-may that caused her, a little later, to commit the indiscretion of entering an exhibition room which she happened to be passing, and buying Kruger a brand-new latest-model Columbia bicycle, which she knew to be the dream of his life, and which reduced her none-too-bulky bankroll by fifty dollars.

It was an impulse and indiscretion that threw scare into her as she walked her way back home, and then brought out some philosophical self-justification.

Glad I did it. Poor kid, what is he ever going to get out of it anyway, with that jumping face of his? No vitality to him. No force. Even less to him, if possible, than to Hugo. Glad I did it. Besides, getting down to rock bottom is what will help me to decide. It's like a storybook. Kurt coming to town in eight days. Oh, God, how can I? How can't I? I can. Why, the security alone. Mrs. Kurt Shendler. Send and charge to Mrs. Kurt Shendler, the little pearl heart, with the gold chain. It is to be a gift to my niece. Emma, I want you to meet your new uncle. Our first present to you is four years at Smith's College—no, it was Smith College, of course—and then four years abroad. Then you are to live with us in our Detroit mansion. No, you didn't refer to your home as a mansion, even if it were one. Our home. Freda, you and Hugo and the boys are to move to Detroit, where Kurt will give Hugo a position of importance in the plant. Your home will be near our home. Not too near. No poor-relation dependence. I hate that. What we give you will be not only the equal of what we have, but very often the superior. Why is it that people who give must always give in smaller proportion than what they themselves have? I should like for you to have a larger house even—a better automobile— Our home will be open to you, but you will have yours. Our home. Mr. and Mrs. Kurt Shendler's. Why, a woman would be crazy, out of her senses, at this time of life, not to crawl gratefully into this golden opportunity. Besides, it went to show, it went to show by now, that she had given the best years of her life, and for what? So that he—Walter—might in the end let her glide out of his existence without even—without even—

The thought, after what had been, of her walking that casually

out of his life, the leaving of the note, the taking of a train, the
ensuing barrage of silence, was one that, flashing over her time after
time during the life of a day, would cause the nap of her flesh to rise,
drenching her in a misery that affected her in the physical manner
of making it hard for her to swallow.

There was something terrifying about that kind of infringement
of the physical into her misery. Sometimes, for a full minute at a
time, she could not swallow, and that sense of paralysis seemed in
a way to affect her breathing, and sweat would break out over her,
and one more day would become one of torment.

Twice, in spite of herself, filled with loathing for her act, she
called at the general-delivery window of the post office. "Anything
for Mrs. Ray Schmidt?" Knowing the while that there was nothing
to expect.

Had she not disappeared? Of course, if he really wanted to find
her! He knew the city of her whereabouts. There was a way. A man
of Walter's resources could find a way. It was simply that he had not
turned his head after her, as she left. The ignominy of that should
be a staff to lead her away from the further ignominy of hanging
around the general-delivery window of a public post office. . . .

Yes, it was well, better, that the bicycle for Kruger had reduced
her roll of bills to a wad. It meant an enforced decision.

I wonder, she thought to herself that afternoon following the
purchase of the bicycle, as she walked her way homeward, twirling the parasol, if anybody else was ever in such a fix. The thing
to do is clear. So right. The thing that is over, so wrong. If only
I could despise him—Walter—as much as I despise myself. God,
what a scare that man gave me, turning the corner so suddenly! For
a second he looked like Walter. I wonder if I can be going a little
mad. He is blond, and doesn't look like Walter any more than I do.
What—how—it is the sun—my headache—

Another pastime of the long, stagnant days was to sit on the
side steps of the Hanck house, with a litter of two-week-old puppies
that had been born to Curtis's fox terrier, crawling about in the sun.
There were five, the shape of enlarged tadpoles with ridiculous little
bellies full of mother's milk, and stick-up tails about the length of

a short lead pencil. The lapful of the entire litter was scarcely a sag in her skirt. They're so little, was her way of explaining to herself the tight, hurt feeling in her throat at the spectacle of the puppies asleep in her lap. They're so little. The tiniest of all, with a black face and a white spot on the tip of its small, frantic tail, had a habit of closing its clover-smelling mouth about her forefinger and pulling on it. There was always the danger of becoming too attached to a dog. But just this one, the tiniest, she took over to her room and made it a bed out of a chip-basket and some pink sateen. Mornings, unable to endure even a sheet for a covering, as she lay bare-limbed, locked in lethargy, the little fellow slept and snored in the crook of her arm, while the sun pressed against the drawn shades and flies buzzed around the chandelier.

"How worthless I am," she thought, as the date of Kurt's arrival climbed nearer. "Why don't I get up and go over and help Freda rinse clothes? I have all the qualities of the bad women you read about in books. I act kept. Women with husbands and children and homes don't lie around in nighties half the day, mooning over dogs. What's the use lying to myself any longer? I'm not fit for anything but loving. I'm not fit even to be loved. Walter, let me slink back into the edge of your life, where I belong, where I'm not even fit to be, except for the one bit of splendor there is about me. My love of you—my love of you."

This sort of thing ended in fits of crying and lying huddled with her pet, until, breathless for the best moment of her entire day, in burst Emma, eager for the service of love in helping her aunt to dress.

One morning, the twenty-fifth of August, to be exact, coming out of the post office, where she had gone this time with something terribly akin to prayer on her lips, she encountered one of the old territory-traveling men of the Cincinnati days, whom she recognized immediately, even under the considerable suet of his greatly increased weight.

"Funny thing, Ray, Roy Ahler told me he thought he'd seen you in town the other day."

Then it had been Roy, lunching at the hotel the day she had

been there with Freda and Emma! She could have sworn that
the tall gray man dining there with what were obviously his wife,
daughter, and possibly son-in-law, was the Roy Ahler of many an
Over-the-Rhine expedition. His carefully averted glance had con-
firmed that suspicion.

"Roy lives here, you know. Quit traveling years ago and went
into the instalment-furniture business. Made a fortune. Youngstown
Furniture Company. And you? Say, you're to the life, Ray!"

"No blarney, Ed. My calendar tells me the same story yours tells
you."

"Living here?"

"With my sister."

"Still Ray Schmidt?"

"Still Ray Schmidt."

"Well, sir, now, what I don't know more and beyond that, don't
hurt me. Anyway, I'm for you. Always was. Question before the jury
now is, are you free to come around to a little penny-ante game at
the hotel tonight? Nixon Stroock is in the town. Remember Nix?
No? Well, he used to hit the Rhine town occasionally. Guess he
came after your time. Well, anyway, good fellow. We're both out
of New York for the same firm. Party is taking place in the rooms
of one of Nix's friends. A Mrs. Dolly Curtis. Good number. Good
crowd. Eight of us. Tickle me, and I know it would Nix, to have you,
Ray. Old time's sake. . . ."

Why not? The evenings in the rear side yard with Freda and
Hugo and the children were horrors. The unrelenting wrangling
of Freda at her children. Do. Don't. Stop. Quit. Even in the dark
Kruger's face twitching like lightning. The loathsome habit of Hugo
of kicking off his shoes and wriggling his toes in his furiously darned
socks. Poor little Emma, tired from her arduous duties with children, sitting with her hands clasped about her knees, and her head
back against her aunt's lap. One needed relief from this to keep from
feeling a little mad. A good game of poker, as in the old days, mild
limit, got your mind off yourself and the menacing imminence of
need of decision.

"Don't know but what I might, Ed."

"Say, that's fine, now. Suppose you come around with me to the hotel. They've got a Wednesday specialty there. Baked shad with boiled potatoes. Afterward we'll join up with the crowd."

There was the puppy up in her room to be fed, and not a telephone either at the Werreneths' or Hancks'. Well, anyway, her shirtwaist felt wilted, and there was always the chance, the off-off-chance, that somehow, some way, there might be waiting that telegram. That special-delivery letter.

"I'll go home and red up a bit, and meet you after dinner, Ed."

"All right. Don't know when I've had such a setting-up as running into you. I've lost a boy in the war. Joined up with the Canadians. Didn't know that, did you, Ray? Hard hit."

"Ed! Oh, my poor Ed! Of course I didn't know. You'll have to tell me all about it first chance."

"Well, same old Ray. Give me half a chance and I'll stand here airing my troubles to you until the crack of dawn. Run along home, girl, and meet me in the hotel lobby at eight. I'd like mighty well to tell you about that boy of mine, one of these days, if you'll listen. Blow of my life, Ray."

The party was all that she remembered such parties to have been back in the old days on those occasions when she had found herself in the suite of "one of the girls." A handful of drummers in shirtsleeves, cigars oblique on their lips, and the girls, usually elaborate creatures, either in evening-dress or strictly proper negligee. A green-baize table. Drinks. Too much gaslight or electricity. A "kitty" for the elaborate supper of salads and sandwiches presently to be served, and almost invariably an upright piano in one corner for those of the girls who did "turns."

Well, what of it? What had she to lose? Off with the old, not yet on with the new. Not yet! At least not for a few days.

Three days later there would come into town, doubtless to this very hotel, a heavy-set, sandy-colored fellow, with fine pigskin luggage and a long Kurt-Sussex car, about which a knot of pedestrians would always be gathering as it stood at the curb, while another knot of reporters waited to interview the "Detroit automobile magnate, honor guest at Youngstown's opening of the Chamber of Commerce."

Under the very roof where she was now sitting playing low-ante poker, Kurt, in three days, would be unpacking his pigskin valise of its personal miscellany. Shaving-mug. Military brushes. Articles of clothing. Pajamas. There would emerge from out of the accouterments of linen duster, good checked suit, the Kurt to whom she, Ray Schmidt, must surrender. . . .

Curious, how suddenly, sitting there holding her five cards behind her stack of red and blue and white chips, the admission, induced by the thought of him under that very same roof, was flooding over her. Kurt, the dear good friend, was one matter. Kurt, the husband—with whom she must presently share hotel suites—

She had known once, back in the Cincinnati days, the legend of a Winton Place girl who had fled from the hotel on her wedding night and never been seen thereafter. Revulsion had put courage into the heart and wings on the feet of that girl. Revulsion would slay her, Ray, that way—revulsion of Kurt—

"I—I'm sorry," she said, and pushed out her chips toward the center of the table. "I—I don't think I feel very well. It's the heat. I shouldn't have come. Not well all day. Please—please—no, Ed. If you try to take me home, I'll not go. I tell you I'm all right. It's just that I'm done-up with this heat. The streetcar in front of the hotel takes me right to my door. Please let me go—alone—"

There were the usual twitterings of the girls, the offices of the men, the kindly concerns.

"Well, let me take you as far as the car, anyway."

"No. No. I am all right, I tell you."

"Take a swallow of that Scotch, dearie, it will brace you."

"No, please."

"Come, Ray, you hadn't ought to go home alone this time of night."

"I tell you I'm all right. It's just the heat."

"Suck a piece of ice, dearie."

"Yes, thanks. I'm so sorry—everybody. Good night—all right now. Feel fine."

How good to be alone! To be free to walk all the way home—all the miles—under the stars—alone—

In the lobby though, as she stepped out of the elevator, a figure with traveling bags in a huddle around his feet was leaning over the telephone operator's desk.

"They must have a telephone. Tell Central the name is Hanck. Hugo Hanck. He works for the gas company. Twelve twenty-one Topeka Avenue. Do your best, miss, to check up on their telephone, or the one nearest to them. I must locate this party."

"Here I am, Walter," she said to him quietly. "Here I am."

36

One knew better than to attempt to tamper with the stemming of tides or oceans or gales; and this thing in her for Walter was ocean and gale. It swept her and there was that. Pride, recriminations, were straws upon the tide. She knew what she was doing was unprideful and turning these weary months into waste, and yet, somehow, had not at her command the psychological tools to follow up her advantage.

She had never quite realized, even with all the weariness of the weary passage of the intervening time until she saw his back hunched there across the counter of the telephone desk, just what a dry lake-bottom life had become, and now there were gushing through her, once more, filling and warming her veins, the released streams of life.

There might be subtle ways of sex and behavior to conceal all this, but they were not her ways. She wanted no penance. The heart flowed with the pathos of his travel-stained eyes and the droop of fatigue around his mouth. And if those were not penance enough, there had been tears in his eyes that instant he had swung around to face her there at the telephone desk.

Then and there he had no terms to demand or offer, no subterfuge to attempt, or advantage to follow up.

"How could you do such a thing to me, Ray? My God, how could you?"

They were seated in an all-night oyster bar across the street from the hotel, where there would be no closing hour to restrict talk.

"Don't ask me that, Walter, any more than you'd ask a crazed person to explain a deed."

"I'll never, to my dying day, forget that afternoon when I walked into the Medes and the clerk handed me your note. It's a wonder I didn't drop dead, Ray."

"Oh, my poor boy! Oh, my poor boy! Oh, my dear boy!" were the phrases that were being borne along the quick stream of her inner sobbing; but she just sat twisting her hands and twisting her lips against the need not to cry there in the incandescent unprivacy of the oyster bar.

"I couldn't have done that to you, Ray, no matter what. Whatever good my trip to Mount Clemens may have done me up to then, I returned to New York a sicker man than I left it; digestion gone, twinges back; a wreck."

Then he had not remained. He had been shot to pieces. (Oh, my boy—my dearest boy!)

"I know now what it means to suffer like a dog in a gutter. You've taught me that, Ray, if it gives you any satisfaction to know it."

It should! It must! Now was the time to follow up an advantage. An incredible undreamed advantage. He was humbled, no doubt of that. Frightened too. Walter needed her! The thing to do now was to keep a stiff upper lip against the flooding tenderness, and demand! How often the girls had said it. The more you demand, the more they respect you. It was a weakness to keep feeling the mind skid off the rail of practicality into the marsh of encroaching tenderness. Now was the moment of advantage. Demand! There were sore hurt places deep down in her heart. Time and time again, the girls, talking among themselves, had asked: "What about you? Suppose a taxicab were to run over him? What about you, who have given the best years of your life? Is your bread buttered? Has he settled on you? Is there a clause in his will? Fool! Fool! He won't thank you. He will think less of you. Fool. Fool. Fool."

"It's been hell, Ray, that's what it's been. We took a house at Deal Beach after we got back, and the Friedlander girls joined us with the children there. That left me free to stay in town when I wanted. To walk the streets in torment when I wanted. To go to the flat and suffer like the dog that you wanted me to be."

The flat! Then he hadn't broken it up. It was there, waiting. Dear, stuffy, poky little heaven—oh, my dear—

"What's the use going into it all? I don't know, Ray, about women. I suppose you're within your rights. I suppose the situation was one to justify what you did. God knows, I don't profess to understand the complicated workings of the whole business. I only know that after all these years, accommodating ourselves as we have to what is what, it seemed to me, well, it couldn't occur to me that anything in one half of my life could have anything to do with your half. You're there. That half is yours. It is as if for you the other half didn't exist. My duty lies in that half just as certain as my duty lies in your half. . . . That's not a bad religion, Ray. Doing my duty all round—"

(Now, now was the time! Yes, what of your obligations to me? To me who have given the best of my life. To me, who am about to continue to throw my life to the winds in order to live on the fringe of yours. What about me, Walter? Must I swallow not only the degradation, which is a lump in my throat—in my being—at this minute, but every lack of consideration as well? What about me, Walter?)

Curious that the words lay unspoken behind two lips that were splinters of wood that would not open. (What about me, Walter? Me. Me. Me.)

"I've been lax in lots of ways, Ray. It usually happens so with a woman as wonderful as you are. A man knows he's not worthy and stops trying."

(What a darling thing to say.)

"I've made up my mind along certain lines, though. God knows there never was a less calculating woman than you. Too little so, for your own good. But I know there are times you must have asked yourself, Ray, just what provision is there for you in my affairs? As a matter of fact, so far as my will goes, there isn't any. Not that the thought hasn't come to me time and time again! It's been because of the delicacy of the situation. How to write you into such a document. Understand? But I'm going to fix all that now, Ray. It's not fair to you and it's not fair to my feelings in the matter of you. Life is uncertain. You're entitled to a sense of security in case anything should happen to me. Problem is, just how to go about it, but I'm going to see a certain lawyer in regard to it right off. That's all that kept me shy of the whole thing this long time. Delicate matter writing you into my will. But don't you worry, Ray. I'd as soon cut off my right hand as see you suffer. . . ."

"Walter, don't go on, darling. It hurts me so. It twists the heart out of me. I don't want anything except—oh, you'll never know what it has been—these weeks—these months—these eternities. If I never knew it before, I know it now. Anything that is right to you, is right to me. It's because I love you so terribly, so senselessly, I guess, that I seem to want rights, observances, conditions that I haven't the right to want. Only go on continuing to need me in your life, Walter, as I continue to need you. That is all I have a right to ask or expect. I see that now."

"Is it enough, Ray, that I am out here?"

"Yes, Walter."

"That I have suffered—"

"Yes, Walter."

"That I mean to try and do everything within reason that you need and want?"

"Yes, Walter."

"That there are certain—er—a—aspects of life—you must have the wisdom to understand and that do not touch you at all?"

"Yes, Walter."

"You've often said yourself, Ray, about—about Corinne—it's our homemade ethics, I guess, but it always helps me—you've wanted as much as I, that she—she shouldn't ever be hurt—"

"I have."

"Then remember that, when certain feelings overtake you. It ought to be a satisfaction to you, Ray, instead of feeling as you do—"

"Oh, Walter, you don't understand. You don't understand."

"Corinne is not complex, Ray. She is as nearly a happy woman as it is possible for a woman to be, and that, in the face of the fact that you and I still have each other. Isn't that—"

"Oh, it is! It is!"

"She has everything, so far as she knows. The deceit hurts us more than her innocence of what is going on could possibly ever hurt her. That is all we need to watch, Ray, you have said so yourself a thousand times, that we hurt no one. That may not always hold water as a text; but since I need you, Ray, with a need that is making me very humble tonight, it is better than no text."

"It is mine too, Walter, to get what we can without hurting, only—"

"No only's now. We're agreed on that. It isn't only in my daily life, Ray, that your being out of it has left such a terrible hole. I need you as my sounding board. I need to think out loud to you. In my work, in my affairs, even in matters concerning my children, it helps me make decisions to have you there—always—no matter where I am. I need you because you are not only one thing, but because you are everything, besides. Come back to me, Ray."

She knew she was going to say it, and she was glad she was going to say it, and she wanted to hurry to say it before the tears might blur it. Madness, perhaps, to say it, but dear beyond telling in the saying.

"My dear darling, bless you for forgiving and taking me back."

BOOK FOUR

37

It seemed almost yesterday that she had sat embroidering, for Richard's fourteenth birthday, the names of the states on the frame that
was to contain the twenty-eight Presidents from Washington to
Wilson, and now here were nearly three additional presidential
terms rolled around and Richard about to be twenty-one.

This fact, combined with his impending graduation from Yale,
was exciting Walter more than anything she could remember since
the quick days of reorganization and immense business adjustments
that had followed the Armistice.

Well, it was no small thing, this coming-of-age of the apple of
Walter's eye, a boy to be proud of, even in a family where every
child had so normally thrived and developed! Irma, at nineteen,
from occasional glimpses and photographs, filled with the promise
of an alien, unoriental beauty that was neither Friedlander, Trauer,
nor Saxel, was already carrying her small head on her shoulders
as if it were a pail brimful with water. And then, across the wide
gap, the five-year-old Arnold. From a newspaper-reproduction of a
group portrait by Halmi, of Corinne and her children, painted when
Richard was eighteen and Arnold two, Ray had cut out the heads
and shoulders of all three of the children, mounting them in a small
album. From time to time there were additions to this collection,
particularly as Richard began to do conspicuous things on the polo-
and debating-teams at college; and at sixteen, Irma's photograph

as Celia in the Spenser School production of "As You Like It" had already appeared in the *Spur*.

Then there were two or three snapshots. "Mrs. Walter D. Saxel and daughter Irma snapped by a *Times* photographer on Fifth Avenue, New Year's Day." "Mr. and Mrs. Walter D. Saxel, Miss Irma Saxel, and Richard Saxel, about to board the S.S. *Mauretania*." And: "Miss Irma Saxel, daughter of Walter D. Saxel, banker, philanthropist, who will sell poppies at the Falkland Hospital Benefit."

Quite a gallery, even while the children were young, which she had managed to eke out of cuttings and clippings, to say nothing of the even clearer word-gallery of their portraits which, down the years, Walter had hung in her mind.

Clearest of all hung Richard's. From his very babyhood he had exhibited qualities that were as admirable and endearing to her as they were to Walter.

"He has a genuine sense of responsibility, that youngster has," Walter had explained to her from the time he was six or seven. "Watches over his little sister as much as his mother or nurses. Tell that boy to do a thing and you don't need ever to give it another thought, because you know it will be done, and right! Wish a lot of men in the bank had qualities like him."

Well, and here was Richard now, twenty-one, a Yale graduate, cum laude, crack polo player in the amateur class, fair at all sports, and no mean debater, about to enter the banking house of Friedlander-Kunz.

Little wonder that his father, ever since his return from commencement at New Haven, had been in a state of excitement that bordered on those days following the Armistice.

"I'll never forgive myself for not insisting that you see that sight, Ray. You and I feel pretty much the same about the pity of having missed education, and this spectacle would have done your heart good, and, if I do say it, the boy held his own with the sons of fathers that can buy and sell me five times over."

"His mother must be proud!"

"She has cause. The boy has come clean since the day he was born. I'm not supposed to say it, because he's mine, but if I had been allowed the pick yesterday of every man on that graduating-platform, my pick would have been the clean-cut young fellow, fourth from the left."

She leaned over on the couch, where, as usual, they were sitting after the table containing the remains of the evening meal had been dragged off to its corner, and kissed him. What a small boy he was! In many ways, as Walter described him, this son of his seemed more the man of banking affairs and worldly concern than his father. But that was because this was the side of his life, in the flat here alone with her, where he could afford to let go. Be himself. Cast aside rigmarole of rostrum, directors' table, husband, financier, philanthropist, and national and even international affairs, into which his peculiar services of vast financial importance during the war called him in firsthand contact with prime and cabinet ministers, and table-conferences with the President of the United States.

Here was her part in his life, to exercise her philosophy of life, that where she was concerned he need have no philosophy of life. To make him laugh. Walter, not notable for sense of humor, laughed here in this flat. To make him play. Walter played here. On rostrums, in his office, even in his own home, he was not a ready laugher. He was young here, capable of the kind of boyish thing that had impelled her to lean over and kiss him for what he had just said about Richard.

"You darling!"

"Now what was there darling about that?" he asked, pleased.

"Just you being you. Honestly, I believe that in lots of ways Richard is older than you are."

"If levelheadedness means anything, he is. Should have seen the way he took the idea of taking his place under Eagan in the appraisal department. Another boy would have—"

"Ah, but you've been such a wonderful influence in Richard's life, Walter."

"I said to him: 'Son, it is a modest beginning, that of appraiser of real estate on which the bank is considering advising mortgages. It is thoughtful, careful work, that requires the kind of consideration you must give the woman and often the widowed investor. I consider the philosophy unsound that a rich man's son needs necessarily to start in overalls. Years of unnecessary hardship may be more destructive than constructive.' As a matter of fact, now that I recall it, I think those were your words, Ray."

Foolish Walter, to look so sheepish! Of course they were her words. She had argued heatedly against Walter's original idea of farming Richard out as runner to a small brokerage firm in Chicago, under an anonymity that, in the end, once his identity leaked out, would mean newspaper publicity and false exploitation. "Let him have his simple beginnings and work his way alone, but why bend too far backward. Starting a rich man's son down at the bottom of the ladder in overalls is fodder for headlines and more fad than fact. Treat him naturally, Walter. There is nothing unusual in any average young man finding himself working as assistant appraiser in a bank. Years of unnecessary hardship can make work more destructive than constructive."

Of course those had been her words! Oh, Walter, Walter; and his constant surprise and embarrassment at finding himself quoting her expressions.

"Comes back at me like a flash: 'I'm glad you're starting me regular, Father. Treat me average. That's what I am, until I prove otherwise, one way or another.' As if it didn't take more than the average to be capable of sizing up the situation like that!"

"You've great joy coming to you out of that boy, Walter."

"Yessir, I think I have, Ray. In fact, I've no kick coming on any of them."

"Indeed you haven't. They're children to be proud of. All this postwar jazz, hip-flask generation you read about doesn't seem to have really touched yours."

"It's not in our ribs, much of that kind of thing. . . ."

How Walter's face had filled out, or was it just from the beaming look it wore when these discussions of his children arose? No, under hair that was plentifully more gray than black, there were soft little jowls to his cheeks now, and even though you could never imagine him stout, undoubtedly the area under his waistcoat had thickened and the old straight look to his back had become slightly saggy.

Strangely, and sometimes a little meanly, she was glad of these inroads into the face and figure of Walter. It made her less fearful of her own mirror. . . .

The trouble with dyeing one's hair to keep the gray down was that after a while, as if too tired to endure under the effort to remain glamorous, it refused to take the coloring. Result, the effect ran crazily to red rusts, greenish tints, with the gray itself persisting through. It was terribly worrisome, because the effect of the dye was to harden and make grim the features without sufficiently eliminating the evil.

It made her welcome, in spite of herself, the little sacs of loose fowl-like skin under Walter's eyes and along his jowls, and the thinning spot that by now was almost bare and shiny on the back of the top of his head. Dear little welcome tracks of time that made her own seem the less terrifying.

"When you beam like that, Walter, you look adorable."

He was annoyed, and rightly, she told herself. It had slipped, a remark that could be warranted to annoy any man, let alone one like Walter.

"Oh, cut that out, Ray. I'm not beaming."

"Well, you don't need to get mad about it, dear."

"No use making a man feel a fool. Women are funny."

"Men are funnier," she said, feeling that everything she was saying was somehow going against his grain, and yet not quite knowing how to right her manner, which, goodness knows, had been well-meaning.

"Walter dear, speaking of funny, I think we need a little more comic relief in your speech for the junior group at the Empire State Club next week. I read it over to myself last night, and it struck me those young men might find it heavy sledding."

"Meaning that my audiences find my talks heavy sledding?"

"Of course not, dear! If you aren't the one to be touchy tonight. That isn't at all what I meant, and you know it. My point is that one who can be as wise and witty at the same time as you can be, cannot afford to be too much one or the other."

As if over and over again there were not this inevitable preamble leading up to the inevitable revision of the cut-and-dried tracts which he ostensibly brought for typing.

"Of course, Walter, I realize that these young men look to you as the symbol of dignified success." (Success, success, that was the noun to wave before him as the white flag of truce! Success. Success. The word made him wet-lipped.) "But my idea is, the more lightly you treat yourself, the more seriously they are going to be willing to take you. It's human nature. I've seen so many of your audiences, Walter, remain a little stiff, if you happened to be saying things about yourself that they would be perfectly eager to say about you themselves, but which they resented coming from you. And then, on the other hand, time and time again, I've seen them warm up after you've given them a laugh or two at your expense, and then eat out of your hand during the rest of the speech. Remember the time you got the entire Bankers' Convention roaring from the very start when you told them how the Maharajah of Something-or-other had mistaken you for his tailor, when you walked into his apartments at the Savoy, in London, with some documents in your hands that were virtually going to change the history of his country?" She had written that, against his protest, into his notes. "Well, that's all I mean here, dear. Get those young fellows with you and for you from the very start. Keep humorous and they'll let you be wise. And if I were you, dear, I'd step on the word 'Hun.' The war vocabulary is already out-of-date and out of hate."

Incredible, the need to keep before Walter the most elementary observations. His inability to withstand the lure of an invitation to indulge in public address seemed to grow with the years and with the prestige of his name on a speakers' list. But his capacity to fatigue an audience, with a spiritless reading of a not always unspirited address, remained static. Strange, because there were aspects of his work in relationship to his public life upon which, in the sanctity of the flat, he could speak with color and authority.

"Walter, let me write that down, just the way you said it. How was it? The buying-power of any given community is—*hors de combat* (whatever that means) if it is-pitted against-a selling-power-so powerful-that it-jeopardizes-the credit—if only you could let go on the platform, dear, the way you do here!"

"There are some who do not think I am so bad."

"Walter, how you twist everything I say."

"I wasn't aware of twisting what you just said of me. In other words, on the speakers' platform I am a dead-cat."

"Why, Walter Saxel, honestly, I could just wash your mouth with soap. Kiss me and take back every word. I think you're splendid on the platform. Getting better every day, and you know it."

"Aztecs of Brooklyn want me for their tenth anniversary."

"Well, brush up the talk you gave the Rochester Aztecs. Same crowd—same spirit."

"Dig that out for me, Ray—will you?"

"Love to. I've got a new wheeze about Brooklyn. Cut it out of the Literary Digest. You get around so much more than I do, honey. Try to keep your ears open for the funny slants. You're all right on the serious banking-side. I just want you to be, as they say at Keith's Vaudeville, louder and funnier."

"There you are again."

"There *you* are again, you mean. Kiss me, and not another word out of you. When you squint like that, dear, you look exactly like little Arnold."

"Speaking of Arnold, of course it's all a bit premature, but Corinne already insists that she wants him to enter Corton. I don't know but what I agree with her."

"Oh, Walter, Corton was all right for Richard, although you know yourself how certain things hurt his spirit there. But Richard is tough-fibered compared to Arnold, and not so easily got at. Richard took his medicine about not being eligible to enter a fraternity, but Arnold will be another matter. They will break his spirit."

"His mother seemed to think just the contrary. He's all imagination and no backbone. The child needs outside contacts."

"But why try to make a polo player out of a silk purse?"

"Why not let him be both? Richard is."

"Because, in Arnold's case, the purse will be torn to pieces."

"Race pride has the buoyancy to rise above race prejudice. [Her phrase.] Let Arnold when his time comes take his medicine about the Corton fraternity situation. Richard did."

"But, Walter, you cannot apply the same formula to two such different natures. I've been sending for catalogues from boys' schools all over the country, Walter, ever since you told me there has been this talk of some day sending Arnold; and the more I read them, and the more you tell me about that child, the surer I am that he ought to be tutored at home indefinitely. Arnold is special, Walter. Don't cut him out with a biscuit tin. Home study and in time, travel, are for his sort of nature."

"Not sure but what you're right."

"I know I am. But all this I'm telling you isn't really my idea. It's yours. You've always been the one to emphasize that Arnold is the sensitive plant."

"His mother—"

"Of course. It's natural. She's ambitious for him, and Corton's the smart school to send him."

"I think I do understand the child. . . ."

"I think you're wonderful with your children, Walter."

"And you're wonderful with me, Ray. But this is what I really dropped in about. Want you to go to the library tomorrow and read up on Abyssinia. North American Archeological Society has been after me to finance that fellow Hickerson who got himself famous down in the Congo country last autumn, and set him up in an expedition to go do some important excavation-work in Abyssinia. Seems to be a good thing, but I'll need a lot of information at my fingertips when I meet the committee."

"Oh, Walter, if only Arnold were old enough to go along! Think what that would do for the boy. That's what he needs—something like that to stimulate his courage and imagination. . . ."

"Oh, I see, poking over dead men's stones and bones in Abyssinia. That would make a hit with his mother! Ray, you're a crazy darling."

"Walter, stop being silly. I mean it. But come, let's get to work on the New York Civic Forum annual-banquet address. Can't you—won't you, Walter, just once forget yourself, forget your audience, your manuscript, and begin to talk—just naturally, the way you do here? Please, Walter, try to deliver without reading from your notes. . . . Get up there before the mirror and try it now."

"Mr. Chairman. Your Honor the Mayor. Honored guests, gentlemen. It is with no small sense of the honor and responsibility imposed upon me that I find myself tonight confronted with—I can't. Give me the notes."

"You can."

"—so vast and distinguished an audience. I remind myself of the man who, walking home one night—Give me the notes. Let me read—"

"I'm here, Walter, ready to help you if you forget. You're going ahead splendidly—"

"—I remind myself of the man—*Let me have those notes!*"

"Don't shout, Walter. Let's try it over again. Just remember that if you forget—I'm here."

"Mr. Chairman. Your Honor the Mayor. Honored guests, ladies and gentlemen. It is with no small sense of the honor and responsibility imposed upon me that I find myself tonight confronted with . . ."

38

It turned out that the hiatus of the months in Youngstown was to divide time and tide into two eras. Not only Ray reckoned in terms of "before and after I went to Youngstown"; but the Walter of those years following, in many ways a kinder and more considerate Walter, reckoned too, subconsciously or unconsciously, in two eras.

"What do you think, Walter? They are going to tear out the ground-floor apartments of this building and put in stores."

"Why, they've been threatening to do that since before you went to Youngstown." Or:

"Ray, did you ever hear me mention a Frenchman named M. Jules Marin, of whom I saw a good deal during the Guerin Conferences in France?"

"Seems to me that was way back before I went to Youngstown; I do remember you used to mention lunching with him occasionally. Why?"

"Nothing. Except I see where he died yesterday in Nantes."

"Walter, I can remember the time when nobody we knew was dead. Now it seems to me that almost every few days somebody drops out."

"Makes a fellow think, doesn't it?"

"Indeed it does. You don't ever seem any older to me, Walter, except in importance. It's when I see you in public that I find myself realizing things that never occur to me when you're just here—with me—as we have been for so many years."

"Funny thing about you, Ray—in this flat time seems to stand still. Same old Ray. . . ."

(Same old Ray. Old Ray. Old Ray.)

"Same old furniture. Same old-shoe of a place. It's when I'm home in the house on Fifty-third Street that the colossal sense of change and time is always with me. The children growing and developing. Corinne's restiveness to have, and to be. Business—change—development, complications, pressure, hurry, and competition all about me. Why, when I think of this town, Ray, the day we walked into each other over eighteen years ago, and think of the changes that have taken place during that time, I sort of feel as if human realization isn't big enough to take it all in, if you know what I mean."

"I do."

"The world my children are going to face, if they live, please God, in the next forty or fifty years, is a mighty different one from the one we faced at their age. We won't live to see how different."

"B-r-r-r. I'm not afraid to die, but I love life."

"While we're on the subject. I—haven't forgotten, Ray, a little subject we once opened, years ago out in Youngstown. Er—matter of will. Haven't forgotten. Life is too uncertain to let a thing like that drift. Certain matters meanwhile have come up in my affairs, the Exchange merger, as you know, which make them more complicated, although fortunately all for the better. I mean to make provision for you, Ray, but in the way that a certain lawyer has got to work out for me so that—well, you know what I mean. No use putting on record any more than is absolutely necessary."

Oh, she had wondered through the years all right. Time and time again, hating herself the while, but nevertheless, as she sat sewing, or devising lampshades, or moving about at the mixing of the batch of cinnamon cookies it was her habit to do each fortnight for the Women's Exchange, which also handled on commission the embroidery and the lampshades, the thought had flown quick as a bird through her mind.

Had Walter ever carried out his announced intention of that dear tender memory of a night in Youngstown? Not that it really mattered—except—why not be honest with herself, it did matter! It mattered a great deal. It mattered for two or three terribly poignant reasons. She had earned the right to inclusion in the last will and testament of the being to whom she had been, if not all, at least many things. And then—here was where she must be relentlessly honest with herself. Not even the bald heads mounted on the short necks of paunchy bodies turned any longer to the spare figure with the metallic-looking hair and the fine lines in which the powder lingered like snow along ledges. A woman whose slenderness had turned lean and whose chic had petered out into neatness. Somehow, admitting these things to herself, the need of assurance about the future became something horridly imperative.

Every so often she found herself wondering what had become of Hattie and Saperlee and various other of "the girls" who had drifted through the scene from time to time. There was occasionally a note from one, Greta, who had occupied a sumptuous flat in the building for about a year who, with her friend, whom she gravely described as the "Old Soak," was living in New Orleans; and once in a while, upon a tip from her, Ray wired down a bet, on one occasion winning five hundred dollars at enormous odds.

But in general, where were those girls? Walter must—must! And then, to be bound up in the close fabric of the last will and testament of a man into whose life you had been similarly bound, was only fair. It was the symbol of your right to take your high place among his dear ones. Walter must. . . .

"There must be a technical way around just the bold procedure of inserting your name into the document, Ray. That would be bad. That's the matter I intend to clear up with a certain lawyer. . . ."

It opened, this subject, the pressure of silent questions that more and more, as she worked, pricked against her consciousness. It was all right, her doing these fancy chores, such as the cookies which she packed into painted tins and sold at a rather close margin, or the padded coathangers, decorated lampshades, and china vases. It took care, along with her rather fair average of good luck at the races, of the not inconsolable item of Emma at Miami University, in Oxford, Ohio.

It was the "principle of the thing" that turned in her slowly, like a knife. Walter, particularly since the Exchange merger, must reckon his fortune in millions by now.

Indeed, always reluctantly, however, where money discussions were concerned, he had told her as much, in reply to an outright question from her the day the Exchange merger was consummated. Everywhere were the evidences of the growing grandeur of his position of wealth. The home in Fifty-third Street, that had been doubled in size by the purchase of the brownstone house adjoining. The period of throwing the two houses into one had been an arduous one of poring over blueprints and architects' drawings, and, for Ray, of exploring large, beautiful illustrated books of Tudor and Italian Renaissance drawings at the library. The central staircase, "winding up like a beautiful woman's two arms," had been Ray's idea, as she had drawn it crudely on the back of an envelope while they sat one evening on their well-dented places on the sofa.

"I wonder," she had more than once thought to herself since, "how many times she must have looked beautiful to him, coming down those white stairs, in her white hair, her white velvet, and her white pearls."

God! Sometimes sitting there at the sewing, suffocation had her by the throat; thwarting, smoky sense of suffocation.

Why, of every aspect of his life, was she alone to remain the dingy one? It was not that the flat, as always, was not the warm cloak of retreat to her that it was to him. That was understandable, dear, warm, old-fashioned corner of security. She, no more than he, would have changed it. What rankled was the consistent fact that never, once, had he permitted the luster of his success to brighten her. At birthdays and Christmas-time, duplicates of the monthly rolls of bills found their way into the fishbasket of the bisque boy on the sideboard. That was all. He had succeeded, all right, in keeping her small and brown and unelegant as a sparrow.

One day, on an impulse he had never repeated, and chiefly because the tines of one of the forks, bent slightly, had scratched his lips as he ate, he sent up a small case of engraved flat silver of conventional design. Another time, during an epidemic of Spanish influenza, he brought her a fur coat, a good quality Hudson seal. Not exactly what she would have selected; but the act moved her deeply.

Otherwise, the same old devices, which Walter never disapproved, of eking out with additional income from handiwork, continued. Not more than two or three times had she been forced to aid and abet her allowances to Emma with contributions from her household funds. "I'm like the fancy woman in the play, tainted money shall never touch the hands of my chei-ild."

But just the same, on the few occasions when she had been short and forced to resort to allowance moneys, as in the case of the ruby lavaliere, she had laboriously gone about the formality of repaying the sum from her Women's Exchange pocket into the household purse.

Strange, strange Walter, you, stinting me out of your plenty. Sitting there beside him in the stale air of a warm May evening, his body stretched out on a sofa, while she sat on a small carpet hassock stitching, it struck her how easily she might hate him, whose family wore so conspicuously the scalps of his munificence. The double house on Fifty-third Street. The summer home at Rye, of twice the magnitude of the old home at Cape May. The prominence of his place and Corinne's, in the listed names of donors, endowers, patrons. The munificence of education, travel, sports, and expensive activities surrounding his children. Lately, too, out of a large sweep of room formed by the merging of the fourth stories of the two houses into a gallery, he had gathered the nucleus of what was to become one of the most important small collections of the Italian and Dutch Masters of the fourteenth and fifteenth and sixteenth centuries.

There were already two Jan Steens, a Carlo Dolci, a Cimabue triptych, an alleged Velasquez, and a Memlinc, smaller than all the rest, but which had cost many thousands more. Ray knew. The bookkeeping, the sending for catalogues, the keeping-abreast with the news of art transactions, had come to be her part of keeping

Walter informed. There were folders of correspondence with Beren-son in Florence, Duveen in London, Zan Marle in Perugia, in her files, and she could recite the names of "schools" not only by rote but in figures of appraisal.

Already, expended in that room across the top of the Saxel home, was a fortune in two or three pictures alone, which, she found herself reflecting one day, would have meant affluence for her for the rest of her life.

Bitterly, before a pride in it that was to become akin to Walter's, began to set in, she could feel about the money expenditure repre-sented up there in that gallery. Why, if he were to turn over to me, in a lump sum, the price of that little Memlinc alone, it would free me for my life; free me from the horrid performance of—the bisque basket on the sideboard.

Yes, sitting there in the warmish May evening, while she stitched away beside him, it struck her again and again how easily she might hate him.

39

It was that summer, just before the closing of the town house and the departure of the household for Rye Beach, that he did what was to her something of redeeming sweetness.

One evening he brought to her, with his own hands, in a small hamper, a young French poodle. He had carried it in a taxicab from a fancier's where he had purchased it. He, with his aversion to bundles and baggage, had brought her this firsthand.

"Why, Walter, I just wouldn't take anything for this! Oh, my little sweety!"

"I know you like dogs."

"Remember the little pug I had back in Cincinnati, Walter? I cried so when it died. I've never since had a pet really of my own except while I was in Youngstown that time."

"I thought he would be company for you this summer."

"Walter, you're a darling."

It was the first admission he had ever made of his cognizance of how dull her summers must seem since the completion of the house at Rye. With his children grown away from the restraints of nurses, and given to riding and driving over the countryside, and the beach so much more restricted, the wise thing had seemed to be for Ray to take quarters at White Plains, a fair-sized town eight miles away. This time she found residence in what was a small hotel or large boardinghouse, situated on the main street, where her presence would not be so conspicuous as it might in one of the smaller houses, set in leafy quiet, that displayed "Furnished Room" shingles, along the pretty side streets.

Always, it seemed, her summers, anyway those that they spent in America, were to be lived on the heated strip of a small town's main street. At least the flat in Cape May, although over a corner drugstore, had been housekeeping quarters. There had been cooking facilities and bright cretonnes over the wintry furnishings, Victrola, and sewing machine. The little hotel in White Plains was of weather-colored clapboards, surrounded by supply shops of many varieties, and clanged into at all hours of the day and night by the insistent note of trolley car bells and motor traffic. No beach nearer than Rye, but pretty country walks along roads that bordered walled-in country estates, and at evening either the motion picture, with soda afterward at one of the many "parlors" which lined the street, or the long after-dinner periods spent in her rooms, at handiwork, beside a rickety table that had a gas lamp attached by rubber tubing to the chandelier.

Long summers, with what there was of Walter arranged something like this. Occasionally, of an early Sunday morning, especially if there were houseguests at Seascape, he drove over from Rye before they were up and stirring, and sat for an hour or so, always with the door left open, beside the square table where she was constantly placing cooling soft drinks. Strained visits, with figures constantly moving across the patently left-open door, and the hot smell of sun, soft asphalt, and leather seats of parked automobiles, coming through the lace curtains.

Right! In such a summer, a dog would be a blessed touch of companionship, during days that, for tediousness, could sometimes be trying almost beyond endurance. Relief from them lay in the semiweekly trips to the city, which she took by train, there to meet Walter in the cool, shrouded seclusion of the flat, on several occasions, when it was possible to arrange his affairs so, remaining there over the period of the weekend, while the city streets lay baking and half deserted outside the drawn blinds, and the high tide of her contentment mounted to the stars.

"Walter, let me stay in town this summer. It's easier for you to come to me here. I will wait. I do not mind the heat. Besides, it is dull and hot for me at White Plains." She did not add, "And more dangerous." But it did seem to her that for the sake of their brief and occasional half hours before the open door of the dingy sitting room, the chances they took for being remarked were unnecessary.

"I want you near where I am," he said doggedly. "I've a sense of something like amputation when you are in another town. Part of me is missing."

That was among the dear things said to her by him which she embalmed in her memory and kept there, as you would a flower in a cake of ice. It made the planning to go to White Plains and the arrangements by telephone for the dreary suite, and the packing away and hanging in camphor balls for a summer that was almost entirely without lure, bearable and even pleasurable. The little dog was going to be a help. He was half shaven, after the manner of French poodles, without pompons above his ankles, and an absurd tuft of pompadour, which had to be caught with a bit of ribbon, to keep a jungle of black wool out of his eyes. Jean Jacques was the name on the considerable pedigree which had come from the fancier's; but somehow, in the memory of a little pug that was gone and of days that were gone, she found herself rechristening him Babe. For the first little while he slept in the hamper beside her, but then, one night, she wakened to find him standing on his hind legs, scratching at the sheets, to be lifted into bed with her. Thereafter he slept at her feet, always in a position so that, through the covering, the flank of his body pressed hers.

"That is a silly name, Ray," Walter admonished her once, before he had had time to become accustomed to it. "Call him by his pedigree name or just Fido or something doggish." She did try for a while, but quickly relapsed into Babe.

"I oughtn't to do that," she soliloquized before succumbing. "There is something too just-right about a person like me cooped up in a flat all day with a poodle named Babe."

Nevertheless, before she left for the country, she was already pressing out his little hair ribbons for him, and keeping them folded in a glove box, upon which she had outlined in pencil, and then embroidered in black-wool French knots, a poodle.

Once she caught herself talking a lingo to him that went something like this: "Muvver's angel-sweet companion. Love oo." And drew up sharply. God, that was awful. "I'll sell you to the black ragman if ever I catch myself doing that again. May I die with a bubble over my mouth if I ever love you too much. You're a galoot. Get out!"

He lay with his nose between his paws, and, regarding her, stared, and staring, blinked.

"Wait until I get you to the country, I'll take you for real walks," she told him, when conscience smote her at her hurried method of slipping a coat over her negligee and taking him down for a brief run up and down the sidewalk. There was less and less reason for wanting to go out, particularly as late spring set in and the streets became glaring and dusty.

Except for the special foods that needed to be personally shopped for Walter—*Schmierkäse,* gluten bread (almost his sole dietetic precaution, which he had followed since his mother's death from diabetes), fresh caviar from a certain Madison Avenue dealer—she had learned the practice of telephoning for provisions. She had even learned the saving device of telephoning Altman's or Lord and Taylor's for wire shades or cretonne covering for the handkerchief boxes she had lately added to the assortment of small objects she offered, on commission, to the Women's Exchange.

Depending largely upon the season and its propinquity to holiday time, her income from this indoor work, which in many ways was child's play so far as actual effort was concerned, averaged about forty dollars a month. Emma, now a sophomore, with advanced standing because of summer extension-work, had written her: "Dearest Aunt Ray, You send me too much. I've saved enough out of what is left every month, to live one whole month without your sending me anything. Oh, Aunt Ray, I am so happy here. Señora Gomez thinks I ought to major in Spanish. I am doing so well, too, in it, and the public schools now feature it in their commercial courses, and there is a big demand for teachers of Spanish. And just think, Aunt Ray, I have you to thank for everything. . . ."

Silly girl, she was not of blood kin, and yet she seemed to have the family failing of lacking either shrewd or shrewish talent in money matters. Another girl, now, would have pocketed the surplus without a word. There were three hundred dollars besides, salted away in a savings bank for Emma. It was part of the sum she had won on the New Orleans tip from Greta, and, on the strength of it, had not ventured to the local tracks any more that season.

"Dear Emma," Ray wrote back, "I want you to take the extra money and buy yourself a nice spring outfit. The snapshot of you on the dormitory steps is good, but I do not like that middy-blouse on you. Buy yourself a good-quality coat-suit, with one of those tricorn sailor hats that are so stylish this season. I will make you two hemstitched dimity blouses with corset covers. Keep yourself neat and study hard. Remember, no one can ever take away your education, once you get it. Knowledge is power. Your loving Aunt Ray."

She made no secret of this, reciting to Walter extracts of Emma's little letters as they came from time to time, and showing him the snapshot of the dormitory steps. "She is not pretty, Walter, in the ordinary sense of the word, but just a fine good girl, and sweet." It was remarkable the consistency with which his interest failed to awaken.

"That's fine. Looks like a mighty nice girl." Not making even the pretense of putting on his glasses, without which he had practically no reading vision left.

Sometimes it seemed to her that he was not even clear as to who Emma was. Some little niece out West, for whom she had a soft spot, was probably what lay lightly lodged in his memory when there arose the subject of Emma.

Well, it was just as well. Emma was the only concern she had that was privately her own. Emma, and now Babe. This cheeky little fellow, the poodle, was possessed of an appetite ridiculous for so small a dog. He liked cheesecake! Too cute. Yessir, ate greedily of the large Torten she was in the habit of keeping on hand for Walter. And another thing he shared with him was his very special appetite for smelts, prepared the way they used to fry them Over-the-Rhine, in breadcrumbs and hot butter. Once she had offered him, off the tip of a fork, a Lynnhaven oyster, another preference of Walter's, and galumph, down it had gone! Funniest little fellow. . . .

The move to the country that summer came a month earlier than usual, because there was some talk of Walter's taking August to go to Aix-les-Bains for the cure. Three weeks a year at the French spa, he declared, could either drive out, or back into the recesses of his bones, for the period of the winter at least, the demon rheumatism. Corinne, of late, had been taking the treatment too, for calcium deposits along her knuckles, which caused them to pain and swell slightly.

"Walter, you eat too much rich food. I cannot watch over you at home and at banquets, but I think I'll cut down some of your favorite meat dishes here. Those heavy steaks and pot roasts, for instance."

"Nonsense," he said, never able to bear the implication of his food indulgence. "I can remember digestive attacks way back in my teens, and I've been rheumatic since I was twenty. My father was full of it."

"No reason you should be."

"Don't concern yourself about things you don't understand, Ray. I have a doctor to advise me about my health. If you find cooking for me a hardship, come out and say so."

She was so hurt it was a full minute before she could trust herself to reply.

"Why, Walter, I didn't mean . . ."

"Of course you didn't. You never do. Only the next time think before you speak. One would think, to hear you, that I'm a gormand. . . ."

"I only meant, dear . . ."

"It's all right. Forget it."

She could not. Tears pressed against her throat for the remainder of the evening, and the marvel of it was, that five minutes afterward he was eating, with unassailed relish, the heavy rich foods she had prepared for him, and later, while she pored with him for hours over art catalogues and the annotations for a public address, her impulse persisted to stretch out her arms on the table, lay her head into them, and cry. Which she did not do.

40

That summer, Richard Saxel had an aluminum-colored Kurt-Sussex roadster, which he drove like a streak about the countryside, and which had come to be a familiar sight in White Plains, whizzing along, usually filled with youth, and the spray of silver sirens on its running board bleating a four-tone chord.

Rushing to her window at the first remote sound of this silver spray of noises, Ray could see the car whizz by her hotel. Frequently, too, it drew up before Doney's Ice-Cream Parlor across the way, a resort popular with the youth of miles around. Sometimes Richard, in white flannel trousers and a pull-on sweater, would hop out, and then, off again in his car, which started almost before he was seated. He was undoubtedly the handsome one of the family, slim and far more impressive in his dark, tan beauty than Irma, who was just plump and pretty.

Sometimes the roaster was so crowded that youngsters sat piled on one another's laps, with tennis rackets propped in clusters between them. On two occasions, Corinne, with her beautiful white waved hair uncovered and trim under a net, and her soft summer dress at variance with the sweaters and togs of the girls and boys, had been in the car. The youngsters had hopped out and stood at attention while her son helped her from the running board. They had swept her into the ice cream parlor in a little circle of deference, her son standing to hold the screen door open, and popping in after, on a sharp slam. There had been pearls, as usual, on her placid breast, and to Ray, even from behind the lace curtains in her room of the hotel, the detail of monogram on the cushion at her empty place in the automobile, the gray felt footrest on the floor, her folded wrap of gray cloth and chinchilla thrown across the nickel bar, were testimonial, somehow, to the ordered rightness that had marked this life.

It was strange, standing behind the Nottingham-lace curtains of that snide hot room, on the snide hot street, gazing across at a car thus strewn with these inanimate objects of Corinne. She so seldom moved with the dimension of a human being, in Ray's imagination. She was just there, pasted like a dominating paper doll in the foreground of everything pertaining to existence.

The second time that Corinne arrived at the ice cream parlor, there were Irma and Arnold also in the car. It reminded her somehow of the portrait that had once appeared in the *Times*, only, of course, they were not grouped, and the children, except Arnold, were grown, and Richard, it was fair to assume, who had worn knickerbockers back in that portrait, must now be in town with his father at the banking house.

From behind the lace curtains it was impossible to get a full glance at Arnold, whom she had never seen before. But it was difficult to conceive that the outline of a small boy in white linen knickerbockers and the sweater with some childish design down the front was the symbol of the knife that had turned and turned in her heart those years ago. . . .

In many ways, it was the most difficult summer of all, what with Richard rampant over the country in his Kurt-Sussex and the possibility of encountering him on all sides. If you so much as took a walk or an ice cream soda, or ventured to the beach at Rye, there was always the possibility of that silver, shining, boat-shaped car, bearing the young Richard at its prow, and, likely as not, a member or members of his family.

It made venturing away from the short radius of the town itself, an indiscretion. More and more it began to seem unlikely to Ray that here, there, everywhere, at concerts, theaters, balconies of banquet halls, public meetings where Walter appeared, spas, European as well as American, gaming tables, casinos, streets adjoining the large hotels where the Saxels were put up, the imprint of her figure had not, by now, somehow begun to sink into the family consciousness. If not into the untroubled, pampered consciousness of Corinne herself, at least into the alert retinas of the children's friends. This tall, gaunt, back-street figure, moving solitarily along the edges of the scene! As the unthinkable question, What would happen, if—persisted more than usual, Ray's discretion began to overtop even Walter's.

One night something occurred at a huge charity fête, held on the lawns of the magnificent Selfridge estates at Greenwich, that caused her heart to stop in its beat.

Plans were afoot for a nonsectarian children's hospital at Percheon that was to surpass in size, equipment, modern scientific facilities, anything hitherto attempted in either Europe or America. Five sectarian philanthropic organizations had joined forces to form a board of trustees, of which Walter was a member. The Selfridge estates, father's and son's adjoining, comprised acreage of vast lawn and woodland, an ideal setting for a charity fête. Charge of admission was nominal, one dollar, although the metropolitan press spread itself at length over ten members of the Selfridge family walking out of one gate of their estate in order that they might enter another, at an entrance fee of one thousand dollars each. Ices were sold from booths; and bricks in the contemplated hospital, going like proverbial hotcakes, were hawked on all sides by young girls carrying brick-shaped coupons in baskets flung by ribbons over their shoulders. From a platform strung with lanterns, professional entertainment and speeches were offered.

"Now, here is your ticket, Ray. All you need to do is taxi over, keep your cab waiting, and come around to the grounds long enough to hear me. I expect to go on about ten-fifteen. It's an important occasion for me, Ray. Certain people of particular value to me will be present. Tell you more about it another time. Has to do with a country-club situation that—well, that is important to me, that is all."

How well Ray knew. The Saxel family, one of the large-estate holders, active locally, pioneers in generous cooperation in beach, county, and township improvements, had not been asked to join the new Exmoor Country Club. Reason, racial. Oh, how Ray wished that in this instance, and in many other similar that had to do with Corinne and her desires for her children, there could have manifested itself in Walter some of the indomitability that had built up that wall of solidarity, outside of which, the greater part of her life, she had stood defeated, but, in spite of herself, admiring.

Here was Walter now, who twenty-four years before had offered himself as so much human mortar to the solidity of this wall, rankling for favor. The unpretty fact of the matter was that the Saxels were standing outside the closed portals of the Exmoor Country Club, wanting in, conniving, even bargaining for social tolerance. It was as if, seeing it happen, a bright and ancient, priceless and venerable something were tarnishing before her very eyes. . . .

But all that beside the point: in addition to the social wedge which this occasion seemed to offer Walter, for Corinne and her children, he wanted Ray there in her capacity of commentator.

"Walter, somehow—it seems so conspicuous my going there— alone—"

"Get yourself some woman."

She was forced to admit that this summer, contrary to her usual facility in picking up a woman friend, she had none.

"Where is that big blonde horse named Mrs. Ryan?"

A Mrs. Ryan had lived in the rooms adjoining hers the summer previous, during the races at Belmont Park, and occasionally they had attended them together.

"I don't know what has become of her. Her friend was a jockey who sometimes rides in England. I imagine they went back."

"Nobody to notice you in a crowd. I've reasons for wanting to inspire local confidence. I'm going to open the drive myself with fifty thousand. You need only show up in time to hear the addresses and mingle with the crowd a little afterward, at the refreshment booths. It will be a crush, almost identical with the fête at Aix two years ago. . . ."

"I'll need a gardenish sort of dress."

"Get it."

Get it! Never the proffered wherewithal to make the getting of it a less laborious scouting about for remnant mill-ends, or odds and ends of material to be put together by ingenuity. Why, the cost of that gray chinchilla-trimmed wrap thrown across the bar of Richard's Kurt-Sussex that day, was three times the cost of her entire wardrobe. The thought evoked a rattle of chilly laughter off her lips.

"If you don't want to come—if it is asking too much—"

"Don't be silly, darling. I was just thinking a dotted mull makes up pretty, and I notice they are dyeing them tan nowadays, just by dipping the material in coffee. Tan-dotted mull with brown ribbon velvet . . ."

"Want you to take notice of a John Estabrooke. President of Exmoor. He and his wife will be there. Tall white-haired fellow, Yankee as Uncle Sam. She is one of these white-skinned, red-haired women. Quite lame. I'll be having something to talk over with you about him in a few days. Also Hale Davis is sure to be there. Want your judgment on that fellow. He has me guessing."

"You know what I already think of him from the way he tried to double-cross you in the Spiegel Trusteeship."

"I've taken your advice on that, but just the same, want you to see him. Funny thing, dear, what it does for me to have you tied to the old apron string. I need the feeling of you around. Don't let me down, Ray."

"I'm not letting you down, darling; only, where we take such elaborate precautions as a general rule, it does seem—"

"Let me do the worrying about precautions."

And yet something happened on that particular occasion which, while it had no quality of definiteness, was to riddle her with dreads.

The afternoon preceding the evening of the fête, there were thundershowers, and, looking out between her lace curtains onto the busy little thoroughfare, she noted with relief, even with the coffee-colored mull spread out on a chair and waiting, that the gutters were running fast waters and the rain came down against awnings and onto automobile-tops with a loud hitting sound.

"It is a straight rain, that means it will be steady and they will have to postpone it," she thought, with a surge of indefinable relief. But along about four o'clock, a hot July sun came pouring through dissolving clouds, and it became one of those sultry evenings, quickly dried, that can follow in the wake of a day that has not been cooled by its storm.

The beautiful clipped lawns of the Selfridge estates were quite dry underfoot, and, except for the red and blue of the buntings having run crazily into the white, there was little evidence of recent and deluging rains.

It was true, the tall nondescript woman in neutral tans attracted little, if any, notice, in the large milling crowds. There were cars parked for a mile and a half down the road, bearing Connecticut, New Jersey, Pennsylvania, and even Vermont license tags. Fords. Hispano-Suizas. And an assortment of family sedans mixed in with Pierce-Arrows, Rolls-Royces, and Kurt-Sussexes.

It was not every day that the general public had the opportunity to inspect the sunken gardens of the twin Selfridge estates.

Once there, Ray felt glad she had come. A watery moon flattened and made gray the lawns, baring them for the laying-on of eccentric shadows cast by tree and building. It was a night the color of a gray moth, with spotted wings. Japanese lanterns strung from tree to tree were the spots. The immense Tudor castle of the senior Selfridge was gray in the moon-wash too, and cast a geometric shadow, black as ink.

There was a large woman, the size of eternity, and in a gray shroud, walking somewhere through this night, and on her shoulder was the gray moth with the orange spots made of Japanese lanterns. Well, anyway, smitten with the beauty, that was the way fantasy had its way with Ray. And the thought smote her further, "I am that gray woman, the color of the background."

It was while she was standing toward the rear of the camp-chairs that had been ranged in rows before the platform, securely tucked into the overflow of standees, that the something happened which gave her once more that indescribable sensation of someone's having caught her heart in his hand on its frightened rebound.

Richard was there. She had spied him earlier in the evening, dancing with one of the young girls who moved among the throng, winsomely hawking the cardboard bricks.

He was in flannels and the light flowed vainly to pierce the heavy black brilliance of his hair; and it seemed to Ray, standing tiptoe behind the fringe of onlookers, that the night was a delusion and that presently she must find herself standing beside a hansom cab at the curbstone of the C. H. and D., looking into the gray eyes of a larger, squarer, handsomer Walter, who was somehow his own son. It did not do to linger more than an instant, but it was the closest she had ever beheld Richard, and, moving on, she actually needed the reassurance of a glimpse of Walter himself, standing beside a sundial, talking to a man she immediately recognized, from his descriptions, to be John Estabrooke, to brush the curious web out of her mind. The stouter, slightly bald, slightly paunchy Walter was hers. . . .

Then, preceding his father's address, during some astonishingly expert banjo-playing, she could see the young Walter (no, no, the young Richard, of course!) through an aperture formed by two heads, standing in one of the side aisles, his indolent but welded young polo-player's body relaxed against a tree, his attention focused upon the fingers of the entertainer as they flashed across the banjo-face.

Once, in the very early years, she had half tried to express to Walter her desire not to try to prevent issue, and had never forgotten the recoil of something in him that was more than fear. Well, whatever the cause of his withdrawal (she believed it to be into the kernel of race), just the same, she might have had to show, for a lifetime of single-track adherence, something as miraculous as that straight young man in the moonlight. She might even—she might even— The thought ran away with her, as she stood in the crowd, and caused her to begin to tremble.

It was then that she saw Irma, who was in white, with small pearls in the scarcely perceptible threat of crease in her white neck, push her way to the side of her brother. A basket of paper bricks hung by ribbons from her left shoulder; and her lightish hair,

Corinne the girl's all over again, curly to a threat of kinkiness, was tipped with moonlight.

It happened just as obviously as you would hold up A-B-C on the linen page of a baby book. There was not a second of it which, out of the tail of her eye, Ray did not see happening. The plump white hand, with a bracelet of seed pearls on it that she had helped Walter select, placed on her brother's elbow. His listening, inclined ear, then startled face. The impulse to turn; the white hand with the bracelet of seed pearls, restraining. The interval of waiting, while the head that had been told not to turn too obviously, holds eager pause, and then the face of Walter's son, swinging to find hers.

It was a face that, even in moonlight, darkened, as it gazed, with a flush that made it look as if it had been slapped. It was, if you can conceive the look when a body feels itself being crushed by a taxicab or run over by a train, the face of someone in the act of being hurt.

That was all, because without a second glance, without waiting for Walter, explaining it to him later on the plea of sudden illness, she slipped through the crowd and out to the station taxi, that was waiting with its flag down.

Never a word, all the remainder of that summer, of the fear that from that day on was nesting high and higher in her heart; but, except to take the Babe for his early and late walks, or to go to town when a chance for a few days with Walter presented itself, she did not leave her rooms again until the end of July.

On that date, some five days after the *Olympic* had sailed, bearing "Mr. and Mrs. Walter D. Saxel, chauffeur, and maid," a Mrs. Ray Schmidt, destination Cherbourg, embarked on the *Saxonia*.

41

"Let me go as your maid," people were always saying to Ray when they heard of these periodic trips of hers abroad. "Oh, don't you want someone to carry your luggage or comb the dog?"

That was well and good from the outside, looking in. Actually, these trips (there had been six of them in all by now) amounted to little in the way of travel. Once, because she had never seen London, she had gone over alone for a few days from Paris, during a six-week stay there at the tiny pension-hotel in the rue Cambon, near the Crillon. Another year, while Corinne and Walter visited the Frankfurt-am-Main Friedlanders, she had taken a Cook's tour of the larger cities of the Continent; but in the main her European trips were largely no more than a matter of changing quarters from the New York flat to a European hotel or pension within easy reach of the large hostelries patronized by the Saxels.

Paris, seen visit after visit, if glimpsed only from an occasional day's tour when she knew that Walter was to be out of the reckoning, or from hotel rooms that looked on a court, and which she failed to leave most of the day for fear of not being in when her guest called, was not the bewitching city of café, gallery, shops, bridges, tower, Madeleine, Louvre, Montmarte, escargots, Halles, Saint-Cloud, Seine, Sauterne, Champs-Elysées, boulevard, and Bois.

Not the Paris that she, Ray, would so have loved: the Paris of terraces and cafés, rue de la Paix, Ritz Bar, dancing at Les Acacias,

dining at Château Madrid, vagabonding among the "bars" and
hotels, restaurants and brasseries, of the town and the Bois. The
American's Paris, of couturiere, Longchamps, Luigi's, and Harry's,
never so much as showed her its face, except from street glimpses
or, occasionally, as she sat down at a sidewalk terrace, sipping her
crème de menthe and watching the ebb and flow of a magic city
whose language she did not speak, nor scarcely understood.

At Aix-les-Bains, Walter's favorite spa of all Europe, it was
better. The Hotel Bernasçon, perched on its hill overlooking the
town and spread of valley, gave one a sense of there being two dis-
tinct townships, an upper and lower, although the little community offered practically none of that larger privacy of Paris. But the
pretty French spa, within sight of the first towering heads of the
Alps, and in many ways as Italian in flavor as in the days before it
was ceded to French soil, seemed, once you set foot on its curative
soil, to reduce to minimum, fears, dreads, old nervousness. A false
security about that, though; because, much more so than in Paris,
Nice, or New York, here the centrifugal life of the place emanated
from the nucleus of the Casino, the bathhouses, the park in the
public square which contained the drinking-springs.

Mornings, at eleven, during the season, there were band concerts in this square, and it was part of the prescribed routine for the
whole of the visiting population, from the large hotels as well as
from the smaller hostelries and pensions, to foregather for the purpose of sipping the waters and strolling or sitting among the pleasant trees, while, gaily as a fountain, the band concert splashed into
the bright morning serenity.

"Aix-les-Bains," Walter was fond of saying, "rests me body and
soul. Quiet enough to get your fingernails out of your palms; not so
quiet that it gives you the jimjams."

"There is something in that, if you live the life of the spa as it
should be lived," Ray had once ventured to reply, but the remark
did not make its dent.

Afternoons at four, the bright performance of music, parasols,
foregatherings of groups for tea and dancing at the Hotel Splendide, Bernasçon, or Europa, helped conceal the creature-fact that

many of the men and women, so seemingly carefree over tea or cocktail, were racked to the bone with infirmities, or the threat of them. Aches-and-Pains was the persiflage-name for Aix-les-Bains. The mode was to flout at your gout and conceal the rheumatic twinge behind good patter. In addition to the English and Americans, there were always, to Ray's endless and insular amazement, maharajas in the most rigueur European clothes, South American magnates, Mohammedan princes, and once, during her sojourn, a queen of Greece.

Evenings, even the hint of infirmity disappeared entirely, and the hundreds who in forenoon had hobbled to their baths or been borne in the mystery of shrouded sedan-chairs through the streets of the Thermal Establishment, seemed to burst mysteriously through the restraints of the flesh, and fling themselves into the burning night life of the Casino.

Oh, there was no use talking, no use denying it to herself, solitude, the quiet reaches of the long, long days she had learned to spend passively within hotel rooms, had not succeeded in downing within her a love of the light, the movement, the gaming, the dining, the wining in the public or semipublic resort. A private party had come to be a bit intimidating to her, but the paradoxical privacy of the hotel dining room, the casino foyer, the racetrack grandstand, where one might see, be seen, was wine of a bouquet more perfect to her than any that had ever passed her lips.

Evenings, from her rooms in a small hotel in a small street that ran directly beneath the hill that held, like a magnificent pack, atop its back, the Hotel Bernasçon, she would begin to see, while the lovely pearly-blue sky that was half Italian was still tinged with sunset, the first reflection of the lights of the Casino.

In another few hours, the big hotels and the neighboring villas would begin their disgorge, and, before midnight, thick crusts of jeweled humanity would form around the strange seductive crater of the gaming-table.

Set in gardens, scented by hills over which Attila had marched, frescoed, shaking its light from the prisms of rows of huge crystal chandeliers as a spaniel shakes its sides of water, there was something about the spectacle of the Casino, sending its luminosity against the sky, that was a clutch of excitement through her very being.

Well and good to remain discreetly at her distance from the bandstand, or to see to it that her strolls through the town and along the upper reaches were carefully away from the direction of the Bernasçon, or were timed to the siesta, bridge, or meal hours of the hotel folk; but there was something about the Casino after dark, when, seated in her room, the Babe asleep at her feet, she could see that glow spring against the heavens, which set her feet tapping of a nervousness of desire to be part of that scene of baccarat and dance, best-dressed cocottes in the world, women with faces cut from polished almonds and lit with the kind of precious jewels you saw in the show windows along the rue de la Paix.

American women, with sleek short hair and rows of blazing bracelets that formed a rigid cuff to the elbow, slim and sheathed in the brief gowns of the period, that, when they sat, revealed the pampered flesh of their bare legs above their web stockings. Men with bands of ribbon across their shirtfronts sat night after night in the platinum-and-diamond crust of the craters: Mohammedan princes, who fed out francs by the thousands to hovering cocottes, American businessmen, British diplomats and consorts, citizens, ambassadors—youth, middle age, and senility of more countries than Ray had been able to retain in memory from her Woodward High School days.

It was one thing to just avoid the public square and popular tea-haunts where you might encounter Corinne or one of her children; it was another deliberately to deny yourself the diversion, sometimes the profit, and always the pleasurable excitement of the Casino.

At Monte Carlo, where the gardens, cafés, gambling-rooms, lounges, foyers, were so varied that the Casino itself was almost a small city, it had all been much simpler. Here at Aix-les-Bains, on those evenings when she knew Corinne to be present, she never ventured into the rooms where the larger stakes were being played, but remained content to take her smaller hazards at the polyglot tables where the croupiers dealt in the pea-shot sums of the pension and boardinghouse crowds.

Townspeople were not admitted to the Casino; but nightly, during the season, there poured from the boardinghouses and pensions conducted by the excluded townspeople, a procession of the transient small fry who were eager to lay their five-franc spots in the outer rooms, adjoining those where such kingly stakes as fifty thousand francs were placed upon a single deal of baccarat.

Hours on end, fascinated, Ray would stand in the heavy fringe of onlookers surrounding these high tables, watching with bright magnetized eyes the spectacle of chance as it held the circles around the green baize in attitudes of strain, expectation, hope, frustration, excitement, suspense, until it amounted to something like indecent exposure to permit these faces, forever being hauled at by croupiers, to reveal themselves to even one another.

The girls on the fringe of these men and women who played and won and lost, in terms of hundreds of thousands of francs, were liked rouged little ghouls of these nightly occasions, hovering at the elbows of the men whose stacks of chips or notes or coins were highest. It was almost an ethic that the male winner must feed into their greedy little jeweled talons the spume of his gains. Cocottes of one country or another, the notorious women of famous men, manikins, prosperous prostitutes, morganatic wives, hung on the outskirts of these gaming tables night after night. One's head reeled with their perfumes, their jeweled arms reaching over shoulders to place bets, their softly breathed profanities, their obscene whispered prayers, their soft hissing-noise of despair and success you could feel in their actual breathings against your ear if, like Ray, you were packed into the table fringe. Spangled birds of paradise pecking at spangled offal. Sometimes, if winnings ran high in her particular segment of the fringe, a stray five-hundred-franc note or a handful of chips flung over a shoulder, often without the head that had motivated the hand troubled to swing, would find itself in Ray's hand.

At first, this had come as a shock; but gradually, as it became apparent that even the smug married women, who to Ray were

criteria for all things, plucked at these backward-flung notes as nim-
bly as the "girls," it all became part of the evening's high pitch.

True, it was not for the likes of Ray, the birds of nondescript
plumage, that these notes actually were intended. But a hand reaching in quickly could flip one. Grabber, keeper!

Then, horrible and inevitable to these tables, was the outer
fringe of the outer fringe, elderly women, with bands of black velvet
worn ornamentally to cover the cables in their necks, their talons
covered with gold rings and clutching onto evening purses of beads
and sequins. Their weaving, witchlike hands and dry-as-powder fingers were what made it a little horrible to clutch for spoils, even if
you never consciously did so unless these spoils were waved almost
literally in your direction. The necky reaching from the last rows
gave one a sick feeling.

Once she found herself caught in an embroil of shrill angry
French which came hurtling at her from a superbly gowned manikin, who, in a carrot-colored wig, had been leaning over the chair of
a special friend, whose reach over his shoulder with a five-hundred-
franc note had seemed so willy-nilly to Ray, eager to play, that she
had let her hand close upon it. Upon the swift avalanche of high
and furious French she had surrendered immediately, of course, and
slipped from the group, ashamed.

But in general, if one stood about patiently of an evening, something in the gay carnival of the gambling spirit usually found its way
to you.

A small fifty-franc stake, perhaps. Sufficient to enable her to
lean in for a bet or two.

One evening, on a hundred-franc stake, she had gone home
with a thousand. But usually her luck was more evasive. Small risks,
small winnings, if any, but a general average profit, because she was
conservative and would dare to quit with a narrow surplus.

This year that Walter and Corinne had come over without the
children, leaving Arnold at one of the summer camps just then
coming into vogue, Richard to his new rôle in the banking house,
and Irma visiting the Mordecai Pooles, said to be the wealthiest
family of Spanish Jews in America, an amusing and daring thing

happened two or three times, between Walter, at play at the baccarat table, and Ray on the fringe.

Without ever the slightest note of recognition between them, he had tossed her of his chips and, leaning over his very shoulder so that they had touched, she had placed them. On the occasions that Corinne did not join him at the Casino—always of course with an impeccable discretion—this was amusingly possible. On the evenings that Corinne, only mildly interested, did join the hotel contingent of wives, she usually merely ambled aimlessly about the various rooms while Walter played, ending by interrupting his game long enough to have him tuck her into the hotel omnibus, which plied between the Bernasçon and the Casino, and take her home. Usually he caught the same bus back to the Casino, resuming his rather moderate game, or watching, with a remote kind of disapproval, the speculations of men like the Mohammedan prince out of India, whose winnings or losings ran nightly into tens of thousands, and who tipped his croupiers sums that were legendary the resort and the Riviera over. Behind the shoulders of this notoriously naughty potentate, who resembled Othello in an uneven walnut-juice makeup, there hung and glittered, like the beautiful and exotic small birds of an aviary, the pick of the manikins, the cocottes, the birds of Paris and paradise, many of whom wore his jewels in diamond, emerald, and ruby service stripes up their arms.

An American woman, reputed to be worth forty millions, had sat opposite Walter one of the nights Ray had so daringly hovered at his shoulder and, without a flicker of her stiff and blackened lashes, or her startling lips, which were painted the color and almost the shape of a large strawberry, had lost to the bank the equivalent of eighteen thousand dollars. And this at one of the more conservative tables.

In such a group, the figure of Walter, the rather short, only slightly stout, graying, and by no means undistinguished figure of the American banker—who, notoriously able to afford a spectacular place at the gaming table, played within a modest budget—was not remarkable. The pearls on his wife were. Even here. And that year, when Irma arrived, wearing the six-carat engagement ring of

Mordecai Poole, II, the Mohammedan prince, famed for his emeralds, appraised hers along with the best of his own.

Yes, the pearls of Corinne were remarkable, even here, and so, in
a war-stripped Europe, were the size of Walter's alleged fortune and
his vast indulgence to his womenfolk and the assiduity with which
his aim in life seemed to be to place himself at their beck and call.
One of the average American big-business men, with not much
grace, but whose families, as their men trailed them so tirelessly
across the high spots of Europe, seemed so sure of their place in the
sun. Spoiled, pampered, overindulged, none-too-reverent families
of men who, with fear of hardening of the arteries in their hearts,
traveled in high-power cars over Europe in search of lowered blood
pressure, while their women acquired Paris wardrobes, impover-
ished noblemen, and imitated accents, which in turn were imitated
on the stages of the music halls of Great Britain and the Continent.

Sometimes, watching Walter's face, from the vantage of a
remote corner of the room, the miracle of the consistency of her
love for this man, which had so long ago passed her understanding, smote her again and again. A face which, graying, became a
Jewish face, sharpening, in the years she had known it, from the
unbattered roundness of youth to plane surfaces and angles. Tri-
angles for cheeks by now, as if the flesh had run downhill off them
into little sacs at the base of the jowls. The nose stronger, and more
prominent and more aquiline, because the face was leaner. A man
unremarkable in a crowd, certainly in that crowd of the world's cos-
mopolites, yet continuing to be remarkable to her, in a way that,
even gazing at him, as he sat, jaws locked, over gaming stakes that
were mere pennies to him, was to feel the something that was akin
to, and even transcended what had washed over her that day at the
curb of the C. H. and D.

It was as if, with her very breathing, as it rose and fell, she could
say over and over to herself, as she sometimes did when she sat
thinking of him as she waited, or sewed, "Darling, darling, darling."
The clock on the mantel, the wheels on the railroad track, could
say that for her. All the little rhythms, the humming of a sewing
machine, the beating of an omelet. Darling. Darling.

It was one of the easy summers. It was a summer that in many ways measured up to and even surpassed the old ones at Cape May, when there had been time for walks along the beach. Come to think about it, this was infinitely better than any other summer. The Meyer Friedlanders from Mannheim and Frankfurt-am-Main, an impressive group of handsome, opulent, and overweight Frauen and Herren, with contingents of daughters, daughters-in-law, grandchildren, maids, nurses, and Fräuleins, had joined their American cousins at the Bernasçon that year. There was scarcely an hour of the day or evening, that Corinne, in her glory, was not occupied with these vigorous and extraordinarily modish German women, who loved to scour the local shops in search of embroidered linen, drive motor-loads to neighboring resorts, and evenings, while the men gathered at the Casino, assemble in the hotel lobbies or gardens for bridge or incessant and animated talk of incessant and animated family nature.

It left Walter more than ordinarily free to lunch in the tiny suite in the infinitesimal hotel buried beneath the hill that shouldered the Bernasçon. A chromo of a pair of rooms that smelled of its carpet, and tasted of its staleness.

But what luncheons could be served there, on a table drawn up beside a window that looked out upon a small garden where guests could sit under tin umbrellas and sip coffee or liqueur! The hors-d'oeuvres *variés*, omelette fines herbes, *poulette en casserole* with all the fresh green vegetables prescribed by Walter's diet. Chianti in its wicker cradle, the long, crisp French bread (forbidden in Walter's diet). Assorted cheeses, served on a board, and from which you could sliver your choice. Fruits, so much smaller and less juicy than at home, but which somehow tasted so much better, especially if you peeled and cut and ate them with your knife and fork, in the killing fashion of these Europeans. It was like a picnic. It threw you into a gay, irresponsible mood. And away from the banking house, away from the affairs that pressed in upon him, away from the more formal routine of the Bernasçon, something let down in Walter. He became younger than she had ever known him in his youth. They became mimes together, aping the Mohammedan prince; aping the ex-mistress of a king, who played her baccarat without ever seeming to open her eyes; aping Mrs. August Friedlander, who wore a stomacher of real pearls and whose stomach was large; aping M. Damlier Printemps, whose monocle was set in a rim of tiny emeralds, and his son-in-law Prince Laski of Poland, who notoriously purchased diamond and emerald bracelets for his mistresses at his father-in-law's world-famous jewelry emporium. One day Ray dressed up the Babe in a spangled shawl, with an aigret of broomstraws on his head, to impersonate a famous dowager, Lady Innescourt, who had a system, and played her *boule* at the cheap tables to constant cabalistic calculations on a paper pad.

And when, so absurd were the antics of the Babe in his scarf, her hilarity became a little hysterical, Walter caught her to him and, in a way that had not occurred for years, kissed her with a flash of youth and an old vitality in his embrace that left her with an old sweet limpness. It was as if the reincarnations of their youth had leaned into these bright fleeting days of this summer at Aix. There was so little talk of the world that lay too heavily upon him. Even the children were scarcely discussed. No public addresses to be worried over and memorized. No typing or scouting about for catalogues or art-dealers' quotations. None of the racking, momentous, and highly special crises of finance that had harassed him throughout the period of the war. Not even the usually daily sheaves of cables from the banking house were permitted to come through to him this summer. As Walter himself put it, this was a case of taking a complete rest or having one for which he was not ready forced upon him.

Ray suspected that part of his docility to this complete business detachment, which was not characteristic of him, was due to an element of scare thrown into him by an attack of acute indigestion that had laid him low during several days of the sojourn at Paris. As a matter of fact, the cause of the sharp gastric attack was easily traceable to his inability to resist the compensations of the table. Before rich foods that were palatable to him, he became the small boy, throwing discretion to the winds and forgetting past after-dinner adversities in the gratifications of the moment.

"I'll have a little of this, even if it kills me," was his almost invariable comment upon surrender.

To demur, or withhold from the table certain of his favorite dishes, such as richly potted roasts, cheese Torten, pickled delicacies, which were sure to incur from him later expressions of regret, was to arouse his immediate irritation, even anger.

"Don't treat me like a child. I know what is good for me and what isn't. My, how I dislike all this interfering." But in any event, the attack in Paris had not been without its effect. "I know what ails me better than those French doctors. The attack had nothing at all to do with the number of those little escargots I ate at Prunier's. It's complete rest I need, and I'm getting it."

Just the same, he was a little chastened that summer at Aix, went through a double term of the cure with a sort of shamefaced regard for his diet that, because it was so boyish, hurt her.

"None of that hors-d'oeuvre for me tonight, Ray. Not hungry for it." The face of the matter, of course, was that he wanted nothing more than the assorted array of salads, tinned fish, cunningly piled artichoke hearts, pickled mushrooms, pâté de foie gras, coiled anchovies with hearts made of their own paste, caviar in beds of ice, endive stuffed with Roquefort; and the pathetic little evasion hurt her. It was not the evasion in itself that hurt, or the self-denial, so much as the idea of the default of the flesh. Why need it be? Especially for him, who felt humiliation. If he had only known it, his debilities, at least where she was concerned, were dear. All the remainder of that summer, as she felt him consciously slowing his pace, observing his diet, leaving the Casino shortly after midnight, attending meticulously to the period set aside for his walks, massages, and rest, her tenderness flowed out to him as it would to a child in a dilemma.

Sometimes, in the evenings, when the women were attending a concert or grand opera at the fine opera house adjoining the Casino, they ventured, by way of one of the little horse-drawn barouches, for a drive along a tranquil old road in the direction of the next town, Chambéry, where trees met to form a leafy tunnel practically all of the way. The trotting horse, the rounded back of the driver, the lazily flecking whip, the lumbering of distant hills against the skyline, Walter's fingers laced into hers, fireflies, tinkle of the semi-occasional horse that passed theirs or the still more infrequent whizz of an automobile, were part of the remote reality seen through eye-lashes that had been recently kissed by Walter.

"Walter"—fingers interlaced—"I love you."

"I love you, Ray."

Clip. Clop.

The driver had a little song which he sang under his breath. . . .

"I love you, Walter."

"I love you, Ray."

Clip. Clop. Neither driver nor his pasteboard-looking horse troubling to ponder at the wintry-looking romance they were drawing gently through the powdery night.

"Walter," she asked him suddenly, during one of these drives, that, as it took place, was being embalmed as precious memory to her, "have you any regrets?"

He had been lying back, his head against her shoulder, his fingers interlaced with hers. "About what?" he asked her, without moving.

"Us."

Clip. Clop.

"When you ask me that, Ray," he said quietly, after a long pause, "you might as well continue and ask if I have any regrets because I have hands, or because my children are healthy, or because there is a sun."

It was she who was silent then, so long that he spoke again.

"You have held my life together, Ray. What force I have would never have been disciplined without you. I don't always admit it, even to myself, but practically everything I am, or everything I have accomplished, has been you. The schooling of my children, the history of my business, the very pictures on my walls have been you. I know that, Ray, and when I am sane like I am now—tonight, I admit it. Me, have regrets!"

The blood began to whir in her ears of the suffusing sweetness of what he said, and yet what she had hoped for was that he would turn the question: "Have *you* any regrets, Ray?"

It was not only that the assurance to the contrary was bubbling at her heart to be spoken, but the question, even though prompted by her own, would have reflected a similar solicitude for herself that somehow she wanted terribly.

What, after all, had she given up in an entire lifetime that could compare with even the stolen sweetness of such an evening as this? "The only ill that can ever befall the perfection of what we have," she told him over and over again, "is that anyone else be hurt by what we are doing, and that we must never let happen." He knew what she meant, and invariably lifted her fingers and kissed them for this. But just the same, if only now he had leaned to her with the question, "Ray, have you any regrets?"

"No, I have no regrets, Ray, except for the lie. There would never have been a way to make her see how this aspect of my life has never encroached upon hers. It has been hard. I have suffered. But I have no regrets, Ray."

(I. I. I. I. I. I.)

"Nor I."

"I have needed you, Ray, every inch of the way."

(I. I. I. I. I. I.)

"And I you."

"I have been happier with you than I deserve."

(I. I. I. I. I. I.)

What if, suddenly, she should throw this hand from her lap, leap from the slowly moving vehicle, and run laughing down the road, thumbing her nose back at him, screaming her derision? That would be madness; the escape of the sense of madness that sometimes pressed against the wall of her being when she felt herself, as now, beating vainly against the walls of his being, as if he were so much mortar and stone. . . .

He lifted her hand suddenly and pressed it against his brow. "I've a headache. I like to feel your hand. I'm so tired, Ray. It rests me to be with you."

For an hour longer they rode at snail's pace along the quiet, tree-laced road, and presently he fell asleep with his head against her numb shoulder, and her palm against his brow.

42

The engagement of Irma to Mordecai II, eldest son of Mordecai Poole, founder and president of the North American Coffee and Mocha Company, brought to an abrupt ending a midsummer that was filled with the little perfections of occasions such as these.

Happening, as she had beheld it happen, through the eyes of Walter, the affair of this betrothal, nevertheless, when it actually precipitated itself, came as a shock to him.

"Why, Walter, you act as if something dreadful had occurred, instead of something which you had not only been expecting, but hoped for."

They had been seated in her little sitting room, reading aloud from the Paris *Herald* the considerable announcement of the engagement party that had been held a few evenings previous in the gardens of the Hotel Bernasçon.

At this remark, one of the familiar gusts of anger, similar to the one inspired by her remark about the back streets of his life, swept him.

"You talk as if I'd been trying to marry her off."

"Nonsense, Walter! But you know yourself, when Irma decided to stay back this summer and visit the Pooles and then come over later with Richard, you suspected what was going to happen. You told me as much."

"You women have a set of mental processes that are beyond me.

You and her mother had this thing arranged in your minds before the two ever met. If I had my way she wouldn't be thinking of marriage for another five years."

She sat very still at that, flushing with a suddenly tapped flood of bitterness and strange pleasure. . . . "You and her mother."

Yes, much of what he said was true. She realized it now. Ever since, through the eyes of Walter, she had beheld Irma and young Poole going off alone, or in groups, to see Richard excel in polo, or skiing at Lake Placid, or dancing in the new ballroom that stretched across the top floor of the Poole town house, the dream of this ultimate alliance had nested in her mind.

As Walter had constructed him in her mind's eye, the eldest child of Mordecai Poole, a chip off the block of a father as renowned in the affairs of Jewry, humanitarianism, philanthropy, art patronage and industry as a Straus, Warburg, or Marshall would add to the already firm structure of the house of Saxel the completion of a tower, and mortar, with a kind of impenetrability that had never failed to awe as much as it had defeated her, that solidarity of a race in which, vagaries of social ambition to the contrary notwithstanding, the clan impulse would not die.

It was right and fitting that a Saxel should marry a Poole. She beheld Irma, through the vicarious mirror of her father's eyes, in an after-war era that was beginning to be littered with the truck of such phrases as "flapper" and "jazz-baby," moving along to the syncopated rhythm of her time, into a destiny as sure and smug and normal as Corinne's. Irma, whose burning, youthful, and at one time really bitter determination to transcend, with the assault of money, certain ostracisms which were galling to her, had been a tempest all right; but tempest in a teacup it had turned out to be. With Corinne, in whom the daughter had aroused ambitions remote to her, the same was true. With the advent of young Mordecai II all that was strangely quiescent now, canceled, as it were. Irma, whose smug Teutonic prettiness was in the image of her mother's, would marry, even as her mother before her, young, well, and within the clan. There would be issue—issue of Walter's issue.

How passionately she, Ray, had desired that marriage, now came over her in a kind of slow anger. Why? In order that the wall which, over twenty years ago, had closed him in, might continue to shut her out. Why? In order that for Corinne, who had everything, there might be even more of the abundance that had filled her arms with children—an abundance that lay crusted in pearls along her plump throat, and which, all unconsciously, was borne out in the dowager perfection of her smug manner.

Why need she desire for Corinne further endowment to the already bursting granaries of her life? Why was she, seated there, in the snide back-street quarters that were typical of the usual mounting he gave her, being barked at for a seemingly inadvertent remark she had made about this impending marriage?

"To hear you talk, one would think I had gone out to make the match."

"No, Walter, no. I only meant . . ."

"You only meant! You only meant somehow to make it appear that what I wished for the girl was to find her a rich husband and marry her off."

"No, no, Walter."

"When, as a matter of fact, it is obnoxious to me. The whole business. No complaint against Mordecai, he's a fine young fellow. But she's too young. Let her wait a few years. I want her at home with her mother and me. It isn't that I don't think this chap is good enough for her. I don't think anybody is good enough for her."

"You're right, Walter. But the real time for the right marriage is when two young people decide for themselves. You did."

He gave her a look at that, as deep, as mystifying, as filled with turgid depths as the pool of unclarified pain she had always carried in her heart concerning a certain Sunday morning and its consequences.

"Well, anyway—she is the dearest thing, Ray. I don't want to seem to say it, because she is mine, but—Irma is the dearest thing. . . ."

"You darling," she said, feeling her eyes fill, and yet somehow sitting carefully away from him, as he stood teetering on spread feet before the window that looked out upon the courtyard with its tin umbrellas.

But the coming of the young people and the subsequent arrival of Mordecai Poole, senior, and his young and second wife, from Carlsbad, put an abrupt end to the rather easily managed scheme of things which had been possible up to then. The Saxel-Friedlander-Poole party now occupied a fine old building, also hotel property, known as the Villa, set well beyond the formal gardens of the Bernasçon, and usually given over to visiting royalty, the Prime Minister of England, personages and their entourages from various lands, who occupied it from time to time during season.

Here, even to the meals, which were served to piping-hot perfection from the hotel kitchens, the party took up a sort of carnival family life, sufficient unto themselves, yet in evidence everywhere—Mordecai Poole, senior, whose resemblance to Bismarck was striking, and his handsome young Viennese wife, driving through the town in a buff-colored, special-body Kurt-Sussex touring car that was conspicuous even for Aix-les-Bains; everywhere, too, you encountered the engaged couple, driving, walking, golfing, or, straight as needles on their mounts, galloping along the bridle paths; everywhere Friedlanders, playing bridge on gala afternoons on the elaborate terraces of the Hotel Splendide, motoring with newly arrived cousins, the Dreyfouses of Frankfurt-am-Main, gathering before lunch in large animated groups around the mineral springs; evenings, the party, or segments of it, flooding the Casino, dining there, on gala nights, at-large special tables, or playing at chemin-de-fer or baccarat with consistent conservatism.

Even young Mordecai II took his winnings up to a point as he took his losses up to a point, and quit. Safety there for Irma. Security.

This much, through the peepholes afforded between heads and shoulders, Ray, on those now rare occasions when she ventured into the Casino at all, had observed from the outer fringe of rooms where the women played lotto and the minors and petty guests played *boule* for stakes that were infantile—to which gambling frontiers she now confined herself.

Saxels, Friedlanders, Pooles everywhere! It made the days,

when she dared not venture to the springs or the band concert or along the streets or into the Casino gardens to sip an ice or frappéd liqueur, long again and dull again and empty of Walter.

It caused the old creeping inertia to grip. It once more afforded time for the writing of long letters to Emma, describing what she could of the historic significance of her surroundings, culled chiefly from the folders in railroad offices; stitching blouses for her by hand, and, on occasional pickings from the Casino, tucking a bill or a trinket into a letter, to supplement the year's remittance for college budget, which long before had been sent her out of combined proceeds from the Women's Exchange and a season at the races that had yielded a slightly credit side.

A summer hitherto all too fleeting seemed suddenly to pause and stand still. There were evenings now, when, deciding against the possible indiscretion of public appearance, she did not even climb out of her negligee into the evening dress required as a badge of admission to the Casino, but had dinner served in the room, where the Babe, leaping into her lap, could yap for each tidbit as it was temptingly held up, before the descent.

Sometimes, for want of the knowledge of French which would have helped her exchange a little patter with the *femme-de-chambre* who spread her bed, the waiter who spread her table, or the petits bourgeois who inhabited this little hotel, so snugly removed from the haunts of the American and English, whole days passed without more than a friendly pantomime with those who served her, or the sound of her own voice admonishing and caressing the day-long doings of the Babe.

In many ways, these long days, wrapped in silence, stagnant with caution, recalled the desolation of that summer at Mount Clemens. Only this, after the weeks of drives through leafy nocturnal roads, the forays into the Casino, there to literally rub shoulders with Walter, the pleasant meanderings through afternoons that were fairly sure to be clear of the possibility of encounters, came with a sense of depressing contrast. She found herself committing the cardinal sin of wishing the passing of time. By noon, it seemed already mid-afternoon. The evenings, up there in the stuffy seclusion of the pair

of rooms, could seem to stand stock-still, so that frequently to fore-
stall them she dressed, in something cool for the street, so that she
could have her dinner in the courtyard at a table from which the
tin umbrella had been removed, and afterward stroll the immediate
neighborhood with the Babe on his leash.

It was during this period, literally to kill time and make less
tedious the performance of consuming that after-dinner period, that
she set about to cultivate her lagging habit of smoking. There was
something about the gesture of sitting beside a demitasse, the smoke
coming in two thin streams of exhalation from her nostrils, that
manufactured a sense of well-being. According to law and order,
you had dined well, wined well, and were at peace with yourself and
your world.

At peace. Sitting there in the courtyard, smoking, little groups
of people in unintelligible conversation about her, the lights of the
Casino beginning to glow against the sky, what beat against her
solitude was not a heart at peace. It was more the weight of a small
killed bird swinging there, whose wounds had hurt it terribly before
it died.

Oh, everything was as it should be. The weight at her heart
was not resentment, it was ache. It was right of Walter to meticulously absent himself these days following the announcement of the
betrothal of his daughter. No one quicker than she to realize the
folly of a careless move. Besides, demands were upon him.

On the last evening she had ventured into the Casino, she had
seen him through a remote doorway sitting in the garden over cigars
and Chartreuse in profound and animated conversation with the
elder Poole and Meyer Friedlander of Frankfurt. From the concen-
trated and always nervous look on Walter's face, she could tell that
their discussion had to do with some form of high finance of banking. A screwed expression invariably came into his features when
he spoke of the banking house whose traditions he was succeeding
in carrying alone. The look of a man not sufficiently sure of himself,
or the stability of his achievement, to relax. The look of a man who
suspects his success to be bigger than he is.

Of course it was right she should not see him during these

carnival times of the gathering of the magnificence of the Saxels, the Friedlanders, and the Pooles.

One evening he did manage to leave the baccarat table for an hour and hurry down the side street to her hotel. She had been bathing the Babe and, seated on the bedroom floor beside a tin tub of soapy water, was engaged in rubbing him dry with an old Turkish towel. Somehow, the spectacle of her there in an old red challis negligee, with the lacy sleeves pinned up to her elbows and the hair down over her eyes so that she had constantly to blow it upward with her pursed lips, made him tender and in one of the moods when he could be considerate. She was darting quickly into fresh clothes, whisking the tub out of sight and adjusting the room back into the immaculate kind of order in which she liked always to greet him.

"Stay the way you are, Ray. Dry the little fellow on the floor. Don't move. I like it."

She sank back on her knees and heels.

"Walter, I had no idea you could get away."

"Neither had I. Couldn't, I guess. Just came. It's the women who are making it this way. No need in the world to call together a league of nations because two young people have got themselves engaged to be married."

"You poor dear tired one. Let me get you something cool to drink. Luckily I took the precaution to buy a piece of ice today."

He waved her back to her position on her knees on the floor. "Stay that way. I like it."

"Why, Walter," she said, looking up at him through eyes that were filled with a sense of his mood of tenderness, but full of unease because she realized that the strand of her hair down over her eyes was a gray one which she had a way of keeping tucked out of sight, "I think you're paying me a compliment."

"I don't know about that, but I do know that it rests me to be here—like this—quiet—little—nobody trying to get anywhere— nobody straining with an ambition, or holding a gun to your head and trying to force you to have a good time. If I had my way, I'd stay here for a month, Ray, with you—and rest—now—like this—"

"You wouldn't, darling," she said, thinking of the discomforts of her mode of living, and then walking over, on her knees, to where he sat on the edge of the bed, and beginning to stroke his hands which were limp on his lap. "But it's nice of you to think that you would. You're fed up."

He made a quick, horizontal cutting-stroke across his throat: "To here."

"It will soon be over."

"Can't be too soon for me. The gabble. Good Lord, the gabble of the women. Their insanity after things. The doilies! What in God's name is it, creates madness in women for doilies the moment there is a marriage on the horizon. The doily brigade. Corinne's mother was the same way. I remember we were launched in our first house-keeping enterprise on a sea of doilies. I want to be quiet. I can be quiet here with you."

"My dear . . ."

"Now, mark my word, Ray. It's a promise to myself. Next year, just you and I are coming abroad somewhere. Just you and I. It can be managed. Some place high and cool and simple and clean and away from feverish people. Switzerland! A chalet that looks out over snow-capped mountains. Peasants. Cows. Eagle-nests. Blue ice. Green pastures. It's coming to me, Ray. I need it."

Even as warmth flowed over her and she laid lips to the hand stretched over his knee, there was that old rhythm at her again, insistent as the click of wheels along rails. I. I. I. I. I. I. It's coming to *me*. *I* need it. What about her? The days of the weeks of the months of years of the stuffiness of indoor routine in the stale air of the chromo interiors with which he provided her. What about the need in her that she felt most keenly when she peered over a wall into a garden, or through a window into a roomful of free-and-easy human beings enjoying free-and-easy social intercourse. What about her? The years of the days with a string to each of them. The hours-on-end of waiting for the beck or the call. The walking in the shadow. The lurking up the side streets. The loneliness that was filled with so many dreads and fears and cautions. What about me? What about me? What about me?

But, instead, she sat there with her lips that were laid close to his hand making little pacifying-sounds that must have been sedative, because presently, without protest, he let her rise and tuck a pillow under his head, lower a light, and prepare him a soft drink of fresh limes, a touch of almond-oil, and grenadine, for which she had brought the almond-oil from America.

"Ah, fine! Beats all your French liqueurs and Haute Sauterne. This tastes like me in carpet slippers."

He was right. How sweet and sure and snug and bright it would be, back there in the flat which was recalled to him by the taste of a drink he had so frequently imbibed there. For that matter, how sweet and right to be here—alone together, with every danger shut out, and dear, warm, rutted habits theirs to enjoy.

"Take off your coat, dearest; you're warm."

"I must go back. They'll miss me. I'm playing fifty-fifty baccarat with old Poole."

"Oh, Walter, I had hoped . . ."

"No. Besides, Corinne has an idea I'm neglecting the Fraus from Frankfurt. There's a trip to Annecy planned for early tomorrow. . . ."

She held out his hat, wanting to say: "What about me? It's been six days of just sitting here alone. It's not that I'm complaining, I understand so well, but sometimes, sitting here alone in the stuffiness, the fear comes over me—honestly, the fear of getting crazy with the sameness of this suspense. . . . Take me to Switzerland now, Walter! I need the change. It's coming to me." Of course, she said nothing of the sort.

"I'll be waiting, dear."

At midnight, against her discretion, but of a restlessness and unutterable weariness of solitude that was born afresh out of her own hatred of seeing him go, she climbed, a little tiredly, into a brown lace evening dress, drew her hair in a new-fashioned part at the side, which she had adopted since fashion's decree against the pompadour, threw on a chiffon scarf, and hurried out through the dark side streets that converged into the brighter one surrounding the Casino.

The way into the lotto rooms and the tables of the minors and petty gamesters was from a side street, separate from the grand entrance through the gardens, where the line of motorcars, motor busses, taxicabs, and horse-drawn vehicles was constant.

For an hour she stood at one of the five-franc *boule* tables, placing one-franc pieces until she had lost twenty. Then for another hour, fascinated as always, she stood watching the small ebb and flow of these backwater tables. Small fry at small stakes. Pastime of the unadventurously inclined. A different picture from the weaving magnificence of the grand salons beyond, where men and women in a single evening lost or won sums which represented fortunes.

And yet it caught her even here. The same lure that used to capture her fancy back at the hazard tables in the back rooms, Over-the-Rhine.

"If I had money, I'm afraid I'd be a big gambler," she once told Walter.

"If you had money you might fly away from me," had been his strange retort. Strange, and yet later, trying to analyze it, she used it often to explain to herself much that otherwise would have been unexplainable, the penury of his attitude toward her.

As she stood there, watching the petty ebb and flow of the franc, the eager greedy hands of the reaching women, which somehow could appear so much more greedy than the reaching hands of the men, desire to play caused her to feel along the edges of her empty spangled purse for a coin which might by chance have clung to the chamois lining.

One ached to be part of that high-tension moment when the *boule*-ball, high-strung as a coloratura's reach for C, skedaddled into place. Ball-bearinged little demon of destiny! The red became one's destiny. The franc piece on the red became one's destiny. One's destiny became the franc. Destiny swung with that skedaddling ball. Planets swung. You swung. Ah, blah!

There were no coins left in her purse, but a gray-haired denizen of her hotel, who looked like an illustrated version of a boulevardier on his uppers, tossed two francs over his shoulder without so much as looking back, as if thus to propitiate the stroke of luck that had just swept him twenty.

It was while she was in the act of placing the two-franc piece on the red, that her lids, as if magnetized, were literally dragged to meet the pair of eyes that were regarding her like two lighted tunnels from across the table. The eyes of Irma. The young, despising, incredulous, wounded, and mercilessly appraising eyes of the daughter of Walter. Beside her, gazing in innocence at the game, stood Corinne. Mother and daughter; and, as paling, reddening, the daughter of Walter continued to impale, with her glance, the frozen eyes of Ray, her arm stole up and lay in a kind of challenging protection along the bare, white, unconscious shoulders of her mother.

As she pushed her way out of that scene of sudden terror, it seemed to Ray that the back streets came running in spokes to the door of the Casino, ready to fold her back into their merciful oblivion.

There was no surprise about it. She had been sitting for practically the whole of the ensuing day, playing solitaire at the center table, which she had dragged over beside the window. Hour after hour, her underlip sucked in and her eyes revolving, as if they had been well-oiled, over the layout of cards, she had sat tucked into the refuge of forcing herself to pit her mind against the small scheme of the game, the idea being not to allow yourself to dwell upon the incident that had turned heart, legs, arms, into sands which were running away, leaving nothingness. The reason she must not allow herself to think was that there was nothing to think about.

Was it possible that all through these years she had ever dreamed it could be otherwise? Other than a fool's paradise? Years ago, at a garden party at Rye, she had known just what she knew now. No. No. No. It was not that simple. Truth of it was, she had never really allowed herself to think. Besides, nothing to do about it. Things as they are, are as they are. Must remain as they are. The thing to do was not to think, to pull oneself together, as if it had never happened; to keep the young, hurt, angered, and loathing face of Irma, as she had laid a protecting arm along the shoulder of her mother, from moving across the lay of the cards and making her feel hot and stifled and full of the sense of a need to do something.

And of course there was nothing at all to do. Presently, when Walter came, as come he would within a day or two or three, everything would go on precisely as it had before. The only possible precaution was to be still more careful—not even venture into the Casino's outer rooms anymore. That was easy. Just a little more careful—and then he came, and there was no surprise about it.

Suddenly she glanced up; he was there. How like his father, as he had stood with one indecisive foot on the curb of the C. H. and D. depot. Precisely so Richard stood now, one foot scraping back and forth as he hesitated.

In the midst of the calamity of what was happening to her, the irrelevant consciousness smote her that, as luck would have it, she was wearing the old red challis, edged with lace which she had let wilt, and that the Babe, with the hair tied out of his eyes with ribbon, was licking a chocolate bonbon she had just tossed him.

Precisely the picture to burn itself, as she had used to sear with her hot needle-point against burnt-wood plaques, into his young mind! The florid-wallpapered room of thick spotted carpet, portieres, and furnishings. The copy of an American all-story magazine, called *Fictionettes*, face down on the stiffly stuffed sofa. One of her washed-out chemises hanging to dry where there had been a bit of sun. The cigarette stubs of a habit acquired within the fortnight, strewn.

This was the kind of scene dished up to boys from college, on larks, who dropped nickels into the slot machines of Cambridge and New Haven. Even her wrapper, when he entered, had been flowing open, revealing her seated with one lace-ruffled pantie-leg flung across the other, a cigarette, which during the last twenty-four hours she had been finding more and more sedative against the rising tide of her nervousness, smoking on the table edge.

"I'm sorry," he said, as she rose, clutching her wrapper together.

It was simply incredible, this flesh of Walter's flesh, there, a man, speaking. Was ever before such an interview as this one about to take place? Son of her spirit, son who should have been of her flesh, standing, an abominating stranger, before her.

"Sit down."

He did, quite simply, and that was a relief, because, whatever of terror and catastrophe was about to be released in that room, he was going to be quiet about it.

And what made it so fantastic, and what made it seem even as repulsive to herself as she felt she was being at the moment to him, was the terrible impulse to take his face between her hands—to feel his head between her hands. And yet, through it, there persisted the strange perspicacity of being able to realize how she must appear to him. One of those frowsy kept-women, who live indoors too much, and who, as the hair begins to streak, the neck to thin, and the veins to bulge, take on that plucked look of old eagles.

Just her luck to have rubbed vaseline into her scalp the night before, so that the hair lay in clumps, revealing scalp. Just her luck—as if it mattered. To the boy sitting there gingerly on the chair edge, in white flannel trousers, pull-on sweater with some sort of insignia of a polo team across the front, twirling a soft white felt hat and with the other hand rubbing frequently over his sleek black hair, she was the anathema of anathemas. His foolish old father's relic of an indiscretion.

All his life, now, he would be branded with the memory of this morning in the back-street hotel room of a French spa that smelled to its very timbers of mustiness and was papered in roses done in the browns and greens of pea soup. The marble fireplace, with its varicose veins, and, on its mantel, as if ridiculously thumbing its nose, a vase of red paper carnations. That horrible unnecessary chemise drying into a shriveled human form across the back of a chair. And then, as if this morning of reckoning were fearful that one taunting detail might be spared to the son of Walter, on the back of the door, in the image of its wearer, hung the old alpaca coat of his father, which she had packed into her trunk the last minute before sailing. There it hung, facing Richard. She wanted to efface it for him. She wanted to efface the morning for him. She wanted to efface the horrible reality of herself seated there holding together the red challis wrapper with the wilted lace, and the Babe there on the chair beside her, licking his sticky chocolate.

(My poor boy. Oh, my poor boy. Sent to propitiate his father's mistress.)

"Let us have this thing out, Miss—er—Mrs. Schmidt, by beginning in the middle. You're sensible, I'm sure."

So this was the curious thing called the new youth. This brittle unembarrassed young voice. This crisp quality that had never been his father's. This accent that gave him "diction."

"I hate like the dickens barging in here, you understand that? As a matter of fact, you have every right to throw me out. Don't, please. I'm sure you won't, being sensible. Lay off Father, Mrs. Schmidt."

She just sat. . . .

"All well and good to say these matters are a man's own. So they are, up to a point. For years we've been letting it happen up to a point. Hasn't been pretty, at that, but at least we took our medicine. We think it is up to you now, Mrs. Schmidt."

"What?"

"To lay off. Save him from making more of a spectacle of himself than he has in the past. Remove this ridiculous embarrassment from my sister's position. Bow out. . . ."

"You mean—?"

"You know what I mean. I suppose if I could steam up a righteous moral indignation about the whole damned mess—pardon me, Mrs. Schmidt—I'd try to shame you with the anomalous position into which you have placed my mother, and, for that matter, us children. But I'm not here in the rôle of either moralist or my father's keeper. I'm here because a very concrete situation has arisen which makes it imperative that I constitute myself a committee of one to request, or demand if I must, that you terminate this ridiculous situation."

Young upstart in white flannel pants and patent-leather hair, for whom her very heart had been bleeding ever since he entered the room; young keg of broken glass sitting there making brittle sounds about life and the secret places of the inner shrine known as heart. As if they were controlled by so many spigots, like those nickel-plated urns from which they served hot coffee in the American drug stores! The incarnation, as he sat there, of the heinous thing known as the "younger generation." She had heard Walter, without comprehending until now, talk about the "hard-boiled young ones" of the day. And now here one sat, not hurt or crushed or wounded. Just cocksure and comprehending and unsurprised. Cocksure and initiated, and so terribly, terribly level-eyed. A nice kind of level eye if you thought about it in one way. Terrible, terrible, if it fastened upon you its fair-and-square gaze with the accusatory look of a private ideal, shattered. . . . She had shattered that, concerning his father; but brittle young men of his training did not out and admit such.

"You cannot, Mrs. Schmidt, continue to make my father the scandal and laughingstock of the world. For years we have had to close our eyes to the shadow of you moving along the background of our lives. Everybody except my mother, who by nature is a babe in the wood, knows. It is not square, Mrs. Schmidt, to continue to make my father, who is a public figure now, a comic strip."

Corinne did not know. *Corinne did not know.*

"And now, as you probably are aware, my sister is about to marry. The Mordecai Pooles aren't any more prudish than the next ones; but, Mrs. Schmidt, surely you must realize that in the face of the circumstance of my sister's engagement and the growing danger of my mother knowing, this public nastiness cannot go on."

If only the floor, yawning, would swallow you up, in your red challis wrapper and slapped heart, before the merciless, unhurt, disgusted eyes of this perfect-shouldered, lean-thighed polo player, sitting there on his high horse. Why, this very quality of his sophistication had been born out of her concern for him. She, Ray, from the back alleys of his life, had steered his development and education away from the softening influences of Corinne. His self-confidence and power of assertiveness and almost terrifying insulation had been born in the stiff experience of his contacts and competition in schools and colleges which she had selected for him. How dared he grind her pain to pulp? . . .

"You must get out of the picture, Mrs. Schmidt, permanently. This you must do out of regard for my father. Out of a sense of the jeopardy in which you place my mother. I wonder if you realize what this would do to her. She is a baby, a woman who has never grown up with a realization, except in a general way, that—if you will pardon my saying it—that your kind exists. She idealizes and worships my father. You dare not destroy that."

(Destroy. Me destroy! Boy, in this strange story of your father and me, I have been at his elbow, conserving, every inch of the way of his life. Boy, don't destroy me, or you destroy him.)

"Remember, Mrs. Schmidt, I have not come here to plead in the name of morality. I may criticize him, but I do not judge. In the years I was growing up and suffered at school and college the noised-about legend of my father and his shadow, it was something I accepted as a kind of humiliation that was to be part of my life. So did my sister. We even learned, in a measure, to understand and tolerate. . . . But now she is about to be married, Mrs. Schmidt, and you have not got the right to jeopardize her desirability in the eyes of the conservative Poole family. Go away permanently."

(Boy, boy, let me talk. Let me find words to say the unsayable. Don't you know your father needs me terribly, even more, if possible, boy, than your mother needs him? Try to see that, Young Beautiful. Try to see the terribleness to him of what you are asking.)

"You must go away, Mrs. Schmidt, without my father knowing. And then, after it is over—the break—I promise you I will see to your—er—proper remuneration."

Oh, the shame of the nakedness of despair she was permitting this young god on his high horse to behold! Her lips were the snake's nest in her face again, and she began to cry, only there were no tears to wet her sobs, and they came on long, hoarse ribbons drawn from an agony of dry throat; and because he was repulsed and horribly embarrassed, he rose and closed the door and stood with his back against it, remotely, fastidiously.

"I wouldn't do that. Why is it that the mention of money is what always creates in situations like these hysteria of one sort or another? All right, if the mention of anything so gross between my father and you is repellent, I rescind. You have the privilege to change your mind later. Only go, Mrs. Schmidt. Save him from the destruction and the ridicule you have it in your power to bring down upon him—and his. He deserves to be saved from you. If you don't go—"

Her crazy impulse was to turn upon him, impishly. What-if-I-don't? What-if-I-don't? There—bah—and shoot out her tongue and do a half-dozen insane antics that were dancing in imagery before her eyes. And yet, somehow it was unthinkable to hear the finish of that threat: "If-you-don't-go—"

"I'll go," she said to him; and then, for fear he might finish his "If-you-don't-go," she repeated it. "I'll go."

Neither was it strange to her that Walter should walk in then. The room was a stage, and he had been dropped his cue, that was all. How like they were, these two dark Semitics, bred well and not too typically of their race, heads mounted on necks that were shorter in the rear, hairy backs of hands, suavity of palms, sensual gray eyes that would practice restraint. The blood that bound the two was thicker than water; it was the thick coagulated blood that bound clans and made imperishable a certain heritage of Jewishness. Walter had it, staring cold-eyed at his son. Richard, who had been on his high and terrible horse two minutes before, was his father's son now, so smitten with horror and surprise that she again wanted to take that sleek head of his between her hands and place her lips against the look of small-boy that had come over the face of young cock-o'-the-walk.

"Get out," said Walter to his son, slow, low, and with his brows clamping down over his eyes like the lid to an iron box.

"I'm not ashamed, Father, of what I'm doing."

"Get out."

"I've the right to be here."

"You have no right here. This is my right—the only right I have ever placed before the million-and-one rights of my family. You have no rights here—none of you—this corner of my life belongs to me—safe, free from every one of you—the only privacy, sanctum, home, I have ever dared claim of my own. Get out!"

The ridiculousness of the going of Richard, like a small boy, whipped!

"Walter, don't humiliate him—he's right—he's right—"

He caught her to him. He kissed her throat. Horrible to her, he clutched at the hem of her red challis wrapper, kissing that. He was trying to say something; but he had no words, and he had no voice, only repetitious whispering-sounds that reminded her of a man having a stroke, and then that hurting, abashing manner of blubbering into her dress-hem!

"I promise you, Walter," she said finally, in answer to his repetitious, only half-coherent mouthings, "not while I live—never will I leave you—never—never."

He began again, still in the clutch of his inability to speak, to kiss and kiss the hem of her challis wrapper.

43

Except for the growing complexity of the precautions, things were strangely little altered by what had seemed, while it was happening, to be so crisic.

Once more in the New York flat, with the sheetings removed from the furniture and the scores of tiny knickknacks abroad once more over the table and mantel tops—the graduated row of imitation-ivory elephants, the gilt filigree parlor set the size of a postage stamp, the three monkeys who could not hear, see, or speak. Souvenir cups and saucers. Bisque figures. Plaster Lion of Lucerne. Gilt Eiffel Tower. Vulgar little souvenir chamber pots and naughty naked little dolls stepping into bathtubs. A layout that had not changed with the years, except that the once modern apartment building had slid back into the quiet limbo of old-fashioned walk-up. The long, dim hallways, lighted now by electric bulbs that had been superimposed on the gas-fixtures, with their pressed-leatherette wallpapers, their disinfectant smells, belonged to an era in apartment-house building that was as dated as bustles or hitching posts.

Not-so-tenderloin flats, some wag had christened the somber old five-storied red-brick relic of the early era of apartment buildings. That would have seemed strange to Ray, had she heard it, because, as a matter of fact, precious little of the old fancy feeling to the place survived; precious little of the old visiting back and forth, with coats flung on over wrappers. Except for one or two families, and there were family tenants now, with whom she had bowing acquaintance as she passed their doorways on her way to take the Babe for an airing, and a Mrs. Hopper on the top floor, with whom she occasionally went to the races, the days of easy informality were gone.

It made time a little longer and a little lonelier, and the closer confinement which she practiced, as the result of what would always remain to her the calamity of the interview with Richard, a little more trying.

The Babe and solitaire helped, and also a new kindness in Walter, which made the horrid occurrence in that back-street hotel at Aix as definite a milestone in their relationship as the affair at Youngstown.

"You overestimate things, Ray," he assured her when she complained of a nervousness induced by too much indoors. "I don't say go show yourself in the first tier of the Metropolitan Opera House, but there is no reason why you cannot go about practically as you have always done. Not to occasions of which I happen to be a part, anymore, but you've plenty of leeway left. That is the trouble with you women. Logic doesn't come naturally to you."

"I do overdo it, I know. And now that Irma is married you'd think I'd feel a little easier, wouldn't you? But curious thing is, I just have a horror of one of these days walking into her and her husband."

"You leave any worrying there is to be done about my children to me. Don't you worry either that another one of them will ever interfere. Richard has reason to know now that this domain of my life is mine! There is only one worry we need have, Ray. Hurting her—would be a calamity."

"But, Walter—"

"What?"

"Nothing."

She had never discussed with him what had transpired that day between her and Richard. She had never been able to deduce how much he knew of what a wagging world knew. She had not even been told of what must have been his subsequent interview with his son. It was as if an unmade bed had been spread over with a smoothed coverlet.

"I'm nervous, Walter. I smoke too much, but it helps," was as much as she could ever bring herself to say on opening the subject.

Once or twice this had evoked discussion, quickly laid by him. For the most part, except for the almost insane confinement to home, actually maneuvering to do her marketing and walking out with the Babe after dark, and sometimes, for days on end, not even venturing that far, but tipping the West Indian hallboy to take out the Babe, she kept up a pretty good front all right. And, no doubt about it, as if cognizant of all this, Walter was gentler.

"Never you mind, Ray. This much I've made up my mind to. This coming summer we're going to take that Switzerland trip together; ours every minute of the time, just the way I've been planning it for years. This summer it is coming off. Arnold doesn't seem to want to go to camp again, and his mother has about decided to go with him and the Friedlander aunts to the Canadian Rockies. While they're on that trip it will be three weeks at Aix and two weeks in Switzerland for us. Pretty nice?"

"Oh, Walter—pretty nice! Heaven!" This plan, perennially made, perennially broken, was perennially a fresh one of no antecedent.

"I want Arnold to see America, first. Richard and Irma had skied in the Alps and motored in the Dolomites before ever they saw the Rockies. Arnold is more American in lots of ways than his brother. Can't so much as get him on a Shetland pony, no matter how much he may admire the polo trophies his brother has won; but he's got his heart set on riding ranges and ranches, and for a little boy that started out to be delicate and too sensitive, we feel pretty fine about that. Corinne is going to stop off with him at some of those Mexican ranches—no dude ones, either. Arnold may not develop into a polo player, but I sometimes suspect him of being just a bit poetic. Fine, if he doesn't let it throw him out of balance."

But just the same, it seemed to Ray she had never seen him

more prideful than he was that same autumn, when Richard's polo team, a Long Island country-club aggregation of which he was captain, won an important international amateur match.

"It's not only because it is a distinguished polo victory, but the boy is part of his horse. Good Lord, even his mother, who turns her head away most of the time for fear he'll crash, sat motionless through the match. Wish you didn't feel so squeamish about appearing around places, Ray. Like for you to have seen that boy ride."

She should have liked it too, although even to visualize herself there, was to induce nervousness almost unbearable.

Irma and her husband would have been there, and young Arnold, whom she had never seen except as a small child that day in the automobile at White Plains. And Corinne.

Why, my whole destiny hangs on the chance of somebody happening to say within her hearing: "There she is. Saxel's shadow!" Every second, every hour, every day her destiny was hanging on that possible eventuality. That was what made the nervousness something to be jammed back like a jack in its box. What if Corinne should come to know? What if? What then? A thousand times a week she asked herself that question. What then? What terrible, indomitable, admirable, cruel, relentless clan-thing would rise in Walter then? The gates of his race would swing together, once the issue came, shutting him and Corinne in, and her out, just as they had swung twenty-five years ago, when there came thundering the need of decision between a Trauer and a Schmidt.

Fear made it easy to be cautious almost to the point of fanaticism. "You'll make yourself sick," Mrs. Hopper was always admonishing her, on those occasions when she came importuning her to accompany her to the races, or here and there about the town. Matinées. Luncheon at the hotels. Motion-picture theaters. "Too much confinement indoors softens the bones—and the character. Humans weren't made to live like that. I'd like to see myself huck in the house for any man. . . ."

Sometimes, never betting more than five or ten dollars, and not

infrequently coming home with a killing that amounted to forty or
fifty, she did bestir herself to accompany Mrs. Hopper, who drove a
small roadster manufactured by the firm for which her "friend" was
city manager.

Warm afternoons at Belmont Park or Aqueduct were pleasant.
You came to know dozens of the women habitués by sight. There
were the bright, gilded followers of the stereotyped variety, who
wrote substantial bets and sent them down by the commissioners
who circulated the grandstand between events, as aids chiefly to the
women, who were not allowed to go into the betting paddocks.

But, for the most part, the women habitués who frequented the
races as a matter of livelihood and routine were, with exceptions,
rather a plucked-looking lot. Women with rouged wrinkles, large,
silver-plated mesh bags, and about their eyes and lips, somehow, a
look of fever.

"You cannot beat this game," they were fond of confiding to one
another, as, day after day, season after season, year after year, city
after city, they continued to foster the feverish dream of one day
beating it.

One day, three or four of them went home with Mrs. Hopper in
her roadster, and because, when they arrived, her flat was infested
with painters, they adjourned to Ray's, where she served beer and
homemade cinnamon-rolls and some of the imported cervelat sausage she kept on hand for Walter.

They sat about the table, five of them, in their bird's-nest hats,
face-veils, feather boas, and their silver-plated mesh bags clutched,
even while they drank. It was easy company.

It's a goddam game to even eke a living out of.

If I could sew a straight seam I'd rather dressmake than follow
the best horse running.

The son-of-a-bitch knew his tip had been scratched when he
sold it to me.

Ladies, that jockey wasn't even sweating at the armpits. . . .

Glancing up as she sat there drinking beer and eating cervelat with them, she saw the mirror above the mantelpiece reflecting
the scene with merciless fidelity. A circle of withering women with

faces that crawled with lines. Women whose gallantly assembled plumage was brighter than their eyes or skins. And of them, so that she in no particular wise stood out differentiated, except for the still impeccable grace of her carriage, Ray herself.

"I am one of these. I must look like one of these women who all seem to have the lean faces of birds with bright eyes and wet broken feathers. I look like a bird. I am necky and beaky and terribly bright-haired, like these women. Why should I be any different? . . ."

Nevertheless, when they left, she began to tinker about with her hair, preparing a complicated shampoo and henna-rinse, which she had learned to administer to herself after an expensive series of instructions at a hairdressing parlor.

There must be some way to avoid the harsh greenish glitter to dyed graying hair when what you merely wanted was to dye it back to its original tints.

Next evening, for the first time, Walter observed: "Are you blondining your hair? Looks like the devil. Why do you women, the minute you get along a little in years, think you need to turn blonde?"

She wanted to say: "But, Walter, if I didn't do that I would be gray. You wouldn't want that, would you?"

Somehow, though, she could not bring herself to tell him that, and so she just sat and glittered.

It was around this period that there came a letter from Emma.

"Dearest Aunt Ray. Commencement is May twenty-seventh. I know it will please you to know that I graduate cum laude and already have a teaching-position in the first-year Spanish and history department of the high school of Newcastle, which is a town of about fifteen thousand inhabitants, not far from Indianapolis, and said to be in a very fine agricultural belt. The salary is sixty-five dollars a month to start, but that is more than it sounds, because I am informed by the Teachers' Agency that splendid room and board can be obtained in one of the first-class private homes of the town for seven dollars a week.

"I know it will make you very happy, after all you have done for me, to see me not only beginning to be in a position to help Mama and Papa and the children, but some day to repay you, dear Aunt Ray, for all you have done.

"Oh, Aunt, if only you could come to my commencement and see me graduate! I think that would make me the happiest girl in the world. We are a class of twenty-two, and it is to be quite an unusual commencement this year, because Shendler Hall is to be dedicated, and Mr. Kurt Shendler, the automobile magnate who donated it and who has done so much for the college, is to be present, and we are all looking forward to a stirring occasion.

"Thank you again for the extra twenty-five dollars you sent me last month, dear Aunt. Mama is coming and perhaps Curtis, because knowing you would want me to, I sent her that money for the trip.

"Oh, Aunt Ray, do try and come. Your appreciative niece, Emma."

Why not? The prospect caught her up in a gale of excitement. See Emma graduate! Kurt would be there. Dear old Kurt, for whom she had not a regret; only the warm desire for the thrill of reunion with a dear friend. He had written her in that vein after the debacle of her behavior at Youngstown. "I understand and shall always regard you as my friend," he had written. And he would. That was Kurt all over. The idea of attending Emma's commencement grew, and made her somehow feel ashamed of the eagerness that crowded over her.

It would be spring at Miami, and from the booklets and pamphlets which Emma had sent her from time to time, beautiful old trees lined the brick walks, and the college buildings themselves were ivy-grown, and she cudgeled her brain to remember whether it was Students' Hall at Miami or one of the institutions in the scores of catalogues she had pored over during the period when Richard was making choice of a university, that had a superb oak tree with an iron fence around it and a brass plate attached, proclaiming this fine old veteran to be over one hundred and fifty years old.

There would be girls in white dresses under black cap and gown, and boys in those absurd little dots of caps, and she would share with Freda the distinction of having claim to the sweet Emma Hanck, who was graduating cum laude.

"Walter," she asked him, after he had finished declaiming into the mirror an address which she had assembled and typed for him to deliver before a large noonday organization of Newark business-men, "Walter, would you mind if I went out to Miami to Emma's graduation?"

"Went where?"

It was as if he could never identify, at first mention, this niece.

"Emma. Emma Hanck. My stepsister's girl. She's graduating from Miami, cum laude. I'd kind of like to go, Walter."

"It's all right with me," he said briskly. And then, as if the idea had penetrated after the words, paused and regarded her.

"Leave me?"

"Silly, just for four or five days."

"Why, of course." But even as he spoke, something in his voice was dropping. "Just you go."

"I'll be back before you can say Jack Robinson, Walter. Emma means a lot to me. I want to see her graduate."

"Natural that you should."

"In a way, I feel about going just like an old mother hen who doesn't want to leave the chickies, but goodness alive, Walter, what is five days? Sometimes I don't even see you in five days."

"Five days is nothing, and you go ahead and make your plans. Just as well, anyway. We're going to see plenty of each other in August, when we get to the Alps."

"Oh, Walter—"

"Just as sure as fate, I've my heart set on it this time."

"I don't dare let my mind dwell on it, for fear it's too good to be true."

"Wait and see."

"It's sweet of you, Walter, to make it all right about my going to Emma. Sure you don't mind?"

"Now, I'd be a fine one to mind, wouldn't I?"

"You'll miss me?"

"There's the woman of it! Wants to be missed more than she wants to go."

"We—nobody could ever have lived more of a home life than we do, Walter. That's why I ask. You're so dependent."

"Never you mind. I'll make out so well that you'll be sorry you ever gave me the chance to try my wings."

"Walter!"

"Can't you take a joke?"

"Of course. You're a dear. I feel right excited, Walter. She's a darling girl. It will mean a lot to her."

"That's fine. Just you go." Still, it seemed to her she detected the artificial plating to his voice, but for fear that her further probing might irritate, let it go at that.

"It's all right with you, then—sure?"

"You heard me say so, didn't you?"

"Yes, Walter."

And so it was arranged, and a letter dispatched to Emma, and another filled with the pleasant miscellany of train schedules to Freda, whose letters were of dubiousness, because her new upper teeth, paid for by Ray, were such a bad fit.

"What are you taking a trunk for?" he asked her one evening. "One would think you were going on a trip around the world instead of an overnight ride."

"Oh, Walter, I've made myself three new summer dresses, and there is one in there for Emma, and they are so crispy I hate to cram them into a suitcase."

"Going out to make a killing, eh?"

She had been mixing him the soft drink of lime and almond-oil, and with the long spoon stirring the contents of a glass pitcher, just stood and looked at him, eyes wide.

"What a rotten thing to say."

"There you go again! Can't take a joke. The Lord certainly left out a sense of humor when he made women."

She sat on his knee, stroking the groomed little gray imperial, which of late years he had cultivated to the nicety of a fine point.

"Walter, it isn't that I can't take a joke, it's just that there are some things so impossible to conceive, that it hurts even to hear them said."

"I'm a dog," he said, "and you're too good for me," and thereafter became his mood so tender, that he would not even let her rise to pour his drink, but with his head against her breast, dozed, relaxed there, and finally slept.

Fortunately, what happened occurred two days before her departure, so there was time to write and wire to both Oxford and Youngstown.

May had come in quite stickily that year, and, according to newspaper headlines, there were already heat prostrations; and beaches, a full four weeks before seasonal expectations, were doing a thriving business.

Because he had asked it, and because these days before her departure, a little heartsick in spite of herself, she had been more than usually indulgent in the matter of foods; there had been Wiener schnitzel for dinner, a dish greatly to his liking, but which she seldom prepared except at his request, because of the almost invariable unease he professed after eating it.

"What, Walter, darling! Another helping? You know who has to pay the piper. . . ."

Extremely sensitive, as he always was, to even the innuendo that his appetite could escape his control, it was not unusual for Ray to be driven to the extremity of pretending that what he asked was not in the house, when, more likely than not, it reposed in the refrigerator.

That night there had been red cabbage, too, which she could concoct with strips of bacon into a delicacy. "Walter, darling, I really shouldn't have served that rich cheese torte after your insisting upon two helpings of the schnitzel and red cabbage. Let's not have dessert, dear. I'll give you a glass of port instead."

"That's right. Tell me what to do. You know how I enjoy it," he said, cutting into the creamy surface of pale-yellow cake that appeared to have the lightness of soufflé.

"I didn't mean it that way, dear."

"That's a delicious torte, Ray," he said, through a mouthful.

"Have some." It offended him to see her hold back. "What's the matter? Getting the diet-craze of crazy women? You're too much of a toothpick as it is. Here, let me give you a piece."

"You're sweet, Walter, but I've had so much . . ."

"To please me . . ."

"To please you," she said, passing her plate and watching him pile it to match the indiscretion of his own.

After dinner, while she dragged away the table and he sat with his port and cigar, he began to fight his usual growing drowsiness, and with the pages of his address propped before him began to memorize.

". . . and I wonder if you realize, gentlemen, the gratification and sense of honor with which I rise to my feet to address an organization of this caliber—realizing as I do to what extent you, gentlemen, stand for the peak of civic and industrial stability—in the midst of a period of financial stabilization—"

"You skipped the 'that reminds me' opening anecdote, Walter!"

"So I did. So I did. . . . and speaking of caliber, reminds me—"

Suddenly it seemed to Ray that there was a cry from him sharp as the explosion of a cap-pistol, and, as she turned, he began to slump in his chair, clutching the front of his shirt between his writhing fingers.

As time and time again it came to her afterward in flashes of remembrance, it seemed to her that they were both remarkably quiet about it.

"Walter," she whispered, and flew to him and let him lop across her shoulder.

"I can't breathe," he said, softly and thickly. "Air."

She lurched him back to his chair as you would a bolster, tore open a window and rushed with a tumbler of water which she had snatched from the table.

"Drink this, Walter."

He was gasping now, and the pallor of jade, and in evident pain, because his feet were twisting about each other and he kept clutching at his shirtfront.

"Walter. I'll call a doctor."

"No. No. No."

Locked in the same fear that must have smitten him as he writhed, she kept smoothing back his hair and running her hand along the cold sweat of his forehead.

"Then lie down, sweetheart. Relax against me."

"I can't," he said stiffly. "I wonder if I'm going to faint."

"No, darling, you're not. You're just in pain and short of breath."

"That's it. I'll be all right."

"Could you drink a little water now?"

"No. Just let me lie quietly. I'll be all right."

Three of the small knickknack clocks which cluttered up the room began suddenly and with absurd prominence to tick roundly and out of time with one another. Between their tiny spans, it seemed to Ray, holding him there, watching his damp brow spring out in globules each time she wiped them away, that long eternities of this terrible waiting wheeled in between the seconds. If only she dared risk his excitement, or his anger, or his—fear, by calling a doctor. Between the eternities of those clock-ticks, she visualized, precisely as if it were held flaming against her tormented eyes, the headline: "Head of banking house of Friedlander-Kunz dies in woman's apartment."

It was as if she had shocked him out of an impending stupor, because he opened his eyes, not quite taking her in for the moment.

"Walter, I will get a doctor."

"I'm all right," he said, and tried to lift himself away from her shoulder.

"Drink this then, darling," she said, and held the tumbler against his shuddering lips. He was sick then, and terribly humiliated, his fastidiousness offended. And she had to assume the high singsong voice of talking to a drowsy child.

"Now it's all over and we're well again, and it's forgotten. So! There! Pillow under his head. There! Purple coverlet that Ray crocheted herself! There! Collar loosed and lampshade just right for no bad glare! There—better, darling?"

"I must have overdone today. Two directors' meetings and then that trip out to Rosmersholm to see Richard play the polo semifinals. Too much—in heat—"

"—of course—"

"—had attacks like this before—pass off—"

"—of course—everybody has—"

"—terrible—"

"—all over now—"

"—must—eat more carefully—"

"—everybody should—"

"—wonderful woman, Ray—"

"—darling—"

"—wouldn't have had it happen for the world—"

"—why not, dearest—here to share bad times—"

"—God knows you have—mostly—"

"—no—no—no—"

He began to whimper, for all the world like a child.

"Don't leave me, Ray."

"Why, of course I won't, Walter."

"I haven't let on, but I wouldn't be surprised—if that isn't what has upset me. Of course, if your heart is set on going—"

"Why, silly darling—it's worth everything that you want me here—"

"I need you so, Ray. Don't leave me . . . don't go to Oxford."

"Oh, my darling . . ."

"Wire them you can't come. Sick. Tell them anything."

"Anything."

"We'll go to Switzerland, Ray, one of these days. You won't be sorry."

"Of course I won't."

"Sure you're not disappointed?"

"On the contrary, I'm happy."

"—couldn't stand your going—"

Crouched there, smoothing his still-damp brow, she was working it all out in flashes. Emma should have the money the railroad fare would have cost. Just as well. The child would need a good outfit to start teaching. It would have been nice going out, but—it was ineffably sweet being needed. How like a small boy he seemed, lying there pale and wanting her. Nothing in the world but an attack of out-and-out acute indigestion from overeating. Strange that she, the fancy one, should always be the one to be let in for the rather brutally plain facts of his life. It was as if, for Corinne, he had troubled to keep up an illusion. Not that she wanted illusion, here at the very core of his life where she belonged. . . .

"Sweet darling," she said to him as he slept.

And even as he floated off, half hearing, his hand closed around her forefinger, holding on.

44

In June, Arnold, valiantly trying to emulate his big brother's polo prowess, was thrown from a pony, and his ankle fractured in two places.

The redeeming side to this catastrophe, as voiced by Richard—whose attitude to his young brother, across the chasm of years that separated them, was a mixture of patronage and paternalism—was that, while it canceled all preparations for the western tour, it did throw Arnold back on the needed resort of spending the summer at school camp, tutoring in an arithmetic course, in which he was trailing.

So once more a default of summer plans, dismaying but not surprising! It had happened so often before, with what seemed by now a consistent perversity.

Corinne, with Arnold no longer able to take his western trip, was going to Aix with Walter, for the cure, which she declared gave her new life for a twelvemonth.

"It's just as if some kind of fate were forever fixing summers for us the way we don't want them, Walter."

"Fact," he said. "I've been banking on this summer being very different from the way it now looks it is going to be."

The thought of the dreariness of the double precautions of the indoor life she must lead this time at Aix came flowing over her.

"Walter, you won't get angry if I say something?"

"Am I as vicious as all that?"

"Now, Walter, you know that's beside the point. Supposing this year I don't go over, Walter. It's hard under the conditions, being at a small place like Aix. I'll stay home this trip."

The old familiar look of hurt and personal affront came in a scowl between his eyes.

"I hadn't realized before that a trip to Europe was a hardship. Of course, if you feel that way about it. Wouldn't think of asking it."

"Now, Walter, dear, please don't go getting sarcastic. You know I didn't mean it that way. I think it's wonderful, of course. It's the conditions I'm talking about. Walter, dear, have you ever thought what it means to be cooped up a prisoner in a small town like Aix, sometimes not seeing you for days, and afraid to go out, for fear?"

"Yes, naturally, but I've been fool enough to believe that it might be worth it. . . ."

"Why, Walter Saxel, honestly, I could spank you. Of course it is worth it, darling, and you know it . . . but . . ."

"I see. But it's not worth it to you."

"Honestly, dear, it is a talent with you to twist what I say into something I didn't even dream of. I only meant . . ."

"I know what you only meant. And you may rest assured there is nothing I want less than to force you into anything against your will."

In the end, propitiating, she had to plead her way slowly, a matter of hours, step-by-step, back into precisely the estate from which she had sought this summer to extricate herself.

"Walter, dearest, it isn't that I don't love to be near you, it is because I do so value it, that I can't bear the thought of chancing—"

"Funny way of showing it."

"But I've tried to explain. . . ."

"I know what you've tried to explain, and you've succeeded, too. It has always been one of my policies, in business and out— no unhappy, discontented people around me. The moment that happens—out!"

"Why, Walter, honestly you—you just make me feel as if I'm going crazy, trying to make you understand. I love Aix, dearest. I love being there just because you are there. I love being anywhere you are, even if I only see you one hour out of a month. I only meant . . ."

"Well then, just what did you mean?"

"I only meant, Aix being so small—"

"Oh, I see—you want me to enlarge it, eh?"

Oh. Oh. Oh. Tears were in her eyes, and each time she attempted the propitiating gesture of trying to take hold of his coat lapels, he pushed her away, unconciliatory.

"None of that."

"Very well," she said, sitting herself down firmly on a chair opposite him. "But just the same, I'm going to Aix this summer and you're not going to hold me back. I won't be punished for saying a little thing that had no meaning."

"You are not going."

"I am."

"We'll see."

"Walter," she cried, making fists of her hands and beating them up and down in the air, "oh, you make me mad. So mad. So mad."

Finally, after hours of this, he permitted his head to be held between her hands, submitted to be kissed, and finally, thawing, took her into his arms.

"You're a bad girl. I oughtn't to let you lick me every time. You sail on the *Saxonia*, July sixth, one week after we leave on the *Paris*."

"My dearest, you have forgiven me—haven't you?"

"What can I do? You're stronger than I am."

"Don't make me laugh, darling."

"Tell you what I'm going to do, Ray. Something you'll like."

"What?"

"Corinne has got it into her head that after her cure she wants to take that Norway and Sweden trip with Irma and Mordecai. I've already begged off. While they're at that, we're going to have our holiday in the Alps after all. I've got it all planned! Zermatt. Blue ice. Cows. Chalet. Peace."

"Oh, Walter!"

"This is one plan that is going through, Ray. Mark you that."

It was easy to be happy after that, regardless or no of whether the trip to the Alps actually would materialize.

By a perversity as benign as it was unexpected, this, of all summers, proved to be one of pleasure and pleasurable surprise.

First of all, for two weeks, Corinne remained in Paris with the Friedlander spinsters to shop, while Walter hurried along to Aix-les-Bains ten days ahead of them.

Long, perfect, always cautious afternoons of drives or walks. Evenings in and out of the Casino, at will. Dinner in her little suite of the chocolate-ochre wallpaper roses, not just hotel cuisine, but served by a waiter trained to bring in dishes steaming hot from the Casino kitchens.

And even up to the day before the arrival of Corinne, Richard, and the young Pooles, they ventured the celebration of a day's motor trip to Geneva, where she purchased a small silver wristwatch for Emma, and, to a delight that was almost childish, was presented with an identical one from Walter, who told the salesman to wrap two—a delight, however, which was to precipitate one of their bitterest quarrels.

"From the way you behaved before that clerk," he told her on the drive back, "you would think that you had never been presented with anything before."

It was on the tip of her tongue to blurt out, "But I haven't, Walter, at least so seldom." But she did not.

"You don't understand German. I do. I heard what one of the clerks said to another."

"What could he have said, Walter? I was only being apprecia-tive. . . ."

"Never mind what he said, but it made me small."

"I'm sorry, dear. It was just the surprise. . . ."

"Precisely what you took pains to convey in the shop."

"What did I say that was wrong?"

"Nothing. It was all subterfuge, which I dislike. Your subtle way of conveying larger dissatisfactions by petty pleasures. I don't know about what—but perhaps because you're not covered with gems."

"Walter Saxel, if I knew the way, I'd get out of this car after a remark like that, and walk home."

"Wouldn't, if I were you."

"You're insulting and horrid, and if there is one thing I am not, and you know it, it's the things you—you are insinuating," she said, and began to cry.

"Oh, Lord, must I always live in a world of women who turn on the waterworks at the drop of a hat?"

"Drop of a hat! You've slapped me in the face. You've hurt me to the core."

"I know. I know. What about me? Innuendoes because I didn't go in there, where likely as not I'm known from my newspaper pictures, and indulge in the conspicuous pastime of buying you an emerald brooch."

"Well, I'll say this for you, I've never known you take any such chance."

It was out! She could have bitten off her tongue, and did press down on it to the limit of her endurance.

"I see," he said slowly. "I see a great deal now that I've never seen before."

"Walter, I didn't mean that! You goaded me to it. Please don't let us have the commonest kind of quarrel a man and woman can have. It's so vulgar. Walter, have I ever mentioned money to you in all these years?"

"You've never had occasion to."

Oh, how she could have unloosed then! The unspoken hurt of years of unnecessary deprivations. The second-rate hotels, from which, when he came to dine, he refused to eat the cuisine. The need to contribute to her table budget out of winnings and pickings from petty traffic with the Women's Exchange. The necessity, always, to speculate with last year's homemade clothes; the fact that for years she had needed, but never achieved, a successor to her one fur coat, long since cut up into strips, so that the least-worn parts could be salvaged for collars and cuffs. The fact that had she gone to Miami, sure as fate, not one extra penny would have found its way into the bisque boy's basket. His unobservance of her self-denials, when he was forever sending her out on the mission of purchasing remembrances for the stenographers and clerks about his office. The fact that at Christmas he sent his favorite candies, crystallized nuts from Bissinger's in Cincinnati, to be consumed later by him, and a case of Cointreau, also to be consumed by him. The fact that, upon her graduation, he had never so much as offered to give her a sum of money for Emma. Not that she would have accepted. It was her proud and secret boast that not one cent of Emma's education had come out of the Saxel coffer. But if only he had offered—oh, there were sore, hurt, bleeding places that he was having the temerity to stir. . . .

"There are some things we had better not discuss."

"Now what do you mean by that? I am not afraid to discuss any subject under the sun. . . ."

"Of course not, dear, but some hurt more than others. . . ."

"Not me, when I feel I've done my part. . . ."

"I've done that too, Walter, where you are concerned."

"Not saying you haven't. But I hate to be made to seem small."

She began to cry quietly into her handkerchief.

"Well, this is the sort of holiday a harassed busy man looks forward to when he tries to escape his affairs."

Without raising her eyes from the handkerchief, she put out her hand toward his, which he withdrew.

"I'm sorry, dear. I was so innocent of harm—just happy—over the sweetness of the gift—"

"Funny way of showing it. A child could see through the sarcasm of the way you acted."

"I—I—oh, what's the use! What's—the—use!" And racked with the scalding tears, knowing them to be only an irritant to him, she tried to check them, and trying, cried the more.

"Walter, whatever I am that is bad, I am not that. If I had wanted the things that money could buy, I could have—"

"Meaning I don't supply them?"

"No, darling, no. I mean, if I were a gold digger— Don't you see, dear, that's why the little silver watch made me as glad as something more valuable might have made another person." Again she could have bitten her tongue, but to her surprise he jerked her into his arms and kissed her with emotion.

"Don't say any more, Ray. I know I'm a dog and you're an angel. Try to understand, dear. Of course, I could deck you with diamonds. But I won't! I want you like this—mine—alone—simple—plain. If I'm a selfish dog, I'm a selfish dog. But I'm going to take care of you in a different way. A way that will never cause you to regret the happiness you have given me. I've something worked out, now. My first act, when I get back to America, will be to take care of that little matter of my will. I take a solemn oath before God, Ray, it will be my first act. A Frenchman gave me the idea—it's all very simple—"

"That is darling of you, Walter. It will mean a lot—that kind of security against the future. But for now, this is all I need or ask, or want, darling—and please believe me when I tell you that the little watch—"

"Don't hurt me anymore by rubbing salt into the wound of my rottenness. We'll have a good dinner tonight, Ray, and after that— after that—"

"Dearest dear."

"It's our last free-and-easy evening before our holiday in the Alps. You won't see much, if anything, of me during the next few days. Corinne and the children arrive on an early-morning train—no Casino tonight, dearest—just us—alone—"

"Dearest dear."

As it turned out, they were forced to spend the evening quietly, because he insisted upon ordering sent over from the Casino kitchens, an elaborate specialty known as canard tour d'argent, a rich concoction of pressed duck, prepared with wine-sauce, and for two hours suffered pangs of dyspepsia that distressed him.

But withal, sweet was the cleansed air of after their quarrel, and pressed against her eyelids and along her throat and against her hair were his kisses, as he bade her good night, his arms still ringing with the passion of having held her for the long, close hours of their intimacy. . . .

It was two mornings following, that her Paris edition of the New York *Herald* arrived as usual by mail, and she opened it to read a first-page headline that, read and reread as she would, did not penetrate beyond causing within her the wildest impulse to risibility she had ever known. Off and off, her mind kept skidding, only to be jerked back to the point of her lunatic-looking eyes.

Head of Banking House of Friedlander-Kunz Dies Suddenly at Aix-les-Bains

Walter D. Saxel, banker-philanthropist, stricken early this morning of acute indigestion. Dies in wife's arms before medical aid can arrive.

Death comes as shock to financial world. Survived by wife and three children.

45

Somebody had stuffed up a rat-hole. She was in that rat-hole. That was one way it had of seeming to her. Then again, she was one of those Russian dolls made out of painted wood, with no feet, but a hemispherical base, so that, topple over as she would, back up she came bobbing. That was quite wonderful. It was apparently of no volition of her own that she rose again after each impact. It was just her being humanly resilient.

Yes, that was very curious. She would never have dreamed she had within her capacity for so much resistance. She would never have dreamed anyone had. The capacity of human beings, the capacity of herself, to go on breathing when the body was little more than a mausoleum!

The mausoleum moving about her room in the little Hotel Choiseul, warming the Babe's food over a spirit-lamp, washing out silk stockings to hang them over an umbrella to dry. The mausoleum was careful to henna her hair, even though she had not been out for four days now. But you could never tell. They might come after her. Need her. They—meaning, oh, my God, they, meaning perhaps a doctor, to say it had all been a mistake. They—meaning Richard, to tell her something that had been left by Walter, for him to tell her privately. They, meaning—well, anyway, they might want her. They might need her. Corinne might!

Corinne was such a baby. Such a terrible baby. Oh, my God,

what a terrible baby to be left, that way. She knew, because Walter had told her some of Corinne's babyish little fears. She knew,
because Walter had told her, without ever realizing that he had told
her, that Corinne, for instance, was afraid of the dark. Away back in
the days before the more common use of electricity, when they had
lived in the Lexington Avenue house, devices had been installed,
so that no gas-jet was ever turned off, but a tiny blob kept burning so that it could be jerked up with a chain. Corinne was full of
fears. She would never put on one of the ropes of her magnificent
registered pearls if Walter did not first test the safety clasps, to make
sure. On board ship, all his meals had to be taken with her, up on
deck, beside her steamer chair, where he fed her as you would a bird,
because she felt half ill. She wanted him home every possible birthday anniversary, and holiday, to meals, and at least once a week,
preferably Friday nights, because it was frightening to her not to
have frequent evidence of solidarity of family. Her superb chinchilla
wrap, for which he had paid thirty-five thousand dollars at a Paris
exposition, had been Corinne's choice because it was such tender
little-baby fur, off an animal that could never have hurt you while
it lived.

If this much had seeped through to her, Ray, think of what she
did not know of the loneliness that must have fallen like a felled
tree, across the heart of the babied Corinne! His solicitudes, his
indulgences, his generosity, born partly, at least, out of the carking
sense of treason that must have been his, had been so constant. Her
life had been cradled and lined in chinchilla by him. His image
must hang aching and glorified in her poor babyish heart. . . .

If things were only so that she could go to her, instead of sitting
bottled like the rat that had been corked into its hole!

And yet to hold back, to make no step, even though the precaution seemed elaborate, would have been the way he wanted it. Terrible to sit there passive, the four days. Terrible. Terrible. Terrible.
And yet that is how he would have wished it.

The Paris *Herald* had carried a subsequent column.

"Private services for Walter D. Saxel, the New York banker-
philanthropist, were held in the villa of Hotel Bernasçon on

Friday—brief address delivered by the Hon. James Reedy, ex-ambassador to Turkey—lifelong friend of the deceased. Tributes were also paid by M. Felix Gateau, president of the Paris Bank of Exchange, Baron Meyer Friedlander, of Frankfurt-am-Main, Mr. David Kuhn, New York banker and lifelong friend of the deceased. . . . The remains, accompanied by Mrs. Saxel, Mr. Richard Saxel, Mr. and Mrs. Mordecai Poole II, will be taken to New York for final interment."

How soon dared she venture out? He would have wanted her to be so sure. And yet it had been two days since that article. Three, since the service. Curious though, how fragments of old memory clung to a brain numbed in a mausoleum! Three years before, a friend of Walter's, a Nathan Dix of Pittsburgh, had died of swift stroke at Aix-les-Bains, and there had been over a week of the agony of procedure. Around dead bodies to be shipped, there revolved elaborate paraphernalia of state. Permit, document, laws of lighterage.

Poor Corinne. Walter had become freight.

Poor Corinne. And so passed the days. The days of the trying to thaw a mind that would not function.

Walter must be lying in a box now, his head on one of those shirred white satin pillows. His body laid out. God, somewhere, had released the dove of his spirit into the blue ozone of eternity—

There had been a poem like that back in the Woodward High School days—anyway, something like that.

If you thought of it that way, the crating and the carting and the loading of the body of Walter was not so bad, but the picture of God catching the white dove of Walter's spirit in His hands, slid about the mind, and wouldn't stay focused—

They must be crating him by now; carting him by now; expressing him by now to Paris. More delay. Permits. Then the boat train. Then the docks. Walter, waiting along the docks, like so much commercial cargo to be hoisted. The poor Corinne, who was afraid of the dark and afraid of the fur of an animal that in life could have bitten. He had sheltered her so—

The fifth day she ventured out, the Babe on a new crocheted

leash she had made for him during those four days, out of the inability of her hands to lie quiet. This must be the way fever patients ventured along after long illness. The legs trembled. The hands felt white and thinner and without stamina. A street gamin, in a black smock, shocked what little strength she felt out of her, as he ran shouting down the quiet little street of the Hotel Choiseul. One had to become accustomed to the feel of air against the flesh; and then, when she reached the square, there was everyone moving about quite normally and apparently happy, in a world that did not contain Walter.

Here it was! Out here was a world that did not contain Walter. He was gone. Walter had died. Walter was dead. Walter was on his way to be buried. Strange that you had never quite fully realized it before. Walter was dead. Somehow, the busy unheeding scene of folk, many of whom had known him, seated about on benches, chatting under trees, sipping the springwaters slowly, moving about in motorcars, strolling, reading, basking, chatting, laughing, proclaimed it more loudly than the silence of the last four days. Walter was dead.

She sat down on a bench, the Babe anchored by his leash to her wrist. The legs trembled so after fever—no, no. After Walter. Dared she venture up the hill to the Bernasçon, and like any interested, casual friend, ask just for a few facts? She was entitled to them! Damn Corinne, who could suffer unimpeded—damn—no, no, no! Frightened Corinne, who was afraid of fur that had belonged to an animal that could bite. There was aloneness for you. Even with her children about her, the aloneness of a woman like that, who had lost Walter!

Walter was dead. Her hands, which were lying palm upward on her lap, opened slowly, as if of their colossal emptiness.

46

All the little clocks ticking at counteraction, and all the multitude of tiny objects, the little filigree parlor set, the gilded walnut with the views of Niagara Falls, the chamber pot, the blue glass bulldog with rhinestone eyes, the bisques, the elephants on their incline, made sort of a hubbub in the room, so that when it came to dismantling, it was a week or two before she could bring herself to strip the place of even the first portiere.

Without the tiny commotion of the knickknacks it would become such an empty room. The first curtain down would make it grin like a skeleton. Those lace curtains that she had always starched and stretched herself, were eighteen years old. So were the green velour hangings with the gilt-braided valance. It was the sort of room which the removal of pictures from the wall would cause to pale in great blotches the size of the frames. Then, too, no matter how you figured it, a few tiny objects were sure to be lost in wrapping and packing. So much tissue! Where could you pack a darling little tea table the size of a postage stamp! Thank goodness the souvenir-spoon collection, eighteen years old now, even though it was not as complete as she could have wished, could now go to Emma. "Altoona" had been the last. Sterling silver, out of a Sixth Avenue pawnshop window.

Surveying them, a thought smote her that made her flush. They were almost all sterling. Some had enameled bowls. The one from

Fontainebleau, with the head of Marie Antoinette etched onto the handle, had cost three hundred francs. Twelve dollars. The average cost was about five. A couple of hundred dollars, perhaps, represented in that collection. Self-nausea smote her. The spoons were Emma's. Had been promised her ever since she was a little girl. Besides, what with her pickings at the Casino, during the summer, and the monthly allowance Walter had left her on top of the ormolu clock at the Choiseul just a week before the calamity, there were still two hundred and seventy-five dollars pinned in an envelope against her rubber girdle. The final month's rent on the apartment would reduce that by eighty-five. That would leave one hundred and ninety. A little frightening, but not too much so. Only a matter of getting one's bearings.

Time was the great factor. That was the reason for holding out against the surrender of the flat for smaller quarters. Here in this lair of over twenty years she was traceable. The giving up of the telephone would be like the breaking of a cable that connected her identity with the very sources of life. The will had been published. An enormous, important, benign will, with regard to both family and charitable disbursements. A beautiful will. There was neither surprise nor disappointment in the omission of any ostensible provision for her. He had never got to it. But somehow, some way, safe from Corinne, there must lurk among his effects, consideration for her; with the best of intentions in the world he had never reached the matter of the will—but somewhere among his effects—if only one could hold out and wait, against the pressure of time and dwindling resources.

The will itself had been one of those which sound as if written for publication. Of course it had to be so. That was what made Walter's dilemma, where she was concerned, so transparent. What if, after the millions to Corinne, the million each to Richard and Irma, the trust fund of like amount for Arnold, the vast sums to philanthropies, the art collection to museums—what if, in among the part pertaining to legacies to relatives, servants, there had come along, "One hundred thousand dollars to Mrs. Ray Schmidt, friend." How dangerous and transparent that would have been. How merciful

that he had been farsighted. But behind all the years of the procras-
tinations, there must lurk among his vast effects, safe from Corinne,
safe from public eye, consideration for her.

He had never failed her—quite. That summer of 1904, of her
despair and shocking plight, a roll of bills caught against the rear of
a buffet had been evidence that he had not failed her. Time and time
again, when he had seemed on the verge of forgetting her steamship or railroad ticket, there, at the last moment, it had bobbed
up, stuck in an envelope on a table or poked into her purse. Dear
darling—

If one could hold out just a second month. One could, of course.
There was still the surplus in her purse. The Women's Exchange
was closed for the summer period, but stacked against that was the
pleasant fact that Emma's earning capacity was about to begin.

Of course, if Walter had somehow provided her with even as
much as fifty thousand, then Emma, whose eyes were none too
strong— But Walter had not yet left her the fifty thousand, so
providentially Emma's self-support as teacher was just this month
to begin.

Curious, the sense of stability it gave her to so resolutely feel
that somewhere, in his affairs, there lurked that consideration for
her. Meanwhile she dismantled the flat slowly; almost the taking-
down of a towel-rack was a rite—splashed with tears.

The justification of her intuition came one warm forenoon
when she was engaged in folding away in a round-top trunk, for
dear knows what ultimate dispensation, an elaborate Honiton-lace
tablecloth which she had made some fifteen years before, and off
which she and Walter, long after it had become a chromo, had
dined such countless times. She had used to spread it over pink
sateen, and there were pink candle-shades to match.

It was the morning that the landlord, to whom she was about to
explain that October the first must see the termination of her lease,
was expected; so that, when she opened the door to a ring, the sight
of Richard there gave her, nearly as anything she could remember,
the impulse to faint. That is, her breathing stopped, and for the
moment consciousness was a mere rush of waters. . . .

"I'll come in, if I may," he said, after what must have been an interval that made him doubt his admittance.

Presently, and much more clearly, as that sense of rushing darkness began to recede, she and this strangely older Richard were seated on the sofa before the open trunk, around which they had awkwardly to detour.

"My father would have wished this," he began. Harshly, she thought.

"Wished what?"

"That I come for this purpose."

"What purpose?" (Dear heart.)

The thing to do was not to be pitied by him. Being staccato helped.

Under his small mustache, which he had developed since last she saw him, he kept biting his full dark-red lips. He was being crucified, sitting here in the flat of his father's harlot; that is how it must seem to him, to whom easy women, without youth, were horrible.

She remembered, from something Walter had once said to her, that Richard upon occasion had discussed an escapade of his while at college. It had flattered Walter and made him feel young with, and secure about, his boy. Well it might have. Richard was the one to sow his wild oats fastidiously, as if each one were one of the flawless, pink-fleshed pearls in which his family trafficked with such munificence.

This was something strange and different to him—hawklike and terrible; and, sitting there opposite him, she found herself trying not to say over and over again to herself, knowing how revolting it would be to him if he knew, "Dear heart."

"I guess you know everything."

"From the papers," she said, on a moan.

"It came suddenly, absolutely without preparation. At ten minutes before five, scarcely dawn, my mother called me from the adjoining room. I had arrived the evening before with her from Paris, where she had met my boat train. When I reached the bed—he was sitting up—quite glassy—color of wax—first thought a stroke. Sent my mother rushing across the hall to my sister's room, for restoratives, while I tried those at hand. In those few moments while we were alone—I don't know how well I can explain this to you, Mrs.—Miss Schmidt—he wanted to speak to me. But his lips and his eyes seemed locked. In those few minutes alone with him, Father was trying to say something to, or about, you. He had that look on his face that he had that evening he found me at your hotel in Aix. I may be wrong, in a way I hope to God I am—but—but Father died with that look on his face for you—"

(How funny. My lips won't move.)

"The point is, everything considered—what Father was to me—what he was to my mother—to my brother and sister—with all his—er—weaknesses—what Father was to us makes his every wish, spoken and unspoken—law. Naturally there was no proviso, in his will. I take it there was no—er—arrangement between you, Miss Schmidt?"

"No."

"He would want you provided for. I know that, from something he said to me in an interview—after Aix. Secretly, between us, I want to continue whatever Father's—er—arrangement was with you."

(Silly dear darling—don't do that with your face as if what you just said was so horrible. It is beautiful to me. More beautiful than anything has ever been. . . .)

"You are good."

"I am fulfilling an obligation."

"I suppose," she said slowly, "that according to the way people look at these things, I should refuse. But I'm not going to. It's like having something left of him. That he thought of me at all—there at the end—puts me somehow in the class with those he loved—"

"How much did my father—what was the arrangement—"

"Two hundred dollars."

"A week?"

"No. Every month."

"You mean—everything—"

"Yes. It had to be more the last few years."

"Oh, my God," he said, and got up and walked to the window.

It made her feel, sitting there, feeling lean and hawklike and as if her eyes were too close together and her thinning nose sharper than ever, that she would like the floor to open and swallow her.

"If it seems too much—don't bother—"

He drew up in front of her. "I need to go now. It's all right. Every first of the month the money will be left for you, in cash, in a plain addressed envelope, in your letter box downstairs. You will understand the need for secrecy."

She wanted to put her hand on his arm, to tell him to be careful of his darling neck at the big international polo-meet, in which, from the newspapers, she knew he was going to play; she wanted, almost beyond the restraining, to draw him down, for just five minutes, onto the couch beside her. He might have something to say that matched more closely with the mood that must have brought him there. If only he would stay. Five minutes.

She dared not ask, because, as she stood there wanting so terribly to put her hand on his sleeve, the door had closed behind him.

47

The day that Richard was killed, outright, in the polo match over which she had wanted to warn him to be careful of his darling neck, such an irrelevant thought quietly struck her, as she read the headlines over a shoulder in a Fifth Avenue bus.

Corinne would now be like a Mrs. Ditenhoefer, who used to live on Baymiller Street. Mrs. Ditenhoefer, with her bare red arms rolled into a muff of her apron, would lean her loose busts over the top of her picket gate, and recite a quick succession of family catastrophes that took your breath away. Within a month, if you paused long enough to listen, Mrs. Ditenhoefer had been widowed, bereft of three children, a nephew—

It often happened that way. How frequently you could hear a widow refer to the loss of her husband and son all within a brief period, or a widower recite the quick and unexpected demise of a wife, followed by a son or daughter.

Death often chose visitations like that. Catastrophes could sometimes seem to come in schools, like porpoises around a ship. Corinne was bereft of a son now. Corinne and Ray were bereft of Richard and Walter. All within a quarter of a year.

Strangely, it was not until she reached home, sodden with perspiration that had drenched her, that another aspect of this terrible tragedy of the beauty and youth of a boy came flooding over her.

As she dumped the contents of her purse onto the table, there dropped out, among the miscellany of keys and a powder puff, two twenty-dollar bills and exactly sixty-eight cents in change. The remains of that first and what was to be the last deposit of the plain envelope into her letter box downstairs.

48

This time there was procrastination neither with herself, nor with her situation.

Within the fortnight, the pale blotches from removed pictures were everywhere on the walls, the windows uncurtained, and all the little objects labeled "elephants," "tinkle-bells," "Eiffel Tower," packed into a wooden case, labeled "Mrs. Hugo Hanck, 1221 Topeka Avenue, Youngstown, Ohio."

The thing to do until she got her bearings was to store away these trinket treasures in Freda's attic. The cost of the slow freight seemed prohibitive, more than their value, but there was something about the sense of them tucked away safely in the top floor of that small house on that stale street in Youngstown, that seemed, utterly without congruity, to make them more definitely her own. The absurdity of the idea of anything tucked away in the attic of such a house being dear or special to anyone besides herself, made it more comforting. And out of the throes of such a move, any bit that brought its modicum of comfort, helped.

The day the dealers came was worse. Fourteen dollars for the cinnamon-colored velveteen divan with the high back, like the hunch of a camel. With its solid-walnut frame and hair-stuffings it must easily have cost Walter two hundred.

"Aren't you ashamed to make such an offer for a handsome piece like that?"

"It's out-of-date and the springs are broken and it has to be re-covered. Take it or leave it."

In the end she took. The folding-bed with the inset desk, three dollars. The extension-table with its timbers crowded with what must have been memories of the countless meals eaten off it, four dollars. Jardinière and rubber plant, whose glossy leaves she had bathed in milk for years, seventy-five cents. Dutch oven for Walter's pot roasts, twenty cents. It had cost six dollars in Macy's basement. Three mahogany chairs, two dollars and a half, each. Small rocker, one dollar. Nine-by-twelve Axminster rug, five dollars. Pair of china, gilt and flowered cuspidors, fifty cents. One china oil-lamp with globe which she had painted with yellow roses, fifty cents. One onyx-and-gilt table, one dollar. One cut-glass punch bowl, glass reflector, and eleven punch-glasses, two dollars. One gentleman's mission chiffonier, five dollars. Bedding, two dollars. One large shaving-mirror, with strop, fifty cents. One carpet-sweeper, fifty cents. One antler's horn chair (curiosity), fifty cents. Inlaid teak-wood taboret, fifty cents.

The galvanized washtub of kitchen utensils she divided between Mrs. Hopper and one of the West Indian houseboys, whose wife was going to have a baby.

One morning that smelled of October, as she sat, in her hat and feather boa, on the packing case marked Youngstown, the express-man came and literally moved it out from under her, leaving her alone in the now empty flat, with the Babe and a round-topped trunk.

There were a stack of neatly piled newspapers and an old art catalogue in a corner, an empty hatbox or two, too pretty in their flowered-paper coverings to toss away, and a coffeepot with only the tiniest of leaks. Otherwise she had swept out and left clean the vacated premises, polishing the windows with a dry cloth and drawing even the shades.

It was like sitting in the middle of last night's dream—or night-mare. What remained of Walter was crammed in the tiny memen-toes of a pair of gold link cuff-buttons she had found in the corner of a drawer of his chiffonier, a leather wallet with his monogram in

gold, a pair of his shoes, patent-leather made-to-order ones, with
steel arch-supporters, all packed into the round-topped trunk. The
remainder of his effects of clothing and whatnot of articles, she had
divided between the delicatessen boy and the West Indian whose
wife was going to have a baby.

The green walls, covered with the square pale eyes where had
hung pictures, stared down at her as she stood there, the Babe and
the trunk waiting beside her. Strangest of all was the absence of the
counter-tickings of the small clocks, quite terrible in fact, that kind
of silence, like the silence of a stopped heart.

Finally, the local expressman came for the trunk, and with only
the look-back of one going to the corner, she followed, with the
Babe, by taxicab, to the furnished room which she had found, by
way of a *Times* advertisement, in an apartment over a Cushman
bakery on Columbus Avenue, in the Seventies.

It was a bright-enough room, with two good-sized windows
looking onto the side street, and the mirror to the dresser reflecting
light. The bed was one of those sleeping couches that under their
invariable green rep covers take on the look of prehistoric monsters.
Within a half hour after she moved in, she had received two towels, a face and a Turkish, from Mrs. Cleveland, her landlady, and
deposited twenty-five cents against a doorkey. Within the hour, the
round-topped trunk had been unpacked, her German-silver toilet-
set spread on top of the dresser, a few of the knickknacks she had
salvaged arranged on the mantel, her dresses, coats, and hats hung
in the shallow closet, and Emma's picture, in communion-dress,
placed on the table.

There remained in the trunk some of the bed linen, some of her
underwear, and, in the tray, Walter's shoes, the cuff links, and the
wallet. By then it was time to go out and purchase sliced beef-liver
for the Babe, which she prepared over her traveler's spirit-lamp. He
sat up for his food quite cunningly by now, yapping each time she
let a tidbit fall into his mouth; but the very first day someone in
the room adjoining rapped sharply against the wall, and since there
had been quite a discussion over the matter of the Babe when she

engaged the room, thereafter she saw to it that his food was fed to him in a dish on the floor.

It was after this half-day of the chores of adjustment that a sense of absolutely nothing to do set in. There was something about this room, nice enough after its fashion, which gave one, however, the sense of a damp bathing suit donned at dawn. It was a room in which you stood about, rather than sat. When footsteps passed her door, she stood tense until they died. Usually they were bound for the bathroom at the end of the hall. The plunge of water into the bathtub was a sound to be heard all over the apartment. Entering the bathroom, the hot steam of somebody else's bath usually smote one. After a while she acquired the technique of its use. Before eight in the morning, and after ten at night, were the best times to avoid the constant turning of the doorknob.

At first, the difficulty about going to the races every day was the Babe. It had been one matter to leave him alone at home in the flat, where he knew his cozy basket in the bedroom, his dish of water in the bathroom, his place on the cushion under the living-room table. It was a different matter leaving him here. It was as if the Babe also found no rest in that room, wandering about and usually ending by raising himself on his hind legs and scratching against her skirt, to be lifted.

A trunk store on Columbus Avenue, where she purchased, at a reasonable price, a wicker hamper with a cushioned bottom and a drinking-cup attachment, helped solve that.

It was a simple matter now, thus avoiding the rulings of trains and streetcars against dogs in arms, to take the Babe along. As a matter of fact, he came to be quite a figure at Belmont and Aqueduct, the women regulars and even the commissioners, stuffing him with sweets until Ray was forced to take a hand, forbidding.

Now there came to her the opportunity to put into practice her theory, often expounded to Walter, that there was a way to "beat the races." Too modest, it is true, in its results, for most frequenters to bother about, but just the same, if you studied your favorite, bet on one or never more than two events, pocketed your winnings or swallowed your loss, letting it go at that, you were fairly sure of a margin of small winnings by the end of the season.

The petty followers testified to that. Men and women, with taut faces, it is true, snide sport finery, nervous twitchings to their hands, dust-gray skins, voices raucous from shouting orders to favorites, but, just the same, the track their sole means of support.

Every morning at eleven o'clock, to avoid Mrs. Cleveland's knowing her affairs, or she might have sent the chambermaid, Ray slid on a coat over her nightdress and scurried to a certain neighborhood stationer's where her racing form was saved for her. It was no small technique, this studying of the day's layout. Allowing for last-minute scratches, which were bothersome, these daily sheets, together with certain sources upon which the habitués relied, were an important part of the technique of playing the races as a business rather than a game. Women, forbidden access to the paddock, could not count on the added advantage of that last-minute opportunity to go down and inspect a horse closely, size up his legs and general condition, pick up the patter close to the post. But, in the main, there was a tight camaraderie among the day-by-day petty habitués. The women in particular, the lean-looking plucked birds of a shabby sort of elaborate grandeur, formed small flocks. You could invariably find them in the same section of the grandstand, buttonholing, trafficking in "tips," marking up their scorecards, and then, as each race began to go its rounds, mounting their chairs, shouting, imploring or deploring as the case might be, and the terrible famished bird-look out in their faces, as the necks of the flying horses began to strain for place.

They were a heterogeneous hard-put bunch, who used "God damn" and "son-of-a-bitch" and "pimp" and "lousy" with frequency and lustiness that at first had been startling. Not all of them, though. There were fantastic and often incredible life-stories tucked under the elaborate coiffures of many of these ladies of the grandstand. Dimmed ladies of the evening. Conventional wives and mothers paying off secret debts. Grandmothers whiling away time of day. Ex-wives, widows, and sweethearts of deceased bookmakers. The "family hotel" idle group, for that money-on-the-side. Then the life-and-deathers.

It was probably in this last category that Ray belonged. It was grim business with her. You bet ten, thoughtfully, having studied your horses with caution and a very certain attention to points. You hoped for only a fair return on your money. If it came, you called it a day, sitting about with admirable restraint, watching the suckers. If it failed, you ventured one more bet, taking your licking with finality, or your success with a sense of relief that made you realize how pinching had been your anxiety.

Sometimes, if the day yielded unusually well, she remained away for as much as a week, but chiefly to relax and freshen up her mind. It was not unpleasant at the grandstand, pleasanter certainly than in the room that never ceased to feel like the damp bathing suit donned at dawn.

For the first months, with ups and downs, on an initial capital of something like one hundred and ninety dollars, she remained consistently ahead of the game, sufficiently so to cover rent and food, and showing something like an average profit, after admission fees, of five or six dollars a day.

Not bad. It kept the mind agog, the horrible demon of loneliness from squatting too heavily on her chest; and, now that her schedule no longer demanded her presence anywhere at any time, it was possible, with one or two of the cronies garnered from the grandstand, to while away an evening at an Italian table d'hôte, or go occasionally to a musical show in one of the first-run Broadway houses.

Then came the shift of season; and, like homing birds, the grandstand women, along with the usual touts, runners, bookmakers, jockeys, owners, habitual followers, turned their faces south. Louisville, New Orleans, Latonia, Miami.

The first time it all seemed too difficult. She not only dreaded the expenditure of railroad fare, the problem of travel for Babe, but there was something went against her grain about leaving New York at this time. Walter was buried there. Without ever having been near, she knew where, to the fraction of a mile, and, beside him, in a grave almost as new, Richard. She would no more have ventured there! But just the same, something was closer to her than it would be in Louisville, or New Orleans, or even in Covington, just across the Ohio River from Cincinnati.

It was sinful to feel like that. All that was near you was the clay of Walter. The pitiful disintegrating clay; and yet, lying there in that room over the Cushman bakery of Columbus Avenue, the Babe at her feet, the darkness oppressing her, it was somehow less horrible to think of him lying out there than it would seem from the distance of another city. Not infrequently she woke to a sense of fingers stroking her face. Pollywoggles she called it, crushing her face back into her pillow to recapture sleep.

But in December, after she had vainly tramped the streets in answer to various advertisements for salesladies, tea-room cashiers, wholesale milliners, insurance agents, and the margin of her reserve funds, a source of constant concern to her, began to narrow, she negotiated a checking-out arrangement with Mrs. Cleveland, whereby she was permitted, more for a sense of anchorage than anything else, to keep a valise of odds and ends at the Columbus Avenue address, and purchased transportation for herself and the Babe to New Orleans.

That was the beginning of years of the rounds of the lean-faced woman with the graying hair that had long since lost its receptivity to henna dyes, and her black French poodle. New York. Latonia. Louisville. Miami. New Orleans. New York.

The touts came to have a name for her, culled from the nameless limbo from whence spring most nicknames. Aunt Bernhardt.

In a remote way there was something of a superb ruin about her. A gaunt oldish tragedy, who seemed to wear a ramrod up her back, against sagging.

49

Dentistry had become so terribly expensive. Why, she could remember back in the Cincinnati days when you had a tooth filled for fifty cents and a bridge for a dollar and a half.

The trouble, she kept telling herself, was the habit "the girls" had of chewing soft sweets during the afternoons. Someone or other was always turning up at the grandstand with a box of chocolates or taffies. It sort of eased your nerves to relax between events over a bonbon and a bottle of pop. Too much candy— sweet tooth—must be responsible for the painful disintegration which had set in along the erstwhile strong double row of her firm white teeth.

One dentist in Louisville diagnosed her trouble as pyorrhea and advised a period of three months' treatment before estimating the amount of salvaging work that might then be done. Anxious as she was to preserve intact what Walter used to call her Phoebe Snow smile, the price of even the preliminary treatments mounted into hundreds. Then, besides, both a dentist in New Orleans and one in New York had advised her to "have them out."

At first this was repelling and not to be considered, but after months of the considerable odds and ends of dentists' bills, for just temporary reliefs, and weeks of nights when she walked the floor with the Babe huddled up against her tortured cheeks for the warmth, she surrendered, and two weeks later, with a temporary "set" in her mouth, began the long period of attempting to adjust the rigid plates to her healing gums.

It was horrible. Grimacing to herself in the wavy mirror of the small hotel room in West Twenty-third Street, where she sometimes put up during the New York runnings, when her old room at Mrs. Cleveland's did not happen to be available, her smile seemed of glass and her gums pink tin.

"Why, I can't go about this way! I'm a hag. My mouth looks better all sunken, without teeth. I'm a hag, this way." She began to cry before the mirror, squeezing her nose with her handkerchief and talking aloud after a habit she had developed. "Why should I care about this mouthful of glass and tin making of me a hag? I only care, sweetheart, not to look in a way that would have been horrible to you. If it wasn't for that, I wouldn't care. Why should I? What have I got to care about, except my Babe? My darling muvver's baby. My gookie angelums Babe."

This last was what Walter would have called a new wrinkle. "A dog is all right in his place, but excuse me from women that slobber over them." This habit had not come upon her consciously. She only knew that even to have attempted to convey in words to the outsider the need in her for the black poodle, would have been to appear ridiculous. Occasionally she met someone whose love of dogs matched in some way with her own, and it was a relief to talk. But for the most part she found outlet in murmuring, only in private, endearments to the Babe that flowed off her lips against her better judgment.

"What would muvver do without her sweetsum bestsum friend in all the world? My patient sweetsums Babe. My good little darlingest friend. Muvver's all."

Usually the Babe, who still wore his hair tied back from his eyes with the bit of ribbon, and whose haunches were shaved, lay with his muzzle on the toe of her shoe as she talked.

Curious thing, but when first he beheld her in her new set of teeth, he lifted back his lips to show his own shining ones and snarled. It was the first time he had ever shown her the slightest hostility, and it almost killed her.

"Why, babykums darling, don't you know me?"

At that he leaped up and began to lick her, filled with atonements and treating her as if she had just come into the room after an absence. Later, facing her cronies at the track in her new smile, she put up a bold front something like this:

"Well, the Babe almost bit me when he saw me in them. I hope you won't."

After the first few weeks it was easier. It came less and less to seem to her, each time she smiled, that the crash of crockery was about to take place in her mouth.

And yet, out of the mental fabric of superstition, lores, occultism, and taboo, woven by years of her contacts with followers of games of chance, it seemed to Ray that, with the advent of the teeth, hoodoo, as she put it, descended, and her luck departed.

Whatever the contributory causes, the fact was that from the day she stood before the mirror of the hotel in Twenty-third Street, regarding the strange new machine-stitched look to the lower half of her face, something in the way of a turn in the tide of her affairs was manifesting itself.

"Lay off thirteen days, and see that you don't see a white horse in the meantime, and your luck will come back on the fourteenth," advised one of the cronies.

The white-horse part seemed easy enough in New York, where motor traffic jammed the streets; but, as luck would have it, a delivery wagon drawn by a fine white stallion was standing in front of her hotel as she emerged with the Babe her twelfth day following her abstinence from the track.

That ended that experiment! The dentistry had cost over two hundred. The inactive twelve days had cost. That always disconcertingly narrow margin was narrowing. The following day she reappeared at Belmont, a jack-of-diamonds folded four times on the inside of her left shoe, for luck.

"If it doesn't beat everything!" did not do much toward solving matters. Perhaps the consistent tie-up in her mind of the dentistry with the reversal of luck, was due to the fact that the several hundred dollars expended on her mouth had reduced her margin to its lowest, subtly reducing, with it, a certain self-confidence.

Be that as it may, she chewed cloves; spat over her left shoulder at the new moon; avoided stepping on the cracks in sidewalks; drank a glass of bootlegged gin with her back three-quarters to the Milky Way; and plucked one of the Babe's hairs, blew it off the back of her left hand, and caught it on the palm of her right.

An old bookmaker who, several years before, had stopped pinching her on the thighs, had a cackle which went something like this:

> Luck's a son-of-a-gun,
> You got it or you ain't.
> Nothing much to do about it,
> You got it or you ain't. . . .

"I ain't," she said to herself one night in the horrid old chronic stillness of her room, and then, as she put it, "laughed up the wrong sleeve."

One day, during this May in New York that had been hateful to her, sending her home as it did almost every afternoon with a fresh debit entry nicked into her unease, a wish packed somewhere in the cold-storage recesses of her mind thawed suddenly and boldly through.

"I want to go and see Walter's grave.

"Why not?" In all probability the house in East Fifty-third Street was closed for the summer. She could have slid into the street herself to fortify her convictions that the family must all be at Rye by now. But Walter would have hated that! Now suddenly, after years of feeling that he might also not want this, it came to her that he might! Surely out of the twenty-four hours of every day of every month of all the years since—there were some brief moments he would want reserved for her to stand over his grave. He would, in all probability, have said of her now, as he had sometimes said in life, when she grew putty-colored from too much indoors, "Don't bend too far backward." How terrible, if in staying too consistently away, she had been bending too far backward!

"I want to go and see Walter's grave."

On a May day she went out by subway, surface-car, and taxi to the Salem Fields Cemetery, situated on the edge of Brooklyn. It was a full mature May, overdeveloped into premature fulsomeness, as if it had great breasts that ached of the surging saps pressing against them.

There were stone gates with Hebrew inscriptions and a phrase in English, which startled: "House of Life." Graveled paths, bordered in orderly rows of the tips of crocuses, bisected the lay of the land, and then began the precise march of mausoleums and monuments, moving handsomely backward in a strange petrified surf of gravestones. Meyerberg. Block. Rothschild. Goldwasser. Becker. Stern. Glauber. Fineberg. Hirsch. Scharff. Wimpfhimer. Kahn. Obermeyer. Bry. Strauss. Bernstein. Zader. Klein. Victorius. Poole. Zacharias. Gerber. Bower. Harrison. Dreyfous. Pearl.

SAXEL

WALTER

DEARLY BELOVED HUSBAND OF
CORINNE TRAUER SAXEL

DEARLY BELOVED FATHER OF
RICHARD
IRMA
ARNOLD

BORN JULY 6TH, 1870. DIED JULY 29TH, 1923.

HE WALKED IN BEAUTY

And beside it:

RICHARD

BELOVED SON OF
CORINNE TRAUER SAXEL
BELOVED BROTHER OF IRMA AND ARNOLD

BORN JANUARY 6TH, 1899. DIED OCTOBER 2, 1923.

GOD LOANED HIM TO US

The mausoleum, in course of construction, on the very crest of the hill, was obviously to be the final grandeur of Walter's and Richard's resting place. A Greek temple, an Old English "S," and part of the "A" and "X," already chiseled against the pediment.

She began to cry, terribly, and make gurgling sounds. May, with the full breasts and the willow trees that drooped all over this beautiful burial ground, seemed standing silent and offended at the grossness of her crying.

Dearly beloveds—

50

Long after she was indistinguishably one of them, she continued to fight off becoming one of them. They were all like that; wary of one another. "Mustn't let myself get like the rest of these ragtags. I'll make a killing and quit."

Once, in Latonia, within a stone's throw of Cincinnati, and by way of a fluke that was the talk of the cronies for weeks, Ray, on a sweepstake, twenty to one, did make a killing.

An old man, named Ed Hofmeister, who had known her back in the days when, as a girl, she had spun the hazard-wheel in the back room of his place Over-the-Rhine, staked her, out of his own big winnings, to one of the most sensational dark-horse events of the year.

One thousand dollars! He had put up fifty for her, and there, one thousand simoleons, clear! A stroke of fortune that was important to her over and above anything that was apparent on the surface. The beginnings of the nest egg on which she could retire. She had dreamed of that, these years. Why, on that she could almost, aided and abetted by small sweepings now and then from the tables, withdraw to a place like Aix-les-Bains. You could live so cheaply at Aix. Infinitesimally so, if you knew the ways and means as she knew them. The place was honeycombed with genteel Englishwomen and women not so genteel, living in pensions and venturing forth semi-occasionally, under the badge of evening dress, for an evening of careful replenishment of their small pensions or widow incomes. You could do pleasant things at Aix. During season, bask in the little park to grandstand music, take tea for a few francs on a tiny plaza, watch the big cosmopolitan world and his women go by, and even during the winters, tucked away, oh, so cheaply, there were rest and memories at Aix, and she was tired—bone-tired. . . .

The night following this scoop, she gave a dinner to Ed Hofmeister, another old fellow named Marty Kaplan, whose father used to play cribbage with Adolph in the house on Baymiller Street, and a woman who, in her day, had been quite spectacular around Cincinnati and Louisville as the beautiful Mary Noalan who had married Ted Mapes, the famous jockey, in a balloon.

It was a gesture expected of her and, as Mary, who was always early inebriated off somebody's hip-flask, put it, "Ray did it up brown, and in true old-time Ray Schmidt style."

She gave this dinner at the Sinton, a new hotel since her time, not far from the site of the old St. Nicholas. Without drinks, which Marty saw to later in the back rooms of Kessler's Café on Vine Street, the check, what with tips and flowers and special requests to the orchestra from Mary, mounted to sixty dollars.

But it was worth it, not only because of her warm glow of gratitude to Ed, who was almost dead even then, old codger, of a liver complaint that was to kill him two months later but, though none of her guests knew it, beneath the brown sequin bolero jacket of her trumped-up evening dress of brown lace, there surged the first warmth of security she had known in many a circuitous weary day of the rounds of Belmont, Latonia, New Orleans, and Louisville.

"You look as handsome as a speckled hen," Ed told her that night. A speckled hen. Her head turned to the mirrored wall of the Sinton dining room. Speckled hen. That was a new one. Speckled hen. Curious how, as they grew older, the lean avian look seemed to force itself through the faces of the gaming women. Well, perhaps along with the others, she was an old bird, too. Over thirty years since she had sat not half a mile from this very site, at dinner— the night she met Walter. The face above the spangled bolero that looked back at her from the mirror was in its way the wattled old majestic face of a sitting eagle.

"Well, boys, well, girls," was going on underneath the bolero jacket, "I may look like a plucked eagle, but this is my swan song. Tomorrow, if you take the trouble to look for me, which you won't, I'll be on my way. New York. Paris. Aix. How sweet to be tucked into the peace of a back street at Aix—at rest—"

"Ray," Ed was saying, leaning his teeming breath close to her face, "you know I've become a rich man since the days you hung around this town, don't you?"

"I certainly do, Ed. Don't know anybody more entitled to it."

"To my way of thinking, a good old one is worth ten times as much as a fair-to-middlin' young one. I don't know much more about you than I did in the old days. Want to know me better? I'm not asking pay for what I did for you in the little matter of the sweepstake. Do as much for any old friend. So help me God, it come clean into my mind, like this: I'll place this bet for Ray for old times' sake and because she's a good old gal. . . ."

"Good of you, Ed. Mighty good."

"My proposition is as separate as hell from the little thing I did for you at the track. I've got a flat on Vine Street, Ray, over Ryan's, nobody's business but my own—private as hell for a night—"

"Oh, Ed, let that part go. I'm not like that."

"The hell you're not!"

"—anymore."

"All right with me. You kind of got me for the minute—the way you always in the old days kind of got every man that ever looked at you—for the minute."

Later, when there were drinks in the rear of Kessler's, he stunned her with the horridness of a kiss the shape of two moist liver-colored lips pasted against the back of her neck.

"I must go," she said, freeing herself, and trying to keep her mouth from crawling of disgust.

"Don't let me detain you," said Ed, making a slow, enormous wink at Mary. "But it's bedfellow-time. . . ."

She got out of the soiled clatter of talk that followed that one, and took a streetcar to her hotel in Fourth Street. There, for the remainder of the night, she packed, bathed the Babe, washed her own hair, and sat in a henna-pack until dawn. . . .

Whenever possible, in her almost routinized cycle of following the races, she omitted Latonia, because of its immediate proximity to Cincinnati. The old town, changed, rejuvenated, modernized, refurbished in those years since its umbrageous hills had closed in her universe, was always her dread.

Here, in the streets of the plateaued city through which the Ohio passed, cutting into Latonia on its southern flank, were the graves of the footsteps of her youth. Asphalt had supplanted the cobbles, gone was the famous old pulsing artery of the canal, plated over now with the smooth face of a boulevard, and, along the streets, scarcely a face that was familiar, and in which she, in return stirred a memory.

In the few times of her return, not once had she found the courage to wander her way past the house on Baymiller. The old store of Adolph Schmidt was now part of the site of a fifteen-story office-building, and Over-the-Rhine mere legend.

One evening she did take the Zoo-Eden trolley car, alighting at the top of the incline for the view of the city which, from the eminence of the Rookwood Pottery, spreads itself like a smoky fan. A city cupped in the amphitheater formed by hilltops, a city of low, smoky, thriving industry, shot with tall buildings, flung with bridges, and long since animated from the small München-like placidity of thirty years ago to this quickened metropolis of Chamber of Commerce buildings, City Hall, Armory, Music Hall, Art Museum, Art Academy, United States government-buildings, hotels, theaters, apartment houses, business blocks, clubhouses, hospitals, churches, schools, and hereditary estates of old families with honored ancestors.

The thought smote her, standing there on the hilltop, that even old Adolph had contributed to the regality of this self-styled Queen City. No appeal on behalf of the Turnverein, the Public Sing, the Music Fest or Opera, had ever found him unresponsive. Back in the days of Adolph, who could sit in Moerlein's beer-garden and keep time with his old head to the strains of Gounod, the Schmidts had done their part in helping create the impulse to crown these hill-tops with the glory of art and music.

Adolph and Lena Schmidt, whose markless graves she could not muster herself to seek out, had pressed their obscure, unhonored strength into the community impulse to lift this Cincinnati from the level of its canals.

Sense of their memories dishonored, sense of shame, recollections both sweet and bitter, were what kept her face averted most of the time she was in Cincinnati, and grateful that nine times out of ten what few faces she did recognize did not in turn recognize her. Memories padded around this town at practically every turn.

There was a curb at the C. H. and D. depot. . . .

51

"It was not to be," repeated over and over again, once more had a way of making everything seem easier.

The first day back in New York, after a morning of purchasing a steamship ticket on a one-class boat called the *American Farmer*, of rushing the Babe to a veterinarian's for a badly inflamed eye, and of trying futilely to locate Mrs. Cleveland of the Columbus Avenue apartment, who had moved, taking with her the old valises that for years had been stored with her, a letter reached her by way of general delivery.

It was from Emma, written just one week previously, and it seemed to Ray, as she read it, that heartache could be more than a figure of speech. The heart could literally hurt. Hers did, in a pain across her left breast.

"Dearest Aunt Ray: Something, sweet Aunt Ray, that I have prayed not to have to tell you is happening to me. It is no good to tell Mother or Father or the boys. They have all they can do as it is, even with my help. But, oh, darling, my eyes! It's cataract this time, over the left. It's all milky now and, dearest, when I close my right eye, I can't see at all. And I'm frightened. And to think it should happen right at the beginning of my teaching year. And I love it so! And they're so good to me here. The eye doctor in Newcastle says the chances are excellent for an operation's clearing it up. But it will mean half a year out—and expense. I wouldn't ask you, dearest of aunts, better-to-me-than-any-one-in-the-world. But you've always been so good. You saved me once. Save me again. I know in your gay life of travel and excitement it won't mean so much to you in the way of sacrifice as it will mean happiness and salvation to me. Sweet Aunt, help me. . . . Emma."

In the moment of receiving that letter she could have laid down her life against the pain of that child. It was as if every bone in her body hurt so that she could feel the outline of her skeleton burning against the flesh.

Those big bright-blue eyes of Emma, that somehow, behind their slightly enlarged irises, had the look of blue flowers under water. An immemorial cry of the old for its young rang through her pain. "And I live on, tired, old, no-good me, healthy and sound, while her sweet eyes are filled with milkiness. . . ."

Give? Her impulse, standing there in the musty hurry of the general-delivery section of the post office, was to flee to this stricken child—her sweet eyes that were innocent. That was what made the pain so all but unbearable. They were such innocent eyes, Emma's were, to be fuddled with cataract. . . .

A passerby, in sporty plus-fours, seeing her bent over her stocking, extracting something, gave her a rude dig in the thigh purposely. There was her handkerchief, containing seven one-hundred-dollar bills, besides the sixty-odd dollars and the steamship ticket in her purse.

No use speculating. Five hundred of it would have to go in a money order to Emma. One might speculate as to whether she could afford an outside or an inside steamship-room, as she had that morning, or whether it would pay to insert an advertisement in the *Times* to try and locate Mrs. Cleveland and the suitcase, but over the destiny of Emma's eyes . . . The money order that finally went to her was for six hundred.

No use pretending, though, that it did not matter. It did, and it mattered terribly. Not so much to her plans. The only appreciable difference, for the moment, was that she changed the outside to an inner room, thirty-eight dollars refund on that, and did not insert the advertisement for the missing Mrs. Cleveland and the suitcase.

But the something that had lifted with the advent of one

thousand dollars was squatting back on her chest. Swept, with the stroke of the pen that signed the money order for Emma, was the sense of the new security of days that were to be spent in the quasi-seclusion of the small French spa that would fold her into the inex-pensive placidity—a placidity, drenched in memories, that at the same time would hold out to her, during season, the one means of livelihood for which, these days, alas, these years, she seemed qualified.

No two ways about it, the change mattered, terrifyingly. It gave one a sense of scare, sailing away with that familiar sense of the narrowing margin.

Live dangerously, the old bookmaker who had ceased pinching her thighs and who was always carrying about, in his pockets, small editions of Nietzsche and Schopenhauer, and pamphlets on religion and science, was forever intoning to belligerents about to lose their gambling nerve. Live dangerously.

The snug security of the life at Aix simply was not to be, at least not for the present. Perhaps all for the best. The headiness of the phrase, "Live dangerously," the elixir of the air of the nine days at sea, made it seem almost providentially for the best. Why not?

Live dangerously. The waving of this phrase helped to give the trip, to which there was to be the finality of residence abroad, the flavor of adventure. If only things could be made to matter again, it would be easy to live dangerously. No use talking; by instinct, by temperament, hers was the nature to crave the very things from which she had been planning deliberately to fold herself away.

Why, if she only conjured up that old exuberant will to live, one could never tell. Poor little Emma's eyes might be an ill wind blowing her good! Nice, Monte Carlo, Vichy—

Play conservatively, but know when to take your dangerous chance! Dress well. Move about. Hordes of glamorous women moved mysteriously through the gilded shades of these spas. And on a hair-pin, mind you, many a one of them. More likely than not, countless of them eked out their glamor by way of living dangerously. . . .

One day, in the solitude of the cabin she shared with a teacher of English in the Berlitz School of Languages in Paris, who had not exchanged a dozen words with her during the voyage, she began a soliloquy which she addressed into the mirror over the collapsible washbowl.

"I am thin and a little gaunt and tragic-looking and the teeth are not so bad anymore and there is a place in Paris where I hear they have a perfect henna-system. People will stare and wonder about me if I dress rightly."

Now and again the peripatetic women of the racing fields had told her that. You look interesting. Dress the part.

Walter had never wanted that. And rightly, of course. It had been so necessary through the years to move like a piece of detached background against the same background. But now—in order to live at all, one must trump up the impulse to live dangerously. . . .

She found herself with a phrase on her hands that had magic to the ear all right, but would not analyze. As she lay in her berth, what mental excitement she had been able to scare up during the day died down, and she began to cry or laugh or both, hands compressed rigidly against her mouth for fear of awakening the Berlitz teacher, who slept in a chin strap, and, in the dim night-light of the blue ceiling bulb, looked as if she were stretched on a morgue slab.

Live dangerously, when her hair was streaked in three colors and would no longer hold even the semblance of dye, and her teeth, two sardonic horseshoes mounted on very pink rubber, were in a water tumbler with a handkerchief tied around it to conceal its contents from her cabin mate. Live dangerously, when she had overheard the steward refer to her as the old bird who shared Cabin 67 with the English teacher.

Oh, yes, live dangerously, when men no longer even glanced up as you passed them on the deck, and when, the night of the ship's little farewell dinner, she had put on her brown net evening dress with the spangled bolero, the low-cut bodice made her feel like one of those female impersonators.

The breasts, drying, left you flat, like a man.

Live dangerously! "Oh, my God," she said, rolling over and away from the spectacle of the English teacher in the chin-mask, "don't make me laugh!"

52

In Aix, as a matter of course, families occupied the same house for fifty, eighty, or a hundred years, and in the meaner of the houses, the smell of the mold of those years was on the stairs and in the upholstery. In the pension of Madame Papatou, which stood like a narrow soldier with arms jammed to his sides, between a novelty store where they sold glass paperweights, with views of Aix embalmed into them, and one of the shops where you purchased cotton-flannel pajamas to wear to the Thermal Establishment, this same smell of must and of dust was kicked out of every one of the seventeen steps you mounted to the second floor.

It smelled, this old house, as if it were alive and had a body odor. Douse her room as she would with eau de cologne, and her pillow with dried lavender to be purchased by the centime, the smell of the corridors and the walls persisted, like live breath. It was a decayed breath, too, filled with old teeth. A horrid way of thinking about it, but then it was that horrid, living at Pension Papatou.

First of all, the walls were all scarred with torn places in the papering, the way she remembered it in a People's Theatre production of "The Two Orphans" in Cincinnati. Lath and plaster showed through and, in the first year, Ray purchased, at a shop where they sold Anderson "seconds," a print of Henner's nude figure that hangs in the Louvre, "Femme Lisant."

Emma would have chosen, she thought to herself while selecting it, the moody bit of "Roman Coliseum by Moonlight," or Botticelli's "Springtime." "Funny thing, I'm just common."

The Henner hung over the naked laths of her high-ceilinged room at the top of the third flight of stairs, and sucked in the odors and became part of the decayed-tooth yellow of Papatou's.

This yellowish tinge, which alike attacked the ancient teeth of the Babe, the linen on the beds, the drinking water, and finally the very flesh, Ray, as she worriedly inspected the aging tints of the backs of her hands and the fronts of her thighs, attributed to "something in the air." "It's this low altitude kind of creates a mold on you. . . ."

Maybe.

Madame Papatou was yellow too, but in a ropy vigorous way that was magnificent. Her squat face, bold in its lineaments as that of an American Indian, was tough as shoe leather. By birth Italian, by marriage Greek, by profession of twenty-eight years a bath attendant at the Thermal Establishment, she was as many-visaged as a totem pole.

There was the craven face she wore when engaged in the massaging, spraying, spanking, soaping, toweling processes she practiced on the American and English women who rode to and from the hotels to the bath in shrouded sedan-chairs; there was the venomous face she wore when a tip fell foul of expectations, and rage transcending greed, was capable of tearing a ten-franc note to bits with her teeth, and spitting it after the donor. There was the spying, suspicious, God-help-you face she wore for Papatou, whose fat hands loved the feel of fat women, and who was as oily as one of the sardelles he held by the tail and swallowed whole. There was the carved walnut of a face she wore for her boarders, and the oleaginous one she wore for her priest.

All day, from the crack of dawn, when the first sulphurous fumes began to rise from the bathhouse, she stood on her widespread bare feet, her stubby body nude, except for a loincloth of wrapped calico, shoulders sweating, hard nutlike breasts still with something of firm Greek beauty left them, horizontally hung onto that terrific old frame, kneading into human flesh.

Half the night she sat in the adobe kitchen of blackened walls, concocting and eating Italian and Greek foods and drinking Chianti, with Papatou, whose feet, when he sprawled them, reached more than two-thirds of the room. Most of the time, though, they rested, bare, in the snarled wool of Marchand, a huge and dirty wolf-dog, who constantly wore a muzzle, because of ferociousness.

There was a great-grandmother too. One of those Italian peasant women who marched through a century of years as if it were a tunnel, blackening them. The gamins about the street called her Ra-Ta-Plan, probably for no more relevant reason than that she stumped about on a wooden leg in lieu of the one she had lost in childbirth, back in those incredible years when that body must still have had fecundity. She was supposed to be one hundred and four years old. Her flesh, which seemed as if you could crumple it to dark powder between your fingers, looked it, but with Madame Papatou all day at the Thermal Establishment, and Papatou, in his oiled mustache, wanting all day to paw the women in the marketplaces and courtyards, she did an enormous amount of housework. She would have done Ray's room too, but something about her was more repulsive than the carrying of her own slops, so by the end of the first year Ray had established the precedent of caring for her own quarters.

And what quarters. Not so bad, however, once you became adjusted, and there was the feather-bed luxury of an enormous four-poster, and furniture of a terrific weight and proportion, that made you wonder how it had ever been tilted through the narrow halls and doorways. Great-grandmother must have remembered, because she had been a young child in that house, but her mind was a ragtag.

At first, Papatou's, where she had to scuttle through black halls, that were tunnels, to an outhouse, and where her allotment of water was lugged up three flights by a pervert neighborhood boy, from whose unmentionable desires she had even to protect the Babe, had at first seemed terrible, then bad, finally not so bad.

There was a patch of courtyard in which the Babe could run, while, high in her rooms, even though Marchand was muzzled day and night, she sat beside the window to keep watch over him. Considering the fact that, in her heart, Madame Papatou carried venom of a jealous and vindictive sort for the Americans and English into whose flesh she had kneaded away practically her lifetime, there was little cause for complaint in that direction.

She was home so little, and then, too, the seeming impregnability of the ear of Ray to foreign languages was rather more of a phenomenon than a remarkable facility of acquisition might have been. With the patter of French and Italian rising all day from the courtyard, Papatou and Ra-Ta-Plan dickering in French, Italian, and Greek, tradespeople in top-of-the-voice sidewalk-conferences, she knew little more than the key words of greeting, passing the hour of day, food names, and elementary servant orders that she had already acquired during the lifetime of Walter.

In a way, particularly now since her months-old decision to return to the States, it was as if she had closed her mind and ears to as much as possible of the tintinnabulation of any tongue save her own. It became a manifestation, this stubborn adherence to her own language, of nostalgia. The tiny *épicerie* where she purchased the major portion of her provisions was run by an ex-*femme-de-chambre* at the Hotel Splendide, who spoke English quite fluently and had married a *valet-de-chambre*. Many of the petty tradespeople in this tiny cosmopolis, which drew its guests from over the face of the world, spoke English in one halting fashion or another.

You lived along all right on English. You lived along all right in general, and all the while it was miraculous that you lived along at all. The margin was so narrow. And yet, withal, there was pride in this admission. In all the stinting, incredibly alone months, she had never, not even counting the traveling expenses of the trip to Nice, fallen below the twenty-five-hundred-franc mark, and that, if you have ever known the bright madness that can overtake certain moments at the gaming table, was achievement. Not once, when the impulse to place just another franc on a color that sure as fate could no longer continue to elude, was perilously near being stronger than she was, had she let slip the iron chain of will which separated her by the margin of twenty-five hundred francs from the

kind of cleanup that sent men and women walking away, even from
the petty *boule* tables, with that God-awful look of no destination
in their eyes. Not once, mind you! Not even that first year, when
she had made the trip to Nice, and it had looked for the moment
as if there she were going to recoup the thousand that Ed had won
for her.

Not once; but if only, alas, that night at Nice, when the shaven-
headed, saber-scarred young baron from Heidelberg had kept shoving her the one-hundred notes every time he took a haul—if only
that night she had not been content to stop at the five-hundred-
franc mark!

But Walter would have played it that way. Walter would have
wanted it that way. It was the safe and conservative way. But the
next morning there had been an item in the paper commenting
on the spectacular haul of this young baron. It seemed that after
she had left the Casino, at one o'clock, following a sag in his luck,
he had rebounded again, enormously. That night at Nice, with a little less caution, she might have canceled these subsequent months
of—well, of near-horror. They had been that.

Long, lonesome stinting months between seasons, when the
Casino and the larger hotels were closed, and wet damp intervals
descended upon the little town of Aix, making it seem moody
as a pregnant woman. Cold-to-the-bone months in that period
when it had become no longer practicable for her to follow a season even so far as Nice; cold-to-the-bone months of sitting in her
high-shouldered room over a brazier that held burning charcoal,
living, cooking, shopping bits of meat for the Babe, whose appetite was growing finicky, as his teeth began to go, dreading the cold
trips through the hallways in a house that boasted not one pipe of
plumbing, and always, always, making out on the budget that was
figured to the franc. So many of them a day, or, if one more today,
than one less tomorrow. Intricate bookkeeping, which had to see
to it, come opening day of the Casino, that over and above the
twenty-five hundred francs stored in her stocking there remained
sufficient to start her off at *boule*.

The clothes were a nuisance. She had a horror of ever taking on, even remotely, the look of the flocks of grandmas-of-the-evening who, like fabled birds of some fabled ether, lit from nowhere and crowded for crumbs around the tables ruled by croupiers. They came with the seasons, honeycombing the pensions, out of sight by day, and venturing out by night in the dreadful finery of mended lace, splitting taffetas, shawls with gaps in the fringe, rhinestones on wrinkles, sequins on old flesh. Women without any more fertility left, whose breasts had shrunk and hung with the flesh dredged, as if water had flowed down a clay hill.

A curious, terribly afraid, terribly avid army, asking desperately, each of herself, as she beheld the other: "Do I look like that? No! A man might still feel himself glad to sleep with me. No! If only I had the clothes. . . ."

If only I had the clothes! To Ray, her brown net dress with the spangled bolero had come to feel like a scab. Horrid, lusterless, the rows of the sewed-on sequins like the tired eyes of tired women, desperately fending off sleep. It was still neat enough, it was still, underneath the invisible patchings, sufficiently presentable to admit her to the Casino as a lady of the tables, but its brownness was horrible to her. And yet, season after season, a yard of fresh malines fluffed up across bare shoulders upon which the powder sat dryly, sequin purse on her arm, lips rouged and lifted back off a por-celain smile to which she had long since become accustomed, this rig constituted, along with her "season card," right to admission to the elaborate halls of her livelihood.

"Do I look like them, Babe? No. No." Standing in her room that smelled of the breath of old bodies, decked out for the third con-secutive year in the brown lace, that antedated, by another brace of years, her dinner to Ed Hofmeister in Cincinnati, staring at her-self in her gaslit mirror, it seemed to her most surely that she did not. A man could do worse! Only yesterday a Frenchman in spats had bought her a glass of port and a package of cigarettes. There had been brown stains on his dirty goatee, but he had rolled his eyes and beckoned backward toward some rooms that were notorious in the town. Repulsive as a crow to her, but it just went to show that there was still life in the old bones. Good life.

She could not very well explain that to the Frenchman with the soiled goatee. She could, however, say it to herself in the night—in the silence of the room at the pension, the Babe wrapped in sleep at her feet.

She could, she must, say it to herself, when finally the days came to be, each one of them, like the black, stripped trees along the promenade in winter, which, one by one, she had to pass on her way to the *épicerie*, in order to buy food in order to live. . . .

53

"Pouf!" as Papatou used to shout when deeply in his cups. Pouf!
You could hear him over the courtyard, with his terrific voice,
like a dishpan that had been struck with a broom handle. Pouf!
Pouf! *L'univers est ma mondaine. J'ai eu toute ma part de la chair de la
femme. Si tu ne croies pas, chérie, que je suis encore homme, viens avec
moi. . . .* If you do not believe, chérie, that I am any longer a man,
come with me. . . .

"Pouf" was how it happened to Ray. "Pouf," she kept saying to
herself in terrible befuddlement directly it had happened. "Pouf,"
just like that.

It could not be, and yet it was. The evidence lay in the certain
and evil flatness along the upper part of the rear of the calf of her
leg. Feel as she would with her instep, where should have been the
neat wad of the margin of twenty-five hundred francs, tucked there
into a folded handkerchief, was only flatness.

Pouf! It had all happened in less than it took Papatou to
shout it.

It was gala night. One of those occasions, frequent during the
season, when the villas and large hotels send down to the Casino
brilliant contingents for dancing and dining and entertainment in
the forepart of the evening, before the gaming begins. A prime minister was entertaining a dinner table of forty. A maharajah and his
American bride had taken a table for one hundred.

It was the kind of evening when the milling color and movement made it possible to venture, even if she owned no club card,
into the large salons, without the attendants, most of whom she
knew and many of whom she dreaded, eying her out.

Usually on the gala nights which each season offered, she could
ooze her way around the chemin de fer or baccarat tables of the
grand salon, there to stand for hours, peering above the bare, jeweled shoulders of women, and the blackcloth backs of men, at the
spectacle of the turning of a card, or the croupier's passing of a
"shoe," which could point the faces of men and women, point their
eyes and lips, and actually their ears.

She never, of course, ventured here anymore to place stakes.
The *boule* tables reserved for the petty players and the minors who
managed their way in by methods all their own, were her limit.

But to gate-crash her way in there to watch a California grower
of citrus fruits lose twenty thousand francs as if it were so much
carfare, or the jeweled blonde of a black Nicaraguan rake in thirty
thousand with an arm banked solidly to the elbow in diamonds and
rubies, was an excitement that never seemed to lose its edge.

That instant before the card flipped from the little box called
"shoe," faces did curious revealing things. The hinges of the jaws
loosened, lines crawled out of secret places of the flesh, eyes became
slits and slits became eyes. Souls stalked out. They did! At the
flipping of the card you could see them flash, banshees among the
erstwhile gravestones of the gambling faces, quick, lightning-quick,
and then back into the tomb of the gambling-hearts. Then the faces
began the pulling-down of the shades, of the eyelids, the straighten-
ing of the mouths, the scurrying back of the momentarily revealing
wrinkles, the pinkening of the pallors.

There was that Heidelberger again! Shades of Nice, the baron
with the shaved head and the cuts all over it and the monocle and
the unmistakable air of a man whose heels would click together
when he kissed a woman's hand. He had slid into a chair just
vacated directly in front of Ray on her tiptoes, peering; and almost
immediately his luck began to be conspicuous, as it had been that
night at Nice, after she had left too soon.

Well, here was opportunity doing the unprecedented. Here it was, knocking twice. The first time she had committed the sickening sin of conservatism at the wrong moment. Yes, here it was again. Heidelberg from the very start holding the deal, or leaning in on somebody else's. Forty thousand francs in ten minutes! Eighty thousand in twenty! One hundred thousand in the half hour! Heidelberg, with no more than a glance at the system chart in the palm of his hand, winning twenty thousand on his twenty-thousand stake. Then three times in succession, nine, nine, nine! Eighty thousand! One hundred thousand in ten minutes! In all her experience, she had never seen it happen. This was the way banks were supposed to be broken in the more spectacular meadows of Monte Carlo, where roulette spun fortunes fastest of all. One hundred and ten thousand francs! One hundred and forty! The crowd, by who knows what subterranean telepathy, was leaving the other tables and pressing harder at her back, and the croupier, whom she knew as M. Topaze, had receded to three little downward slits, mounted on pallor. Two eyebrows and a tiny waxed mustache. One hundred and seventy—eighty—

"What is his name?" she asked of an American whose elbow was piercing her rib, as he slowly edged his way in front of her. She had known it once from the newspaper columns at Nice. "What, please, is his name?" The American did not reply. Often she found that to be the case now. People did not reply. Not particularly because they wanted to be rude. It was just that her voice did not seem to matter.

One hundred and ninety—

"*Qu'est-il, monsieur? Allemagne, n'est-ce-pas?*"

This time the question came from a manikin whose back, bare to the waistline, was sunburned to henna and whose marcelled yellow head was precisely the perfection of a small egg on end.

"Oh, pardon me, mademoiselle. Baron von Hufstangel is his name. Biggest manufacturer of medical instruments in the world. *Permettez-moi, mademoiselle*. Stand in front of me. You can see better—outrageous luck—phenomenal—"

Two-hundred thousand—

Full flash, like a sword out of its scabbard, there leaped her impulse—an impulse slightly impeded by the ridiculous necessity of having to stoop, in that pressure of crowd, for the franc-notes that were banked in her stocking.

"Permit me, please," she said, on the baron's picking-up of the card, reaching between the shoulders of the manikin and the American, to place twenty-five hundred francs on the table.

There on the green felt, in a neat pile between the croupier and the baron, was the contents of the wad of twenty-five hundred francs that one instant before had been resting in its neatly folded clean handkerchief against the calf of her leg.

The spinning silence was your head, it had a thin high sound—it became, the inside of your head, a bicycle race with the riders on a slant—it became Richard leaning off his pony for a polo stroke.

Oh, la-la! Ten-spot! Baccarat!

The baron had lost.

"Pouf," said the manikin, whose bare back was suntanned to henna, "his luck has gone up in smoke."

Pouf, just like that. Pouf! Edging her way out, every time Ray said that "Pouf," a bubble formed like a bit of glassine paper over her mouth. Pouf!

54

The contents of the valise that had been swallowed into the limbo that contained Mrs. Cleveland, was on her mind.

No telling what was in that bag. She could not remember exactly; ends of laces, jabots; slightly worn petticoats from the days when she still wore them; a couple of sheer nightgowns, needing new yokes; fans, feathers, odds and ends; two books on Italian primitives; and, strange to remember, quite a pretty pincushion doll, half-finished, a bisque head and shoulders mounted into a yellow-silk sawdust ball.

Not much, each in itself, perhaps, but the persistent thought held her that the aggregate might be considerable. Oh, yes, there was the burnt-wood toilet set that she had cast aside years ago, with "R.S." on each piece, and the poppy design brightly colored.

That burnt-wood set, the percolator, binoculars, especially such objects of metal, could doubtless have been disposed of to no mean advantage by the *valet-de-chambre*, husband of the ex-*femme-de-chambre*.

He had already begun the process of selling off for her various of the small objects she took to him from time to time. An alarm clock. She had two. An umbrella with a sterling-silver handle. The silver toilet set had gone, too. For one hundred and fifty francs. It had cost forty dollars the day of the opening of Stern's new department store on Forty-second Street. One hundred and fifty francs!

That low-watermark price made her begin to suspect the *valet-de-chambre*. But what could one do? It was not New York, where you knew the ropes, so to speak. It was simpler, but doubtless vastly more expensive, to entrust these small enforced sales to Anatole, who charged commission.

Every time she wrapped an object in a bit of the Paris *Herald* and hurried through the streets with it to the shop of Anna and Anatole, she had the absurd feeling that under her arm, in the shape of an alarm clock, for instance, she was carrying part of herself, detached, and for sale. Here's my heart, ticking. Sell it, Anatole. Here's my arm. It is pure silk and has a sterling-silver handle. Sell it, Anatole. It should bring one hundred francs. It cost twelve dollars, American money, at Wanamaker's. Translate that for him, Anna. Twelve dollars at Wanamaker's. Not so long ago either.

Actually it brought eighteen francs.

Low. Disgusting. Degrading. Close personal things like a nice dimity nightgown scarcely worn, and laundered in all its pleats and underlaid in pink tissue, five francs. One franc for a little silver dachshund, with bristles on his back, which had been given her, back in the Cincinnati days, by a traveling salesman for a hat concern. There had been other such objects; a black-enamel thimble with white polka-dots, which had brought one franc; a blue-enamel bracelet bangle, two francs. It was somehow quite frightening to even let the mind dwell on that. . . .

A great deal might have been frightening if you let it be. Didn't intend to let it be.

In a way, looking back, it was simply beyond credence. The margin swept away like a leaf on a fast current. It had happened so quickly. It had happened so terribly. And yet one dared not be frightened. The thing to do was to profit. That was it! Profit by the rigors of this experience. As old Jim Culbertson, a Cincinnati sheriff, used to say, many a good man was saved and made by having the daylights scared out of him. Well, the daylights were scared out of her, all right. But there was a way out. Didn't exactly see it at the moment, but there was a way out. Probably have a good laugh over it some day. Those things take time.

Could have been worse, too. Fancy trying to live on a few francs a day in New York! But that was precisely what you could do in Aix. Thank God, Papatou, who was always in some sort of frightening arrears with his madame, had a way of egging room rent out of her three and four weeks in advance. He had been paid for the entire month just two days before the advent of the Heidelberger. Thank God for that.

All sorts of food substitutions that could even be made to seem amusing, were possible. Cabbage cutlets, browned to look like veal. Flour soups, with the bread sliced and toasted as if for *petite marmite*. Except that the Babe, rascal, silliest of precious darlings, would not have the wool pulled over his eyes. Meat once a day for him, and don't you fool yourself! Try to deceive him, if you could, on bread and a brown-flour gravy which had been mixed over chicken feet.

Besides, never again would she permit herself to pick chicken feet out of refuse pails. It looked shocking. It was shocking. God, it made her shudder down into her hands. Never, never again would she succumb to so degrading an economy. Served her right, too, the Babe sniffing her concoction, had turned up his nose and walked off. . . .

It was easier and somehow more decent to practice abashing denials of one's self. Chicken gizzards, necks, veal bones for the Babe could be purchased from the chef of a grimy little restaurant down the block that sold her about a candy-sackful for a sou. Refuse, but at least not from the bin. For herself, a *petit suisse*, lentil mash, or a surprisingly tasty soup of cabbage, a carrot, an onion, and a dash from a bottle containing kitchen-bouquet.

It kept her thin and a little underfed, precisely what her preachment to Walter had been for years. "Make it a rule, Walter, to get up from the table a little hungry," and then the continuous paradox of her preparing him the rich bakings, broilings, and fryings, which, when they had her turn of the spoon, had been so palatable to him.

There was a way, all right, to get on her feet. She was a little shocked; oh, yes, no doubt of that. Shot to pieces, as the saying went. But Rome was not rebuilt in a day. Or was it rebuilt? Anyway, once you got your head clear . . .

It was really quite amazing, and yet it hurt her terribly the way in which the Babe simply would not remain out of her lap.

"Please, Babe. Muvver's worried. Let her think."

Scratch, scratch, his little old feet with their extremely long nails, since it was all he could do now, in the way of exercise, to waddle around the courtyard, clamored at her skirts.

"No, Baby. Ray must think, darling." God, how Ray must think and think and think!

Scratch, scratch, scratch.

"Oh, for goodness' sakes, here! Muvver has a mind to go down and make old mean wolfhound Marchand eat her baby up. Now are you satisfied?"

In a way, it was blessed to hear him breathe out with satisfaction and feel the warm sag of body through her skirts. Sometimes noonday waned into dusk as she sat with him thus, and in spite of a frenzied rhythm of the phrase, "I-must-think-I-must-think," the brain remained a dead thing. "Lump," she cried to it. Lump it remained, seeming to lodge against her brow as inert as the Babe in the bowl of her skirts.

Just the same, come evening, and like a slow-motion picture of a fire horse making beeline at the clang of the bell for his trappings, on went the brown net dress with the bolero of sequins, accompanied by the ritual of the powdered neck, the touching-up of the lips along the chilly teeth, the laying-on of the spots of rouge.

It gave something akin to vigor and hope to feel the old shoulder straps slide into place, to feel the chest bare and powdered and revealed, as if its breasts were not two drooping wrinkled sacs.

Daylights scared out of her, yes! But only that she might profit. Good lesson. Never again. One of these nights, a hundred francs, a louis, who could tell, handed back by a prodigal winning hand—and presto—pouf!—success.

It had to be. People simply did not get into predicaments like this without getting out of them. The high-divers, the spectacular gamblers whose brains, after they had been blown out, got into the headlines, were one matter. So were the drug-and-drink habitués of the tables. Monte Carlo, Deauville, Paris, had their Bluebeard chambers of legends like that. But the ordinary run-of-the-mill people who were content to earn livelihoods around the tracks and tables of Europe and America, they dropped out, of course, and became difficult to account for, like pins, but so did people in other walks of life. No, the run-of-the-mill folks whom she knew, simply did not get into predicaments like this without getting out of them—head up, too.

Picking those chicken feet out of the refuse can had been unnerving. Disgusting to have stooped to that, for a matter of fifty centimes. Suppose Papatou had seen it. The Babe had set her right to such obscene economies, turning up his darling little black-rubber nose. No, the question really was how to get things moving.

With twenty-two francs, some centimes, and a few sous to your name, and what aiding and abetting you could do by way of the sale of a few objects, the dilemma amounted to this: Risk ten or twelve of those precious francs at *boule*. The thought of that was terribly frightening to one so recently burned. There was not sufficient of the indomitable in her for that. Better to wait. Bide one's time.

The young American fellows, off on summer vacations, were beginning to throng in now. College seniors most of them, minors, who, gaining their entrance cards by jolly outrageous devices, played *boule* in the outer rooms and cast about their ten-franc pieces in magnificent imitation of roués.

She could, if she would, go up to one of those fellows, and all in the spirit of jest say, "Big Boy, stake me," yet knowing she couldn't, she couldn't, any more than she could go up to one of the girls, the old girls to whom she had more than once tossed a franc or two, and ask. Nonsense, of course she could! One can do anything that is sufficiently necessary. Besides, she herself had given in response to no more than the look in an eye. The pinched look in one of the pinched faces of one of the grandmas of the evening. What was to prevent her going up to one of the youths . . .

Nothing. Everything. The everything was that, for the life of her, the words would not come. She had tried. Evening after evening she had put on the brown net, and skirted the edge of the *boule* tables, now that all these cocky American college boys with their sure humorous faces and in such exaggeratedly well-fitting evening clothes, were everywhere in evidence.

Big Boy, little stake? Bring you luck. Stake a lady, there's a Big Boy. They were so crammed with easy hilarity, these youths, and with easy pity, for that matter. That would be terrible. . . .

Really though, serious for the moment as matters seemed, the impudence of the Babe was cute. Just once again she tried a con-coction of the meat-extract over bread stewed in some of her own vegetable soup. "I guess not," said the Babe, turning up reproachful eyes and little rubber nose. "I guess not." Pride. Out-and-out pride. He made her feel snide again and scamper to get him the sackful of giblets and odds and ends from the chef.

That evening, after hours of watching and hovering on the edge of *la boule*, she finally placed a franc piece on seven, and with the chance to win back thirty-five, lost.

"Walter!" What a sickening thing to have done. To have blurted out a name as if you were calling someone. Of course, no one heard, or hearing, listened.

But just the same, it was a lesson in the need of holding on to oneself.

55

The hateful Anatole. Even though she seldom saw him, and transactions were carried on through Anna, he came to have a most horrible and symbolic significance. He was the disappearing medium
through which vanished the Honiton tablecloth, the turquoise
beads, the pearl fleur-de-lis, the German-silver coin purse, the opal
ring, the handful of tiny porcelain knickknacks, the embroidery
scissors, the little gold wedding band which she had bought for
herself almost thirty years before and used sometimes to wear for
convenience.

And for what? For no more than the price to keep ahead of her
rent, which she meticulously did, still three and four weeks ahead. It
was the one out-and-out security, other expenditures susceptible to
constant shaving-down here and there. Lentils and barley for boiling into soups. *Petits pains.* Cheeses (the *petits suisses* in their silver
wrappings cost fifty centimes). They were nourishing. Occasionally,
a bit of veal. Giblets, fresh necks, gizzards, and not infrequently a
wing or liver thrown in, for the Babe. How the rascal could gobble
them, as if they had cost nothing, and no matter how bountiful
his meal, always licking his chops for more. It was lovely to see
him eat. It gave one a vast sense of his confidence in you. Come
what would, the little black rogue knew that there would be no such
thing as jeopardy for him. It was lovely to feel the completeness of
that confidence.

Otherwise, there was something pretty downright frightening about the dilemma as it lengthened. One of those vicious circles, in which a person can sometimes find himself. There was a way out, of course. If everyone who found himself in the vastness of a vicious circle remained there, the world would end. A way out, of course, but one could not go on selling trinkets indefinitely. There was a well-defined limit to the trinkets. The room at Papatou's was stripped, by now, of its "Femme Lisant" and of the bisque cherub which had swung from the chandelier of her flat for over twenty years. It had brought a franc. Because of the nick in the nose, Anna had explained. It was a dear nick in the nose. Walter had done it once, swinging his cane. . . .

Sitting the interminable days through, when she scarcely ventured out, except with the Babe when she was sure that Marchand, whom she feared even muzzled, was chained, she thought a lot, irrelevantly, about the nick in the nose.

It had happened one evening when he had burst into the flat after a banquet to a visiting Belgian patriot and financier, waving his cane with enthusiasm over the success of the address she had so carefully edited for him. How like a boy! There had been chopped liver for him that night, a delicacy for which she had journeyed down to a Roumanian delicatessen on Delancey Street. He had eaten far too well, of course, and in spite of the fact that after the repast he had importuned her to never again permit his overindulgence, became offended when she did remonstrate at his second cup of coffee. Dear darling . . . digging his grave with his teeth. . . .

God, one simply must not sit there, hour after hour, reliving such moments as the nick in the cherub's nose.

The maddening continuous foreign whine of voices from the courtyard! The din that was suddenly terribly alien. She wanted home these days, with a nostalgia that was twisting. With so much in the way of the strategic next move to think about, irrelevant pictures kept cluttering up concentration. A spring afternoon at the Fifty-ninth Street entrance to Central Park, with the first buds spangling bushes. Belmont Park, with her horse running to form, and sun drenching grandstand and faces that were familiar to her.

Walter at Cape May, on a moonlit strip of beach. The cinnamon-brown velvet sofa, after the table had been dragged away, his head, tired, against her. . . .

"Snap out of it" was a new one she had heard the American college boys use at the Casino. Snap out of it! Yes, but how? The thing to do was to bide one's time and the good break would come, but the biding came high. Food. Francs going out and, except for the tiny enforced sales of the tiny objects, nothing coming in.

Something sweet did come in. A letter, written in the full power of restored eyesight.

"My dearest of dear Aunts: Just because I never write anymore does not mean that you are ever far out of my mind. You lead such a gay, wandering life, that you sometimes fail to supply us, naughty dear, with sufficient address. But now that it is Aix, indefinitely, as you put it, I hasten to tell you that I love you and owe you everything and am back at my work and have had two promotions and my eyes are splendid. And from what the doctors tell me, I have every reason to feel they are permanently so.

"One of these days, no matter how little you want it, or need it, I am going to treat myself to the great joy of slipping my first one-hundred-dollar check into a long envelope that will bear the homely return address of Newcastle, Indiana. These long envelopes will reach you from time to time as I feel able, dear Aunt, so be sure and keep me advised of any change of address. Not that a hundred of them could ever really repay you, but the rest you must take in the payment of love. We are all well, and don't forget that if you ever need a new maid or a secretary, your loving niece is eager for a glimpse of Europe."

There was no good letting go the impulse to laugh—it would have been a horselaugh—it might have been a bray—

A strange thing happened. There was an Englishwoman, a Mrs. Meserick, who lived in a pension on a street that backed up against Ray's, appreciably more of a commodious hostelry, except that there were railroad tracks in front of it. Sometimes they sipped vermouth together at the sidewalk table of a little sawdust-strewn *buvette* they both frequented, and on one occasion Mrs. Meserick, pressed, had borrowed a dozen francs. Mrs. Meserick was seventy, had eked out her living from the gaming tables of the cycle of spas for fifty years, and, on the countless occasions of street mendicants approaching them, was kind, if only with sous.

The day that Ray, pressed by the prospect of having to dispose of certain objects that were almost unbearably close to her, finally sought out, in really great travail, Mrs. Meserick in her lodgings, there was a group of gamins about the sidewalk and a gendarme at the entrance to the little room.

Mrs. Meserick had died in her sleep.

She tried, in a frantic and therefore extremely unconvincing fashion, to make it understood to the gendarme, in a roomful of seemingly irrelevant people, that the deceased had owed her a dozen francs and would have wanted that sum to be paid immediately out of what was left. . . .

It struck her, after she had been somewhat firmly shouldered by the gendarme down the stairs, how shockingly futile and even horrible had been her demand. Fancy walking into the apartment of a dead friend in America and requesting the payment of a petty debt. Oh, she needed to be at home—she needed to be back at home to get her bearings. . . .

The terrible fact of the matter was that by now she was faced with the crisis of selling possessions that were not possessions at all, except in the sense that hands and knees and heartbeats are possessions. There were the silver watch that Walter had bought that day at Geneva, his gold cuff links, the pin-seal wallet, and the pair of patent-leather shoes, with the arch-supports.

They were revenue; the cuff links alone, even allowing Anatole's rascality, would pay August's room rent. That was important. Even with the prospect, once the tide turned, of breaking up any day for the homeward sailing, the security of the roof was important. It kept off the sniffing suspicion of Papatou that all was not on even keel. It kept the infrequency of her comings and goings unremarkable, it kept the nose of any possible suspicion of not all well, sniffing elsewhere.

Once, when she had not ventured downstairs for five days

except, when Marchand was chained, to the courtyard with the Babe, Papatou had come knocking at her door to inquire in pantomime if all was well. After that, such lapses ceased to be lapses, and became matter-of-course with Madame l'Américaine.

Madame l'Américaine was biding her time and yet biding, when, with her footsteps seeming to echo in the hollow of her head, she turned her face toward Anatole with the little silver watch from Geneva in the palm of her hand.

Walter had bought her that and buckled it around her wrist. Almost his sole personal gift to her. They had even quarreled over it and that somehow was what made it easier to part with it first. His voice, though, that in the end had been forgiving, must be prisoner in it. Next to the personal things which he himself had worn, the cuff-buttons, the wallet, the shoes, it was her dearest link to the inexpressibly dear—for sale. The meaning of my life. The power of myself to hurt. The power of myself to be glad. The sweetness of my memories. For sale. Here is my silver watch. Locked into this silver watch is something that cannot die. Anatole, if you knew that, you would not cheat.

This was rank sentimentality, the mealy self-indulgence of trading on easy emotions.

Anatole, if he knew that, would not cheat! Anatole, if he knew that, would cheat her to her very eyeballs! The way to handle Anatole was to make him understand the futility of trying to put anything over, where the value of this watch was concerned.

"Anna, tell Anatole I expect seven hundred francs for this watch. Swiss movement. Good as new!" It brought four hundred.

Four hundred francs for the watch! It had cost eight. She knew because she had bought one precisely like it for Emma. Four hundred francs. She felt like banging, one after the other, the fat cheeks of Anna, as she handed over the paltry sum. But of course one did nothing of the sort. What she did was to buy veal, *petits pains*, sugar, of which the larder had been empty for a week, alcohol for the spirit-lamp, shoes, fresh malines for a shoulder-scarf, face-powder, Castile soap, giblets for the Babe, and, hurrying home, cross the palm of Papatou with the sum total of next month's rent.

So much for that, except that it left her, as to francs in the
pocket, precisely where she had started. Then it struck her that the
thing to do was to wound an already open wound, which she did by
carrying the next day to Anatole the gold cuff links and the wallet,
for which he brought back to her precisely the amount of the watch.

The ridiculous fancy had her in its clutch, the sentimental fancy
for which she flagellated herself, that while she had the shoes, the
patent-leather ones with the faint cracks across each, where his
weight had pressed and his foot had curled in the walking, it really
was not so bad about the watch and the cuff links. (If only you could
stop crying nights!) There were the shoes! They were wrapped each
in a strip of canton flannel, in the drawer of a chest that was now
about empty.

Thank God, they, the shoes, were too trivial to be negotiable.
The thing to do now, what with another month's lodging clear, was
to make her tiny beginning. Five francs to bring in ten. Ten, twenty.
And so on, by a process which Walter had once explained to her in
terms of compound interest. Countless gambling fortunes had been
started that way. At the *boule* tables, too, mind you.

There was the classic story of the Frenchman, M. Poiteau, baker
in a patisserie at Rouen; sent to Aix through the largesse of his
employer for a cruel rheumatic complaint; placing twenty francs on
the *boule* table on the first of a month, and leaving Aix six weeks
later with one hundred thousand francs.

On twenty thousand francs—on ten—she could buy security
from this heritage of fear. Twenty thousand francs—when there
were less than four hundred in the wad of her purse underneath
the pillow.

Walter—if you had only realized—you could have spared me
this. . . .

56

Around that long outer *boule* table were no few grandmas of the evening! Along about eleven o'clock, in finery that hung from the racks of their shoulders, they came, in ones, along the spokes of side streets that radiated toward the Casino. They smelled of frizzled hair and old dress shields and Chianti-spots on yokes and laps that had been pressed with a too-hot iron. They were ladies, for the most part, with loose skin hanging in sacs along the underparts of their upper arms, and strong isolated hairs growing out of their chins, and cheekbones on which the pleated flesh had been laid over with rouge that squatted lightly, in the same detached fashion of the henna-dye that refused any longer to align itself with the frizzed coiffures.

They stood out in the pattern of gallant ruin around the table, no more cruelly etched, however, than the waxed, burnsided old boys who rolled their eyes to make them appear naughty, and pinched at ladies' legs underneath the tables, to conceal their impotence. Pretentious relics of better yesterdays, most of them, in machine-stitched toupees and shirtfronts time and time again chalked over.

A frieze of old valiants with porcelain smiles, trying to hide fear of paresis with the look of seeming to still be lascivious.

Do-I-look-like-that? No. Do-I-look-like-that? No. God, what if . . .

The youngsters, by contrast, were what heightened the effect of crow and crone. Fellows actually scarcely beyond the period of their first long trousers; older brothers, themselves still surprised with the dawn of down along their jowls, who had been obliged to prove their majority in order to obtain entrance. American boys with allowances or incomes or spending money. Younger brothers. A seventeen-year-old dauphin to a long-since-overturned throne. A duke's youngest son. The twenty-year-old twins of a South American copper king. Legend had it that it was not unknown for youth on a lark to put its small brothers into their first long trousers and gain them entry here. Youth, cutting its gaming and gambling-teeth at *la boule*. The buzzing at their shoulders of the scenting bevy of cocottes.

The South American twins, restive of the traffic in petty francs, and eager to graduate to the tables of man's estate in the rooms adjoining, played night after night to the limit of the stakes permitted, and tossed their coins like feed to sparrows.

Occasionally, among the frieze of onlookers, Ray caught one or two of them; once a ten-franc piece, which she placed and lost. It was horrible, hovering, night after night, around those South American boys, and, occasionally, at the more conservative shoulder of the duke's youngest son, or the American boys who kept up a running and extremely local patter of colloquialisms. Red-hot mama! Hotsy-totsy! Atta-baby!

There was one, the seventeen-year-old possessor of an entrance ticket that had been maneuvered, and heir to a rubber-heel fortune that would have bought the entire principality of his running mate, the Bulgarian prince with the Oxford accent, who had a habit of clicking his fingers and exclaiming, "Hot dog, snap out of it!" at whatever turn in the tide of the affairs of this strange company of men, women, and grandchildren.

He was a crazy-haired youth, with a birthmark strewn over one cheek, and hands that seemed to fly in all directions, as he raked in his winnings before the croupier should shovel them toward him. Sometimes, to the hilarity of the onlookers, the odd chip or the odd franc flew so wildly that it struck a bystander quite willy-nilly. One night a chip danced right down Ray's low bodice and lodged there against the bare flesh. She fished it out, and with it, won five francs, and with the five won ten, and with the ten lost ten.

After that, she hovered chiefly in the vicinity of the willy-nilly rubber-heel prince, placing her bets cagily over his shoulder, reaching for any chance flying foam from his chips.

It would have been comparatively a simple matter to go up to this youth and banter some francs out of him; so many of the cocottes, to say nothing of the crones, were constantly at him. One quickly learned to beg alms in the spirit of carnival, for fear the specter of need should show its head, offend your patron, and turn him away, cold.

The crones did it. The cocottes did it. Even the old men. But somehow, for the life of her, hovering there night after night, in the brown dress with the fresh malines scarf, the laid-on circles of her rouge that might have been placed on her cheekbones with a rubber stamp, the porcelain smile, the slightly palsied habit of her head to shake, the neckwattles held by a brown velvet ribbon, like pea-vines to their stick, she could not bring herself to out-and-out ask. Hover, yes! Hover, until the tables were half deserted and of weariness the lids hung over her eyes like bat-flesh.

The blond son of an Alabama patent-medicine king, said to be already keeping the gilt-haired danseuse of a Paris music hall, who played his stakes at the baccarat tables in the rooms where his youth forbade him, had a way, toward the end of an evening, of tossing a handful of coins straight up into the air, and laughing with his big, firm white teeth at the pecking crows.

It was part of the spirit of carnival to scramble for coins that would buy giblets. . . . One evening, in the tussle, a man's heel came down on her thumb and caused the blood to spurt out. That was pretty bad. Not the wound, which healed rapidly, but somehow the picture she made to herself, on all fours, her back bare and with a ridge down its middle, which she could never quite reach with a powder puff, fingers groping among cuspidors and table legs and feet-of-the-evening, for rolling coins.

Ugh! That was somehow, in a remote and highly unpleasant manner, equivalent to the lapse she had allowed herself the day she had actually permitted some neighbor children (it might easily have been Papatou) to see her pick chicken feet out of a refuse can. Simply must not let such things happen. Never again. The blond boy from Alabama could toss his coins. Let the others crawl in that horrible panorama of carnival.

The thing to do was to pull herself out of her dilemma. Nothing ventured, nothing gained, and yet the days passed, and out of that dwindling four hundred francs from the cuff links and wallet, it was difficult to risk next day's security by planting so much as another franc piece, the hand simply refusing to dig down for one, into the dilapidated finery of her evening bag.

Now, if only that sweet freckled American youngster over there, who always seemed to have so much spending money, and who played with the delight of a child, could even suspect that by staking her to a hundred francs he might be starting her on— Nonsense! How could he suspect? Merely because she stood across the table from him, smiling. He never smiled back, chiefly because he never looked.

Perhaps the reason youth no longer looked back was out of deference for the little habit she had taken on lately, of nodding her head. She had noticed it quite suddenly one day at the Casino, while standing opposite a long mirror. Why, her head was shaking! She was nodding at herself without meaning to nod at herself. Silly, quit it! But on she went nodding. Nervousness. Old Mrs. Winninger, on Baymiller Street, had been a great nodder. Palsy. Well, cut it out. Then for days she did not nod again, and suddenly, there she would be at it again, without knowing. She took to wearing a tiny jet ornament on the side of her hair. It was easier to tell when the nodding began, by the twinkling of the jet.

Well, anyway, if one of those nice kids, without her having to go up to him, would toss her a stake. You simply dared not go down into the narrowing wad in that old sequined evening bag. You dared not. . . .

Curious, though, how comparatively little frightened, deep down, she was! Walter had once told her the legend of a man lost in the snows of an Alpine pass, who had dared, within half a mile of a lighted hut, to let himself become pleasantly sleepy, and, succumb-ing, had perished. The thing to be was frightened—unsleepy. The thing to keep yourself was frightened. Act! But how?

One day, sitting with the Babe in the sag of her skirt and looking from her steep window into the courtyard where moved all day and had their being, the strangers of that strange world down there, an idea did auger through into her mind.

Why not present herself in just the plain facts of her dilemma to the American consul? Silly, there would be no consul at a place like Aix. Well, better still, why not appeal to some of the dozens of Americans now registered, at the height of the season, at all the better hotels of the town? Not necessarily at the Bernasçon. God, not there, or even the Splendide, but there were dozens of wealthy Americans registered at the Europa or Astoria. Go to one of the well-fixed Americans, the man of the family if possible, or, if need be, his wife. Simple. To the point. I am an American woman, stranded abroad. A loan of two hundred dollars would put me on my feet in no time, and enable me to return to my home in the States. Even if I do not put it to you very desperately, I am in need. Will you help me?

Why, of course! Time and time again, to women at the track, to women in the flat building, she had given help on lesser provoca-tion. Anybody would. An American who thought nothing of losing thrice that sum at a table would be quick to come to the aid of a countrywoman. Somewhere in Paris, or was it Berlin, there was an organization for just that purpose. If only one knew just where. But there was humiliation about that, and besides one needed creden-tials. Here, in a gaming resort, anyone was likely to find himself in a dilemma! The thing to do was to get into something chic, feel chic, be chic, and go boldly. Time and time again, she rehearsed it, aloud before the mirror, as Walter used to. I am an American woman, temporarily stranded abroad. Please forgive what may seem a presumption, but I know you will understand. A loan of a hundred or two—

No use! No use. The spas were riddled with that type. The women in mended finery temporarily on their uppers. It took a something, to go find out these Americans visiting abroad, the very parents of the youngsters who were cutting their teeth at the *boule* tables, that she did not have in her makeup. She could no more, when it came right down to the doing, have presented to one of them her predicament! Why, the very words would have congealed upon her lips, and there was that fear, which was beginning to haunt her these days, that her head might begin to quiver. That would be terrible. Get your head set back square on your shoulders—then go!

The Babe had begun to regard her, when her head started to shake, with something a little mystified lying in his milky old eyes. Once or twice he tried to lick her cheeks. It was not pleasant, though, licking a cheek that was filled with tremor, because after each attempt he sat back and just looked his mystification.

"I won't do it anymore, Baby. I know it is horrid. Lookie, darling. See. Muvver will wear the little jet aigret, and the minute it begins to bob, Muvver will know. Don't mind Muvver when she nods, darling. Lots of people do it. Mrs. Winninger—healthy as anything, used to nod her head, too. Just that little nervous way. Horrid. I'll quit."

That was the beginning of a week that ended in a way for which, by all processes of deduction, she should have been prepared, and yet somehow, when it came, the breath was literally knocked out of her.

Literally that, because she had refused to so much as take stock of the dwindling contents of her purse. Something would happen. Something had to happen. Height of the season and all that. People did not remain in dilemmas like this. And then, when it came, this Saturday morning, to hurrying down the street for giblets to prepare for the Babe, there were exactly forty centimes in her purse when she opened it to dig for a franc. Literally, then, her heart missed its beat, or whatever anatomical hiatus is ascribable to the shock that takes place under such external stimulus. In the bright light of a faultless morning, an array of soiled, worthless-looking coins, such as one is in the habit of tossing to roadside youngsters, stared up from her palm.

"*Encore—dix centimes*," said the chef of the restaurant, handing her the sackful of leavings and scraps. *"Dix centimes,"* and held up his ten bloody fingers.

"Chez moi. No more. Left money at home. *Argent—chez—moi.* Bring tomorrow," she mouthed at him, with her lips folding back against her chilly teeth with all the amiability she could muster. "Next time. . . ."

Then something happened, which sickened, enraged her, so that she began to shout profane sentences which she did not know she harbored.

The chef opened the paper cornucopia, extracted three or four of the scraps of meat, tossed them into a refuse pail, and handed her the remainder.

"Dirty, stingy Frenchie! Wop! Piker! Stingy-gut! Damn dog! We Americans may be money-mad, but we're not money-mean. Ugh, you dirty little sardine, you're not worth canning!"

God, that was common. That was fishwife. The chef had yelled back at her, too, with an obscene gesture. That was fishwife! Hurrying along the street, the giblets beginning to dampen through the newspaper, reaction set in that continued to horrify her. How could I have? It's all right for these fishwives around here. They're forever hollering. But me. How could I have? The dirty little oily sardine. Taking those few scraps out of the mouth of the Babe. It isn't that I care about those few scraps. There will be more and plenty. The Babe will eat better food before he dies than that old sardine ever saw! It's just that it scares one that life can be mean, like that. Taking those scraps from the Babe. I should have thrown them back at him. Dared not—those scraps—

They boiled up though, with a warm well-flavored smell that permeated the room. Just as good, it struck her suddenly, as the general smells that permeated the hallways and courtyard of the pension. Americans were squeamish. Why, it was well known that in France, even before the war, the peasantry bought horse-meat, ate it, liked it. Just a matter of what you were accustomed to. A place on Vine Street, in Cincinnati, used to specialize in eels. Rather share of the Babe's giblets, stewed up nicely with onion, than eat eels!

For her lunch, that day, she ate a portion of the giblets, helping it down with generous chews off a *petit pain* and plenty of hot sweetened coffee. It went down, and, as she put it, stayed down; and that afternoon, meticulously keeping the day to normal, and filling in every second of it with some chore of the hands, she bathed the Babe, rolled him dry, played an absurd game which he loved, of squatting on all fours and making lunges at him, combed up his front-hair into a pompon above his eyes, which she screwed with red ribbon, and, seating herself by the window to watch, sent him down, through the corridors, alone, to the courtyard.

It all happened so suddenly that trying fantastically to live it over, in its horror, in its terror, in its heartbreak, it seemed to her that instead of leaping out of his kennel where he had become unchained, Marchand, as she stood leaning out of the window, looking down, must have sprung from her own forehead, and landed straight, sure, and fanged, on top of the prowling little Babe, whose nose had been snooping along a fence edge.

All the world, as he landed there, became the delirium of barks. The short sharp terrified barkings of the Babe. The long tunnels of barkings from the wolf, Marchand. Their duet—*ye-ye—woof—woof*, and suddenly the distant bayings of the town's dogs, everywhere. Her own voice shouting. Then the instantaneous miracle of many voices, many figures, her own cries streaming behind her like a waving banner, as she tore through the halls. Dust. A Babylonian moment of the Babe on his back, his mouth open, a red furnace flecked with white foam. The wolf-dog, whose teeth were fastened in the just-combed wool underneath the Babe's throat, and who would not be beaten off by Ra-Ta-Plan with a broom!

"Coming, Baby!"

There was simply no end to the corridors; the stairs; the darkness which she knew inch by inch, flying up to try and impede her with the hallucination of steps and doors, where there were none. "Coming, Baby!"

There was quite a circle in the courtyard; and, of all people, the little hunchback tobacconist from next door, who could not have weighed ninety pounds, was standing, holding off the black

Marchand, from whose jowls red spittle was dropping; and there in the center of the yard and the silence, with his head curled under him, and his body risen to a hump, the Babe!

"*Tenez! Ne touche pas!* Madame, do not touch! He eez in pain. He weel bite!"

"Not me. Let me go!"

"Madame!"

"Oh, my God, he snapped at me, didn't he! That's because—his throat—look—his throat—he has two mouths! That red is where his throat is ripped—his head is halfway off! It will drag if he walks. What makes him jump that way—like a chicken without its head! Baby—my sweet—let me go. God damn you—strangers you—you'd see him starve for ten sous. When he gets well, I'll sick him on you—dirty bitch Marchand—do you hear—you all—I hate you—let me go—"

"Madame, you must compose yourself. It will be more merciful to keel—"

"Who are you? What do you want? What do you know about anything?"

"I am a guest in zee next pension. I have seen the black dog in the kennel jump—I follow—"

"Oh, my God! Something is wrong here. Some conspiracy among you. No, you don't! No, you don't! He's mine. See, if you don't believe me. Now you touch him, if you dare, the way I'm touching him. Bah—you—you all—enemies—strangers—skinflints—leave me alone—"

The Babe had not snapped this time, even as she scooped him, bloodred about the head, into her arms, and could feel through her lap, against her legs, against her breasts, against her arms, the quick warm wet of his blood.

But his head! His head kept dangling over the crook of her elbow, and the Babe had two mouths. His own gasping one with the lolling tongue, and the red gash across the throat, half-severing his head.

"Get me a doctor." No one moved. They must have thought

that was a frog croaking, from the way the voice in her felt, and so she tried to lift it, quite idiotically, she thought. "Get me a doctor—someone—"

"Madame, eet is no use. Eet is best he should be killed *immédiatement*. He suffers. Eef you will go away I will see to it that mercifully he eez—"

How you hated him. God, how you could have gored the little English-speaking skinny, even as the Babe had been gored. "Go away—you—go away, all you strange greedy faces—leave me alone—I will take him up—I will cure him."

"Madame, you are not kind. Hear how he suffers—"

He's bleating. He's bleating like a little lamb. My lamb. . . .

"One merciful hit over the head will put him in peace. . . ."

You thought you were going to faint this time, sure, but the warm feeling of the blood pressing through your corsets was what revived you.

"Babe, don't moan. They want to kill you for it. Babe, upstairs alone—you can moan. Not here. See now, you gapers! It's all right. Everything is all right. Warm water and rags and—why, there weren't so many gapers anymore. The wolf-dog, damn him, God damn him, was being bathed in a corner, and someone must have fainted, because there was another little knot of folk. But it's all right—everything is coming all right. Here, you—skinny—see, I've got his head back on. I'm holding it on. I'll hold it on until the doctor comes—sh-h-h, my lamb, don't bleat. That is what will make them want to kill you. That's what makes them faint. Don't cry, Baby. Old man—you—the doctor— What is that?"

"This, madame, eef you will be so kind—it is a club that with one blow will put your little dog out of his misery. Madame, you must, eef you will be so kind—eef you will go—we will do this act of mercy—I myself will even do it, eef—"

"Go away! Go away! Oh, God, there was that head slipping again back into the hallucination it gave of the two mouths. Babe, do not scream so! Babe, look at me! You want them to kill you? Is the wound too terrible for you to live? Must I? No. No. No.—You see, that was a lick he gave me with his tongue! My dog licked me with his tongue. If anybody has to kill him after that, I do! Not you. Not strangers. If I do, he'll know it's all right. Not you! Babe, look at me. Do you understand? My darling. My black curly innocent, have no fear. No strange hand shall do it. . . . Give me that club! Babe—one for the money—two for the show—three to make ready, my darling, four for to—go—"

My, how many stairs—will I ever stop falling—

57

The shoes lay in the empty drawer, wrapped each in its canton flannel and with an expression to them as if they had features. The left one was more streaked with lines, like a human making a grimace of pain. "Ouch," it seemed to say. That was practically true, because, when tired, it was characteristic of Walter to bear down on his right foot in order to relieve the chronic gouty twist that resided in his left.

The sending-along the shoes would ultimately have been the simple matter it deserved to be, except for that grimace. Of all the objects that one by one had gone the way of Anatole—the cufflinks, the watch, the wallet—the shoes continued to represent the peak of anguish. Perhaps because they were the last. With them would go the tie of every tangible thing that had been Walter's. With them would go out of the house, out of the room, out of the days grown so tormentingly quiet, the last evidence of his almost breathing presence.

He would have been the first to laugh this off. An old pair of shoes. Don't be ridiculous. You women—God-awful sentimentalists. There was undoubtedly that aspect. You were ridiculous, sitting there in the center of the silence, as it milled around, feeling the anguish of carrying those shoes to Anatole.

There was something funny and undignified and unpretty about shoes that had been worn. And these seemed to say, in the tone she had heard a hundred times over, when the wince came, "Ouch!"

It was hateful to sit there feeling ridiculous. For two days, now, she had held out against the tightening little knot that had ceased to be active hunger and lay in an area of chill against the pit of her stomach.

The thing to do, while waiting and gathering forces for the open-and-aboveboard presentation of her situation which was to be made to one of the Americans at the Europa or Astoria, was to realize on the shoes and tide over this inertia.

The death of the Babe had been the almost irretrievable setback. The days since had taught her the insanity of daring to let anything connected with that scene nest in her memory. Things were about to move along all right once more. Just a matter, now, of mustering up the strength to get past this supreme absurdity in her inability to sell the shoes. Plenty of Americans, indeed the average, once you had the strength back and the vitality to feel chic, would be glad to tide over a countryman. His throat had been ripped until it looked like a mouth, and above the two mouths were his eyes— stop it! Stop it! All this talk about the human mind being able to stand so much and no more, nonsense! I don't intend to let mine go—what is it the American boys around the *boule* tables call it?— ga-ga! I don't intend to go ga-ga. Not much.

What if one could sell one shoe and keep the other that was saying "Ouch"? There was comedy for you! Sell one shoe and keep the other that was saying "Ouch"! I can't give them up. I can't give them up. I can't give them up in the morning. If you sang it like that, to the tune of "I can't get them up, I can't get them up, I can't get them up in the morning"—there was a laugh in that.

It was not that she felt hungry; there was only the chilly knot. But one had to eat; all there was to it. For two days now, six meals in all, there had been only the milky water left over from boiled rice. Extraordinary to have thought to save that. Loathsome, as it went down, but undoubtedly nutritious. Or was starchy water bad for one? You dared not even think of it one way or another toward the third day, because of the feeling of the throat closing against it like a heavy door. Besides, it did not do to let that tinge of Chinese yellow creep into the eyeballs and against the skin.

Fool. Idiot. The shoes themselves, lying there in that drawer, in lieu of the good hot soup, the fromage, the *petits pains*, the sale would bring, must be crinkling with the laughter of ridicule.

At two o'clock of the fourth afternoon, because it seemed to her that what she had awakened out of, with her arms outstretched, and her head lying on the table into them, was more of a prolonged faint than a nap, she carried the shoes to Anatole who, two hours later, returned her six francs. Three francs each.

58

This was the first time in all her life that anything of such a nature had happened to her, and, please God, it would never happen again.

The affair with Anna and Anatole had made her nervous. Fancy their daring to jeer her out of the shop that way, when she protested at the six francs, and in the very face of the loiterers and drinkers at the tables in the *buvette* next door. That in itself was sufficiently shattering to cause to happen what did. That and those silly indigestible buns, with raisins poked in, that had caught her famished fancy as she passed the patisserie. The buns were heavy and made her feel sick, even as they went down, but now was not the time to be fastidious. The Americans to whom she intended appealing would be kinder if she looked a bit chic and well-nourished. Life was like that. The same way, you could hope for a handout of francs at the Casino, chiefly if you looked as if you did not need them.

Anyway, it was the combined nervousness and the indigestibility of the buns. At two o'clock, in the dead of night, she had awakened suddenly, and all on the instant realizing that the warm lump of the Babe was not at her feet, and that the drawer in the chest was now empty of the shoes, there had gone, curdling through the stilly decorum of Papatou's, great spinning spirals of cries, one topping the other, thinner and higher, like mounting rope before it hurls out to become a lasso.

"Oh, my God," she cried, sitting up in the dark and slapping her hand with great force against her mouth, "this is terrible. Stop! Stop!" And still she could not, and still the cries kept mounting, and with them horror of the self who was creating this perfectly dreadful commotion.

It was unthinkable to cry out like that in the strange night of a strange country, and worse to keep on, even after there were steps in the corridor, and, worst of all, she could not stop. . . .

"The banging against the door will help me," she kept moaning in her mind, as the cries kept mounting and the banging sounding. They were like the slaps, those bangs, which you administer to a strangling infant, and presently, as the banging continued, the yells did subside. They were the most terrifying and confusing sounds, these, emanating from herself, she had ever heard. Even after they had subsided, it was as if she sat huddled there in bed in the midst of a silence that had been terribly shattered. Lunatic-sounding and resounding noises lay strewn about the place in a silence that was almost more unbearable than the ripping sound the cries had made as they left her head.

"What have I done? Oh, you—out there—it's all right. Everything is all right. Very well, I'll open the door. You must forgive it, please. You see, I dream sometimes. Won't you come in?" This was terrible. They were seeing her with her face all toothless, and the old brown wrapper flung on over her nightgown was really by now quite a sight. When once taffeta silk begins to split . . .

There was Papatou in a night-rig of striped underwear and a pointed cap that was enough to wring a laugh out of even her horror, and the half-dressed figure of the boy who had always worried her so on the Babe's account, a couple of dim figures from rooms down the hallway, and, holding a lamp so that it showed her stocky and enormously muscular figure, which was attired in a one-piece chemise of unbleached muslin, Madame Papatou.

My, she was terrific. Thewed like a short-necked ox, muscles coiled in the calves of her legs and the uppers of her arms, sixty-five if a day, the color and texture of red soil, rain-washed.

"Excuse it, won't you, please? I must have had a bad dream. *Mal rêve.*"

What were they saying to her—of her? The voice of Madame Papatou, filled with questioning grunts: *"Voilà madame, qu'est-ce qu'il y a? Êtes-vous malade? Rêvez-vous? Qu'est-ce qu'il y a avec vous à cette heure de la nuit?"*

Papatou, his old fat stomach bulging in his ridiculous underwear, and his eyes unnice, as they roved the torn places of her robe and gown. The dim eyes of the curious, hanging like faintly lit grapes in the background. Oh, my God, were they thinking her crazy? . . .

"I'm ever so sorry, Madame Papatou. *Je suis triste.* Dream. *Rêve. Je ne suis pas malade, comprenez-vous? Mon petit chien—je pleure pour mon petit chien*—my dog—I weep for him—"

They had wept with her, that day in the courtyard, this strange assorted mixture. Grief should be a great leavener. *"Je suis triste, mes amis*—sad—I am sad—*mon petit chien—mon pauvre petit chien*—my heart hurts while I sleep—and I cry out—*pardonnez-moi*—"

They were kind, these strange alien faces, behind which thoughts went on in a language not her own, and to whom she was as mysterious as they to her, Madame Papatou even remaining after the others, to knead with her terrific hands, in a vigorous massage along her body.

"Bien, madame, n'est-ce pas? Good. *N'est-ce pas?* Goo-od."

"Oui. Oui. Bien, madame, but a little lighter—please—"

"Bien, madame?"

"Oh, *très* good, *madame.* But I—*je suis*—much better—ouch!"

"Bien, n'est-ce pas?"

"Yes. Yes." If only she would stop kneading. Those terrific fingers working into the hollows of her neck, along her thighs, under the very vertebrae of her spine. "Ouch—please—"

"Bien, n'est-ce pas?"

"Oui. Oh, my God, not so hard—"

"Bien, n'est-ce pas?"

"Oui, but—"

"Bien?"

Of course, to have forgotten! What lack of diplomacy, when of all times her rent was beginning once more to be due in a week, it was unwise to let the slightest duress show itself. There was a franc and ten centimes in her purse.

"Here, Madame Papatou, *merci bien.*"

"*Bien, madame. Merci. Bon soir.*" The terrific Papatou, placated, slipping the coins into the pocket of the chemise, taking up her lamp and going. "*Bien, Madame—maintenant vous restez bien.*"

This was no good. Nights like this took it out of one. There began a parade through the mind. Playing jacks on the Auths' steps in Baymiller. A boy named Charley Schermer, who had once sprung upon her from Clagmeyer's alley, as she passed it one day when she was scarcely more than eleven, and said unmentionable things to her. Adolph's fat knee, which had jounced her up and down on it, detaining her with caresses, when she was eager to be off to play. Kurt's nearsighted blue eyes, desiring her. The small old-fashioned rocker, in which her mother had loved to sew, and which Tagenhorst had spirited off to Youngstown. The low gleaming of Cincinnati, beheld through the two smokes of twilight and factory, from a spot on Walnut Hills called Ingleside. The hum of the hazard-wheel in a back room, Over-the-Rhine. Hamilton, Ohio, as you stepped off the C. H. and D. into a drab red station. Voices at night along the canal. Woodward High at noon, when boys awaited you at the corner. A drummer in Wielert's asking you if you were innocent. The fatty look to Freda's face, as it lied about the baby. The Stag Hotel, with fresh window boxes of bachelor's buttons, as she had passed it one spring afternoon, wearing the last word in a piqué skirt, the new "rainy day" length. The barrel figure of Adolph, singing at Turnverein. Walter, the night he had come bearing the Babe in the hamper. . . .

Sh-h-h-h! She must have cried out again, this time from the rim of a very light doze. Simply must not do this. Besides, the time had come to plan. No more procrastination. Old Mother Hubbard, she went to the cupboard, to get her poor dog a bone— Thank God, Babe's cupboard had never been bare. But now the cupboard was bare all right. Well, here goes. The Americans, tomorrow. The brown tweed suit with the turban still had its quality of chic. Now,

now, give the devil his due, she still had style all right. Country-woman in dilemma. Small loan would tide over . . .

It was bright noon when she awoke, without the headache which had tormented her at intervals during the night, and feeling ready for what lay before her.

But in spite of presenting herself at the Hotel Europa, about two o'clock, just as the dining room was filled, and running her eye over the register of little white cards, she did nothing as planned. Each white card bore a name. Reinhardt. Plant. (There had been Cincinnati Plants. Fine conservative large family. But somehow—well, somehow, one didn't approach a Plant this way.) Greer, Drey-fous. (Dreyfous, French or American? American Jews are generous. Still, it might be a French Dreyfous.) McCaffry. (Good name.) Stedman. Opdike? (There had been a Maggie Opdike at Wood-ward High. Trashy people, who would grow rich trashily.) Swan. D'Artagnan. (There had been a character in the literature course at Woodward High, named that—D'Artagnan.) Vaselli. (Italians.) Sir Hubert Grenbole. (No, one could not appear on her uppers before a Sir Hubert.) Ryan. Ponscarme. St.-Beauve. Levi.

She drew back her lips then, that had not breakfasted, and directed a smile to the *porter* which she realized was her glassiest.

"I wish to see Mrs. Levi."

"Mrs. Levi and her daughter, they have checked out theese morning for Paris, madame."

"Oh, yes. Oh, yes, of course, I see. They did say something about it." Couldn't very well say then, "Mrs. Ponscarme will do, or Mrs. St.-Beauve." (Besides, you could not in a thousand years approach a Mrs. St.-Beauve.) The thing to do was to move grandly out through the lobby, with the vista of diners showing in the din-ing room beyond, or, quick as a flash, he might suspect. One of those women who peddle lingerie, with samples of the materials in their handbags, or a solicitor for an automobile-touring company. There was an idea. Somewhere there must be positions like that open. . . .

The day drifted, and strangely without hunger or concern. The *boule* tables did not operate at the Casino in the afternoons, but the garden was pleasant, and there were benches where one could sit without needing to order drinks.

She wondered a little how she looked, seated there on an iron bench, with her handbag, to which she had applied shoepolish, on the seat beside her, and the corners of her lips nicely up. Not bad. She could tell her head was not nodding, because, when it did, it jarred her headache, which was returning, but not enough to matter. Certainly she did not look the part of having lived through last night—or, for that matter, the night before that, or the night before that, before that. . . .

A tall, rather gaunt, wide-shouldered, narrow-hipped woman, with a face that was filled with little valleys, but molded, withal, in a certain grandeur. A ruin, if you must, but one with a straight back.

The sun wore down, and chill came up, and it was time to go home and dine and rest and dress. Time to go home and rest and dress. Why, in God's name, for the sake of a cheese-bun, which had made her ill at that, had she let go those shoes? The one saying "Ouch!" It would be simpler, even with the Babe gone, to go back to that room now, if the chest of drawers were not empty of those two patent-leather— God, this was lunacy! To sit thus in a garden, with laughing, strolling, normal people moving past, dreading to go back to a room because the last possession of a dead man's shoes were no longer in it! Of course one went back. Rested. Dressed. There was a sign up at the Casino entrance. *La boule* tonight. It was always there. Baccarat. Chemin de fer.

But somehow, passing out on her way back to the pension, there was something about this sign! The placard, "*La boule* tonight," which she had passed a hundred times without heeding, had winked, beckoned her in some unobtrusive way that had snagged her attention.

Really the effect was not so bad. Curious she had never thought of it before. Talk about necessity being the mother of invention! With the bolero jacket left off, from which the sequins were peeling like scabs, the brown net gave the effect of the new, daringly low neckline and sleeveless mode so many of the American and French women were affecting that season. It left the arms bare, and, with a little pinning and arranging, gave the rear effect of a waist-deep "V."

Took little things like this to buck one up! Why, if some women had that back—if the famous French actress who was recuperating at the spa and who only wore rhinestone straps for the rear part of her bodices, had that back . . .

It was still a stunning back, except for the ridge, and had the same length and taper to it of the "stylish" figure that had caused many a head in front of the old Stag Hotel to turn.

Just all the difference in the world, leaving off that bolero. The aigret in the hair was not much good. Passé. All the lovely young, these days, were wearing their heads either docked and marcelled to the perfection of every strand accounted for, or low and plain and sleek, without ornament.

For a long while, before the mirror beneath the gas-fixture, there was the question of the small jet ornament. On. Off. Better off, no doubt of that. Younger, and the jet made the hair look brassy. . . . But it helped to know the ornament was there. Sometimes, without it, even in the mirror-lined rooms, the shaking of her head remained unnoticeable to her. With the jet, the little dancing of the beads was like a signal. Not only could she see, but they made a tiny noise, when her head got to nodding.

It was horrid to nod. See a doctor about that. Nerves. Old lady Winninger had it for years. . . .

Curious, what a habit food was. Now that the headache was gone again, and the exhilaration had come with the effect of the refurbished gown, she was downright hungry. Two glasses of water assuaged that, and the conviction that there would be food later at the Casino. It was going to be that kind of night.

Sure enough, as if for a corroborative beginning, there seemed to be more of a crowd than usual, about *la boule*. More youngsters. Apparently a whole new contingent of American, college-appearing fellows, with sleek heads and faultless ties and some of the really adorable and ridiculous pomposities of the precocious minor. There were cocottes aplenty, too, like sparrows alighting for crumbs. Not the very young, who hovered in dazzling flocks around baccarat and chemin-de-fer. The older pecking daws were out here in the *la boule* rooms; older, but more meticulous to be gay.

There was that handsome young Klinger! A Pittsburgh Klinger, whose father, at the moment, was the subject of a loud divorce scandal that was being enacted at Nice. He was the one from whom she had caught the twenty francs once, and had the nasty encounter with the French girl in the carrot-colored woollen wig.

The bolero jacket off, was very effective. One moved through the brace of mirrors, feeling long, bare, nice arms and tapering back. . . .

Walter had always been very much the husband where her décolleté was concerned. "Cover up your shoulders. What is the idea of all that nakedness? Don't like it."

A young fellow, also American, was tossing his coins about in a fashion she had not seen duplicated since the South American twins. Up went his shower of coins, like sparrow-feed. Gatherers on the sidelines, keepers.

The trouble about horning into the group was that they were almost all French girls around him. They squabbled so, and were apt to become ugly. . . .

There was one fellow seated between two waxed old Frenchmen with false shirtfronts, an English lad in horn-rimmed glasses, a repeater, playing a system time after time. Number five; number five; number five; number five. Sometimes the first winnings of these fellows playing a system exhilarated them to the extent of passing a five-franc piece, willy-nilly, over their shoulders, for luck. After half an hour, as she waited, suddenly and with an empty-handed gesture he pushed back his chair and walked off. . . .

"Heigh-ho, poor kid. Hard luck. Better next time."

Farther along, a Parisian in burnsides, looking like a riding master, was winning. Naughty old boys like that, though, did not distribute indiscriminately, if at all.

The young Americans were the darlings. There was one, with a sleek tan head and a face that must have caused the admission clerk to look thrice at his passport. A fledgling, not, as yet, as they would have put it in the elegant phraseology of Baymiller, dry behind the ears. A darling, winning too, and chaffing with his colleagues, and being generous in a way that had already attracted a little flock of French girls to his elbows.

Well, why not? She was as much of the spectacle of the evening as any of them. Who were these French girls, with the unwashed-looking necks, and the burnt hair, and the elaborate décolleté, to keep shoving her back to the outer fringe? Besides, these darling, reckless, naughty little boys, cutting their citizen-of-the-world teeth, were her countrymen! That tan-haired boy, there, the darling! A mere baby playing hooky from his crib and winning so recklessly with the luck of an innocent abroad, was her compatriot. God damn the pecking greedy daws between her and him. She was hungry! Her head, of just shameful degrading creature-hunger, was nodding like a nail file when you hold it between thumb and forefinger and pluck the loose end. She could see, in the mirror, the dancing of the jet. She was hungry, with that caved-in feeling that made one see everything twice. The way to treat these pecking daws was to peck as they pecked—shove as they shoved—push as they pushed. If need be, scratch and claw as they could claw—there—now—this way, boy! Me! That's the boy!

It landed, swift and sure into the outstretched talon of her hand, without the youth so much as glancing back to see its destination, and causing a little gasp, but no contesting, among the girls.

"Arnold mustn't throw away his five-hundred-franc notes like that," sang one of the colleagues, "or Mama'll spank. Irma'll spank!"

The shock of that went home so quietly! Like a bullet that enters a breast without pain. Why, of course, that was Arnold. That was Arnold, who only yesterday, at Mount Clemens, had been tucked away under the heartbeat of his mother. She might have known it. That was Corinne's hair—that was Walter's Arnold.

There were five hundred francs in her hand. The joke of having died and cried over the shoes that said "Ouch!" Here was something more directly from the flesh of the flesh that had been Walter. Five hundred francs as if from the dead hand of Walter, by way of the live hand of his son. Catch me giving these up. . . . Catch me.

Papatou declared to the officials it was the sight of the long envelope from America, from New-cas-tle, Indeeana, to be exact, that had been lying untouched, halfway under the door, for three days, which first jerked him to the realization that Madame l'Américaine had not been seen so much as scuttling through the corridors to the outhouse for almost a week. That, and to quote him literally, the faint stink of death which had seemed to seep out as he applied eye to the keyhole.

The old miser of an Américaine! She had died from lack of food, her dry mouth open, with a bubble, as if of glassine paper, spanning it, and, all the time, a five-hundred-franc note plastered to her bosom like a porous plaster.

Printed in the United States
by Baker & Taylor Publisher Services